THE CALL OF THE RIFT
VEIL

JAE WALLER

Published by ECW Press
665 Gerrard Street East
Toronto, Ontario, Canada M4M 1Y2
416-694-3348 / info@ecwpress.com

Editor: Susan Renouf
Cover design: Erik Mohr (Made By Emblem)
Cover illustration: © Simon Carr/
www.scarrindustries.com
Maps: Tiffany Munro/
www.feedthemultiverse.com
Author photo: © Rob Masson

This is a work of fiction. Names, characters,
places, and incidents either are the product
of the author's imagination or are used
fictitiously, and any resemblance to
actual persons, living or dead, business
establishments, events, or locales is entirely
coincidental.

LIBRARY AND ARCHIVES CANADA
CATALOGUING IN PUBLICATION

Title: Veil / Jae Waller.

Names: Waller, Jae, author.

Series: Waller, Jae. Call of the rift ; bk. 2.

Description: Series statement: The call of the
rift; book 2

Identifiers: Canadiana (print) 20190111585
Canadiana (ebook) 20190111593

ISBN 9781770414570 (hardcover)
ISBN 9781773054193 (PDF)
ISBN 9781773054186 (ePUB)

Classification: LCC PS8645.A4679 V35 2019
DDC jC813/.6—dc23

The publication of *The Call of the Rift: Veil* has been generously supported by the Canada
Council for the Arts, which last year invested $153 million to bring the arts to Canadians
throughout the country, and is funded in part by the Government of Canada. *Nous remercions le
Conseil des arts du Canada de son soutien. L'an dernier, le Conseil a investi 153 millions de dollars pour
mettre de l'art dans la vie des Canadiennes et des Canadiens de tout le pays. Ce livre est financé en partie
par le gouvernement du Canada.* We acknowledge the support of the Ontario Arts Council (OAC),
an agency of the Government of Ontario, which last year funded 1,737 individual artists and 1,095
organizations in 223 communities across Ontario for a total of $52.1 million. We also acknowledge
the contribution of the Government of Ontario through the Ontario Book Publishing Tax Credit,
and through Ontario Creates for the marketing of this book.

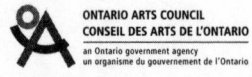

For Douglas

"When I'm at my best, I am my father's daughter."

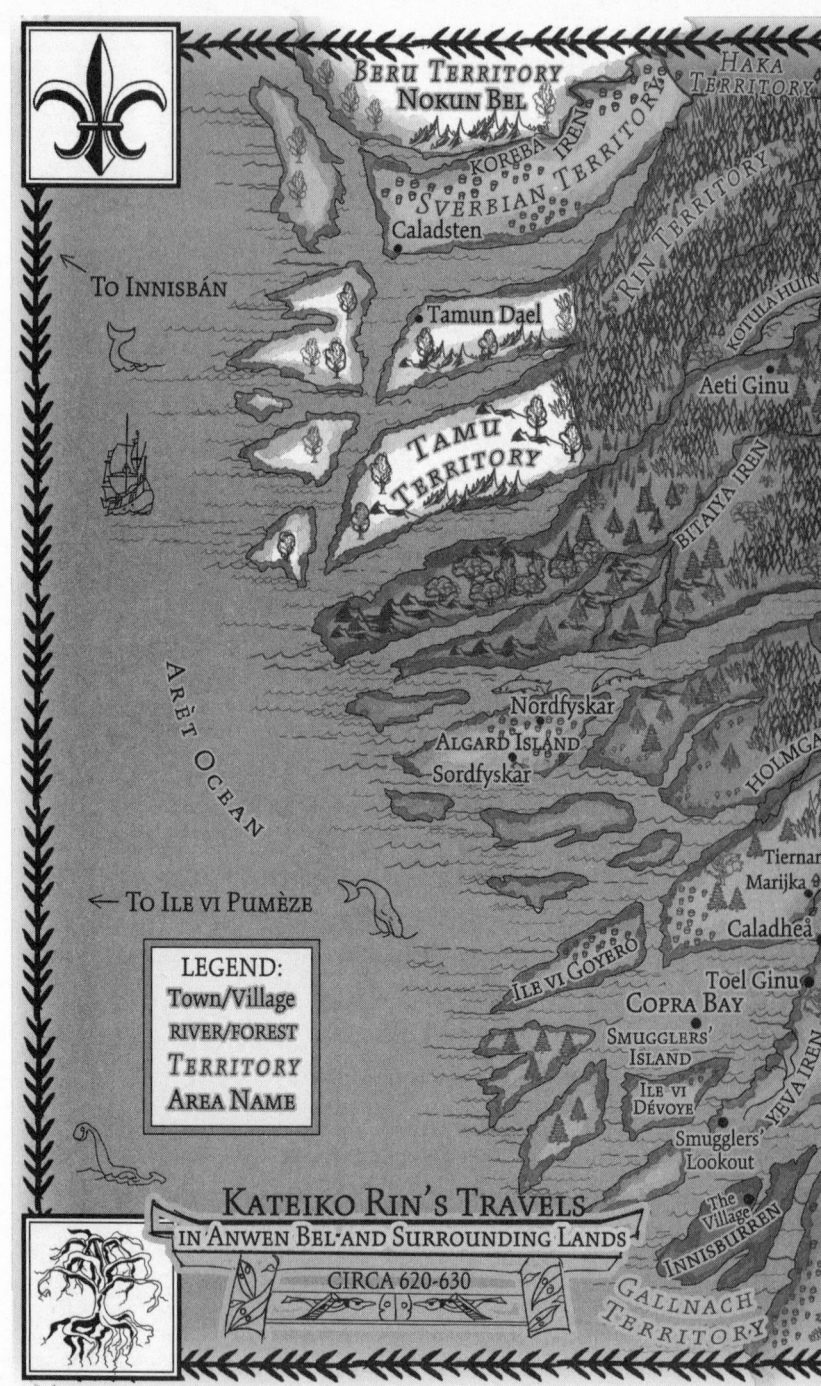

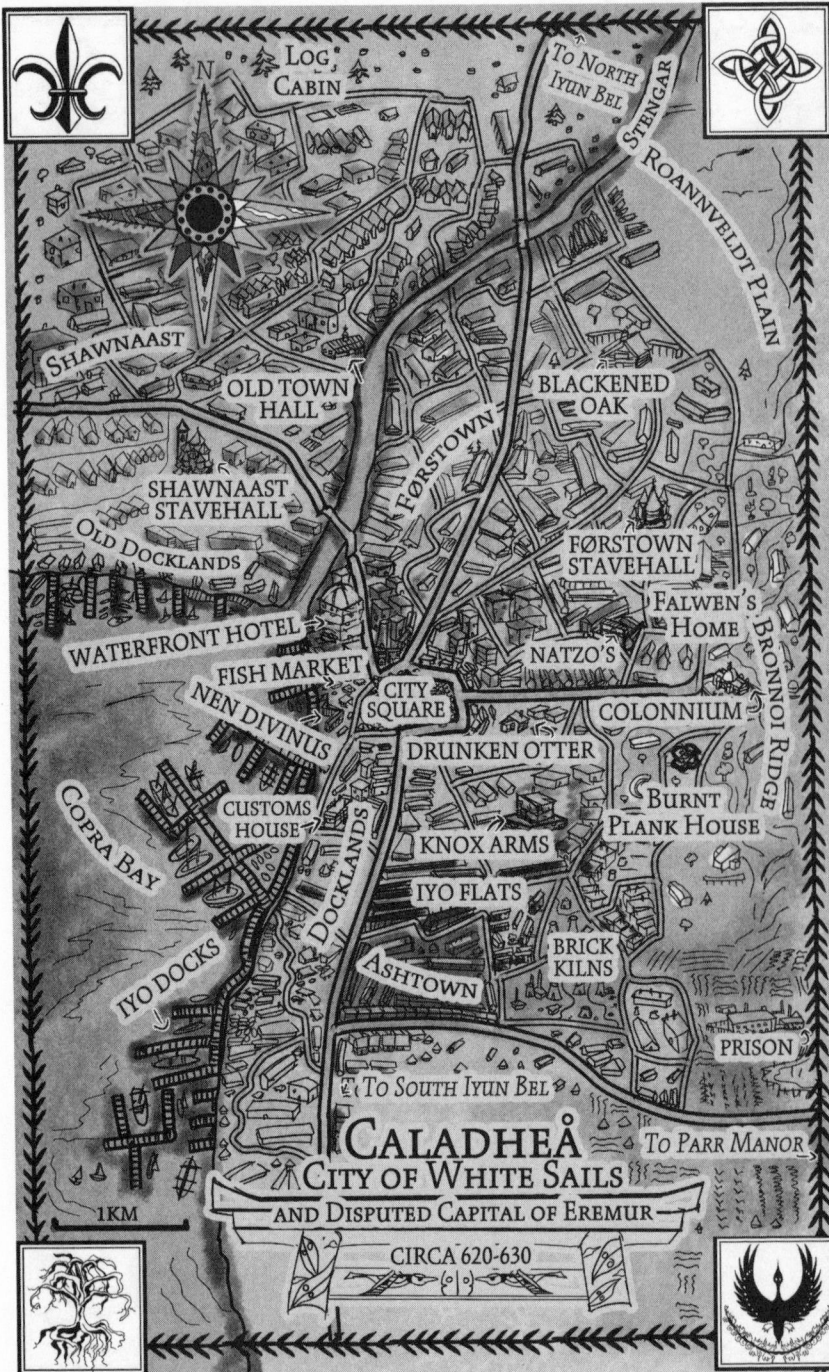

CALADHEÅ
CITY OF WHITE SAILS
AND DISPUTED CAPITAL OF EREMUR
CIRCA 620-630

1.

RUTNAAST

"Salmon? That's what you're looking forward to?" My cousin Dunehein laughed behind me in the canoe stern. "Thought you'd say your friends or a proper bed."

"Not just any salmon." My muscles strained with each stroke of the paddle. Droplets streamed off the wood. "Hot from the smokehouse, oily, flaky, and steaming, with that sweet, hazy scent of burnt alder."

Right now, all I could taste was salt. Sea spray kept my leggings and shirt constantly damp. To our right, snow-capped cliffs rose like crooked walls. To our left, the inlet's far bank was a green smudge wreathed by mist.

I glanced over my shoulder. Dunehein's brown hair stuck to his face, escaping its braid. "What do you miss? Dry clothes?"

"Holding my daughter," he said. "And my wife. Don't tell her she comes second."

"Hah, I'm *so* telling."

Dunehein flipped cold water at my back. I shrieked and dropped my paddle. He snorted with laughter.

"*Kaid*," I swore and leaned over the gunwale. Our boat rocked and listed precariously close to the water. Slimy seaweed spilled in. My fingertips brushed the paddle, only for it to float out of reach. I stretched out with my mind, calling the water around it, but the heaving current pulled it back.

A canoe veered toward us, its dolphin-head prow cutting through choppy waves. Ilani, a thin-faced girl around my age, plucked my dripping paddle from the surface. "Don't you Rin learn how to paddle?"

"It needed a wash." I yanked it from her grip.

She rolled her eyes. "A few more days until home, then I never have to hear your voice again."

Her boat glided ahead to the other two canoes in our small fleet. I flicked my fingers. The seawater that had pooled around my boots swirled into the air. I nudged it into Ilani's craft and through a gap in the sealskin protecting her bedroll. Her older brother, Esiad, twisted to look at me from their canoe stern. I held a finger to my lips, and he grinned.

Esiad and I were antayul, trained to call water since we were children. Our skill was marked by the fan shapes tattooed just below our collarbones. His was faded by a few more years than mine, and arrow scars dotted his chest and back.

"Don't stare," Dunehein teased. "You know Esiad's taken."

"Shut up."

Of everyone in our fleet, I was the only member of the Rin-jouyen, our confederacy's oldest but smallest tribe. The others were from the Iyo, the largest. For now, both jouyen lived at the Iyo settlement of Toel Ginu. There, in the damp chill of a late summer dawn a month after the Blackbird Battle, ten of us had packed our canoes and hugged our loved ones goodbye.

I'd argued against Dunehein coming. He had a newborn daughter and a limp from a wound that still bothered him, but he'd out-stubborned me. We were used to travelling together — paddling the same canoe, collapsing in the same tent, waking at sunrise, and still not wanting to strangle each other.

Officially, this had been a trading trip. We'd paddled up the inlet to Ingdanrad, a settlement built deep in the mountains by ith-erans, the immigrants who settled in our lands. Their mages had dug underground homes, workshops, even a university where they studied everything from theology to metallurgy. Above ground, fields of golden barley rose up the settlement's terraced slopes.

Everyone on this trip was used to dealing with itherans — I spoke fluent Coast Trader and decent Sverbian — but half the people in Ingdanrad spoke neither. We'd haggled by pointing and occasionally laughing at offers. I'd been glad of Dunehein's pres-ence then. No one wanted to challenge me with a burned, tattooed man the size of a grizzly at my side.

Now, finally, we were returning to Toel Ginu, bringing some-thing more valuable than the coins in my purse, more dangerous than the steel blades under my canoe seat. Our real goal had been information on Suriel, the last known air spirit. Why he'd been silent while his human soldiers, the Corvittai, mutinied and attacked us earlier that summer. Where he'd been since then. If any humans still followed him.

As we travelled homeward, the mountains softened, turning green with dense rainforest. Foam churned against our dolphin prow. Paddling an Iyo canoe felt like wearing someone else's clothes, but in the bow, I could see the kinaru carved inside the hull — wings spread, long neck outstretched, like the Rin bird inked on my left arm. Dunehein's Iyo wife had carved it into the auburn wood after he had married her, a quiet tribute to his Rin origins.

"Ai. Look out." I nodded ahead.

A pair of rotting masts jutted up from the water's surface. We steered around them, gliding over the shipwreck. Taut ropes still snapped in the current. Greenish-white sails billowed underwater. I couldn't see deeper than the upper rigging, but when we'd passed it before, Ilani had swum down and found corpses and Sverba's pale blue flag. I tapped two fingers to my forehead in salute.

Last winter, Suriel had sunk half the ships on this inlet in a windstorm. Rutnaast, the only major port between Ingdanrad and Toel Ginu, had fallen to a Corvittai attack the next day. Sea traffic had abandoned these waters after that, along with many of the area's survivors. We'd seen just three intact ships on our whole trip — a galleon carrying plows and harrows forged in Ingdanrad, a heron-prowed canoe from a southern jouyen, and a cod trawler.

Ilani stared into the cloudy water. "Think Wotelem would let me swim down again? There's stuff to salvage."

Esiad snorted. "Whatcha gonna do, porpoise girl? Haul crates up with your flippers?"

"Hush," Dunehein said. "Mereku's back."

An osprey streaked across the grey sky. The bird dove and struck the ocean with a plume of water. A tanned woman broke the surface, flipping black hair out of her face. Mereku hauled herself into a canoe. "Ship coming," she called.

The foremost canoe spun and looped back. We manoeuvred together, holding each other's boats so we didn't drift apart. Wotelem, the Okoreni-Iyo and second-in-command of their jouyen, wound up next to me. Esiad dried Mereku's clothes with a few waves of his hand.

"Armed and moving fast," she said, shivering. "Shot crossbow bolts at me when I flew too close. Their shields have Suriel's kinaru sigil."

Dunehein swore. "Corvittai. Guess we only killed their army, not their navy."

Esiad squinted back east. "They're not here by accident. Someone in Ingdanrad must've sold us out. They don't want us passing on what we've discovered."

"We can lose them on the creek," a heavily scarred man said.

"Too far." Wotelem closed his eyes, lips moving in a plea to his ancestral spirits. "Make port at Rutnaast."

Mereku's mouth twisted. "I'd sooner step into my own grave. Suriel's stench is all over that place."

"It is the last place they will expect us to go."

Grudgingly, Mereku shifted back into her osprey form and launched off the prow. No one else argued. Wotelem's callouses and wind-worn skin proved his time on the sea, but if that wasn't reason enough to obey him, the okoreni band tattooed around his arm was.

Our canoes shot across the water. My arms ached, but I pushed on. Landmarks on tree-lined peninsulas slid past — a massive fallen salt spruce, a rowboat lodged between cottonwoods, Rutnaast's crumbling lighthouse.

Broken boards floated in the harbour. We glided over the wavering silhouette of a seaweed-mottled ship, sideways with its mast on the ocean floor. Our fleet ran aground on a stretch of gravel sheltered by evergreens. I leapt into the shallows and held the canoe while Dunehein climbed out.

"Ilani, Esiad, Dunehein, Kateiko." Wotelem split us from the others with a sweep of his hand. "Search the town. Retreat if you see anyone. We will hide the boats and meet you on the granary road."

I dug my belt out from under my bedroll, buckled it around my waist, and sheathed my knives and flail. Dunehein strapped a double-edged battle axe to his back and picked up a lumber axe. We touched the carved kinaru in our canoe, our private ritual.

Sverbian immigrants had built Rutnaast as a trading post a century ago. With the discovery of silver ore nearby, it had swelled into a mining town. I was the only person in our fleet who hadn't been here, but I knew plenty about Sverbians. I'd lived with one. Loved one. Attended his wedding and his wife's funeral. Tiernan Heilind, the burning man who was never mine.

We climbed over the ashy rubble of cabins. In the docklands, a pier lay underwater, pinned down by a capsized ship. Warehouse doorways yawned dark and hollow. An elk flag, its scarlet dye already faded, twisted at half-mast outside a two-storey log building. I sounded out letters etched on the window. *Customs House*. Fingernail-sized scratches scored the porch like someone had been dragged outside.

Dunehein gripped my shoulder. "Better keep moving, Kako."

We fanned through dirt streets speckled with puddles. Wind and rain had smoothed the mud. The town was a loose grid, its steep shingle roofs orange in the setting sun. The stench of rotten hay oozed from a stable. Farther inland, I glanced through a door hanging from one hinge and saw burlap sacks strewn across the floor, tables upended, a broken baker's paddle by a stone oven.

The sacred stavehall's arched windows were shattered, its west wing a pile of blackened timber, its bronze bell cracked on the cobblestones. The gable carving of a leafless nine-branched tree was criss-crossed with gashes. A rusty nail pinned a bloody white cleric's robe to the door.

I'd heard so many people speak of Rutnaast. Refugees, soldiers, Iyo who once traded here. But *his* voice filled my head — Councillor Antoch Parr. His words that day he berated his colleagues in Council

Hall for ignoring Rutnaast's pleas for help. By the time the navy had arrived, there was nothing left to save.

"I don't get it," Esiad said at the far end of town. The streets converged into a dirt road that wound north into a shadowed valley. "Three thousand people lived here. You'd think someone would've moved back."

"Not if they believe it's haunted by Suriel." Ilani slung her bow over one shoulder. "We're done. Let's go."

"Wait." Dunehein held up his lumber axe. "You smell that?"

Esiad's nose wrinkled. "Reeks like rotting seal."

I scanned the valley mouth, a tangle of waist-high ryegrass. It had grown wild without livestock to graze it. Then I heard buzzing. I clamped my hand over my nose and pushed through the yellowing stalks, following the trail of flies.

A man lay face up in the grass, his skin black and patchy. He was Sverbian, judging by his trousers and tunic. Crossbow bolts stuck out of his chest and leg. Maggots wriggled across the wounds. I choked back vomit and waved the others over.

Ilani gagged. "How long's that been there?"

"Ain't near long enough for a massacre that happened last winter," Dunehein said. "Probably a looter caught by the itheran navy."

I crouched by the body. "These bolts aren't military issue. Look at the fletching. The feathers are cut differently."

"How do *you* know?" Ilani asked.

"I have friends in the military. Point is, if the navy didn't kill him, who did?"

"If any Corvittai were lurking, we'd be dead already." Dunehein pulled handfuls of grass aside. "More bolts here. Looks like they came from the north."

Esiad drew an arrow from his quiver and climbed a hillock. I followed with one hand on my throwing dagger, Nurivel. The logged valley gave us a clear view of the dirt road leaving town. It crossed a creek via a timber bridge and forked on the far side. Both routes zigzagged into the hills.

I pointed at the fork. "Where do those roads go?"

"North to a silver mine, northwest to a tannery," Esiad said. "We sold furs there last year."

"Come on," Ilani said. "Wotelem's waiting."

Esiad didn't move. "Maybe we should—"

He choked and toppled back. I spun. He tumbled down the hillock, a bolt in his stomach.

Ilani screamed.

Something streaked past my head. I swept my arm in an arc. A crescent of fog swirled up, shielding us from view.

"Back south! Hurry!" Dunehein scooped up Esiad as if the younger man was light as goose down.

I skidded down the slope. Bolts thudded into the dirt. I leapt over one and kept going, my braid streaming behind me. *Run. Just run.*

We wove down laneways, around stacks of logs, anywhere we had cover. I cleaved apart a pond, holding the water aside until Dunehein caught up. We stumbled to a halt in a dark alley. Dunehein set Esiad down and collapsed into the mud.

Ilani knelt by her brother. "Esi. *Esi!*"

"Move," I snapped, fumbling through the leather purse on my belt.

She shuffled aside. Of us all, I'd spent the most time helping healers. I pressed gauze packets of dry bogmoss to Esiad's gaping stomach. The bolt had torn his flesh when he fell. The moss swelled with blood, reeking like mouldy timber.

Esiad coughed. Red froth bubbled from his mouth onto his bare chest. He wiped it off his antayul tattoo and stared at his dripping fingers. I gritted my teeth and started binding the bogmoss in place.

An osprey whistled. Mereku landed on a wagon, talons scraping the wood. She leapt off and shifted to human in midair. "What in Aeldu-yan happened?"

"Ambush," Ilani said. "We have to reach the others."

"You can't. The Corvittai ship's in view. If they see you, we're all in danger."

Ilani whirled on her. "Then what do we do?"

"Ask the aeldu for a blessing." I knotted the last bandage. "Esiad's already bleeding into his lungs. I can't mend that."

"You're wrong." Ilani shook me so hard my teeth cracked together. "You're wrong! *Fix* him!"

"Ai!" Dunehein hauled her off me. "You think we'll let him die?"

Mereku sighed. "The stavehall's just ahead. Wait there. I'll tell Wotelem where you are." She was gone with a few flaps of her wings.

I crept to the alley end. The cobblestone courtyard by the stavehall was empty. I beckoned to the others — just as a bird screeched.

"Nei!" I cried, snapping my head up. Mereku tumbled through the sky, one wing limp. "Nei, nei, nei!"

Pain tore through my shoulder. I reeled back. A bolt had struck me. Another burst through a wall, raining splinters.

Ilani dashed up, arrow nocked. "Where are they?"

I scanned the courtyard. "There! On that roof!"

Her hands moved in perfect rhythm. One man went down before he could reload. She turned on another, hammering him with arrows. He dropped too.

A bolt skidded across the ground, leaving a furrow in the mud. I saw a reflection in a puddle. A third archer stood in the crumbling bell tower. No way could I throw my dagger that high.

I thrust my arm up. A water whip shot three storeys into the air and curled around his leg. I yanked. He plummeted through the air and hit the cobblestone with a *crack*.

I wanted to throw up. I focused on the broken bell instead, trying to block out the red smear in my peripheral vision. When nothing else happened, Ilani rushed back down the alley to Esiad.

"*Kako!*" Dunehein called.

I turned. His eyes widened.

He threw his lumber axe. A man dropped a few paces behind me, the axe in his chest. A dagger slid from the man's hand and clattered into the gutter.

All I could hear was wind and the gurgle of the dying man. Blood oozed across his jerkin. Then I realized why he looked odd. Sverbian clothes, blond, pale. Every Corvittai I'd fought had darker colouring.

Dunehein drew up next to me. "Kako, one of us has gotta reach Toel Ginu. They need to know what we learned in Ingdanrad."

"We should find Wotelem first."

"He could be dead already. Ilani ain't gonna leave her brother, and you've got a better chance of making it than me. My leg's still no good."

He was right. That didn't make it easier. I climbed onto a windowsill, gripping the roof as I peered over Rutnaast. The last rays of sun lit up the bottom of heavy clouds. Just beyond the lighthouse, a ship glided across the water, white sails billowing.

I dropped back to the ground. "Let me say goodbye."

Esiad's eyes were unfocused, wandering from the plank walls to the sliver of indigo sky overhead. Ilani sat with his head in her lap, stroking his black hair. I knelt and took his cold hand. His breath came in shallow gasps.

I forced a smile. "Too bad we can't go fur trapping together like we planned. You Iyo boys are more fun than our Rin. But you'll be back soon, haunting us from Aeldu-yan."

He grinned, his teeth red.

"There's something we Rin say." I touched the dolphin tattoo on his upper arm. "Today you flew."

Shakily, he returned the gesture on my kinaru tattoo, blood running down its ink wings. He understood.

Dunehein led me through the streets, muttering instructions as he peered around corners. We were a few blocks away when Ilani's tortured wails reached us. I closed my eyes and whispered a death rite.

We stopped at the edge of town. Our planned route to Toel Ginu had been to paddle a network of creeks, but it'd take too long even if I could reach our canoe. I had to go by land. Beyond the mat of forested hills were the plains, and from there, rolling farmland. It'd take a person thirty hours to walk if they never tired. I hoped to be there in less.

"Kako. Little cousin." Dunehein gripped my arms. "You know why I'm rejoining the Rin, right? Not just for my daughter, but for you. To make up for the nine years I wasn't there."

I hugged him, ignoring the pain in my shoulder. The top of my head barely met his chin. "Don't get stabbed in the leg again. I'm not carrying you around Toel."

He patted the battle axe on his back. "I'll take down anyone who gets close. Gotta do my brother's weapon justice."

"He'd be proud."

"If I . . ." He hesitated. "If this is it. Take care of my wife and little girl."

"You know I will, Dune. Always." I spread my arms like wings. "Today we fly."

I paused atop a hill to look back. Warm light flickered above the horizon, casting pink smudges on the dark ocean. Someone had lit the lighthouse pyre. I wondered who'd been hiding there, if they knew they were signalling a Corvittai ship, or if they thought it was the navy on patrol.

My paws hit the forest floor, springing off spruce needles. I longed to sprint, but couldn't with my wounded shoulder, and anyway, the instincts that came with my wolf body knew better. I had to pace myself. Run without sleep, without food, with as little rest as possible.

I hadn't known Esiad well until this journey. As the only antayul in our fleet, we'd spent a lot of time together. It hadn't taken long to figure out what he loved most. Canoeing, his family, and the Iyo girl he planned to ask to marry him. She'd want to know who killed him. I wouldn't be able to tell her.

Run. Just run.

2.

TOEL GINU

I slid through wet grass into a muddy hollow and flopped over. No sleep, just rest. Toel Ginu was a couple leagues away. My wolf ears could sense it, a distant cluster of voices like a fleck in my vision. Shaggy mountain goats bleated nearby. The hot scent of their blood made my stomach growl. No sleep, just rest . . .

"*Gåtag! Skytten húnd!*"

Some Sverbian goatherd, yelling at his dog — no, at *me*. I leapt up and veered toward the rainforest bordering the plains. Trees loomed in front of me, hazy green through the mist. *Run. Just run.*

The forest flickered. My eyelids drooped. Rain fell into my ears, eyes, rolling off my fur. I wanted so much to curl up in a hole. Never move. Never open my eyes.

Smoke, fish oil, burnt alder. The scents of Toel Ginu wafted through the dripping trees. There — a wooden stakewall. The new

Rin stockade. Raw timber under a canopy of rioden trees, ditches flooded with rainwater.

I burst through a tangle of bushes and collapsed with a whine. Shouts, the groan of a gate, squelching boots. Someone knelt next to me and spoke.

I willed my body to change. Silver fur melded into tanned skin. Hands. Feet. "Fendul," I gasped.

The woman slid warm hands under me. I flinched when she touched my braid, though after she saw me attune, one more taboo didn't matter. "Get the okorebai!" she called as she carried me into the stockade.

People leapt up, staring past us, watching for my companions, who weren't coming. The woman took me into a dim plank house and laid me on a crackling grass-stuffed mattress. Firelight sputtered into life. The vaulted ceiling bowed in and out of focus.

Fendul froze in the doorway, hand on his sword hilt. "Kako."

His face blurred, but I'd know him anywhere. Perfect posture, cropped black hair, lines tattooed around his upper arm. Only the Okorebai-Rin had those marks.

He crossed the room with long strides and sank to his knees. "What happened? Where are the others?"

"Rutnaast." I coughed. Someone pressed a mug into my hands. I choked down water. "Corvittai. Sverbian archers. Esiad's dead."

Fendul turned to the woman who brought me in. "Ready every Rin warrior who can fly. Double the gate guards. Send a runner to the Iyo plank houses. Tell the Okorebai-Iyo her brother's delegation has been attacked."

"Fen—" I sat up and groaned. I had no time to be tired. "He got one."

"What?"

"Suriel. Got a rift mage."

Fendul folded his hands over his face. "Aeldu save us all."

I grabbed his arm. "Remember this name. Iollan och Cormic. *Say* it."

"Iollan och Cormic. I'll remember. Now rest."

"Wait, Fen." My voice cracked. If he didn't return . . . While I was travelling, I'd thought of a thousand things I wanted to tell him, but they slipped away. "Be careful."

"I will." He rose, pulling away. "We'll bring everyone back. I promise."

I crouched on spongy moss, hidden by curtains of green witch's hair that draped from pine branches. Ash floated through the trees and brushed my skin like soft rain. The sun glowed red, so hazy I could look at it without blinking. Acrid smoke burned my lungs.

A silver wolf nudged its companion with its nose. Pawed at the motionless body. Dried blood had caked the black wolf's fur into rough spikes, the pine needles under it stained dark. The silver wolf whined, a quavering plea.

I reached through the curtain of lichen. I knew now, looking back, that the aeldu would bless me with the silver wolf's body within a day of this moment. The wolf gazed at me, tawny eyes flat in the smoky light. It lifted its head and howled.

I woke with a gasp, chest heaving. My hands felt heavy as anchors.

A man knelt facing away from me. Rumpled black hair, empty knife sheath on his belt, curled dolphin tattooed on his arm. I knew the constellation of arrow scars on his back. *Esiad.*

He turned. His stomach was smooth. Whole. Blood dripped off the bone hunting knife in his hand. A silver wolf lay on the dirt floor, half its pelt cut away.

"Stop! *Stop!*" I grabbed at the knife and missed.

Esiad grinned, holding his blade out of reach. "Fitting, ain't it?"

My hands trembled. "You're dead."

"Whose fault is that, ai?"

"You were bleeding into your lungs! I couldn't fix you!"

"*She* would've taught you how."

Marijka stepped out from behind him. She looked like a drawing from my book of Sverbian folk tales. Pale as ghostblossom, blonde hair pinned up, a head shorter than Esiad. A dove next to a raven. Her bodice and white dress were bloodless, unmarked. No trace of Parr's slender knife.

She sat on the bed. The mattress sank under her weight. I heard her breath, saw her chest rise and fall. She just looked at me. Her eyes were vast skies, soft and empty as a winter day.

The first time I saw Marijka, I thought she was a shard of moonlight. After her death I tried everything I knew to keep her in this world. Begged my aeldu to let her stay. Screamed at her gods not to take her across the ocean to Thaerijmur. Spoke her name in the moonlight. The Sverbian legend of the white woman said she'd appear.

"Maika." I took her hand.

She pinned my elbows down. I squirmed. She was strong for someone so small. For a spirit.

"I didn't know what he'd do." Tears pricked my eyes. "Please, you have to believe me. I'm sorry!"

"You led Parr to her." Esiad pressed the tip of his knife to my shoulder. The pain was distant, slight as a nettle scratch. A red drop welled up.

"Stop!" My throat felt tight. Marijka held me in place, her face blank.

"Your aunt's gone because of you, too. They all are." He stuck the knife into me again. "Fendul's father." Again. "Nili's lover." Again.

"Yironem's friend." Wolf blood rolled down the blade, mixing with mine. "You led them south. Straight to Parr and the Corvittai."

The air felt heavy, crushing me into the mattress. Esiad kept going. One jab for every Rin who'd never go home. Every elder who raised me, every youth I swam with, everyone whose blood was in the ground outside the stockade walls.

Cool air drifted over my skin. It was too dim and grey for me to guess the time. My skin was scrubbed clean, my hair freshly braided. Nili or Hiyua, my adopted sister and mother, must've done that while I slept.

The bed I lay in wasn't mine any more than this was a Rin dwelling. Two months now we'd been borrowing a visitors' plank house from the Iyo. The place felt blank as polished wood. Bare walls, unpainted lanterns, no makiri figurines on the mantelpieces to watch over us. Just Behadul's sword mounted over the largest hearth. Fendul had chosen not to wield his father's blade, keeping his own instead.

"Ai, she's awake." Nili limped over and lowered herself onto the next bed. "Done fighting me and the healer?"

"What?" I looked at cottonspun bandages on my shoulder, then recalled drinking tulanta to numb it before our healer, Barolein, stitched me up. "Oh. Sorry. I thought . . . the aeldu were here."

Her smile faded. "Did you see Parr?"

"Nei. Others." I traced the blanket, searching for the raised threads of silver fir branches, but the fabric was smooth. Right — my mother's blanket was still in my canoe in Rutnaast.

Nili pulled off her boot and rubbed her calf. Her arrow wound from the Blackbird Battle had gotten infected. Barolein had cut away the dead flesh, leaving a palm-sized hollow on her leg.

Outside, voices melded with the crackle of flames. "Where's Yironem?" I asked.

"Rutnaast." Nili scoffed. "Our mudskull brother volunteered. Fendul agreed if Yiro stays out of combat, but we've seen how well he listens."

Yironem's a good archer, I almost said, but he was also only fourteen and gangly as a fawn. Esiad had been a grown man and one of the Iyo's best archers, and that didn't save him. Still, I understood Fendul's decision. With only a dozen Rin who could fly, he needed them all. After the Blackbird Battle, we'd debated for days before raising the age limit for combat to sixteen. It was too late to save Yironem's best friend. That battle had changed Yironem in a few ways.

"Wait. They left flying," I said. "So now people know Yiro . . ."

"Attunes to a kinaru, yeah. He hasn't got the hang of it yet. Took out the archery targets with one wing. Everyone went rushing outside. Half of 'em thought Suriel's kinaru were attacking, half thought it's a sign from the aeldu. The elders keep shrieking that we dared keep it secret."

Dunehein's wife, Rikuja, also came by. She'd been living in our plank house to help out even though she wasn't Rin yet. She held their baby in a bundle of woolly goatskin. I cooed over how much dark hair Sihaja had, how big she'd gotten in a month, how she could grasp the bark cord woven into her mother's braid.

Rikuja settled on the foot of my bed. "Better not hold her until your shoulder heals. Aeldu willing, Dune comes back with at least one arm."

My chest tightened. "I'm so sorry, Rija. I didn't want to leave him—"

"I know, love." She squeezed my hand.

"Fendul said you have news, Kako," Nili said. "Something about . . . Ulan? Olan?"

"Iollan. Thank the aeldu Fen's better with itheran names than you."

She waved at Hiyua across the plank house. "You'd better tell our tema. She's in charge while Fendul's gone."

Hiyua came over and kissed my hair. She and Nili were twins a generation apart, all curves on hard frames, their dark brown hair pulled back into long tails. "Good to see my other daughter again," she said, smiling. "The Okorebai-Iyo wants any info you have, but I refused to let her disturb you."

I was grateful for more than the rest. I'd gotten used to Wotelem's rigidity, but his elder sister, Tokoda, was a different matter. Even without a weapon, she could silence a room of arguing people from every jouyen in our confederacy.

"Well," I began, "Ingdanrad's mages don't know much about Suriel's whereabouts. We met a few scholars from the Kae-jouyen who study saidu, and they think he's in the eastern mountains, but they can't track him. They haven't seen any Corvittai since the Blackbird Battle, either. Instead, the mages told us about Iollan och Cormic.

"Iollan trained as an earth mage, but his obsession was theology. He wrote the book that Ingdanrad scholars use to explain rift magic. Tiernan immigrated from Sverba to study under him. It . . . didn't go well. Iollan kept pushing the law with his research, so Tiernan left with Maika when she finished her medical training. They never mentioned Iollan to me.

"Then, five years ago, people started finding runes of Suriel's kinaru sigil all across the rainforest. But the Kae scholars say saidu can't make runes. A human mage had to be working for Suriel, trying to open a rift into the void between worlds and marking runes at the test sites. Ingdanrad swears it was Iollan."

Hiyua sank onto the bed next to Nili, cradling her badly scarred left arm. "They're sure it wasn't Nonil?"

The Corvittai captain no one had heard of until he brought an army to destroy the Rin. Nonil was fixed in my memory. Slumped in the saddle, an orange glow lighting up trails of smoke. I'd named my flail Antalei — waterfall, destroyer of fire — after shattering his ribs with it.

I shook my head. "The mages knew Nonil by his real name. He was a young Ferish soldier named Alesso Spariere, who defected to Ingdanrad and served in their militia in exchange for learning fire magic. He was in Ingdanrad when the runes were set. Iollan wasn't. Plus, Nonil never studied rift magic. He just liked setting things on fire."

"Spariere," Rikuja repeated, shifting Sihaja in her arms. "So Nonil wasn't Parr's son."

"Nei. Anyway, three years ago, Iollan got caught doing illegal experiments. *Really* illegal. Ingdanrad threw him in prison and melted down the key. A few months later, Nonil quit their militia. Soon, the mages realized he'd left to carry on Iollan's work. Suriel formed the Corvittai to protect him so he didn't get arrested, too. In one move Nonil leapt from low-ranked soldier to an ancient telsaidu's prized hand."

"A traitor defects twice," Nili muttered. "Who's surprised?"

"Thrice, actually. I always wondered what tipped him over the edge toward mutiny this summer. Turns out it's the same reason he stopped trying to recruit Tiernan." I stared at the vaulted ceiling. "Suriel didn't need them anymore. Iollan och Cormic had just broken out of prison."

Nili swore. Hiyua silenced her with a glare.

"Is—" Rikuja hesitated. "I'm just saying, it was Nonil who attacked us. Is Iollan really so dangerous? For a while you thought helping Suriel open a rift was a good idea, Kako. You thought he'd leave our world and the wars would stop."

"Then I got Maika killed."

Hiyua put a warm hand on my shoulder. "That was Parr's doing."

"Still. Suriel said he's trying to reach the void because other saidu don't want him in this world, but there's another reason he didn't tell us, something from before our jouyen woke those other saidu. I've got no idea what else he might've lied about. I don't know how Iollan plans to open a rift, if he can close it, or what might come through from the other side. The mages wouldn't talk about the experiments that got him locked up, which can't be a good sign. And now they have no idea where he is."

"So . . . what happens if we find Iollan?" Nili asked.

"We stop him if we can," I said. "Kill him if we can't."

Before we built the stakewall, I could stand in our plank house's doorway and glimpse Iyo buildings through the trees. Beyond them was a strip of ocean that changed from blue to grey to teal with the weather. In the other direction, salt spruce covered the dense green understorey. Rain slid off rubbery leaves sheltering deep purple berries. Sparrows and waxwings hopped among the branches. Once, I saw a mountain cat crouched in the bushes, gold eyes watching me.

Now there was only an oval of sharpened posts bound tight around the visitors' buildings like the ribs of a canoe. Most of our life happened within the stockade. We'd converted the stable into workshops, cleared land for combat practice, strung up canvas tarps for shelter.

When the clouds cleared, Nili and I lay outside on woven bark mats to watch the star rain. She won our bet for spotting the first falling star. After four straight years, I suspected she was lying, but I paid her a pann anyway.

"So," Nili said, balancing the iron coin on her nose. "You met Gallnach people in Ingdanrad, right? What're they like?"

"Weird. Both men and women wear long skirts they call wool-wraps. And they all smell like barley."

She snorted. The coin fell.

We'd grown up hearing about Gallnach, the first itherans in our lands. Their homeland, Gallun, was a group of islands overseas. Three centuries ago, they settled in the eastern mountains near Iyo territory. Sverbians who arrived later spoke of them as a curiosity — strange people who carved symbols in rocks and lived in the earth.

Tiernan and Marijka always dodged my questions about Gallnach. Wotelem was the one who filled in the gaps as we'd prepared for our journey. Gallun was once governed by druids who used runes and nature rites to defend their lands. Sverba conquered them and banned magic so they couldn't rebel. Desperate, several druids fled and built Ingdanrad as a refuge.

When other itheran races began fighting for land here, Ingdanrad declared neutrality and accepted anyone who wanted to study magic. I wouldn't have thought teaching potential enemies was wise. But after Sverba claimed this, too, as their territory, it was new Sverbian mages who managed to keep non-druidic magic legal. Without them, I could be arrested for calling water to wash my hands. Marijka could've been executed for sealing someone's wounds.

In Ingdanrad, I'd asked an old friend of Tiernan's how he learned magic, since all forms were still banned in Sverba. She told me that a few druids who stayed in Gallun married Sverbian soldiers, starting a long line of mixed-blood warriors who practised in secret. They trained Tiernan. Yet another thing he never told me.

Nili started tossing her coin in the air. "What do Gallnach look like? Are the men lush?"

I smacked her. "They look like Sverbians. Shorter, but they

sunburn just as easy. I could only tell them apart by their clothes. Or names. Iollan's second name means 'son of Cormic.'"

"He's Gallnach? I thought all Corvittai are Ferish."

"The ones who fought under Nonil were. I guess Suriel takes whoever's useful."

"Aeldu save me. Dunno how you keep track of it all."

I glanced over at her. "How're you holding up?"

"Surviving." Nili took two drummer's wristbands from her purse. Even in the dark, I knew they were embroidered with rioden needles. "I should leave them at Taworen's grave. But it feels like as long as I don't . . . he might walk into the stockade and kiss me. As if the last two months were a bad dream."

We lapsed into silence, though it was never truly silent at night. Voices whispered through the scrape of branches. No words, just a rise and fall of sound, faint as rippling water. Sometimes they grew louder. The memories came in waves, crushing my lungs, like being slammed into a wall over and over. Every night on the trip to Ingdanrad, in our cramped tent, Dunehein had held my hands in his massive ones until I fell asleep.

Who do you hear? he asked once.

Your brother, I said. *Your mother, these days*. And Parr. Always Parr.

A mournful wail shuddered through the forest. The gate guards seized their javelins.

"Was that a loon?" Nili whispered.

I folded my hands and blew into the gap between my thumbs, making a high whistle. The reply was instant. And loud.

"Kinaru!" I leapt to my feet.

Nili snatched up her bow and dashed toward the firepits. Our plank house door swung open. Hiyua stepped into a pool of firelight.

A bird glided across the sky, blocking out a swath of stars. Branches bowed under the gust of air. The kinaru thumped down with a colossal splatter of mud. Its mottled neck rose over the sod roofs, its webbed feet leaving prints big enough to bathe in.

"Yiro!" Nili rushed to the bird.

Two figures slid off his back. An Iyo woman with a bandaged knee and our scout Mereku, arm limp, face a swollen mess. The kinaru shifted into Yironem, scrawny and dark-haired.

"Yiro!" I called. "Is Fendul with you?"

He pulled out of Nili's embrace. "Yeah — he was right behind us—"

An eagle landed, a goose, a kingfisher. No crow. Heat rose inside me, pressing against the back of my eyes. My whistle echoed off the stakewall.

Nothing. Just whispering voices. A star streaked overhead, plummeting toward the horizon.

Then, from high in the trees—

Caw. Caw.

3.

AUTUMN EQUINOX

Fendul shifted and hit the ground feet-first. He was bruised, cut, covered with blood and dirt. I flung my arms around him. He knotted his fingers into my hair.

"Fen. Are you okay? Is Dunehein—"

"He's alive. I'm fine. Just not built for speed." Fendul looked past me, coughed, and stepped back. "Sit. I need to speak with you and Hiyua."

The few people who weren't staring at Yironem were watching us. Fendul gestured them indoors while I settled on a log bench. Hiyua picked up a forgotten blanket and draped it over my shoulders.

Fendul lit a stone lantern. Its carved holes cast triangles of warm light around us. "The others will be here in a few days. They're bringing the canoes back with our dead." He slumped on a bench. "Three Iyo lost besides Esiad. No Rin deaths. We found the delegation under siege in the stavehall. Wotelem was holding captives so attackers didn't just torch the place."

"Were they all Corvittai?" Hiyua asked.

"The sailors were. The archers who set the ambush didn't seem to be, but we figured out why they're in Rutnaast." He took a jagged, glittering rock the size of a crabapple from his breeches pocket. "Silver ore."

I gasped. "The mines — they were abandoned after the massacre last winter—"

Fendul rolled the ore around his palm. "We found a dozen itherans working a mine. The guards they planted in town weren't proper soldiers. Probably why they had crossbows. Easy to use."

That's why they didn't shoot right away. They didn't want a fight. Cold horror crept over me. They might've let us leave if I hadn't discovered the rotting body, if we hadn't looked toward the mines.

"What did you do with the captives?" Hiyua stood over Fendul like a mother about to scold her son.

"They slit their own throats." He looked at his hands. "Aeldu knows what they expected us to do that's worse."

Her face softened. "And the miners?"

"Wotelem's taking them to the prison in Caladheå. Let itherans deal with their own. If we executed everyone who stole from our lands, we'd have to cut down half the forest for funeral pyres. We couldn't understand them anyway."

"Wait," I said. "What language were they speaking?"

"Honestly, I'm not sure. But we found these in their camp." Fendul passed me a roll of papers.

I untied the string, releasing a shower of grit. Angular black lines formed rows across the sheets. "What are these?"

"I hoped you'd know. I didn't get a chance to show Wotelem, and nobody else with us can read."

"I've never seen these symbols. They're not Ferish or Sverbian." I held a paper up to the lantern. "But those archers looked — *oh*. Oh, shit."

They stared at me. For once Hiyua didn't reprimand my swearing.

"They were Gallnach dressed as Sverbians. I bet they struck a deal — the Corvittai took the mines, the Gallnach worked them, and they split the profit. Which means these papers could be linked to Iollan och Cormic."

I drifted in and out of sleep all night, giving up when early risers started moving around the plank house. Next to me, Fendul's bed was empty, perfectly made with embroidered kinaru wings curving across his blanket. I dug through my rioden chest for a waterproof bark cape. Rikuja, her shirt unlaced to feed Sihaja, said good morning as I passed. I checked the firepits, then the workshops. No Fendul.

Akiga, the eldest surviving Rin at fifty-five, stopped me at the stockade gate. Only after I threatened to get Hiyua did she let me pass, declaring Hiyua would have no time for an adopted daughter's whining once she had grandchildren to look after. Akiga took every chance to point out she was the only Rin with grandkids, even though it meant reminding us most adult Rin were dead.

The forest was washed in green. Straight west, neat rows of Iyo plank houses lined a peninsula that dropped away as cliffs. A stone archway led to an island where black stumps surrounded the shrine ruins. I went southwest instead, stepping over logs and lichen-spotted rocks.

Fendul sat at the edge of the forest peeling bark off a branch. Water dripped off his hair and ran down his skin. Coastal mornings were cool, but men went bare-chested into autumn to show their tattoos as long as possible. He'd never admit it, but he also took pride in the sunken scar that ran diagonally from his shoulder to the bottom of his ribs.

"Don't you ever sleep?" I asked.

He sheathed his knife. "It's the only time I have to think."

"Oh." I stepped back. "Sorry—"

"Kako." He took my hand.

I eased down next to him, sinking into thick moss. "Why are you out here?"

"Trying to get used to the view."

The sky over the ocean was inky blue. Rock pillars rose from the water, wreathed by fog. "We're not going home, are we?"

Fendul shook his head. "I thought we'd beaten the Corvittai down. But if they found Gallnach allies, we need allies, too. Tokoda agreed to let us winter here."

"You're okay with leaving our land unguarded?"

"The Tamu-jouyen offered to guard our border in exchange for hunting rights. I sent a messenger last night to accept."

His voice was steady, but I knew he'd struggled with that decision. Rin had lived and died in the rainforest of Anwen Bel for thousands of years. Wildlife grazed vegetation that grew on our burial grounds. Hunting rights meant giving away the blood of our people. We'd only ever granted that right to the Iyo.

I pulled my cape tighter. "What do we do about the Corvittai?"

"Tokoda's looking for a Gallnach to translate the Rutnaast papers, and she sent word to the rest of our confederacy about Iollan. We decided not to involve the Caladheå Council."

"Good. I don't trust them after Parr. Besides, if they know an outlaw druid is on the loose, they'll probably kill every mage they find and identify the bodies later."

Fendul spun his peeled branch. "You know we have to tell Tiernan. He was Iollan's acolyte for a year."

A sigh escaped me. I'd promised Tiernan I wouldn't return to him. "I'll get an Iyo to drop by the Blackened Oak. The innkeeper can pass a message on."

"Then if that's settled . . . I need your opinion. I want to ask Hiyua to be Okoreni-Rin. It feels odd asking someone twice my age to be my second-in-command, but I could use an elder's guidance."

"Do it. The Rin like her, and the Iyo know her. Plus her son attuned to a kinaru. No one can complain about her bloodline."

His cheeks flushed. "I thought you might be offended I didn't ask you."

I laughed. "The okoreni takes over if you die. The jouyen would throw me out. Aeldu knows who they'd choose instead. Akiga? We'd be back to executing itherans and sending twelve-year-olds into battle."

"Right. Well." He shredded a cottonwood leaf. "Speaking of . . . things I've asked you."

I knew this conversation would happen. He'd been patient, but I owed him an answer.

Marriage had been my planned escape from Anwen Bel. When that fell apart, I drifted. Betrayed Tiernan, my first love. Killed Parr, my first lover. In the wake of that wreckage, Fendul said the last words I expected. *Marry me.*

I closed my eyes, listening to the waves. I used to watch ships sail past and daydream about fleeing this coast, but it was time to stop drifting. Fendul had given me a second chance. Didn't lecture me, didn't pretend my decisions were okay, just accepted them. Kept my secrets.

I touched his right arm, the ink I'd marked to complete his

tattoo. It'd still been bleeding when he proposed. Twenty-one, the youngest okorebai in generations, leading a jouyen into war.

"You asked me two things. One was to stay with the Rin. To that — yes."

He smiled, dawn breaking after months of night.

"To the other question . . ."

I had plenty of reasons to say yes. I loved him, even if I wasn't *in* love. Being around him was as natural as breathing, and he was lush enough I wouldn't mind the physical side. But no matter what I said, it wouldn't be for myself.

"What do you think will happen?" he asked softly.

"The jouyen will turn on you, Fen. Everyone calls me a deserter."

"Not everyone." He dropped his handful of shredded leaves. "Remember how many Rin have family here, people they hadn't seen in years. You did what my father was too proud and too scared to do. You led us south."

"Now we can't leave."

Fendul touched my elbow. "We have a chance to fix things. End a century of violence, rebuild the Rin, do it better this time. I need your help. I need someone brave and determined, who reminds me to be those things, who cares so much it hurts. They'll turn on me if I marry anyone less than that."

I pushed off the moss and straddled him. His rain-soaked breeches were cold. I traced below the huckleberry crest tattooed on his left arm, leaving a band of water where my fireweed crest would mark his tanned skin.

"Kako," he whispered.

I looked into his dark eyes. "Can we give it time? Let people settle in for winter. In a few months, if things are going well . . . then yes. I'll marry you."

The Rin-jouyen felt like a tree rebuilt from broken branches. Nearly everyone had taken orphans as apprentices. Nili had three embroiderers, all siblings. Rikuja taught woodcarving to twins. Barolein, our only healer, was assigned the two most skilled antayul-to-be. Hiyua took care of the younger kids. There weren't many. Our birth rate had dropped to almost nothing.

Every antayul except me had apprentices. Even a fifteen-year-old girl taught her younger sister. Water-calling was too crucial to lose. I'd expected to train two young girls, inseparable friends, on my return from Ingdanrad. Instead, Fendul asked me to train Yironem.

"But Yiro's grown up as a dancer!" I said. "His initiation's in four days!"

Fendul shrugged. "It's what he wants. And he's your brother now."

After my shock wore off, it made sense. The kinaru shawl worn for ceremonial dances must've seemed a ghost of his real wings. Still, it meant leaving the role his father had taught him, and becoming an antayul would dictate everything from how he wore his hair to who he could marry. It was also far easier to learn young, which is why most antayul started soon after they learned to walk. It'd be months before Yironem could nudge a droplet.

From then on he was my constant companion, a shadow with rumpled hair and deft hands. He watched me dry firewood and boil ropeweed to make fishing nets. As we skinned game and washed roots I explained how to sense water, to pay attention to its taste, smell, feel, temperature. He rarely talked, and wriggled like a worm on a fishhook after sitting still too long, but at least he followed directions.

Lessons were combined with chores. We spent a day hammering dried meat into powder, mashing cranberries, mixing it all with softened deer fat, and shaping it into slabs for camp food. Autumn fishing began early on the coast, and several Iyo had already gone to the rivers.

Dunehein returned at dawn on the autumn equinox. His left ear was gone. My cousin was crumbling, a mountain worn down by storms, but he still lifted me off the ground like I was an arrowhead-leaf doll. His smile as he held baby Sihaja made everything a little easier to bear.

It was rare the Rin weren't home for the equinox. Normally we'd open our shrine, calling our aeldu back for winter. Instead we heard drums echo up the coast all morning from the new Iyo shrine, slow and heavy like a heartbeat. We hung fire-red blazebine on the stakewall and white flowers on the doors to brighten the place.

Our ceremonies were planned for afternoon. The Rin had no surviving drummers, so Fendul had invited select Iyo to perform. Airedain was invited on my request, but his uncle Ranelin said he'd travelled to Crieknaast. I'd given up hope until I heard his voice at midday.

"Ai, Rin-girl! Your guard won't let me in." Airedain stood in the stockade gateway carrying a drum under one arm. The Iyo dolphin crest adorned the drumskin. He was partly in regalia with curving blue lines painted across his chest and black cloth knotted around his wrists, but still wore his usual breeches and boots with his dark hair spiked up like a shark fin.

Akiga pointed her javelin at his head. "*That* is unacceptable. Unmarried men should have short hair." Her own hair was perfectly braided with bark cord woven among grey strands.

"Airedain persuaded his elders to make up with the Rin," I said. "Without him, we wouldn't *have* this stockade."

"That's no excuse for breaking regalia. My grandchildren would bathe in itchbine before participating in a sacred ceremony looking like that."

Ignoring her, I pulled Airedain into the stockade. Away from the gate, he said, "Aeldu save us. I see why you left. Even Tokoda's given up making me cut my hair."

I gave him a quick hug, hindered by the bulky drum. "Why were you in Crieknaast?"

"Working in a Sverbian lumber camp. Tokoda wants eyes in the eastern mountains in case Suriel starts messing with rift magic again, and I'm one of the only Iyo who's seen another world *and* speaks fluent Sverbian. You shoulda seen me hauling logs next to bearded itheran lumbermen." He laughed.

"That explains this." I poked his arm, more muscular than I remembered. He wasn't such a skinny sapling anymore.

We assembled by a pond a respectful distance from Toel Ginu. Auburn rioden framed the shore, their branches mirrored in the rippling surface. Fendul stood on a boulder. Airedain and the other drummers formed a semicircle around him, their drums strapped to their hips. Water lapped at their boots. Drumbeats boomed through the trees, calling our aeldu from every burial ground across the coastal rainforest.

Hiyua was initiated as okoreni, then all four youths who had attuned over summer were initiated as adults. Yironem received the outline of a kinaru and Hiyua's ropeweed crest on his arm. The tattoo would be finished the next day in a private ceremony. Dunehein was next. Burns from the shrine fire had twisted his kinaru tattoo, but he'd asked to have it fixed to mark his return to the Rin. Six Iyo including him and Rikuja had volunteered to join our jouyen.

"Wait," Barolein said after Rikuja and the others had been tattooed. He helped Mereku to the pond. "There's one more."

Mereku could barely stand. Her arm had to be amputated after Rutnaast, and one shoulder was a bandaged stump. "Okorebai, I'm sorry this is so sudden," she told Fendul. "But the arm with my Iyo crest is gone, and if that's not a sign, I don't know what is."

Fendul waded forward and touched her remaining arm. "I accept. Today you fly. And for all days to come."

I pulled Fendul aside after dinner and hooked a tiny wolf makiri next to his crow amulet. I'd made it by twisting a scrap of snare wire. "Don't tell anyone where you got it."

He smiled. "People will figure it out."

I didn't see much of him during the evening festival. He was busy greeting Iyo visitors. Nili and I gathered a group of kids and showed them how to toast hazelnuts in a flagstone firepit. For her, it involved chucking shells at Yironem until he got her apprentices to slingshot them back. I coated a handful in ice and slipped them into the pile he was throwing. Nili shrieked when one went down her shirt.

Airedain came around twilight, one hand behind his back. He nudged me. "Am I allowed in your plank house?"

"Sure, but why—"

"Don't ask. Just lead the way."

I pushed open the door. He ducked inside, his spiked hair brushing the frame. The room was cool and dim. People were packing up blankets, cloaks, weapons. We'd fit everyone in one building by putting extra mattresses on the floor, but now that we had more members, we were finally splitting into another plank house.

Airedain glanced around, recognizing my bed by the fir branch blanket Dunehein had brought back. "Sit. Close your eyes."

I obeyed. There was soft rustling, the smell of burning fish oil, then he said, "All right. Open."

I gasped. A lantern flickered on the shelf by my bed. The translucent vellum was painted with thin black conifers, the brushstrokes so precise I could feel the rough bark and scratchy needles. "It's beautiful."

He grinned. "Ladder pines. Thought they'd remind you of home."

I touched the delicate wood frame. "Did you make this?"

"Yeah. Ranelin taught me to paint. You know, drum crests and stuff."

"My gift's not nearly as impressive." I dug through my sealskin pack and held out a bottle of golden liquid. "You said you like Gallnach whisky but can never find any. I found some in Ingdanrad."

Airedain threw his head back and laughed. "You know me well, Rin-girl. Tell ya what. I'll save it for when you visit me in Caladheà."

Back outside, Dunehein wandered over with Sihaja in his arms. She clutched a fistful of his elbow-length hair. I wasn't sure who was happier — him or Rikuja for getting a break from child care. He thumped down on a bench and shouldered Nili. "So now that your tema's okoreni, you're next in line, ai?"

She groaned. "Don't remind me. Maybe it can skip me and go to Kako."

"It's temporary," Akiga said. "Aeldu willing, the okorebai will take a wife soon and give us a successor within a year."

I dropped an armful of kindling, scattering it across the flagstone. Nili gave me a *look* before kneeling to help. My family were the only ones who knew about my engagement.

"Bit soon, ai?" Dunehein said casually. "Fendul ain't even seeing anyone. Besides, Rija and I weren't ready to have a baby right away."

"Rin don't have that privilege." Akiga lifted her chin. "We have a duty to ensure the jouyen's survival."

Nili snorted and muttered to me, "Easy to say when you're too old to pop out any more kids."

"We're at war," I said to Akiga, gripping a branch so tight it cut into my hands. "An okorebai's partner is supposed to fight alongside them."

Akiga fixed her gaze on me. "Our jouyen is dying. Whoever the okorebai marries should be ready to accept all the responsibilities."

I jerked up. "I'm going for a walk."

The gate guard didn't stop me. People had been coming and going all night. I strode away from the stockade and breathed in salty air. I couldn't afford to get in arguments. Fendul was counting on me.

Footsteps rustled in the underbrush. Airedain drew up next to me, thumbs hooked on his belt. "Ai. You okay?"

"Fine. Just . . . couldn't listen to that anymore."

"Wanna go see my family? My tema's here from Caladheá. She was asking about you."

Dots of firelight on the coast guided us through the trees. The Iyo side of Toel Ginu, housing over a thousand people, hummed with voices. We were near the plank houses when a shout came from the firepits. I peered into the gloom. Hundreds of faces stared back.

"Oh shit." Airedain backed up, pulling me with him.

Ilani strode across the dirt. "How *dare* you come here. Liar! Traitor!" She shoved me.

Airedain caught me before I fell. "What's with you?!"

She spat at my feet. "You could've saved my brother. An itheran taught you healing. I saw you buy medicine in Ingdanrad."

"They're just painkillers, antidotes, simple things," I protested. "Even Marijka couldn't close Esiad's wound with those!"

Ilani jabbed the scar on Airedain's ribs. "Marijka saved *him*."

My mouth fell open.

She shoved me again, hard. I hit the ground, air bursting from my lungs. Airedain grabbed Ilani.

"Don't touch me, pigeonfucker," she snarled.

Someone wrenched them apart. It took a moment before I realized who'd arrived. Grey braid, crossed arms, okorebai tattoo.

Tokoda looked from Ilani and Airedain, restrained by grim-faced Iyo warriors, to me in the mud. "One question, Kateiko Rin. Was there anything you could have done to heal Esiad?"

"Nei. I can only fix scrapes and headaches. Esiad's wounds were way beyond me."

Wind whistled across the bluff. Tokoda studied me, then pulled me up. "Ilani, wait at my plank house."

Ilani scowled. A warrior led her away.

Tokoda gripped my shoulder. "Five Iyo, including Ilani and my brother, the okoreni, survived the Rutnaast siege because you reached us in time. They owe you their lives. Forgive my people our grief for those we lost." She left.

"How'd Ilani know about Maika?" I asked.

Airedain avoided my eyes. "Let's not talk here." He led me down the bluff, away from the light and noise. We stopped by an old salt spruce where we'd watched the waves two months ago.

He slumped cross-legged onto the dirt. "After the Skaarnaht riot last winter, Ilani asked who healed my stab wound. Today when I got back, she had all these questions about how. I just said Marijka was a herbalist. Figured if she kept her magic a secret while she was alive . . . well. I didn't mean to make Ilani think *you* could do it. Sorry, Rin-girl."

I sank down next to him. "Most people wouldn't cover for an itheran."

"Marijka saved my life. There's a few good pigeons."

"What Ilani called you — was that—"

"Yeah." Airedain laughed hollowly. "Sleep with an itheran and suddenly you're the village freak."

He'd call me a freak if he knew I slept with Parr. They'd kill me.

4.

SALMON

"How can there be no one?" I said the next afternoon as Fendul and I knotted scratchy rope into fishing nets. Rain cascaded off our canvas shelter. Ditches overflowed with muddy water, draining toward the sea.

Fendul didn't look up. "No one we trust. Tokoda found a few people who can read Gallnach, but we have no idea what we're handing over in the Rutnaast papers."

"So I'll go to Caladheå and ask my friends—"

"No. I need you here."

"Fen, maybe the Corvittai took Rutnaast for more than just the silver mines. Suriel needs damaged sites to open a rift into the void. If they're moving toward Toel Ginu, the war will follow."

"I know, Kako, but it's in Tokoda's hands. This is her jouyen's land. I'm just trying to keep our people alive."

I watched the bustle in the stockade. People packed blankets into bedrolls, checked over paddles, stacked bark baskets. At dawn tomorrow, five Rin would canoe down the coast to the river mouth of Yeva Iren to fish for our winter stores. Tokoda had given us permission to share her plank house's fishing grounds.

"Fen." I waited until he looked at me. "We should go to the salmon run."

"I can't leave the Rin-jouyen that long."

"Hiyua will be here. The people leaving need you more. They'll be living right among the Iyo, not with a stakewall between the two jouyen. I don't know what Ilani would've done to me if Tokoda hadn't been there."

Fendul opened his mouth, then closed it. He leaned against a hemlock, rubbing his tattoos through his plain woolen shirt. Nili would've loved to show her skill embroidering for an okorebai, but he always said there was more important work to do. "What about Yironem? You're supposed to teach him water-calling."

"We'll take him. He's not . . . handling all this attention well." Just that day, he'd snapped at another boy for saying good morning.

For a moment he just gazed at me. Then he picked up his net. "We'd better finish these fast, then."

We left in long seafaring canoes, our unmarked prows rising high above foaming swells. The Rin were safer in anonymity. Airedain, his cousin Jonalin, Wotelem, and a few other Iyo travelled alongside us in dolphin-prow canoes. Most others were already at the fishing grounds. The rough ocean kept driving us toward cliffs studded with pines that grew horizontal from the rock. Farther south, slopes of green conifers were veined with brilliant yellow where cotton-woods grew along streams.

We weren't the only ones out for salmon. A pod of blackfin whales swam by, skimming the waves, silhouettes longer than our canoes. One leapt into the air, smacked the surface, and drenched us with salt water. Yironem couldn't stop grinning.

I smelled alder smoke as we approached Yeva Iren in late afternoon. Its muddy delta split the forest into wedges, each river arm lined with smokehouses. White clouds puffed through stained plank walls. Tokoda and Wotelem's building was on the south arm, and Airedain's was just upriver, identifiable by their family crests carved on the doorframes. We dragged our canoes away from the high-tide line and roped our tents to a stand of cottonwood.

Daylight was too valuable to waste. Fendul went straight to the weirs, stake fences that stretched across the river with lattice panels to control the flow of salmon. He stood on a narrow bridge using a long-handled net to catch the trapped fish. Yironem and I filleted them and hung them over burning woodchips in Wotelem's smokehouse. We'd divide the catch based on how long each family spent fishing.

After dark, we shared oily meat-and-cranberry slabs, not bothering to light a fire. I dried every Rin's clothes before they went to bed. No one questioned Fendul and me sharing a tent. We'd done it every year as children, being the only kids in our plank house without siblings. Yironem shared with our canoe carver's younger brother.

That was our life for days. Choking on smoke, eyes watering, reeking of salmon. Wet clothes, blood up to our elbows, fish guts trampled into ankle-deep mud. Wolves and bears plucked wriggling salmon from the water. The first frost bleached the riverbank sparkling white.

One blustery afternoon, a fishing trawler shuddered into the river mouth, flying the scarlet elk flag of Eremur. I wiped salmon blood from my knife, told Yironem to stay put, and ran down the bank. Fendul met me on the way.

Four men vaulted overboard and waded into the shallows. They all had matted blond hair and windburnt faces. Their patched jerkins looked Sverbian. They stopped on shore, surrounded by Iyo levelling blades at their chests. A man with pale blue eyes raised his hands.

"We've come to trade for salmon, that be all," he said in accented Coast Trader. "Who's in charge here?"

Fendul didn't move. The wrong person learning his identity would be a death sentence.

Wotelem stepped forward. He never carried a weapon at Toel Ginu, but here he had a spear, silver as the streaks in his braid. "Where did you sail from?"

"Caladheå. We went to Toel Ginu first." The blue-eyed man gave Wotelem a thumb-sized stone dolphin. "Your commander sent us with this."

"Why would the Okorebai-Iyo send you here? Caladheåns can fish the Stengar."

"It's not enough." The man removed his wide-brimmed hat. "Please. We fled Rutnaast last year. So many farms were razed by Corvittai that food be scarce. Our families won't survive winter."

Wotelem lowered his spear. "Wait there." He pulled Fendul and me into a cluster of brown-barked hemlock.

"I heard similar reports when I took those miners to prison," he said. "Three thousand refugees living in shacks in Caladheå."

Fendul frowned at the men huddled in a circle of swordpoints. "They're not our responsibility."

"We need to prove we're on their side," I said. "Some itherans still think we're behind the Corvittai attacks."

"Kateiko is right. If they return empty-handed, it looks like we want them to starve." Wotelem flipped over the dolphin to show us marks painted on the belly. "One red, five black. My sister agreed to sell a sixth of our plank house's portion. You must decide for your jouyen, Okorebai-Rin."

Fendul's lips pressed together. Sharing food was a determiner of political standing in the Aikoto Confederacy, a sign of the wealth a jouyen could afford to spare. We'd have to match the Iyo or damage our reputation further. Already we balanced on a needlepoint.

"We'll manage, Fen. We know how to handle winter." I gripped his hand.

He pinched his temples. "Fine. A sixth."

The itherans relaxed once the Iyo blades were away from them. They unloaded goods from their boat and spread them on pine needles. Fendul and I picked over axeheads and sawblades, copper pots, skeins of goat wool, tins of salt and spices, coils of snare wire, weighing up what the Rin needed.

"Good thing you're armed," the blue-eyed man told me as we waded into the river carrying baskets of smoked salmon. "My cousin's fishing village on Algard Island just got hit by raiders. They took everything that weren't nailed down."

I shuddered. We would've paddled past that island if we'd gone home to Anwen Bel. "Who were they?"

"Gallnach sailors. Those woolwrapped scoundrels won't work for a living." He shook his head, stowing a basket in his boat. "The navy cracked down on piracy in southern Eremur. Drove 'em up this way."

"Have you heard any names? I'm looking for a druid named Iollan och Cormic."

"Sorry, miss. Never heard of him. But I'd keep those close if I were you." He jabbed a thumb at the weapons on my belt. "Slippier than eels, the Galls are."

"I've been thinking," Fendul said that evening as we gutted salmon. "Sverbians in the north knew our ways. We never had to learn theirs in any great depth. Once you came south, Kako, you learned all sorts of things from Tiernan."

"Like how to bake rye bread," I said. "Very useful without rye."

He gave me a reproachful look. "I'm serious. You're the only Rin who's lived with itherans. What do we teach our children so they can survive now?"

I unsheathed Antalei. The flail's spiked head swung on its chain. "My mother taught me how to crush ribcages. My father taught me how to slit throats. When I inherited his throwing dagger, *you* taught me how to use it. That's how I survived."

He winced. "Sorry."

I focused on the silvery fish in my lap. "Reading. That's what I wish I knew better. I can barely read a newspaper or fill out a form to meet the Officer of the Viirelei, our own representative to the Council. Everything itherans do is written."

"Don't do it." Airedain didn't look up from the alder block he was chiselling. Bright red woodchips fell into a basket at his feet. "Send kids to school, I mean."

My brow furrowed. "Tiernan enjoyed it back in Sverba."

"Different for pigeons, ain't it? I had to use a Sverbian name and cover my tattoos. Couldn't speak Aikoto in class. The teacher made us stand in the corner for mentioning the aeldu. Can't count how many fist fights I got into with itheran kids."

"I won't send Rin kids to Caladheå anyway." Fendul looked thoughtful. "Airedain, could you teach them to read?"

"Probably. But it'd take years, and I don't plan on moving back to Toel. Sorry."

I chewed my lip. "What if we hired a schoolteacher to live with us? Then we could set the rules. Maika's village over the mountains did that."

Fendul shook his head. "Itherans don't move to Toel Ginu unless they marry in."

Airedain finally looked up. "I know one who might take the job. Viviwen Hannehl, a Sverbian girl I was seeing. She got fired from her last school 'cause she refused to treat Iyo kids like shit."

Fendul was silent. Eventually he said, "I'll talk to Wotelem," tossed his last salmon onto the pile, and headed to the weirs.

Night folded around me, blacker than the inside of my eyelids. Yeva Iren's swirling weight outside the tent crushed my senses. Voices cocooned my body. Not the living — these were older, deeper, the whispers of people who'd forgotten how they once spoke. I sifted through the tangle of blankets until my fingers touched embroidered fir branches.

Canvas rustled at my feet. Cool air washed over me. Fendul unbuckled his belt and set his sword next to my weapons. I reached out with my mind, weaving through the wool fibres of his shirt and breeches, drawing out the water.

"Thanks," he whispered as he slid under the blankets.

Most nights that'd be all. He'd never mention his bleeding callouses or the stiffness in his legs from balancing on a weir all day. I'd fall asleep listening to rain and his slow breathing. At sunrise, I'd crawl outside, and he'd be in the smokehouse adding more woodchips.

"What'd Wotelem say?" I ventured.

"Viviwen can live in Toel. I'll get Airedain to offer her the job after the salmon run."

"Oh." Silence. "Fen . . . I'm sorry for getting all bitter earlier."

"It's fine."

"Nei. It's not. You're doing everything you can, and . . . " I rolled to face him. "I freaked out when you mentioned teaching 'our children.' I know you meant the jouyen, but Akiga's calling for a natural-born okoreni."

He paused. "So you . . . don't want to have children with me?"

Heat flooded through my body. This had to be the least romantic discussion on the topic ever. "I don't want to with anyone. That's one reason I left home last year. Isu was pushing me to marry, rebuild our numbers."

Fendul shifted in the darkness. His breath warmed my cheek. "I'm trying to fix things, Kako."

"You can only do so much. This *world* is broken. It whips people raw until violence is all we know."

His hand landed on my arm. "I know how much you'll sacrifice by marrying me. But I don't ever want you to feel forced into something, or . . . like you have to hide your feelings. We're in this together."

I reached out, finding scratchy wool. I trailed my fingers up and stroked his jaw, ear, hair. Fendul stilled. The strands were short on the sides of his head, but long enough on top for me to run my fingers through. I'd only ever touched his hair in mourning.

I'd already made my sacrifices. Tiernan was sunlight on water, shattered when I touched the surface. Parr was a bonfire doused by my storm. I rose burnt and naked in his ashes. Love was nothing compared to saving my people.

"What about . . . ah." Fendul ducked his head. "Do you also . . . not want to . . . sleep with me?"

"Oh, Fennel." I smiled, glad it was too dark for him to see.

"Because I'd understand — I mean, we're not—"

I kissed him. He tensed, then settled into it, his chapped lips exploring mine. He tasted like alder smoke. Our first kiss in a dusty farmhouse had been brief, a question. This was an answer.

Memories stung me. Tiernan's cracked lips, rough beard, rain on his cold face. Parr's dark eyes, glittering rings, the spice of his cologne. Nothing else surfaced. No panic, no lust. Instead, I sensed something dormant like frozen sap. I had a long winter ahead before it'd thaw.

5.

FATHER'S SON

A week later, a rest was called. The salmon were waning, and some families were returning to Toel Ginu. We paddled to the central arm of Yeva Iren for a last meal together. Everyone hunted or foraged something — sour crabapples, bitter cranberries, geese from a migrating flock, mushrooms of every shape and colour, nut-sized duck potatoes. We clustered by bonfires on the riverbank, sharing bottles of clear rye brånnvin bartered from the Sverbian sailors.

Airedain played a flat handheld drum with his arrowhead-leaf crest painted on the sheepskin. Aliko, a Rin weaver with the voice and smarts of a songbird, sang a canoe shanty she couldn't get away with around children. Her smile faltered when Fendul left with an unimpressed look. She'd never given up on catching his eye.

When the brånnvin came Yironem's way, he spluttered but kept it down. An older Iyo boy thumped his back approvingly. Hiyua would tan me alive if she knew I let her fourteen-year-old son drink. I felt stretched thin, a pelt pulled tight on a drying rack.

"Ai, Rin-girl." Airedain nudged me with his drumstick. "Still in there?"

"Hmm?" I hadn't noticed his drumming had ended. Aliko had moved onto a drinking song loud enough to wake the aeldu.

Airedain followed my gaze. "Worried about your little bro?"

"A little." I rubbed smoke from my eyes. "I've tried getting him to open up, but . . . maybe I'm too close now that I'm family."

"I could try. Yironem talks to me a bit. I know what it's like to have your best friend's blood in the ground." He heaved himself off the log bench, dropped his drum in my lap, and started splitting more firewood.

I held his drumstick up to the light. It was double-ended, smaller than his standard leather mallets. "Is this an itheran drum?"

"Yeah. A moor drum. Liam helped me make it."

"Emílie's son? The boy you work with at the Knox Arms? I've only seen him play with single-ended sticks."

"Moor drums are banned in Caladheå. Some goatshit about druidism."

I choked on my spit. "Iyo-boy, is Liam Gallnach?"

Airedain paused, slinging the lumber axe over his shoulder. "Yeah. Keep it quiet. Last time Sverbians found out, they beat the shit outta him."

"But I've heard him speak Sverbian. He's fluent—"

"So? I am, too."

I grabbed his tunic sleeve. "You work with a family of them? Why didn't you tell me before I went to Ingdanrad?"

"'Cause you woulda repeated it to Wotelem, and aeldu knows who he'd tell. Then Liam gets jumped by some fucking pigeon with a knife. Again."

"Wotelem wouldn't betray your friend—"

Airedain laughed. "You sure? There's a reason most Gallnach stay in Ingdanrad. The Sverbian-Aikoto alliance from the Elken Wars was just that. No other nations."

"Then why tell me now?"

"Starting to wish I hadn't."

I let his sleeve fall. Maybe he was right. I trusted Parr, and Marijka was dead for it. "Look, I don't want to argue. I just need your help. When Fendul was in Rutnaast, he found papers written in Gallnach. They might lead to Iollan och Cormic. We need them translated."

"Liam can't read Gallnach. Says there's no point learning when everyone writes in Trader."

"What about Emílie? Fendul will keep their secret, I promise."

Airedain exhaled. "Sure hope your okorebai's as decent as you think."

We tracked down Fendul, who listened to my proposal, then shook his head. "No. It's impossible."

It felt like he'd slapped me. "No? That's it?"

"I can't hand the papers over without telling Tokoda where they're going. Even if I do, how would we explain any info we find? Lying to another okorebai is a rapid descent back into civil war." He nodded at Airedain. "Your jouyen says I'm my father's son. That Behadul broke the Aikoto alliance, and I will, too."

Airedain lifted one shoulder. "Yeah. People talk."

"So what do we do?" I demanded. "Ignore that Iollan's trying to tear a *hole* in our world? What about the Gallnach who raided Algard Island? They could be working with the Corvittai, too."

Fendul rubbed his temples. "What do you expect of me, Kako?"

I folded my arms. "I expect more, Okorebai."

*

My eyes watered. There wasn't enough time between batches of salmon for the smoke to clear, even with the smokehouse door propped open to let in grey morning light. Rows of raw fish hung from the rafters, a garden of orange flesh and silver scales around my head. The only sounds were rain beating the roof and Aliko humming.

I plucked a salmon from the basket at my feet, then paused. Voices. Shouting. I ducked under the hanging fish and stepped over woodchips to the door. Aliko gasped behind me.

A red-sailed cutter bobbed in the river mouth. Itheran archers lined its bulwarks, crossbows aimed. A man with pale skin and rusty hair stood in the bow yelling in broken Sverbian. Iyo and Rin lined the bank, a bristling wall of blades and bows.

"He says drop your weapons." Wotelem set his spear on the muddy ground. "They will not harm us unless we resist."

The Iyo followed suit and stepped away from their weapons. The Rin didn't move, waiting on Fendul. His face was set like wood. *You're not Behadul,* I thought. *Don't force a fight.*

The rust-haired captain shouted. A bolt shot across the river and went through Jonalin's shoulder, spraying blood across the dirt. Fendul dropped his sword.

I shoved Aliko back into the smokehouse. "Go to the next river arm," I hissed as I pried a plank loose in the far wall. "Tell them to come armed. Don't be seen. Mereku was shot while she was attuned."

Aliko nodded. A second later, a yellow-breasted waxwing sped out the gap into the rain. I pressed my fingers to my lips. Sending someone into danger never got easier, but I'd never make it across the river.

Through a crack in the wall, I watched the itherans wade ashore. They wore jewel-toned woolwraps over their trousers, the draped cloth floating around their thighs, and a mix of leather and rusted iron armour, likely stolen. Sixteen soldiers plus four who stayed on the ship. Eighteen of us. The other Iyo on this arm of Yeva Iren had left for home at dawn. The raiders must've been watching.

The captain barked orders in Gallnach. They shoved everyone into a line, forcing them to kneel in the mud, and stripped them of money, hidden weapons, everything but clothes. A man with a thick brown beard snapped the cord around Fendul's neck. I bit hard on my tongue as he pocketed the crow amulet and wire wolf makiri. A man with a scarred eye headed for the smokehouses.

I stepped into the doorway and tossed Antalei at his feet, followed by my knives. "Just raw salmon inside," I said in Sverbian, hoping he understood.

"Your cooked fish." His accent was heavy. "Where?"

I froze. We could never replace it by winter. If our trappers got injured or killed — if Rin children had to forage alone—

The man yanked me outside and backhanded me across the face. I slammed into the mud. His boot struck my ribs. "Where?!"

I rolled onto my back gasping. He put his foot on my throat. Rain blurred my vision. I pointed upriver toward the storage sheds we used to keep out bears.

The rust-haired captain strode over and peered at me. They spoke rapidly, voices rising, hands cutting the air. The scarred man lifted his sword to plunge it into my heart.

An ice shard formed in my fist. I stabbed his calf. He stumbled, collapsing onto me. I shrieked. His hands were on my hair, *him*, the man about to kill me, touching my spirit. Raindrops froze into ice, driving into him, crackling across his skin.

"*Helid!*" The captain hauled the scarred man off me and grabbed my cloak collar. "You. Girl. We take you, too."

"No!" Fendul leapt up. A raider slammed a dagger hilt into Fendul's head and shoved him back down.

A dozen reasons they might want me shot through my mind. Translator, cook, female "companion."

The captain toppled next to me. Blood gushed from his severed spine. Airedain stood behind him, lumber axe in hand.

An arrow thudded into the scarred man's chest. He reeled, slipping in the mud. I didn't need to look for the archer. Yironem.

Shouts broke out. Both sides surged at each other. Fendul wrested a man's mace away. A Rin woman shifted into an eagle and launched at a raider, tearing his face with her talons. Bolts streaked through the air.

A man rushed at me, sword raised. I grabbed my hunting knife from the mud. An arrow grazed his face, sending his swing wide. I dragged him to the ground and slit his throat.

I shoved him away, holding back a scream. I couldn't stop this. Every awful possibility unfolded in my mind. Fendul dead, Yironem, Airedain—

The river.

Water spilled over the banks, running high from the autumn rains. I threw my mind into the centre. Its weight crushed my lungs. I saw everything like I was underwater, spinning, torn apart by the current, flowing through weir lattices toward the ocean. The raiders' ship was an eclipse on the surface. I flung myself against its hull with all my strength.

The ship vanished. I saw straight through it to the far shore. Soaked spruce, a carpet of yellow leaves, the muddy bank I'd seen every day for half a month. I knew what this was. The *shoirdryge*, the world that split from ours ten years ago, a place where the raiders weren't here. Yet I still felt the ship in the river like a knife in my gut.

Someone yelled my name. Everything snapped back into focus.

Waves crashed into the ship. It rolled, its barnacle-studded underbelly rising. The Gallnach archers onboard dove into the water. Everyone else whirled at the sound of snapping timbers.

I thrust my bloody knife toward the far bank. "Surrender! You're surrounded!"

Aliko and a dozen Iyo stepped from the forest, a weaving line among the spruce. Yironem emerged from behind the smokehouse, an arrow nocked. Fendul had a knife to the throat of the man who took his amulet.

The man raised his hands. He shouted at the others. They dropped their weapons, spitting curses.

Airedain drew up next to me, the axe in his grip. "Well played, Rin-girl."

Fendul shoved his captive to the ground and strode toward us. His shirt dripped red. "Go find Emílie."

6.

BRONNOI RIDGE

Hours of running later, I padded to a stop in a grove of skeletal alder. Rotting leaves assaulted my wolf nose. A coyote slunk through the shadowy trees after me. Airedain rose into his human body and wrung rain from his tunic in silence. No one coped well with their first kill.

Two men from Airedain's plank house were dead, as was the Rin woman who attuned to an eagle. Six Gallnach went with them, maybe more. Only two archers had made it ashore after I capsized the ship. It scratched at my brain, not knowing if other deaths were on my hands.

Our boots squished in the shallow stream that was once a road through the harvested fields around Caladheå. Hundreds of camp-fires flickered between us and the ocean. After the Rutnaast massacre last winter, a village of refugee shacks had sprung up by Caladheå's docklands. It'd grown over the year, creeping inland along the edge of the Ashtown district.

A log guardhouse loomed from the darkness. Its lantern glowed in the mist. An Elkhound in grey armour stepped off the porch, cursing when he landed in a puddle. We handed our identification cards over as his partner emerged from inside. It was strange hearing gliding Ferish accents after so many months. I pulled my borrowed cloak tight, covering my bloodstained clothes.

Once again, I was grateful Falwen, Officer of the Viirelei, had registered me as Iyo. The Blackbird Battle had caused a surge of newspaper articles about the Rin. Supposedly we were Suriel's true followers and bewitched Ferish soldiers into joining the Corvittai, then slaughtered those who rebelled. Or, according to another newspaper, we were an extinct viirelei nation who rose from our graves to get revenge for the Elken Wars.

The first guard handed our cards back. "Where are you headed?"

"Home." Airedain's voice was taut. "You know I live here."

"*She* doesn't."

The other guard rapped his spear against his partner's breast-plate. "A young viirelei taking a girl home at night? You know what they're doing. Let 'em have their fun."

Ashtown was cleaner than usual, the coal ash rinsed away, though the stench of fermented cod and stale urine lingered. Airedain and I slunk past red-brick buildings with iron-barred windows. Most people in this district were recent immigrants who could only afford to live near the brick-making kilns. I used to think they were all Sverbian or Ferish. Now every itheran who passed could've been Gallnach.

Light poured from the Knox Arms. Airedain dodged the cascade of rainwater from a gutter and pushed open the heavy doors. Inside, two men onstage pounded drums strapped to their hips, Liam played a handheld frame drum, and two women tapped their feet to their fiddles. The pub was furnished in salvaged wood and metal, with shelves of brånnvin bottles above barrels of Ferish wine.

We wove past damp, staggering patrons into the kitchen. Heat rolled over us from the stone hearth where a mountain goat roasted on a spit. A woman with arms thick as casks stood at a stained table chopping rutabaga with a cleaver. Even in the sweltering room, she wore the wool bodice and white dress of Sverbian women. Sweaty curls of blonde hair stuck to her neck.

"There he is!" Emílie wiped her hands on her apron and seized Airedain in a hug. Then she looked at him closer. "Whoa now. What's wrong, lad?"

He couldn't meet her eyes. "Let's go upstairs. Kateiko knows."

Emílie snapped her fingers at her elder daughter, a teenage girl with twin braids. "Maeve, mind the roast. If anyone stumbles in here, beat 'em out with the broom."

She lit a candle and led us up a zigzag staircase. It opened onto a room just big enough for a table and three beds. I guessed her daughters shared one. On the shelves were spools of thread, newspaper clippings, and varnished boxes painted with floral patterns. Nothing would've looked out of place in a Sverbian home except red wool hung on the wall, looped into what I now knew was a druidic knot.

Airedain told her about the raid and the Rutnaast papers. When he finished, I said, "I promise to keep your secret, Emílie. To make it even, I'll tell you mine. I'm Rin, not Iyo."

Her eyebrows shot into her hair. "The nation with that blackbird crest like Suriel's? I see why you'd keep that hidden. Well then, let's see these papers."

I opened the waterproof elk bladder on my belt. Emílie pushed aside a bowl of cranberries and smoothed the dusty sheets on the table. She read them twice, read the backs, and sighed.

"It's a port log. Earliest date is right after the Rutnaast massacre. Ships brought supplies in — food, lamp oil, mining tools — and hauled silver ingots out. No mention of Suriel or an Iollan och Cormic."

"That's it?" I sank into a chair. "Does it say where the silver went?"

"Tírcattil, which just means Cattil Territory. No idea where that is. You didn't get a captain's log?"

"Nei. The Okoreni-Iyo scuttled the ship in Rutnaast, and I sank the one at Yeva Iren. This is all we have."

Emílie flipped a page over again. "What else do you know about Iollan?"

"Thirty-eight, brown hair, shorter than me. Emaciated with a long beard when he broke out of prison, but he's probably healthier now. Born in Ingdanrad, so he doesn't have a Gallnach accent."

"That could describe my late husband and plenty of others. But I'll ask around." She rapped the table in front of Airedain. "You back for work, lad?"

He rubbed his neck. "Can it wait a few days? I ain't supposed to be back until mid-month."

"Sure thing." Emílie thumped his shoulder. "C'mon downstairs. That roast ain't gonna eat itself."

Maeve lent me a dress and woolen underskirts. The hems only hit halfway down my calves, but it was better than wearing a dead man's blood. I burned my shirt and leggings in the alley.

Airedain's home wasn't far, but we took side routes to dodge Elkhounds and drunken itherans. Inside his flat, I sifted through a rioden chest and tossed his spare tunic and breeches at him, then looked away while he changed. When I turned back, he sat against the brick wall like he'd melted down it. His keys, fan knife, everything from his pockets lay jumbled on the floor. The oil lamp cast his face into harsh shadow.

I'd never seen him like this, even when his best friend, Nokohin, died. Anger I could deal with. Silence unnerved me. I lit a fire, threw his bloody clothes in the iron stove, and sank down next to him. Stone makiri — ospreys, dolphins, otters, all carved by his sister — watched from a shelf.

"Did you understand what those Gallnach argued about?" I asked. "When they had me pinned down?"

"Yeah." For a moment that seemed like all he'd say. Then, "One wanted to kill you as an example. The other refused to kill a woman."

"Oh." I picked at a splinter in the floorboards. Rain pattered on the shutters.

Finally, he spoke again. "After Noko's death . . . I kept thinking, maybe if I was there I coulda saved him. But that's bearshit. I'm used to fist fights, not war. So this summer I started training with Iyo warriors, then with Crieknaast's militia guarding the lumber camp."

"Really?" I'd noticed he looked different, his sharp edges padded with muscle, but had chalked it up to working in the camp. "Why didn't you tell me?"

"It's different for you Rin. Your parents gave you a flail when you were a kid. Me, I started working in my tema's shop when I was twelve. That's how I was taught to look after my family. I've been trying to figure out if becoming a warrior is the right choice."

"And if no one knew, you could still back out?"

"Yeah. Today, though . . . I almost lost you and Jona, too. But I didn't. So there's my answer, I guess." He picked up his fan knife and snapped the blade out from the auburn handle. "Does it get easier? Killing people?"

"Not really." I ran my nail along the bone edge of my hunting knife. My last weapon had earned its name — Kohekai, the blood bringer. I'd never forget the grotesque marsh of the scarred man's blood pooled among mud and grass. "I don't want it to get easy, to forget what it means. I name my weapons after they take a life. It helps me remember."

Airedain scoffed. "It was a fucking lumber axe. Not even mine."

Maybe words weren't enough. What could I say to someone who took a life to save mine?

I loosed his fingers from his knife and placed his hand on my matted hair. His eyes widened. He curled his fingers into strands that had been part of me for years, witness to everything. They carried secrets I could never speak.

Airedain ducked his head. "Dunno about you, but I need to get really, really trashed."

I spent more of the night awake than asleep. At dawn, I gave up, sitting on Jonalin's bed as I untangled my hair. Airedain slept with one arm across his chest, covering the edge of his drummer tattoo. He'd offered to walk me to his mother Segowa's home, then offered again after half a bottle of vodka. I didn't mind staying. He'd taken care of me more nights than I cared to admit.

Once there was sunlight, I mixed brassroot flour into dough and fried it in a pan of fish oil. I was washing dishes when Airedain woke holding his head and muttering curses. I dumped my purse on the table. Identification stamped with rearing red elk, coins etched with elk sigils, balms, flaking herb packets. I needed a better way to carry things.

Airedain caught the vial of willowcloak tincture I tossed him. "You're nicer than Jona."

"I'm eating your food. Seems fair."

He swallowed the tincture and flopped back onto his ash-grey caribou blanket. "So, Rin-girl. Where do we look for Tírcattil?"

"Everywhere," I said around a mouthful of flatbread. "I'll talk to Iannah on her day off tomorrow. For now, ask around if there's silver showing up anywhere, news of raids, or . . . I'm not sure. Weird rift magic stuff."

We split up, arranging to meet later at Segowa's embroidery shop. I approached the Blackened Oak in the old Sverbian quarter with a knot in my stomach. Nhys, the innkeeper, was friends with Tiernan. He was too polite to mention the past, but I wouldn't stay at the inn again.

"I brought Tiernan your message about Iollan och Cormic," Nhys said in the cellar, surrounded by ale casks oozing a malty smell. "He melted a kettle with his hands, packed up, and left. That be the last I've heard."

"Where'd he go?"

"Ingdanrad, to find out how Iollan escaped."

"Kaid," I swore. "Does he know I got attacked out that way?"

"Aye." Nhys sighed under his bushy yellow beard. "But Tiernan knows better than anyone how dangerous a rogue rift mage is. He didn't go alone, at least. He and Rhonos Arquiere sailed with the navy."

Small comforts were better than none. Rhonos had kept his promise to look after Tiernan. And Tiernan had his fire magic back, to the misfortune of his kettle. He'd been so cold when I left. Extinguished.

Nhys promised to keep an ear out for mentions of Tírcattil. I had less luck elsewhere. An Elkhound shooed me from the dock-lands after I peered over a clerk's shoulder at a port logbook. The elderly Ferish owner of the city square bookstore muttered as I lingered in cramped aisles looking at atlases. It was useless. I didn't know if Tírcattil was a town or island or even in this province.

Almost every merchant in the square sold imported goods. Damask cloth, bricks of tea, glass bottles with labels I couldn't read. A crisp, summery scent drifted from crates of fuzzy orange fruit. The price of one could feed a family for a day. It was the kind of place stolen silver would appear, but a jeweller reeking of musty cologne pretended not to understand my questions about his suppliers.

Segowa's shop was my only respite. In the back room, surrounded by bolts of dyed wool and crates of leather, I stripped off my borrowed dress so she could measure me for a new shirt and leggings. I picked black wool to hide the inevitable soot and mud. Cold wind breathed through the shop walls. My fingers were too numb to lace my bodice back up.

"Stupid itheran clothes," I muttered.

Airedain, waiting up front, leaned around a stack of crates. "Move your braid." He pulled the laces tight and knotted them.

"I figured you'd have more practice getting women out of their clothes," I said, but he didn't laugh.

"I'll get these to you tomorrow," Segowa said, cutting wool with a bone knife. "You'll need them in this weather."

"What do I owe you?" I sifted through a handful of coins. A single silver half-sovereign and two copper quarter-sovs among grimy iron pann.

Her eyes passed over my palm. "I'll take it out of your next payment for furs."

"I won't have furs to spare this year. There are more than thirty Rin kids without winter clothes."

"Then I'll wait." She smiled, soft but heavy, like grey clouds. A bell tinkled and she went up to the front.

Airedain leaned against the wall, arms folded. "Find anything about Tírcattil?"

"Nei. Nothing. And I'm out of ideas until I talk to Iannah."

"Same here. Though I did track down Viviwen Hannehl. She agreed to take the teaching job. My uncle Ranelin will take her to Toel day after tomorrow."

"Oh," I said, startled. I'd forgotten. "Thanks."

He chewed the inside of his cheek. "If we're done for today . . . can I take you somewhere?"

I was baffled when we headed east into Bronnoi Ridge. The entire district was Ferish, with cobblestone streets wide enough for horse-drawn carts to pass and clean enough it didn't reek constantly. I only came here to visit Iannah or deal with politicians at the Colonnium. The trouble from Elkhounds wasn't worth it otherwise.

Airedain stopped by a timber fence between two red-brick buildings, a bakery and a millinery with felt hats on display. The fence was too high to see over. He glanced up and down the empty street, pried open some loose boards, and slid through the gap.

"Where in Aeldu-yan . . ." I followed, clutching my cloak so it didn't snag.

I gasped. A scorched plank house, its sod roof overgrown enough to feed a herd of goats, stood in a courtyard enclosed by windowless brick. Waist-high grass brushed the walls. The kinaru crest over its door was so perfect only a Rin could've carved it.

"The building from the newspaper," I breathed. Last winter the *Caladheä Herald* reported a plank house had been found in Bronnoi Ridge, a remnant from the old Aikoto district. "How'd you find it?"

"Wish I could say I spent days searching for you, but I just asked Ranelin if he'd seen it while flying over the city. Itherans think it's haunted. They're scared to knock it down."

I ran my fingers up the doorframe, reading the carved crests.

Too many were from ended bloodlines. This was our third war since the Ferish torched our district and built on its ashes. Just above my head, I found tall, proud fireweed. My father's crest tattooed on my arm. I clapped a hand to my mouth. "Airedain. My family lived here—"

He nodded.

"Have you been inside?"

"Just looked in." He tugged open the door. Lichen flaked off the blackened wood.

I stepped into the dim room, meeting the smell of mildew. Water dripped from the ceiling and pooled in circles. Beds and rioden chests lined the walls. I moved as if in a dream. The plank house was decaying into earth, returning home.

Wooden makiri gazed at me from mantelpieces. My ancestors had left their sacred guardians to protect the building. I ran my fingers over the glossy curve of a bluejay's wing, then glanced at Airedain in the doorway. "You can enter. The makiri won't bite."

He ducked, careful not to let his hair touch the frame. His footsteps were soft on the dirt.

I stood under a hole in the vaulted ceiling and stared up at grey sky. *This is Aeldu-yan. The house of the dead.* The voices were so clear that if I looked back down, I half-expected to see a spirit staring back.

Airedain was silent so long I wondered if he'd left. Then he said, "What was it like? Right before you killed someone the first time."

"Fear." I closed my eyes. "Not for me. For Nili. I . . . couldn't imagine life without her."

"That's how I felt. When those raiders wanted to take you away." His voice sounded odd. He stepped closer and tipped my chin up. Falling water skimmed his nose. "Kateiko."

Warmth fluttered in my chest. I loved hearing him say my name, not just *Rin-girl*.

Some nights last spring, we'd lain on his bed, shoulders touching, an empty vodka bottle between us. I could've curled against him, listened to his heartbeat, breathed the pine resin he used to spike his hair. But we'd both been getting over Sverbians who didn't share our feelings. We needed friends more. Then I disappeared for three weeks, mourning Marijka and caring for Tiernan.

By the time I returned, Airedain had moved on with Viviwen, so I moved on with Parr. I didn't blame him. The way I lived then, alone in the woods with a horse and a flask of brånnvin, he'd probably thought I left Iyun Bel. He was a lake I passed and never expected to touch. Now I was back on his shore, staring into his dark brown eyes.

He kissed me, hard and desperate. My body locked, bracing for the marble fireplace Parr had pushed me against. It wasn't Airedain's mouth on mine. It was a dead man's. I stumbled back.

Airedain looked like shattered glass. "Ai. What's wrong? Aeldu save me, if I just fucked everything up—"

"Nei." I swallowed my panic. He'd be furious I slept with Parr. "It's just . . . Fendul asked me to marry him."

He froze. "What did you say?"

I felt like if I breathed, I'd cry. At least I could kiss Fendul without freaking out, even if he made me feel nothing else. *Because* he made me feel nothing else.

Airedain's shoulders sagged. "I knew you two were close, but . . ."

"It's not like that. It's political."

"For both of you?"

My answer died on my lips. Fendul claimed he'd never been in love, but maybe he didn't want to scare me off.

Airedain dropped onto a rotten mattress. "Yeah. I get it. An okorebai, a real warrior, the most powerful person in your jouyen. Not a hard choice."

"Is — that what you think I *want*?" I stuttered. "Fendul asked for my help. I'm trying to protect the Rin. If you think so little of me—"

"Nei, I — fuck. Sorry, Kateiko." He ran a hand over his hair. "I'm just pissed. Not at you or him. At life. I just figured it out yesterday, and I'm too late."

Damp air weighed on me. I sank onto a bed across from him. "I tried, you know. After Tiernan and I fought . . ." I touched my neck where his sword cut me. "I came to see you. Jonalin said you were out with Viviwen."

Airedain laughed bitterly. "Figures. She was a mistake. Good schoolteacher, yeah. But a mistake."

"What happened? You were still together when I left for Ingdanrad."

"She used me to piss off her parents. You know, bring home a tattooed viirelei from the slums." He slumped forward, hands folded behind his neck. "What if I'd been home that night?"

I wouldn't have gone to Parr. His voice wouldn't whisper things that made me want to chop off my hair because he'd touched it. *Darling girl.* Airedain and I would've had one night together before learning the Rin came south. Maybe I would've stayed in Caladheå. Missed the Blackbird Battle. Never killed Nonil. Then we'd be hunting him and Iollan both, a fire mage and an earth druid working together to tear open the world.

No room to look back. Only forward. I'd made my promise to Fendul. Tiernan had been lost for years searching for *what if*.

7.

TÍRCATTIL

I spent the night at Segowa's flat in Ashtown. Nothing good could come of sleeping in Airedain's home. Segowa didn't ask questions. Maybe she'd pry it out of him later.

At midday, I waited outside Natzo's, Iannah's favourite noodle shop in Bronnoi Ridge. I spotted her down the street, sword at her hip, auburn hair in a bun. People swerved around her like insects dodging a hawk. The pressed blue coat and fawn breeches of her guard uniform kept anyone from looking too long.

She approached me with measured steps. "Hey, Koehl." She claimed that Sohikoehl, the Sverbian second name on my identification, was far too long. "So you didn't get lost in the mountains."

I rolled my eyes and hugged her. Maybe it was my imagination, but she felt less rigid than usual. "So you didn't get killed on duty."

Iannah pulled a kinaru makiri carved of faded red alder from under her collar. I'd given the necklace to her before I left for Ingdanrad. "Something was looking out for me."

Natzo hollowed out wheat rolls and filled them with noodles so we could carry our lunch. *Spianèʒi te choionne* was the least spicy Ferish soup, but my eyes still watered as Iannah and I walked northwest. Shacks hung with ropes of laundry lined the Stengar banks. Children netted sickly fish in the muddy river. Iannah gave her last chunk of bread to a knob-kneed boy begging on the bridge.

We sat on a grassy hill near a stavehall with steep shingle roofs. The Shawnaast district was once a separate town until Caladheå grew into it. A few original Sverbian buildings were intact, their timbers dark with age — lumber mills, stables, the old town hall and armoury. Most residents were Ferish now, living in identical brick rowhouses. Iannah liked Shawnaast because it was the farthest she could get from the Colonnium, where she worked and lived.

"Checked the provincial mage registry?" she asked after I told her about Iollan. "All sorts of info in there."

"Falwen looked. No entry for anyone matching Iollan's description. Ingdanrad mages don't come to Eremur much since, well, a bunch got murdered here."

She had no idea where Tírcattil was. "Not sure it matters. It's probably just where those Gallnach miners offloaded the silver. Iollan might have nothing to do with the place."

"That's . . . the opposite of what I hoped to hear."

"Follow the raiders. They've hit fishing villages all over the coast. Could be selling food to the Corvittai."

She did have news. The war was at a standstill. The Corvittai had fought so hard to control Dúnravn Pass, and now it held no magic, no storms, nothing. Suriel was silent. Combat had fallen to skirmishes near Rutnaast as the military cleared out Gallnach miners. Iannah muttered that someone must've been bribed to over-look the mines until now.

We spent the afternoon poring over every detail I knew, matching them to snippets she'd overheard from politicians and sol-diers. By the time the sky faded to violet, we had nothing. I knew I should find Airedain, but I couldn't bring myself to look for him. When I admitted why, Iannah just raised her eyebrows.

I flopped backward onto wet grass. "Do you think I'm doing the right thing, marrying Fendul?"

"You know what I think about Airedain." *Deadbeat alcoholic* had been her exact words.

"He's changing. But him aside, you said I let men control my life."

Iannah lay next to me. "This is different. You're making a com-mitment to your people."

"What about you? Still committed to the Colonnium?"

"Looks like it. Every guard quits, dies, or gets promoted. Not planning on the first two."

I scoffed. "You really want to stay there forever? Six hours of sleep on a hard bunk, twelve hours standing guard for councillors who don't know your name?"

"Parr knew my name." She folded a blade of grass. "Wish I could get deployed in the countryside. Barely remember how to navigate by the stars."

"Really? That bright one is my people's guiding star. See how it's the tip of a cross? That's the sword of the tel-saidu." I traced a line along the blade to a cluster of four more stars — crux in the centre, pommel at the far end, left and right sides of the hand guard. "In Rin legend, spirits fight with real weapons."

"That constellation's an emperor in Ferish mythology," Iannah said. "Arms wide to embrace the world, feet together at the bright star. All I remember is one star's called Nonil. Must be where Alesso Spariere got the name."

I jerked upright. "Wait. Months ago, Rhonos killed a Corvittai carrying map coordinates that said 'Nonil.' It was for navigation, but not by astronomy like he thought. The coordinates were a Corvittai camp in Dúnravn Pass. Nonil's territory."

Iannah sat up. "If Spariere chose his new name after joining Suriel — Cattil Territory isn't just a place. Cattil's a *person*."

She was moving before I could reply. I scrambled down the hill after her. She wound through dark streets and banged on a door painted with *Lis Libres te Quintes*. When nothing happened, she banged harder.

A man leaned out the window above us and snapped in Ferish. Even spoken angrily, it flowed in a way other itheran languages didn't. Iannah stepped under a street lamp to show the elk sigil on her coat. The man's head disappeared. A moment later he opened the door, candlestick in hand, waistcoat unbuttoned.

"I need to see an astronomy chart. Council business." Iannah pressed five pann into his hand, enough for a good meal. "For your trouble."

He grumbled and stepped aside, eyeing me. The shop was tidy, with leather-bound books on polished shelves and illustrated tomes open on display. A ship's wheel hung over the staircase entry. The man climbed a ladder, took down a roll of parchment, and spread it on a table. Ink animals cavorted across circular grids. Iannah stared at the man until he slunk away, leaving the candle.

She skimmed the chart and tapped a five-star cross drawn over a crowned man. "Cattil's a star, too. Clever. Nobody would connect the names to Suriel without knowing both Ferish and viirelei astronomy."

"And the odds of our races working together are pretty much

none." I doubted a Rin had ever set foot in this shop. "What do you bet Cattil is Iollan?"

"One problem with that theory. The other stars in the constellation."

"You think Suriel had five mages?"

"Captains, maybe. Iollan's neither soldier nor sailor, but someone's been coordinating with these raiders."

I frowned. "That . . . makes sense. Parr claimed his source wasn't Nonil, but it wasn't Iollan, either. Iollan was in prison then. Maybe Parr's son is a Corvittai captain after all."

Iannah's finger slid across the drawing. "Nonil, the emperor's left hand holding a dagger. Cattil, his right hand holding a sextant. Nonil helmed the army, so Cattil probably helms the navy. Then Peimil, the head. Arril, the heart. Quinil, the feet. At a guess, the head is highly academic while the feet move among the people. The heart would be Suriel's most trusted captain."

"Any of those could apply to Iollan. We don't know enough about him."

Iannah shrugged. "So we find out more."

Sleet turned to drifting flakes as I walked back to Ashtown. The snow was early. Every winter was colder than the last, but this year I understood what it meant. The world was swinging out of balance with so many saidu dead. Even Suriel, wherever he was, wasn't controlling the wind anymore. The only gusts came from the ocean where other tel-saidu lived, too far away to have been woken by the Rin. They went on sleepwalking through their duties, creating weather systems that barely reached the coast.

The Iyo gathering place was across the street from their row of two-storey flats. Rioden branches burned in its windows, dripping hot sap onto the sills. Mourning beacons. I stepped into the smoky building and found more than a hundred Iyo standing in clusters or huddled on bark mats between red-brick columns.

Airedain was with Jonalin and two other young men sharing a bottle of brånnvin. I didn't know how to talk to him now without crossing the line marked by my engagement. At least Jonalin was well enough to have made the trip back from Yeva Iren. His sleeveless tunic showed bandages across one shoulder where a raider had hit him with a crossbow bolt.

Segowa waved me over to a hearth. Salmon roasted on a grate over duck potatoes nestled in the coals. "Have you eaten?"

"Nei. I will later." I brushed snow off my hood. "Who are the beacons for?"

She lowered her eyes. "Two more Iyo died of their wounds after you and Airedain left Yeva Iren. One was the Okoreni-Iyo's elder son. Our warriors just brought the news along with captured raiders."

I breathed deep, steadying myself. "The captives — do the Iyo still have them?"

Segowa nodded. "In the carpentry workshop. The Elkhounds won't take them until daylight."

Follow the raiders. Once they went to prison, not even Iannah could get me access. I crossed the room and had a whispered exchange with Airedain. We went outside to the field behind the flats. An Iyo woman stood guard by the workshop, a plain building with wide doors for moving lumber.

I raised a hand in greeting. "I need to speak with the captives on behalf of the Rin-jouyen."

She heaved open a door. Being the Okoreni-Rin's daughter had its uses.

Clay lamps cast yellow pools on the walls. Two burly Iyo men watched over a row of itherans slumped on the floor, bound to thick rioden logs. I searched the raiders' faces until I found the brown-bearded man who had surrendered. Seeing them like this, shivering, streaked with dirt, I didn't have the energy to hate them. They were probably refugees like the Sverbians who had traded for our salmon.

At first, I'd asked Airedain to help translate the raiders' broken Sverbian. He had a better idea. He spoke enough Gallnach that if I could get the raiders talking to each other, feeling safe in their own language, he might overhear something useful.

I stood out of reach, Airedain beside me, and spoke. "The things you've been stealing. Where are they?"

The bearded man just looked at me.

"Did you sell them to Cattil?"

His mouth twitched.

"What do you want? Food? Blankets? Messages sent to your families?"

The boy next to him shifted his leg and winced. His knee was bent at an odd angle under his woolwrap.

"You didn't treat their wounds?" I asked the Iyo guards.

"He just got that," said one, a drummer with half his hair in a bun. "Tried to escape."

"Stay still," I told the boy. I knelt on the dirt, pushed his wool-wrap aside, and felt his knee. His trousers were tight over the swollen flesh. "I have to cut the cloth. Okay?" I mimed it before drawing my hunting knife.

He didn't move as I slit the fabric and peeled it back. The skin underneath was a sunset of purple and red. Gritting my teeth, I slipped his kneecap back into place. His face twisted, but he stayed silent.

"Tell me about Cattil," I said. "Is that who your ship captain wanted to kidnap me for?"

He hesitated. The bearded man glared at him. The boy snapped back in Gallnach. They broke into rapid speech like grating bones, punctuated with jeers from the other raiders.

"Shut it!" An Iyo guard swung his sword in an arc.

I showed the boy a tulanta vial from my purse. "For the pain. If you talk."

"Poison," he muttered with a thick accent.

"It's safe. Watch." I tipped a drop onto my finger and swallowed the sour liquid. "Do you know these names? Arril, Peimil, Quinil?"

The boy scowled.

I closed my hand over the vial. "Your loss."

Airedain and I left, our bootprints churning the snow grey from the underlayer of coal ash. Alone in an alley, I asked, "You understand any of that?"

"Some," he said. "Sounds like they trade with Cattil, but they're scared shitless of her."

"*Her?*"

"Yeah. Whoever it is, it ain't Iollan."

I'd never seen a female captain among itherans. Then again, Suriel wouldn't care. I exhaled, forming a white cloud. One name down. Three to go.

I'd hoped to find out more before leaving Caladheä, but Fendul expected me back. Ranelin, Jonalin's father, offered to take me to Toel Ginu along with Viviwen. When I returned to the Iyo gathering place in the morning, Airedain gave me a bowl of roast squash and salmon. We sat on a woven bark mat eating in silence.

The door swung open with a swirl of snow. An itheran stepped inside holding up her skirts. She must've walked the whole way through Ashtown like that to keep her hem clean. She reminded me of a snowshoe hare — white shawl, white skirt, white knit bonnet, all white except the canvas satchel over one shoulder. She spotted Airedain and waved.

"That's Viviwen?" I whispered.

Airedain nodded. I looked from her neatly pinned brown curls and ironed clothes to his ashy breeches and rumpled crest of hair. Once I would've teased him. Once he might've laughed.

"Miss Hannehl!" An Iyo boy of about seven dashed across the room and tugged on Viviwen's skirt. "Look!" He pulled her over to a bucket of water holding a toy canoe. He raised his hand. The water churned, tipping the canoe as if in a storm.

Viviwen smiled and clapped. "You've gotten so good! Where's your tema and temal? I'd love to see them again."

I raised my eyebrows. I hadn't expected an itheran to know our casual family terms.

"She was his teacher this spring," Airedain said quietly. "Refused to punish him for calling water."

"Yet she treated you like shit, using you to upset her parents."

"People fuck up." He picked at our bark mat. "I think she took this job to make up for it. Ain't gonna be easy living in Toel."

"If Fendul accepts her." I rose and stretched. "Guess it's time to go."

Airedain rose with me. "When will you be back?"

"Depends how much I'm needed in Toel." I pulled on my cloak, then paused. "One more thing. Iannah's from a blacksmith family, and she's got connections here in Caladheå. She'll help you get a proper weapon. Next time you won't need to save someone with a lumber axe."

8.

SECRETS & LIES

Viviwen could barely stand when we reached Toel Ginu. Whatever she'd eaten for breakfast was in the ocean. Ranelin went ahead to bring news of our arrival while Viviwen rested at the docks.

Once she recovered, I followed her up slick zigzagging steps cut into the cliffs and through the forest, where her iron-buckled shoes sank into mud thick as porridge. Her skirt wouldn't stay white here. My new black clothes from Segowa were hasty work, unfitted, but they were warm and sturdy. My knee-high boots, coated with cottonwood resin and trimmed with caribou fur, kept out everything from wind to water.

I handed Viviwen a ribbon on the way. "Braid your hair. It's considered humble."

She flashed a shy smile I couldn't return. It reminded me of Marijka pinning up my hair the first time I went to Caladheå.

Akiga let us through the stockade gate, her eyes creased with wariness. Children peered out from behind buildings. A canoe sat half-carved on blocks. The archery field was empty. Nili limped out from the textile workshop, muttering about the hollow on her calf where Barolein had cut out the infected flesh. She hugged me and looked at Viviwen with bewilderment.

"Where is everyone?" I asked Nili.

"Gathering duck potato on the islands. Fendul says we don't have enough salmon to last the winter."

"He sent Rin over the ocean? After we got attacked at Yeva Iren?"

She shrugged. "Raiders won't bother going to uninhabited islands. I hope."

Bitterness wreathed me like fog. Fendul had promised that we would make decisions like these together. I led Viviwen into our plank house where Fendul and Tokoda waited by the central hearth, Wotelem on one side, Hiyua on the other with a toddler on her hip.

"Okorebai-Iyo, Okorebai-Rin." Viviwen curtsied, then as if suddenly remembering, raised her hand. "It's an honour to be invited to your settlement."

Tokoda returned the second gesture. "For your safety, I advise you not to stray into the forest. Wildlife is the least of our worries." She nodded at Fendul. "I leave the rest to you, Okorebai."

I waited until she and Wotelem left before whispering to Viviwen, "Don't worry. You won't see much of her."

Fendul stood straight-backed, stone-eyed. "I trust you agree to our terms. Three sovereigns a month plus room and board. Kateiko will go over the subject matter with you. You'll be accompanied by a Rin during lessons, and discipline of children remains in our hands. Is that clear?"

"Yes, sir," Viviwen said.

Hiyua beckoned, shifting the round-cheeked boy on her hip. "We sectioned off part of our other plank house to give you privacy. I'll get you settled in."

"Take her to Barolein first," I said. "She could use something to soothe her stomach."

Viviwen smiled gratefully. Hiyua gave me a quick kiss on the hair. They left, and then it was just Fendul and me.

Fendul couldn't meet my eyes. "Kako. About the Rutnaast papers . . ."

I crossed my arms. "You wouldn't let Emílie translate them until a Rin died?"

He flinched. "I won't apologize for being cautious. The truth is I wasn't just worried about lying to Tokoda. I don't trust Emílie. That's twice her people have attacked us unprovoked, and I don't know her allegiance. All we have is Airedain's word."

"So you don't trust Airedain? You hired Viviwen on his suggestion."

"With Wotelem's support. Emílie doesn't have that. Plus she owns a pub near the docklands, so she could be in contact with Gallnach raiders. For all I know she's already told them we're after Iollan."

"Why didn't you bring this up when I asked? You didn't give Airedain a chance to defend her. You just insisted Tokoda was holding us back."

Fendul rubbed his temples. "I'm trying my best, Kako. When I asked you to marry me . . . we talked about alliances. But I've got six other Aikoto jouyen, two other confederacies, and three itheran races to deal with, and we've fought them all at some point. One wrong move is the end of us."

I sank onto a woven bark mat. "Trust *me*, at least. I'm supposed to become your wife. Talk to me. Don't shut me down the moment I suggest something."

"I'm sorry," Fendul said, so quiet I barely heard over the crackling fire. He knelt and took my hand. "I was afraid you'd think I'm paranoid like my father, but . . . maybe I *am* like him. Proud and too cautious."

"Oh, Fen." I touched his crow amulet, nestled against my wire wolf makiri. He'd been so close to losing them in the raid. "Promise me one thing. From now on, no secrets, no lies. Not from me."

"I promise. Absolutely."

My face grew warm. "In the name of honesty . . . um . . . Airedain kissed me. Two days ago."

Fendul's brow furrowed. "That's all, though? You didn't . . ."

"Nei. I told him about you, and he backed off."

"Good." He smiled. Then, with the grace of a canoe dragged over stones, he kissed my cheek. "I'm glad you're back."

Now that we weren't busy with the salmon run, I set aside an hour every morning to meditate with Yironem, like my mother had when teaching me to call water. Most days it meant sitting in the rain. We spent afternoons helping Viviwen. She began teaching the youngest children since the older ones were preparing for winter. All her books were in Sverbian, so I lent her my Coast Trader collection of folk tales to read aloud. She demonstrated writing with charcoal on soft inner bark. Hiyua supervised, mostly to keep kids from running off, but I soon realized she was watching the lessons.

Akiga refused to let her grandchildren participate. Fendul overrode her. He declared loudly that if we were living near enough itherans to get attacked by them, we'd better be able to communicate with them. I soon realized Akiga was on gate duty not because she had the most combat experience, or because our shrine was in another rainforest, and she had no work as a shrine carver, but because Fendul didn't want her anger near the Rin kids. A little boy, sniffling, told me Akiga said itherans could steal his spirit by touching his hair. It took me hours of insisting that three *very* kind itherans had touched my hair — Tiernan, Marijka, and Iannah — to convince the boy to attend lessons with Viviwen. I didn't mention Parr was the fourth.

"Look," Nili said one night, pointing down the plank house with her embroidery needle.

Barolein sat on the floor with his healing apprentices, demonstrating on a slab of raw shark how to irrigate a wound. Mereku sat nearby singing to a young boy in her lap. Her shoulder stump had scarred over like a tree knot. Every so often she and Barolein smiled at each other. Every time, his face flushed, and he forgot what he was saying.

I stifled a laugh. "When did *that* happen?"

"Right after she joined the Rin," Rikuja said. "Barolein took over her care from the Iyo healers, and . . ."

Nili grinned. "Go Mereku. She's, what, thirty-six? One arm and she still snagged a younger man."

"We'll see." Rikuja frowned at the axe handle she was carving. "Barolein only lost his wife three months ago. I wouldn't be ready to move on if Dune's blood was so recently in the ground."

Sobered, Nili watched Orelein sharpening his chisel. Orelein, Barolein's younger brother, had asked Nili to marry him the spring before last. She had said no. It took almost a year before she moved onto Taworen, a Rin drummer — only for Taworen to fall in the Blackbird Battle.

On clear days, Viviwen ate with us by the firepits. She balked at dipping food into smelt oil, which she said tasted like rotten whale mashed with rye malt, but was content eating whitefish and berries plain. After seeing her slog through mud in buckled shoes, the leatherworker made her resin-coated boots. She made toy owls for his children in thanks. The owls had painted hazelnuts for heads, pine cones for bodies, and feathery rioden needles for wings, glued together with pine pitch.

Gradually Viviwen began to tell us about her life. She had begun teaching when she was sixteen to help support her eight siblings. After the school fired her, Airedain got her work as a barmaid. I smacked Nili for asking about their breakup. All Viviwen said, in her little snowshoe hare voice, was she never meant to hurt him. She'd kept working at the Knox Arms while he worked in Crieknaast, but now he was back. So, nineteen, with no prospects of marriage or another teaching job, she'd come to Toel Ginu.

Cold set in. Ice covered the ditches when I woke each day. The one hare that wound up in my snares had thicker fur than I'd ever seen at this time of year, halfway between its brown and white coat. It'd be a good winter for pelts if I could find the game. Iyun Bel had been heavily over-trapped by itherans.

"Where are you going trapping this year?" I asked Dunehein one morning while he stood watch at the gate. The canoe workshop was near enough I could stand under its roof and talk to him, holding his daughter Sihaja in a bundle of otter furs.

He shrugged. "Haven't decided. Why, wanna come?"

I chewed on that thought. It'd be an excuse to search the wilderness for Iollan and Suriel, unquestioned by itheran soldiers. If Yironem came, I could keep up his antayul training and he could fly us out of danger.

"Be good to have help. Esiad was gonna come, until those Gallnach takuran put his blood in the ground." Dunehein thumped the stakewall. Slush slid off and splattered everywhere. "Anyway. Wet winter ahead. The marsh rats built their dams high."

I held my hand into the gusting sleet. Every winter since the Storm Year tested our limits more as the temperature dropped and precipitation rose. Ingdanrad's mages guessed our world was losing heat and gaining water, maybe to and from other shoirdrygen. The few surviving saidu in this region weren't strong enough to repair the barrier everywhere. If Suriel tore a rift into the void, and our world's natural elements — heat, water, earth, air, everything that gave life — disappeared through the rift into that nothingness, we might never get them back.

Sihaja fussed in my arms. I kissed her tiny nose, red from cold. *This is the world we've forged for you.*

The first group of Rin that'd gone to gather duck potato on the western islands returned with half their baskets empty. Storms had knocked down hundreds of trees, causing streambanks to erode and collapse on underwater potato patches. The second group found streams flooded with salt water that had killed the vegetation.

"You shouldn't have sold our salmon," Akiga told Fendul.

9.

SCHISM

I was asleep when I heard the scream. I flung aside my blankets to see Rikuja hurrying down the plank house, lantern in hand, shirt unlaced from feeding Sihaja. Nili rose groggily. The bed between hers and Hiyua's was empty.

"Where's Yiro?" I cried at Rikuja.

"He was gone when Sihaja woke me — I thought he was at the latrine—"

Another scream, short and shrill. I seized Kohekai, my hunting knife, and burst through the door. Snow shocked my bare feet. Lanterns burned at the stockade gates among swirling flakes. Shouts came from beyond the stakewall, too muffled to understand.

Akiga blocked the gate with her javelin. "Not until the okorebai says—"

"Move!" I wrenched her aside, knocked the crossbar from the gate, and ran — careening through the forest, stumbling over roots, cracking thin layers of ice. Conifer needles jabbed my soles. Moonlit leaves fluttered like birds.

"Stop!" came Yironem's voice from a thicket. "Leave her alone!"

I swung around a massive spruce. Two hooded figures kicked a heap on the ground. Yironem grappled with a third, a male judging by the build. I smashed Kohekai's handle into the man's head. He stumbled, taking Yironem down.

Someone tackled me. We spun, colliding with a tree. I lashed out with my knife, lost in a tangle of cloth, branches, needles. In the dark, I couldn't tell where one person turned into another. Kohekai was prised from my hand, my arm pinned behind me.

"You're not part of this," a soft voice said into my ear.

I froze. Aikoto words. Iyo accent.

Yironem rolled through the muck, a flurry of elbows, knees, fists. His opponent's hood was off. I could make out dark cropped hair. The man pinned Yironem down, striking again and again.

"That's my brother!" I rammed my elbow into the man holding me. "We're your fucking allies!"

A female scoffed out of sight. "Not these days—" She cut off with a gasp.

Fendul emerged from the trees. He hauled the man off Yironem and slammed him into a tree trunk. "Enough. Or I will repay this triple, I swear as Okorebai-Rin."

Hiyua strode up holding an irumoi. The glowing mushrooms on the wooden rod cast dim blue light across the thicket. Dunehein closed in on one side, Nili's ex-lover Orelein on the other. Nili dragged the Iyo female forward.

Ilani. She clutched a bloody hand to her stomach. My work. The proof was on my knife.

The man holding me swore and let go. In the watery light, I

recognized him as Makoril, an antayul in his early twenties. Fendul held Ganiam, an Iyo stonecarver.

Yironem struggled to sit up, stretching toward the limp figure the Iyo had been battering. "She — is she—"

I rolled her over. Her chest rose in shallow gasps, but her swollen face looked inhuman. "Viviwen?"

Fendul shoved Ganiam forward. "Take them to our stockade. Send for the Okorebai-Iyo."

Orelein prodded Ganiam along with his bow. Dunehein grabbed Makoril, his hand wrapping all the way around the slender man's arm. I'd never seen more disgust on Nili's face as she supported Ilani. Hiyua tried to help Yironem up, but he pushed her away. Blood flowed from his nose.

Fendul crouched at Viviwen's side. The braid she'd worn for half a month had come undone. He pulled off his wool shirt and folded it around her to avoid touching her loose curls. She gave a strained moan as he lifted her. Only as I searched for Kohekai did I realize the forest floor was covered with trampled, disintegrating paper. I picked up something that felt solid. A book, cold and dripping.

Akiga watched silently as we entered the stockade. Fendul carried Viviwen into our plank house and set her on an empty bed. Her bonnet was dyed red, her shawl torn and coated with mud. Barolein paled and sent his apprentices scrambling for supplies.

Ilani, demanding an Iyo healer, refused to let Barolein do more than put bogmoss on her stomach. I wrapped my numb, cut feet in a blanket. Ganiam and Yironem were a motley of black eyes, split lips, and purpling bruises. Makoril's skin was streaked with cuts under his tattered shirt. Damp black hair hung over his eyes. He must've married recently and begun growing it out.

Fendul sent the onlookers to our other plank house and forced the Iyo to their knees by the main hearth. His hands shook. "Explain."

"Ask the Rin brat," Makoril said in his soft voice. "He'd love to tell you what he learned from the pigeon."

Yironem flushed. "We were just talking—"

"She was reading." Makoril pointed at the sodden book I'd found. "From *that*."

I peeled two sheets apart and studied the bleeding ink. I only knew a few symbols, but it was enough. "It's . . . a theological book. About Sverbian religion."

I felt a flood of understanding. Tiernan had taught me about Thaerijmur, the distant land where Sverbians believed they sailed after death. Yironem was looking for anything that might connect him to people he'd lost or killed. His best friend, father, oldest sister, the Corvittai he shot in the Blackbird Battle.

"Bet that's why the pigeon came to Toel," Makoril said. "She'll try to convert Iyo next."

"It's not her fault," Yironem burst out. "I asked her to teach me—"

"Takuran spirit traitor," Ganiam muttered.

"You will not use that language here," Hiyua said coolly. "Least of all to describe my son."

Ganiam laughed. "Ai, need your tema to defend you, kid?"

Fendul grabbed him by the throat. "Yironem held his own in a fist fight despite being ten years your junior and has shown more honour and courage in battle than you ever will." He raised his voice. "Ilani, Ganiam, Makoril. You assaulted two Rin, plus an itheran living here on my invitation. You are banned from a hundred paces of our stockade."

"You can't ban us!" Ilani cried. "It's our land!"

"Consider yourselves lucky," Tokoda said from the doorway. Snowflakes blew in around her. Her eyes went from Ilani holding bogmoss on her stomach, to Makoril laced with cuts, to Kohekai at my feet, its blade streaked with blood. "The Rin are not known for mercy."

"I didn't know they were Iyo," I said. "Their faces were hidden."

Tokoda beckoned to them. "You three, come. Okorebai-Rin, we will talk in daylight."

Ilani staggered up and pressed her fingers into the spongy bogmoss. She marked bloody streaks down my cheek. "You let my brother die in Rutnaast. Only fair we got a few hits on yours."

Dunehein grabbed me before I could react. Tokoda stood with her arms folded until the Iyo men got Ilani outside.

The moment the door shut, Hiyua touched Fendul's shoulder. "Okorebai, how did the Iyo know Yironem left the stockade while our guards were unaware?"

"Akiga knew," Yironem said. "She caught me climbing over the stakewall last night. I didn't think she saw Viviwen. She promised not to tell if I left again."

Hiyua's mouth pressed into a line. She strode outside, her tail of dark hair swinging.

I yanked on my boots. We followed her to where Akiga was barring the gate behind the Iyo. She turned at the sound of our footsteps.

Hiyua seized her shirt. "You knew. You knew my son was out there and did nothing!"

Akiga grabbed Hiyua's scarred arm, trying to push her away. "He wasn't in danger—"

"How would *you* know?" Hiyua shoved her into the stakewall.

Akiga gasped for air. "I just wanted the itheran to leave. Your boy wasn't meant to interfere."

Hiyua released Akiga with a look like she'd swallowed rotten meat. "You're a disgrace."

A crowd had gathered by the plank houses. Someone threw a torch on a snowy firepit, followed by pine pitch crystals that blazed like fireworks. Fendul stepped into the spitting light. "Viviwen Hannehl broke no laws," he said. "She did us no harm. I hired her to teach our youth about itheran ways and language, and she was doing exactly that. Her presence isn't up to you, Akiga."

"She has no place here," Akiga said. "Our ancestors lived with itherans once in Caladheå. It ended with Rin bodies in the ashes of our plank houses."

"Ferish caused the Bronnoi Ridge fire," I said. "Our ancestors saved a Sverbian stavehall from burning. You'd know that if you talked to any Sverbians."

"Akiga, you betrayed us." Fendul drew his sword. "Kneel."

Her hand went to her grey braid. "You wouldn't dare."

"I'd exile you if we could spare a single person. Kneel."

"I am the eldest Rin. I watched you and your father be born, boy. You dishonour me by relegating me to gate duty, ignoring my advice, refusing me apprentices. You put my grandchildren in the hands of that itheran—"

"I am your okorebai. *Kneel*."

Akiga stared at him over the flames. "No. I challenge you as Okorebai-Rin."

Silence choked the stockade.

An elder had challenged Fendul's family's leadership during the First Elken War. When that elder lost the vote, he took Rin and Iyo dissenters to form the Dona-jouyen, who, decades later, would return to kill most of the Rin. Three people had challenged Fendul's great-great-grandmother after the Bronnoi Ridge fire. She scraped a win by agreeing no Rin would live in Caladheå again, ending our role in the Sverbian-Aikoto alliance.

Holding a knife by the blade, people said about okorebai challenges. No jouyen faced one without a cost.

Fendul nodded, jaw clenched. "Make your case."

Akiga faced the gathered Rin. "Our last okorebai sided with itherans and led us to war with our own families. His son leads us down the same path. Fendul sent two Rin on a dangerous trip to Ingdanrad, sold our food to itherans, then invited one to live among us. They would have us betray our aeldu and forget our history. Our ancestors are everything we've ever been.

"Fendul chose Hiyua as okoreni, a woman whose daughter Nisali abandoned us last year, whose son, Yironem, turns to foreign beliefs and defiles the kinaru body our aeldu gave him. Kateiko — Hiyua's adopted daughter, Fendul's most trusted advisor, and our most noted deserter — just stabbed an Iyo to defend an itheran. Our leadership is not loyal to us. They will lead us into nothing but ruin.

"We have a duty to guard our land and culture for our descendants, but one battle could end the Rin. Fendul has been far too lenient. We must be tougher than ever. We must raise our children to fight, not read ink symbols. We cannot survive unless we rebuild our numbers. Everyone will have until summer to bring a partner into the jouyen. After that, I will negotiate marriages."

Nili's jaw fell. Yironem gripped my hand like he was trying to crack a hazelnut.

"This is our future. We must make sacrifices. My children died defending all of you." Akiga swung her javelin in an arc. "I've already arranged marriages for my grandchildren when they attune. Fendul will turn twenty-two soon and has not yet given us a natural-born okoreni. Where is his commitment?"

"Right here." Dunehein lifted Sihaja from Rikuja's arms. "In our children he fights and bleeds for. In the stockade he built to protect them. In the Aikoto alliance he renewed. Don't claim he isn't committed."

Fendul drove his swordpoint into frozen dirt. "Do you want to risk another schism, Akiga? The one with the Dona-jouyen spilled far too much blood."

"The aeldu spoke to me. This is our path." She planted her javelin next to his sword. "Our future depends on it."

Fendul stepped back into the darkness. "Rin, make your choice. You know what I stand for."

Everyone who'd attuned had to vote. Nili, Yironem, and I stood behind Fendul. Hiyua, Dunehein, Rikuja, and Orelein came with us. So did Aliko. Her lifelong interest in Fendul was one-sided, but at least she was loyal.

More than I expected went to Akiga. Each one made my stomach wrench. Most lived in the other plank house with her. She might've been building support for months.

"How can you choose her?" I demanded of Akiga's side. Snowflakes sizzled around me. "She'll get us all killed! Is that the sacrifice you want?"

"Compromise," our tattooist told Fendul. "Get rid of the itheran, and I'll vote for you."

"Viviwen will leave when she's able," he said.

At the end, two groups faced each other across the fire. Thirteen votes for each.

"My brother's not here," Orelein said.

His older apprentice dashed into our plank house. An owl hooted as we waited. Barolein emerged, pulling water out of the air to wash Viviwen's blood from his hands.

He grimaced. "So the decision's on me."

Everything we'd worked toward could be gone in a single night. We'd be back in the spiral of violence Fendul and I were trying to end. No one would live long enough to marry.

Barolein rubbed his forehead. "I didn't want to come south this summer. Thought we should wait out this war with Suriel. I feel justified since I buried my wife days after we got here. I treated more wounds in the Blackbird Battle than I ever expected to see in one place, yet I'm supposed to choose between two people who both supported coming here. I wouldn't vote for either of you if I had the choice."

His eyes lingered on Orelein, his last relative, then Mereku, the one woman who'd made him smile since losing his wife. "But we're here now. We've got to live with Iyo and itherans, and I'm about to stitch up a Sverbian girl's head. What happens when her family finds out? If soldiers come for the Iyo who assaulted an itheran? You think Tokoda will let us stay in Toel Ginu after that? If this is how you solve problems, Akiga, I don't want to see what you do with a jouyen behind you."

Barolein tossed his knife at Fendul's feet. "May the aeldu guide you, Okorebai. No one else can."

Fendul moved into the firelight. Snowflakes melted on his skin, glittering over the tattooed lines on his arm and the scar across his chest. He seemed to be every Okorebai-Rin at once, a thousand layers of himself. He cracked Akiga's javelin over his knee and pulled his sword from the ground.

"Kneel," he said.

Akiga sank into deepening snow. Fendul lifted her grey braid, wound with the bark cord that marked her as a shrine carver, and slashed through it. She wrenched like he'd sliced into her chest. He tossed the braid into the fire, filling the stockade with the reek of burning hair. The pride and memories of her ancestors turned to ash that drifted away into the night. Severed bark cords hung at her neck like tendons. She lifted her face to the sky, speaking silent words to the aeldu.

I walked alone through the forest, stepping around barren bushes laced with frost. I set a lantern in the snow where Fendul and I had sat the morning I agreed to marry him. The ocean broke against the cliffs like an argument. The spirits of the dead, our aeldu, buried outside Anwen Bel were meant to return to our home shrine, but it felt like they were still here, sensing there were no living people to return to.

Help me. Tell me what to do. If the aeldu heard my plea, they ignored it.

Footsteps crunched. Fendul drew up next to me. "That could've gone worse," he said.

"What'll happen to Yiro?" I asked.

"It's up to Hiyua. Sneaking out was stupid, not illegal."

"And Akiga?"

"Confined to the stockade."

I gazed at the ocean. Snowflakes drifted past the cliffs, falling off the edge of the world. If I swam straight from here, I wondered if I'd find Thaerijmur or Aeldu-yan first. "I can't do this, Fen."

He touched my arm. "We knew it wouldn't be easy."

"Viviwen has two broken ribs and eight stitches in her head because I suggested hiring an itheran. Ilani could be *dead* if my knife landed different. Aeldu save us, the Iyo still haven't forgiven us for killing their relatives who joined the Dona. If they kick us out for this, the Rin will blame both Akiga and me."

"The Rin chose us, not her."

"They chose you."

Fendul pulled me to face him. "I'm giving my whole life to these people. You're all I have. I won't let them take you from me."

I looked into his dark eyes. "Fen . . . did you mean it when you said you'd never been in love?"

He stiffened. A cold breeze brushed my hair against his waist. "Kako . . ."

"No secrets, no lies. You promised."

"Honestly, I don't know. I . . . feel better when we're together. I think about you more than anyone else. But I've never had a romance to compare to. I'm not sure how that kind of love is supposed to feel."

I rested my hands on his chest. "Did you come to the salmon run just to be with me?"

Fendul's heart quickened. "It crossed my mind we'd share a tent. But I know you look forward to the run. It's the one time each year we can leave everything behind. After Ilani picked a fight with you on the equinox, time away seemed like a good idea."

Something unfurled in my mind, an algae bloom colouring a lake green. "All this time, I worried what the jouyen thought." I drew back, leaving icy air between us. "But it's not them."

His brows knit together.

"Everything Akiga criticized you for was my idea — Ingdanrad, Viviwen, selling our salmon. You'll never know if you're doing something because I suggested it or because it's the right thing to do."

"Tokoda and Wotelem agreed to all those things."

"What happens when they don't? Will you trust me over them? Tokoda's been leading the Iyo for twenty-five years. I keep fucking up, Fen. I don't know how to lead—"

"Kako." Fendul held my shoulders. "Plenty of okorebai marry for love. They manage."

"Most are married for years before becoming okorebai. They

don't figure both out at the same time. We can't risk tonight happening again. One more mistake will be our last."

A slow tide moved across his face, receding to show barren sand. I wanted so much to hold him until the hurt on his face eased.

"I'm sorry, Fennel," I said.

"Do you think it could ever work?"

"Maybe. Once this war's over. But we can't live waiting for that possibility."

He pushed my hood back and stroked my hair. "I wish I'd . . ."

"What?"

"Kissed you more. While I still could."

A smile nudged my lips. "I haven't left yet."

Fendul slid a hand behind my head. He pressed his lips to mine, our breath mixing in a white cloud. His arms were one place Parr's spirit couldn't touch me. I wanted to remember this forever — cold hands, snow on our faces, chapped skin, the rhythm of waves. A night that happened because of all we survived and all we left behind. We'd held a knife by the blade. Better we bore the scar than the entire jouyen.

When the lantern went out, Fendul unhooked my wire wolf and pressed it into my palm. Our engagement was over before the jouyen knew it existed. I traced the smooth wings of his crow amulet, then slid my fingers down his scratchy wool shirt to his heart. The spirits of every Okorebai-Rin flowed in his veins. He'd never be truly alone.

We walked back hand in hand, letting go before we reached the stockade. Nili and Dunehein were the only ones in our plank house still awake. I unfolded my fist to reveal the wolf makiri. Nili hugged me. Dunehein wrapped bulky arms around Fendul and thumped his back.

"I failed them," I whispered to Nili. "Fendul, Yironem, everyone."

"Nei." She pressed her hands to my hair. "We only fail people when we stop caring."

10.

HAFELÚS

In the morning, Hiyua told me Yironem was confined to the stockade for a month. We couldn't even go to the docks to work on water-calling. Instead, we climbed onto the roof of the canoe workshop and lay in the snow while everyone finished breakfast. The only person in sight was Dunehein at the gate, tossing his battle axe from hand to hand.

"I get it, you know," I said. "About Thaerijmur and the dead. I went through the same thing with Tiernan."

Yironem's brow crinkled. "But you're . . . you."

"What, your sister?"

"Nei, I mean, most Rin attune to birds. You didn't. I'm supposed to be . . ."

Perfect. Someone so devout the aeldu blessed him with a kinaru body they didn't even give okorebai. Legend said the first Rin were born from a kinaru egg. Jouyen branched off over time, taking other animals as their crests — dolphin for the coastal Iyo, fox for the southern Yula, seagull for the nomadic Dona — but every member of the Aikoto Confederacy carried the blood of the mother kinaru. The oldest aeldu.

"Who are you afraid of letting down?" I asked. "The living or the dead?"

Yironem shrugged. "Both. I kept thinking if I got initiated as a shawl dancer, I could ask my temal's spirit why I'm a kinaru. What to do with that body. Do I fight? Do I *refuse* to fight 'cause the kinaru it came from didn't attack us? I didn't want anyone to know my second form until I figured it out. But then Dunehein got stranded in Rutnaast, and . . . he's practically your brother, which makes him mine, too. I didn't know what to do. I just went.

"Suddenly everyone knew about my kinaru body. Before we broke the siege, Aliko wanted me to ask her tema what it's like in Aeldu-yan. After, Ilani asked me to talk to Esiad. She thought since he attuned to a raven, he was . . . close to the Rin. I said I couldn't. She screamed at me. When we got back to Toel, people touched my hair. Just to be with their dead."

"Nei," I breathed. "How did I miss that?"

"You and Tema were busy with the Okorebai-Rin. Anyway, that night I decided to quit dancing, make people realize I can't do what they want. But they kept pushing. Especially after a Rin died at the salmon run. When Viviwen came, I was curious how itherans talk to their aeldu, but she says they don't. So it was all for nothing. And now Viviwen . . ."

"Barolein says she'll be okay. But there's one thing I still don't understand. Why become an antayul?"

"Water always responds." He glanced at me, his brown eyes bright, and sat up. "Ai. Let's try that training game."

Skeptical, I formed a water disc above his head. He had to guess without looking when I froze it. So far, he hadn't gotten it right once.

"Now!" Yironem jerked his head up as ice crackled across the disc. He broke into a grin.

Laughter bubbled out of me. "What changed?"

"I felt it during the okorebai challenge. While you were shouting at everyone and boiling snowflakes. I . . . felt the same as you. And for once I didn't want to hide it."

Something settled into place in my mind. Tiernan believed I kept seeing the shoirdryge because I learned to focus on other worlds. He was the only itheran I knew who heard the dead. Maybe calling fire or water taught us to sense other things below the surface. Maybe becoming an antayul was exactly what Yironem needed.

I rumpled his hair. "You're gonna be okay, kid."

Iyun Bel was shrouded in white when I went to check my trapline. Hopping wrens left tiny prints on the snow. The only colour was red ribbons tacked to trees to mark my snares, which were buried so deep I had to dig them out. One held a thick-furred pine marten. The wire had broken its neck quick and clean. Sometimes the aeldu's gifts were clear.

On the way back, I stopped at the Rin burial site by the junction of two frozen streams. I sank to my knees by Isu's grave. Frost nestled in the grooves of her tiger lily crest carved on an ancient rioden. I'd almost said yes the first time Fendul asked me to marry him, so I could tell Isu before we buried her. I drew my fireweed crest in the snow next to Fendul's huckleberries, then wiped them away, apologizing.

Dunehein stopped me on my way back into the stockade. "Your Iyo-boy's here. He wants to talk to you."

Airedain came out of my plank house. Two matched daggers hung from his belt — proper weapons, finally. They were a good choice, easy to carry and conceal, and his drummer training meant he'd be good at dual-wielding.

"Ai, Rin-girl." He traipsed over, hands in his pockets. "Glad you're back. Thought I'd have to wait with my sister."

"How bad are things in the Iyo?" I asked.

"Ehh. Don't go near our plank houses. Tokoda's exiling Ilani, Ganiam, and Makoril to the Nuthalha Confederacy until spring. It's so far north, hunters walk onto the frozen ocean and wrestle seals into traps."

"What if Elkhounds come looking for them?"

"Yeah, about that — Viviwen promised not to tell anyone that Iyo attacked her."

Dunehein lifted his eyebrows. "She looks like death walking. Ain't no hiding that."

"I told her to say Gallnach raiders did it. See, thing is . . . her parents don't like our people, so they think she's teaching Sverbians up north. They're so worried about feeding eight other kids, they were happy she got room and board. Didn't ask questions."

I hugged Airedain. "Thank you," I said into his jerkin.

He stood stiffly until I let go. "There's something else. Jonalin and I were gonna do it ourselves, but . . . I know a way to look for Iollan och Cormic."

"What? How?"

"Bódhain, the Gallnach harvest festival. You wanna find a druid, that's the place to be."

"Bo-yin?" I rolled it around my mouth. "Where is it?"

"Two places. You can bet Iollan won't go back to Ingdanrad. The other festival's on Innisburren, that big island in Kae-jouyen territory." He drew a map in the snow. "See — down around the peninsula of South Iyun Bel to the border at Burren Inlet. Innisburren's in the inlet mouth. A night and day of sailing with good wind."

"And *you're* going?"

"With Emílie and her family. Working." Airedain drummed on his legs. "Could bring you along, Rin-girl."

I kicked snow over the map. "I'll ask the Okorebai-Rin."

Even though our engagement was over, Fendul stuck to his promise and considered the idea without immediately refusing. He hated it. I reminded him Iollan had been out of prison for four months and we had no leads. He said Ingdanrad would send mages to Innisburren and I didn't need to go. I pointed out that contacting them could be useful, especially if Tiernan had made it to Ingdanrad.

He agreed on three conditions. One, I wouldn't attack Iollan. It was a scouting mission only. Two, another Rin had to come. Nili volunteered, saying she'd give her bad leg to get out of the stockade. Three, we told Tokoda.

Expecting that, Airedain had Emílie's permission to reveal that she was Gallnach. Emílie's condition was he only brought people he trusted. Amazingly, Tokoda wasn't angry Airedain had already gone to Bódhain three years in secret. She gave him a tired, patient look that spoke of things private to the Iyo-jouyen. He wouldn't take his combat test to become a warrior for months, but she seemed to respect him like one already.

"Kako," Fendul said as I did up my bedroll. "You are coming back, right?"

"Always." I touched his crow amulet. I'd broken that promise to Tiernan, but my connection to Fendul couldn't be severed.

We told the Rin-jouyen it was a simple trip to Caladheä, looking for news and delivering textiles to Segowa's shop. Nili gawked as we walked through the city. Brick walls, cobblestone streets, coal smoke in the sky. We stopped at the Iyo gathering place and made sure people saw us, proof that we were here, then went to find Emílie's ship.

The docklands were crowded at dusk. Wind-chapped itherans set sail to catch fish for the morning market. Ferries brought passengers from up and down the coast. A bald clerk walked the piers, jotting notes and directing captains toward the sandstone Customs House. Emílie's son, Liam, and Jonalin were loading casks onto a herring drifter. The *Seakip*, with two masts and peeling black paint, was a sparrow of a ship next to the four-masted merchant galleons flying flags from Ferland and Sverba.

Liam vaulted over the bulwark onto the pier, swept into a dramatic bow, and kissed Nili's hand. "Captain Carrégind at your service. I had no idea Kateiko's friends are so lovely. Tell me, how're you enjoying our fine city?"

Nili scrunched up her nose. "I've killed things that smell better."

He smirked. "You don't live in the capital for the smell. Music, women, and paved streets — that's why I stay. And my beloved family, who'd better get here soon or they're swimming."

"He's you, but charming," Nili told Airedain.

Liam's Gallnach name must've been och Carrég, but evidently, he used the Sverbian version to blend in. It didn't work perfectly. His nose had been broken, and he wore a knife on his belt I doubted was for gutting fish.

"How'd you learn to sail?" I asked him. "I've never seen you near the docks."

"Spent my childhood on the water around Innisburren. My grandfather built the *Seakip*. We sold it when we moved to Caladheå, but the fisherman who bought it lets us borrow it a few times a year."

"Don't port clerks question a herring drifter loaded with alcohol?"

He jangled coins in his trousers pocket. "Little of this goes a long way."

His family showed up soon after. Emílie carried a wicker basket of food in each hand. Maeve, seventeen but tiny, struggled with heavy waterskins. Orla, fifteen and still in school, carried a pile of blankets. I'd often seen her hunched over a slate and chalk in the Knox Arms kitchen. She brightened when I introduced Nili.

"Kateiko talks about you all the time," Orla said. "She said you once killed two ducks with one arrow. And you can spit squash seeds farther than anyone in your nation." Nili looked pleased.

Liam took first shift at the helm. The bowsprit pointed at a strip of red sunset as we left the harbour, then veered south, plunging through foamy waves. Billowing sails caught snowflakes that swirled through the fading light. Maeve and Orla went into the cramped cabin to sleep. The rest of us sat on casks, trading smoked salmon and flatbread for salted goat and barley loaf.

"Tell us about Bódhain," I said. "Seems late for a harvest festival."

"Ah, well, we harvest the barley crop later in Gallun." Emílie leaned back against the bulwark. "It's the day of the dead, see, when souls return home. We bake extra bread and burn it, then boil ale so they can drink the steam."

"Your dead *eat*?" Nili asked.

"Not much. We only feed them once a year. Anyway, the Caladheå Council banned our rites to guide souls home from the otherworld. My husband passed away three years ago, mother of mountains bless him, so we buried him on Innisburren and do the annual rites there. Lots of families do the same."

"People must notice every Gallnach leaving the mainland at once," I said.

"They notice, all right." Liam pushed up his sleeve to show a long scar across his forearm. "From a Sverb soldier, big yellow-bearded bastard who survived the Dúnravn massacre. He blamed our druids for what Suriel and the Corvittai did. The day after we got back from Bódhain, he came to the Knox with a knife."

"And left without some teeth." Airedain cracked his knuckles.

Nili shook her head, ribbons flying. "I wouldn't move to Caladheå. Nothing's worth living in fear."

Emílie thumped a cask. "This is. Ships sink, crops wither, livestock die, but alcohol's a solid market. The worse things get, the more people drink. Innisburren's safe from most things, but it's all farmers and fishermen. Too poor and scattered to frequent a pub."

"Most things?" I echoed. "What *isn't* it safe from?"

"Depends on the date," Liam said. "The barrier from the otherworld is weak on Bódhain. Ain't just the dead who cross over."

That's why Airedain expected Iollan to show up, I realized. It was the best time to open a rift.

"Mostly it's Folk you need to worry about," Liam went on. "They seduce you or drown you, depending how they feel. But there's also lake spirits, soulhounds, bansídhe, shapeshifters—"

"Known here as anta-saidu, wolves, wailing women, and us," Jonalin said. "I've met sailors from all around the world. They all tell stories. We can shift forms, but we're not spirits."

"Let's set something straight." Emílie's voice had an edge. "You don't question our beliefs, and we don't question yours."

Jonalin didn't flinch. "Not saying you're wrong. Just that whatever your ancestors saw in Gallun might not be here."

"Or the people who saw something else didn't live to tell." Emílie stretched, her cloak tight over her brawny arms. "Time to get some shut-eye. Feel free to kick us out of the cabin later. You'll need the sleep."

Nili and I wandered up to the bow. Fog rolled across the dark water, so thick I could only see the faint halo of light where I knew the boys were in the stern. I leaned out into the sea spray and said, "Ai. Should I tell Airedain I ended things with Fen?"

She eyed me. "You gonna sneak off during Bódhain to tap him?"

"Aeldu save me. What, you think he's Folk, going to seduce me? Nei, I just have enough secrets."

"Tell him when we're back on the mainland. Neither of you need distractions right now."

I glanced up at red sails glowing around the masthead lantern. Tiernan's sword, Hafelús, was named after the torch on the ferry to Thaerijmur. I couldn't shake my unsettled feelings.

11.

BÓDHAIN

I woke with a stiff neck and cramping legs. Next to me, Nili's head was pressed against the cabin wall. Airedain and Jonalin were scrunched on the other bunk like fiddlehead ferns, Liam on the plank floor in between. I stumbled outside into a soggy grey morning. Maeve and Orla waved, bundled in wool blankets.

At the helm, Emílie pointed ahead. "There ya go, lass. Innisburren."

Farther south than I'd ever been. The hills looked like someone sponged white paint above the ocean. Dark lines of trees planted for windblock ribboned through snowy pastures. Red-sailed cutters and cod trawlers loomed out of the mist, all heading toward Innisburren.

"How'd your people survive here so long?" I asked. "You couldn't have escaped the Elken Wars."

"Our druids put magic so deep in the island the rock sings," Emílie said. "Sverbs and Ferish both tried to uproot us. Gave up when their soldiers kept mysteriously dying. 'Course, we live here with the blessing of the Kae nation. If they wanted us gone, I reckon we'd have trouble holding the place."

Nili ducked out from the cabin, shivering. "Forget history. Airedain said something about disguises. They better be warm."

Emílie looked us up and down, in fur mantles, cloaks, and knee-high boots. "They'll fit over your clothes. Maeve, show 'em a guise. There's a good girl."

Maeve pulled a black bundle from a basket, unfolded a hooded robe with a gauzy muslin veil, and held it against Nili. The fabric gusted in the wind. "You can wear mine, Nisali, and Kateiko can wear Liam's. They'll just be a bit short."

"The Folk hide their faces when they come out of the sea," Emílie explained. "Grief lures 'em, but if they think you're Folk, too, they leave you alone, so we wear guises when we're in mourning."

I wondered if Airedain had a guise. This was the first Bódhain after Nokohin's blood met the ground, as well as Esiad's and so many other Iyo. There wasn't a spare guise that fit Jonalin's broad shoulders, but I doubted he was scared of Folk.

"What's your plan?" Emílie asked as the boys emerged yawning from the cabin. "We'll keep our ears open at the festival, but the island's twenty leagues tip to tip. Can't search the entire place in a day."

"Jona could before he got shot." Airedain thumped his cousin's shoulder. "He'll scout as long as possible. I'll see if I can get drunk people to talk. What the girls do is up to them."

I hesitated. "Would it . . . be okay to watch druids guide souls from the otherworld? Seems like the best place to look for Iollan."

Emílie nodded. "Just stay out of the tomb valley. Move slow, stay quiet, and *don't* talk to anyone else in guise. Mother of mountains willing, nothing and nobody will bother you."

We followed Innisburren's coast. Far inland were smudges of

rainforest. In early afternoon, we steered into a cove that curved out of sight. Emílie and her kids were letting us off early to avoid questions in the village.

The *Seakip* shuddered into a lopsided dock. Airedain and Jonalin hopped over the bulwark first, then Nili and I climbed off. A plank cottage missing shingles stood above the tide line, ringed by dune grass poking through the snow. Rusted wire fence surrounded a garden plot. Brass wind chimes tinkled on the porch.

"Whose house is this?" I asked.

"Ours." Emílie gazed at a boulder painted with white symbols. "Remember, for Gallnach, the new day starts at sundown, but some Folk sneak through early. So be on guard and stay out of the water."

We waved goodbye. Airedain climbed the rocky shore and shouldered open the cottage door. The front room was empty except for cabinets and a stone fireplace. White rectangles on yellowed shiplap walls showed where pictures had hung.

"Nice place," Nili said. "They left this to open a pub?"

"They don't talk about it," Airedain said, "but Emílie had twin boys after Orla. Didn't reach half a year. Pox, I think. Her brother died in the navy that autumn, her mother of fever soon after. Four deaths in as many months. Emílie's father refused to wear a guise, called it a dumb superstition. But that Bódhain, he disappeared without a sign. Hadn't been drinking and the *Seakip* was still moored. Two days later, he washed up where that rune boulder is outside. Drowned right here in good health and good weather."

"Sounds like he drowned on purpose," Nili said. "People do awful things in grief."

"Maybe. But I ain't gonna tell Emílie that. She sold the *Seakip* and built the Knox with the money. Said her family would never work on the ocean again."

People believe what gives them comfort, Tiernan had once said. Easier to blame spirits than believe someone you love abandoned you.

Airedain picked at some bread he was eating. "They'd been in Caladheå about a decade when Emílie's husband died. That's when I started coming to Bódhain. She asked me to take over Liam's drumming at the festival, but I think she wanted me to keep him away from the water."

We dressed after lunch. Liam's guise fit snug over my marsh rat mantle, the bell sleeves covering my hands. I wore my belt outside the robe, knives in easy reach, but stowed Antalei in a cabinet. The flail's sheath was too recognizable. Nili strapped her bow and quiver to her back. Brass clasps held our veils in place. I felt uneasy not being able to see properly through the muslin.

Airedain undid a cloth bundle holding his flat moor drum. He wrapped the thick blue cloth around his body like a cocoon, belted it, and let the top half fall so it hung to his knees. I'd never seen someone put on a woolwrap before. He buckled his new daggers onto his belt.

"Aren't you expected to wear a guise?" I asked. "After Nokohin . . ."

"Like Emílie said. I don't question their beliefs, they don't question mine." He squinted at his reflection in a frosty window, fixing his windswept hair with a clay pot of amber paste. "And Gallnach tip better when I wear a woolwrap."

We followed a winding track along the cove, walking in ruts left by sleighs. Mountain sheep with curling horns browsed shrubbery behind fences. Snowshoe hares, supported by thick tufts of fur on their feet, scampered over white ridges. It seemed odd to see so much game until I realized shepherds had probably killed all the predators on the island. Wolves included.

The track eventually sloped down toward the village. Stone buildings were clustered on the bank of a frozen river. Around them, radiating out like wheel spokes, were rows of crude timber shelters draped with sailcloth. Bright-cheeked kids played tag or threw snowballs. Ships crowded the harbour — tied to piers, pulled onshore, anchored in the cove, packed so tight that I could've leapt from deck to deck.

A family with squawking children passed us going the other way. The parents smiled at Airedain. Their freckled daughter ran up asking to see his moor drum. Grinning, he showed her the painted arrowhead leaves and pushed up his sleeve to show his matching tattoo. The adults' eyes slid past Nili and me as if we didn't exist. When their youngest son peeked at our veiled faces, the mother snapped in Gallnach and shooed him on.

"Question," Nili said. "How will we find each other again? Kako and I aren't even recognizable."

"Hold out your hands." I wrapped bands of water around her and Airedain's wrists. "Tug on that if you need help — *ow!*"

Nili stopped pinching the water. "Just testing."

Jonalin stepped into a pine stand. An osprey flew out and perched on a stone fence. I made a band around his scaly ankle above the talons. He took to the sky, soaring west. We weren't much of a search party — two uninjured people, a bird recovering from a bolt wound, and Nili with her bad leg.

Airedain gave us directions to the tomb valley, then headed into the village while Nili and I looped around it. People called to familiar faces, laughing and embracing. Guised figures clustered together, still and silent, warming mittened hands over fires or holding babies swaddled in black. Their robes looked like charcoal smears among the golds, wines, storm blues, and cinnamons of the Gallnach dress. Everyone else looked past them. It seemed a lonely way to mourn.

Kae moved among the crowd, tall and dark-haired, in moss-green woolwraps that matched their heron crest. The people I couldn't identify were probably mixed-blood. Two kids argued over a wooden sword in a stream of Gallnach interwoven with the Kae dialect of Aikoto.

I wondered if Tiernan was here searching for Iollan. He didn't believe in spirits enough to wear a guise, but it was a way to move unnoticed. We could brush past each other and never know.

Past a bridge over the river, an icy track did hairpin turns uphill toward the tombs. Nili and I followed a grey-haired man leading a mountain ram. I felt Airedain and Jonalin's water bands in the distance. Clouds blazed over the western ocean by the time we reached the rim of a round valley, steep and smooth as a bowl. Figures waited around an unlit pyre in the centre.

Rough-hewn rock slabs, pink in the fading light, were set into the valley walls. The west ones stood open to reveal yawning tunnels. Two druids in hooded brown robes moved around the valley perimeter. The near druid faced a slab and raised his arms. With a groan that shook the earth, the stone swung outward, leaving a furrow of exposed dirt. The druid marked a glowing rune on the slab and moved on to the next one.

Aikoto didn't have a word for stone-callers. *Edimyul* was closest, akin to edim-saidu who turned dirt into trees and back into dirt. Even then it was just a concept, an impossible thought, like drinking air.

"Why are they ignoring us?" Nili said. "We could be Folk."

"That's the point. Folk drown people, right? If you ignore them, they can't lead you to the water."

"Then why bother hiding in these?" She pulled at her veil. "My breath is frozen onto it."

I melted the frost. "Grieving people are vulnerable. Doesn't matter if it's all lies. Imagine a spirit promises to take you to

Aeldu-yan, says you can bring people *back*. You'll see your temal and sister again — your blood sister, not me. You can hold Taworen again. He'll be alive, warm, breathing. You can marry him. Have kids. The spirit says you have to go tonight, while Aeldu-yan is open. Do you follow it?"

Nili didn't answer.

"Exactly. It's easier to avoid the offer."

When each tomb was open, and the sun slipped below the hills, the shepherd led the kicking ram forward. A druid slit its throat, then laid it atop the pyre and set torch to tinder. Low drumbeats thudded through the valley. Steely pipe music rose in long wailing notes and shattered. In my mind, I saw trembling turquoise light the night Tiernan and I stood outside in the house of the dead.

My water bands strained at me. The itch of a vision rose in my skull. Snow drifted through the air, blown off the hills. The shepherd had moved. I blinked, and he snapped back to where he'd been. So in the shoirdryge, after years of that world diverging from ours, he was in the same valley doing the same rites.

I pulled off a glove and stuck my hand in the snow to shock away traces of the vision. Maybe the barrier was weak on Bódhain between parallel worlds, not the living world and a spiritual other-world. If the druids had called any souls out from the tombs, I hadn't seen them.

The music faded. The druids climbed the hillside with torches and passed us on the track. I studied their faces under their burlap hoods. A golden-haired young man and a Kae-Gallnach woman. They wore red wool pendants of the diamond-shaped druidic knot. Drummers and pipers followed, then the shepherd and horse-drawn sledges hauling enormous steel drums.

I stood ankle-deep in snow listening to their fading footsteps. Wind swept across the barren hills. It was a good spot for rift magic, damaged from years of earth-calling, but Iollan would be an idiot to try anything here. The runes probably kept away more than Folk.

"Let's go back," I said. "My toes are numb."

Our veils made it impossible to see in the dark. I took Fendul's irumoi from its case on my belt, holding the glowing mushrooms high as Nili and I edged back down the icy track and over the bridge. Crowded as the village lanes were, people parted around us. It seemed subconscious, like they happened to lean away to hear an elderly relative or grab a stray child the moment we passed. Farther in, among stone buildings laced with frozen vines, a half-dressed couple curled together in an alley. The girl's eyes flickered to my veil and away. She left her arms around the boy. I was a ghost, glimpsed but not acknowledged.

In the village square, wool-capped men tossed the shelter timbers on a bonfire that crackled higher than the shingle roofs. People approached through muddy slush, lay bread in the coals, and tipped ale into the flames. It steamed up into the sky. They had food to spare for the dead. Innisburren was untouched by the war with the Corvittai that had destroyed so many mainland farms.

A boat workshop by the river served as pub for the night, its wide plank doors propped open with boulders. Long tables with checked cloths strained under dishes of meat, fish, and bread. Square-nosed dogs sniffed for scraps. Smaller eating tables spilled through the pub doors into the square. Emílie and Maeve bustled around serving drinks. They looked natural, at ease. Home again.

Airedain and Liam sat outside the pub, moor drums propped on their thighs, beating a lively rhythm with double-ended drumsticks. They switched fluidly between striking the sheepskin and tapping the maple frames. Orla played a tin whistle. An older man held a leather bag fitted with steel pipes. Its thin tune shivered like the wind chimes at Emílie's cottage.

I tugged the water band around Airedain's wrist. He jerked up, whispered to Liam, and followed us into a shadowed alley. The music resumed.

"How's Jona?" he asked. "Still moving?"

"Yeah. He's west, but I'm not sure how far."

Airedain rubbed sweat off his forehead. "Ingdanrad sent druids. Emílie just talked to one. They swept the village and left to check any sacred sites Iollan might be using."

"Did she ask about Tiernan?"

"He's in Ingdanrad, going through everything Iollan wrote on rift magic. Tiernan's ranger friend wasn't allowed in."

Rhonos. So Tiernan was alone. He'd be safe within Ingdanrad, but he was a danger to himself these days, reckless from mourning Marijka.

"Try checking the harbour," Airedain said. "Awful lot of Gallnach people around Emílie doesn't know."

Sailcloth banners snapped in the wind along the harbour. Hollow turnip lanterns carved with runes lined the gravel shore. A few people leaned off piers and tossed herring into the sea. Fish bribed the Folk to stay in the water, Emílie had explained. A girl screeched when an otter popped up and caught a herring. Nili shook with silent laughter.

I was starting to think Jonalin was right. Anyone who walked out of the ocean was probably an Aikoto who'd been swimming in their attuned form. I might've drowned itherans, too, if they threw raw fish on my head and then pretended I wasn't there.

Nili rested her leg by the waterfront buildings while I moved along the shore. Distant drumbeats melded with the soft tide. Parents carried babies and dozing children. Folk kidnapped sleeping people, it was said. My eyelids felt heavy. I'd slept poorly after the okorebai challenge and on the *Seakip*. Tracking the water bands was far harder than it should've been. A year ago, I'd made a necklace for Nili out of wire and water droplets, and been able to keep it intact even when she was in another rainforest.

A dark shape caught my eye at the end of a pier. A guised figure faced me, unmoving.

I stared back. The ocean shimmered. The moored ships were different. I distinctly remembered a cutter with the black-and-red Gallun flag, now gone. I leaned sideways. The guised figure vanished. The cutter reappeared. I straightened up, and they reversed, as if the shoirdryge was a tunnel straight down the pier.

I sank into meditation so I wouldn't pass out like I had the other times. *Breathe. Feel. Extend.*

When I leaned over again, the figure remained. I turned in a circle. Ice floes floated down the thawed river that had been frozen a moment before. Dead grass stirred across hills that had been covered in snow. Guised people drifted along shore, but none wore Nili's bow or quiver. There was hollowness in my mind where her band had been.

The figure on the pier beckoned.

Something deep inside, a fishhook in my gut, pulled me toward it. I planted my boots in the gravel. Folk weren't real. Aeldu-yan wasn't real. But if I was wrong—

An arrow shot through the guised figure. The figure winked out.

Pain rolled through my head. The arrow vibrated in the hull of a cod trawler where it'd landed. Nili stood onshore, fingers on her bowstring. She strode toward me. *Move slow, stay quiet.* It must've taken all her willpower not to run. I met her halfway and nudged her droplet necklace so she'd be sure it was me.

"You saw it," I whispered. "That figure—"

"Yeah." She pulled me into the village. "You lose all the water bands or just mine?"

"All." I must've maintained her necklace through force of habit.

Nili dragged me through busy lanes. Airedain was at the pub clearing tables, woolwrap swishing. His smile looked stiff. Nili nabbed his arm. He dropped an armload of mugs into a tub of soapy water and ushered us behind casks stacked along the wall.

"We lost Jonalin," Nili said. "No idea where he is."

Airedain swore. "What happened?"

I slumped against the wall. "Gallnach don't see Folk. Maybe in Gallun but not here. They see *other people* in parallel worlds. And one saw me."

"You think Iollan did something? Messing around with rift magic?"

"Maybe." I rubbed my eyes through the veil. "Or the barrier's just weak tonight. I don't know."

Airedain hooked his thumbs over his belt. "We've got something. A drunk itheran keeps flashing silver coins. They're unmarked, no provincial sigil or anything, which means they're untraceable. Pirates use them sometimes. This man's trying to impress girls, so Maeve chatted him up. He just emigrated from Gallun. Says a woman offered him good money to protect a druid and 'rough up some bastard Sverbs.'"

I gasped. "Cattil. She's hiring mercenaries overseas?"

"Plenty of people wanna leave Gallun bad enough they don't care who pays their way. Cattil must've sent for them with the first lot of silver from the Rutnaast mines, but it takes months to sail there and back. These must be the first to arrive."

"We have to talk to that drunk man alone," Nili said. "Where's a safe place nearby?"

"Emílie's sister has a boathouse," Airedain said. "Upriver, village-eside. Ram's horns mounted over the door. Can't miss it."

"Find a guise and meet us there." Nili stashed her bow and quiver among the casks.

Airedain pointed at a husky man with a shaved head and thick beard. "He's the one. See ya soon."

The mercenary was telling a story to a table of Gallnach roaring with laughter. We waited while he finished another round of barley ale. When he staggered off to relieve himself, Nili glided forward, hiding all but a trace of her limp.

We followed the mercenary into an alley. Nili beckoned. He paced forward like a mountain cat on the hunt. She circled him, trailing a gloved finger across his chest, murmuring Aikoto words he had no chance of understanding. He slid his hands around her waist. She lifted her veil as I wreathed mist around her face.

The mercenary jerked back. She'd transformed her eyes into their fox form, slit-pupilled and tawny. She smiled with long canine teeth and pulled him toward the river.

The boathouse was outside the village, standing on weathered stilts frozen into the river. No one was in sight. Nili led the mercenary through the door — and a guised figure seized him by the throat.

I stuffed my bell sleeve in his mouth as he shouted. Nili wrested his sword away. Airedain, his captor, hauled him against a mooring post and bound him to it. Quickly, I took stock of the building. Open at the riverfront side, letting in a wash of moonlight.

"Ask about Iollan och Cormic," I told Airedain.

His voice came from under his veil, a short string of Gallnach. I didn't need to understand the mercenary's reply to know it was all cursing.

"Try Cattil," I said.

The man's tirade cut off.

Airedain repeated my questions. I paced the creaking deck. Nili sat on an upside-down fishing skiff, stretching out her bad leg. The murmur of the festival went on. I wouldn't torture the mercenary, but the longer this took, the more likely it was that someone would notice him missing.

I stepped off the deck onto the open river. Its surface was lumpy as cobblestone from ice floes freezing together. I melted a wide circle. Water rushed past underneath, misting in the night air. "Bring him here."

Airedain untied the mercenary and dragged him to the deck edge. The man yelled, twisting and biting. Airedain forced him onto his stomach, half off the deck, his beard grazing the water. Nili pressed his swordpoint to his back.

Ice splintered around my melted circle. I'd tipped a delicate balance, too focused on not having another vision. Floes detached and spun in the current. I thrust my mind into the surface, willing it to hold, and beckoned. The man snarled. Loud cracks sounded out as more ice broke up. Foaming gaps opened up across the river.

The mercenary thumped his foot in a yield. Airedain wrangled him back against the post. He sat limp, head down. Icicles hung from his beard.

"Start again with Iollan," I said, returning to the deck.

Airedain slowly translated. "He's never heard the name but says a druid who broke out of Ingdanrad must be Peimil. That's who Cattil hired him to protect."

Peimil, Suriel's archmage, the head of the emperor constellation. "Is Peimil here?"

"Nei. The only other Corvittai on Innisburren are this man's shipmates. They were supposed to meet some of Cattil's men to get orders, but the men didn't show. He doesn't know where anyone else is."

"What's he know about Cattil?"

"Her real name is Fíannula ó Brennen. Born in Gallun. She controls the Corvittai fleet — what's left of it." Airedain nudged the mercenary to keep talking. "She faked being Peimil's half-sister to visit him in prison and pass him messages, then she smuggled him out by ship."

Cattil, Suriel's navy captain, the constellation's right hand holding a sextant. "What's she look like?"

"He's never met her. She sent someone else to recruit in Gallun 'cause she's wanted overseas for war crimes against Sverbians. All he knows is she got branded for smuggling, so she burned her arm to hide the brand."

I winced. "Where's Tírcattil?"

"He ain't sure. Cattil abandoned it and relocated when Peimil broke out of prison."

"Who are Arril and Quinil?"

"Arril commands the other Corvittai captains. That's all he knows. No one's mentioned Quinil."

Arril must've been Suriel's air captain, the constellation's heart. The only itheran in history to gain a tel-saidu's trust and the authority to command kinaru. The birds never fully obeyed Nonil. Quinil, the constellation's feet, was still a mystery. No hint if Quinil or Arril could be Parr's son.

The mercenary looked up. He spoke faster, pleading.

"He says he's got nothing against us. His village had a truce with Folk." Airedain's throat caught. "Then Sverbians razed it. Cattil offered him revenge, but he just wanted out of Gallun. We can take his silver, weapons, whatever Folk use, if we let him keep his ship and his life."

I turned away. "You brought us here. It's your decision."

"He hasn't hurt anyone." Airedain fished through the mercenary's jerkin and took his coin purse. "I'll tell him to go south with his crew. There are other immigrant settlements there."

He spoke in Gallnach as he untied the man's bonds. The man didn't move, as if expecting a trap. Nili kicked him. He bolted.

Airedain held up the coin purse. "What should I do with this?"

I shrugged. "Split it with Jonalin. It was mined from Iyo land, after all."

Nili dropped the mercenary's sword. "Ugh. I feel dirty. He reeked of alcohol, and he saw part of my attuned form, and I think he wet himself—"

"I can toss you in the river," I said.

She gave me a two-hand salute, bell sleeves and all.

12.

PROMISES

Jonalin returned safely along with Ingdanrad's druids, who thanked us for letting the mercenaries go. Gallnach were their kin, just caught on different sides of a war. We stayed a day to catch up on sleep, then loaded the *Seakip* with crates of frosty mutton and lamb, tubs of root vegetables, cheese wheels, and barley sacks wrapped in waterproof canvas tarps. Emílie couldn't afford to run the Knox Arms on Caladheå's food prices.

"What's with burning those shelters in the bonfire?" Nili asked as we sailed back.

"It represents the burning of our homes," Emílie said. "Six centuries ago, a Sverbian warrior queen named Rånyl Sigrunnehl invaded Gallun and razed villages that wouldn't hand over their druid. The sailcloth banners at the harbour represent people who fled by sea. Still happening today."

I imagined the fury the Gallnach must've felt. Fleeing all the way here, building a new home, only for their conquerors to follow. No one had managed to drive us out of our homeland, but we paid the price for staying.

We returned to Caladheå well into the night and unloaded cargo onto a horse-drawn sledge. "Stay awhile," Airedain told me as we walked behind it. "My tema likes having people at her flat. Says it's too quiet otherwise."

"Things are a mess in Toel," I said. "It's bad timing."

"Always is, ain't it?"

I stopped. Wet snowflakes fell around us. It'd been bad timing when he was with Viviwen in summer, when I was with Fendul in autumn. It always would be unless we were honest. "I have something to ask you."

Airedain faced me, hands in his breeches pockets. It felt like I could seize a clump of soft heavy silence.

"The Okorebai-Rin and I aren't engaged anymore. So I wondered if you're . . . seeing anyone."

A grin split his face — pure as a glacial lake, brilliant as moonlight breaking on its surface. "Only the beautiful girl in front of me."

My lips twitched up. "Wait. I'm not promising anything. I just thought you should know."

"Ai, no rush." He took my hands. "Being around you is enough for now."

I gazed at his leather gloves, fitted with Segowa's careful stitches. "I've been thinking . . . I don't truly *know* you. Your family, your friends, your life."

"Sure. Let's start there."

I smiled. "Okay. But first . . . say my name."

"Rin-girl?"

I shoved him.

Airedain laughed and caught me up in his arms. "Kateiko," he murmured, sending a flutter through my chest.

His breath frosted on the cropped hair over my forehead. I was about to protest that this wasn't waiting, but he just kissed my nose, then led me hand in hand down the sledge tracks, still grinning.

In Toel Ginu, some Rin had tried to switch plank houses to live with who they voted for. Fendul forbade it, not wanting to divide us further, but he couldn't force people to get along. The tattooist's younger sister, who'd been flirting with Yironem all autumn, now ignored him like he was in guise. Fendul and Hiyua spent hours in conversation working out how to manage the jouyen. I didn't get involved.

Dunehein had left to trap in Anwen Bel where game was more plentiful, so I took his gate watch. Nothing ever seemed as slow as those days on duty, wearing a bark cape and wide-brimmed hat to keep off the sleet. Checking my trapline was my only break. Orelein had made me snowshoes by bending boiled alder into droplet shapes and lacing them with stiff rawhide. My legs ached from the heavy shoes and odd gait, but for all my efforts, there was little in my snares.

When Viviwen was well enough to return to Caladheå, I seized my chance to see Iannah and Airedain. The canoe carver and I paddled Viviwen back. Her bonnet covered the bare spot where Barolein had stitched her scalp. Airedain had arranged for one of his Sverbian friends to accompany her home and pretend to be from the island where she was meant to be teaching. As we said goodbye, Viviwen hugged me, avoiding my braid.

"I hope your brother will be okay," she said. "I'm sorry for causing so much trouble."

Iannah was at Natzo's staring out the foggy window. I gave Natzo four pann and pointed at a steaming vat of *spianèɀi te choionne*. A bowl of wheat noodles cost only two pann a year ago. While he ladled my soup out, I looked over hundreds of spoons hung on the brick walls and chose a brass one with a handle shaped like a feather.

I edged onto a stool across from Iannah, bumping a man in a patched coat. "What's wrong?"

Iannah gripped her steel spoon like she was wringing it dry. Her green broth was untouched. "I'll tell you later."

After lunch, we walked to our favourite park in Bronnoi Ridge, where the shovelled paths were sprinkled with gravel for grip. We brushed off a bench and sat on the cold stone. Snow laid smooth as cotton across a frozen pond.

"Nonil's men knew this land," Iannah said as I told her what I'd learned in Innisburren. "Most had lived here for years. Relying on new immigrants means Cattil's desperate, and she can't hire more with their income cut off. Military's got the Rutnaast mines locked down." She rested her elbows on the bench back. "Seems odd that mercenary knew nothing about Quinil if that's who does the legwork."

"Maybe there isn't a Quinil."

"Or there *was*. Before these new recruits arrived. What if it was Parr?"

I stared at her.

"Think about it. His son could be Arril, the commander, who sent him to recruit Tiernan. Someone gave Parr a kinaru to ride—"

"You can't *give* anyone a kinaru. They're sacred birds, not sheep. Besides, Parr pushed the Council to declare war on Suriel."

"So people wouldn't suspect him. The military knew someone was leaking info. Parr was ex-military. The leak stopped after he died."

Politics is a game no one wins, Tiernan had said. Still, Parr had played it better than most. "Well, it doesn't matter now. Iollan's who we need to find."

Iannah shrugged. "I'll ask around the barracks if anyone's heard the name Peimil. When do you leave Caladheå?"

"Tomorrow." I gazed at the pond as I told her about Akiga's challenge, the end of my engagement, and figuring things out with Airedain. "You going to lecture me about commitment again?"

"You going back to the Rin?"

"Of course."

"Then I won't lecture." She folded a gloved hand over mine.

I rested my head on her shoulder. The park felt blank — somewhere I had to be nothing, do nothing, feel nothing. A patch of wilderness surrounded by brick walls that kept everything out.

"About before. At Natzo's." Iannah tapped a copper elk pin on her collar. "I got this last month for disarming a man who attacked a councillor. I have seniority in my guard unit. Almost nine years' service, clean record, top of my academy year. My captain just retired and gave his position to someone else."

I sat up. "Why?"

"He says soldiers won't listen to a woman."

"That's ridiculous. Cattil runs the Corvittai navy. Tokoda commands every Iyo warrior. A female okorebai led the Rin in the Second Elken War."

"Your people also let female soldiers marry."

I rolled my eyes. "Force us to, more like. Tell you what. You guard my stockade, I'll take Council Hall. How hard can it be?"

She flipped me off the bench into the snow.

✳

At sundown, I went by Segowa's embroidery stall. She said Airedain would be at the fish market. Leaving the shelter of downtown, I braced myself against a cold wind bearing the familiar fishy smell. People huddled under long open-air shelters that lined the shore. Snow fell, bright against the dark clouds.

The stone counters were sparse. Few fishermen risked winter seas, especially a winter this wet. Two purplish crabs scuttled around a steel tub. Men and women in fur coats haggled for halibut and shellfish. A woman with a thick golden braid filleted a lingcod as big as she was, its turquoise flesh unfolding around her knife. She smiled at me and held out a vibrant slab.

"Nei, thanks, I was just looking at the colour—"

"She's deaf." The man beside her tapped his ear. He had an anchor tattoo on the inside of his wrist. "If you speak slow, she can read your lips."

"Oh!" I returned her smile. "The colour is pretty. Like glacial lakes." As I turned to point toward the mountains, I saw a grimy boy with his hand in a bucket of sardines.

"Hey!" The tattooed man cuffed him. Silvery sardines spilled across the flagstone. "Rotten thief. Get going or I'll call the Elkhounds—"

"Wait." In an instant, I took in the boy's torn clothes and gaunt face. I dropped an iron tenpann on the woman's counter and tossed a greenling at the boy. He caught the fish and ran.

The woman pressed a tin coin into my palm. One side had the same crown as a sovereign, but the other had a leafless tree instead of two elk.

"Is this from Sverba?" I asked.

Her head bobbed. I tried to hand it back — it felt wrong to take change for something I hadn't haggled on — but she refused to take it.

At the end of the market, Jonalin stood filleting a dogfish. Normally, he kept offcuts for bait, but today he set them out for sale. Maggots wriggled in the bait bucket instead. Airedain grinned, signalled he'd be a moment, and went on wrapping surfperch in butcher paper for a customer.

"Aren't you back working as a dockhand yet?" I asked Jonalin.

"Took too long to heal. Some itheran got my job." He rolled his shoulder. "Better money in fishing these days anyway. Prices keep going up."

"I didn't think you needed the money after Innisburren."

"People died for that silver. Aire and I don't wanna use it."

Their fish were barely frosty by the time they sold through. Jonalin wiped the counter and headed to their canoe, but I said to Airedain, "Let's go for a walk."

Even in the cold and dark, people fished off piers. We wandered through the docklands toward the Stengar river mouth. Lights glowed from a waterfront hotel, four storeys high with ornate gables and wrought-iron balustrades. A timber fence surrounded its grounds. Refugee shacks pressed tight to the outside of the fence.

I showed Airedain the tree coin. "A Sverbian fishmonger just gave this to me. I've never seen one."

He held it up to a street lamp. "Can't get away from this crown. As if we'd forget Sverba calls Eremur their territory. They could sweep in here and erase the Council, just like they wiped out the druid assembly in Gallun."

"Tiernan and Marijka never mentioned what happened to the Gallnach. They must've known."

"It's the same shit over and over. Itherans bring their wars here and all claim they're right." He passed the coin back. "Can't feed the ones we've got, but they keep coming. They're killing the salmon run. Not enough left to respawn."

I laughed bitterly. "We can't respawn, either. The Rin had thirteen thousand people once. Now we have sixty-five."

"Itherans got my ancestors, too. The Stengar was our fishing grounds once. Our smokehouse was right where that hotel is. The brown pigeons destroyed our salmon weirs so they could send barges upriver."

"Really? I thought your family always fished Yeva Iren."

"Didn't seem worth mentioning. Not like we can go back."

"Nei," I said, thinking of Fendul. *Only forward.*

One evening after I'd returned to Toel Ginu, I opened the gate for Orelein hauling firewood and heard a coyote yowling behind him. I dashed outside. The coyote bounded over a snowbank and shook melted snow all over me. I laughed and shoved Airedain away with my boot. "Piss off!"

He shifted back, panting. "You asked to know my family better. Best place for that is our plank house."

It was tempting to kiss him, but I didn't want to encourage anything yet. We traded news until the end of my shift. Airedain had set aside his distrust of Antlers and met Iannah at Natzo's. She'd checked Eremur's naval records. A Gallnach woman had been branded for smuggling stolen weapons six years ago, possibly Cattil under an alias, but there were no other details.

After Aliko took over my post — she had remarkable aim with a javelin for someone who kept missing her mark with Fendul — I invited Nili along to Airedain's plank house. Seeing Yironem's dejected look at being left behind, we begged Hiyua to let him out of the stockade for a night, reasoning it was the safest way to rebuild trust with the Iyo. With a look only mothers can give, Hiyua said we were responsible for him.

"You know, I wasn't sure about you," Airedain's sister, Lituwa, told me later. "But even I can't get my brother to visit. Maybe you can make him stay in Toel."

"Ai, we're not—" I stammered.

"Please! He won't stop smiling. Anyway, better you than Ilani or that itheran schoolteacher."

I choked on my tea. "*What?*"

"Viviwen Hannehl? Aire must've told you—"

"Not her!"

"Oh. *Oh.*" Lituwa backed away. "I'm going to check on my son."

I breathed deep. I was in another jouyen's plank house where everything I did reflected on the Rin. Isu's scolding voice crackled in the hearth. I whispered in Nili's ear, put on my cloak, borrowed a lantern from Airedain's grandmother, and said to Airedain, "Outside. Now."

Cold hit like a wave when I opened the door. The lantern swung in my hand, glowing from holes punched in the tin cover. I strode down shovelled paths toward the forest.

Airedain jogged after me. "Rin-girl, what in Aeldu-yan—"

I spun and pushed him against a tree. Snow tumbled onto our heads. "You were with *Ilani?* The girl who attacked me, Viviwen, *and* my brother?"

"Wh— everyone knows that. You saw me dancing with her on the spring equinox."

"That was *her?* It was my first time in Toel! I'd never met her!"

"Fuck." He thumped his head against the tree. "Fuck! Listen, it wasn't serious. We slept together once, last year."

"Your hands were all over her *this* year!"

He winced. "I was drunk. And lonely. But we didn't hook up again, I swear. Besides, back then she wouldn't have attacked a Rin. She's messed up over Esiad dying. I felt sick when I heard what she did to your little bro. Hated myself for ever touching her. Nuthalha lands aren't far enough away."

I knew that exact feeling with Parr. The land of the dead wasn't far enough. I set the lantern on a stump and lifted my face to the drifting whiteness. "You don't have the best record with this kind of thing."

His face crinkled. "Don't you trust me?"

"Not enough."

"Wow. Okay. I'm gonna pretend that didn't hurt as much as it did."

"You're friends with itherans, lovers with them, but you fight them an awful lot, too. It's not always self-defense. What would happen if the Rin and Iyo fight? We have before, remember? The Dona woman who killed my mother had Iyo ancestors. Now you're training to be a warrior, too."

"Shit." He exhaled a white cloud. "*You're* scared of *me*? Everyone in our confederacy is freaked out by Rin warriors."

"It's different when I don't want to fight back." I touched the sword scar on my neck. "Tiernan promised he'd never harm me. Then he got angry."

"I couldn't live with myself if I hurt you."

I looked up into his brown eyes. "Have you ever hurt an Aikoto?"

Airedain's mouth twisted. "Once. This wasn't how I wanted to tell you, but . . . my temal left when I was a kid. Ditched us to marry some Kowichelk Confederacy woman. That's why my tema moved us to Caladheå, to start over. Anyway, one of my cousins talked shit about it, blamed my tema for being a bad wife. So I broke his nose."

"Oh," I breathed.

"My tema showed me the back of her tongue for that. I'll never hurt an Aikoto again." He set his hands on my waist. "I've fucked up, Kateiko. A lot. But I don't wanna be that anymore, and I ain't Tiernan. So I'll wait until you trust me, as long as it takes, this winter and the next and the next. Just give me a chance."

13.

LOCKDOWN

Airedain promised to visit Toel Ginu again in a week, but the day before he was meant to arrive, Fendul came by the gate and asked me to go to Caladheå for him. He wanted Falwen, Officer of the Viirelei, to find a schoolteacher to replace Viviwen.

"Your trip to Innisburren gave me the idea," he said. "Apparently lots of Kae attend itheran schools. The Rin agree as long as we hire a full-blood Kae."

I hadn't known he'd discussed it with other Rin. "It'll take a while," I said. "And isn't this Hiyua's job as okoreni?"

Fendul pinched his temples. "Kako . . . Nili won't talk about Airedain. That only means one thing."

I stepped back, stunned. "You're getting rid of me?"

"I won't force you. Just give me time before I have to see you with him."

It was risky to canoe the ocean alone, and my snowshoes were too slow for such a long trip. I left as a wolf, running on ice-hardened drifts. Once I hit farmland, I realized my mistake. A delicate snow crust balanced atop winter rye. I sank and floundered as if the stalks were seaweed twisted around my legs. I settled for walking on the road as a human and pushing into waist-high drifts when sleighs approached. What took four hours by sea took nine on land.

In Caladheå, horse teams packed the snow by dragging huge weighted rollers down the streets. Hired boys shovelled alleys. When I asked a blue-coated Antler at the Colonnium gates for an appointment form, he slid a paper through the bars and said to return it tomorrow.

I headed to the Knox Arms next and waited for Airedain in the humid kitchen. Emílie gave me a bowl of vinegar-soaked cod and squash in exchange for washing dishes. When the pub faded to a hum, Airedain came through the half doors and collapsed on a stool. I pushed aside tins of salt and sugar to spread my form on a counter. He read it aloud for me, stumbling on the longer words. I filled out the form with a borrowed quill, leaving black smudges, asking Airedain how to spell things.

In the morning, I returned my form to the Colonnium and waited. Snow gathered on rearing stone elk mounted on the gate pillars. Inside the grounds, two councillors in black gowns passed the fountain where Parr and I used to talk.

Finally, an Antler crossed the courtyard and spoke through the gates. "You have an appointment at two o'clock, five days from now."

"*Five?* Does Falwen know I represent an okorebai?"

"Was it on your form?"

I couldn't press the issue without explaining why I, registered as Iyo, was here for the Rin-jouyen. There was a faster way to get inside. I hurried to Natzo's to catch Iannah. But after I slid into a seat across from her, she smiled. It looked unnatural, like she'd forgotten how. A wooden spoon lay by her green broth.

"Airedain came by last week asking about you," she said. "I might've implied you're fed up waiting for him to propose."

I was sure of two things — that they hadn't discussed that and that Iannah wouldn't smile if they did. I played along while scanning faces. A young man in a blue wool coat read a newspaper while eating with Iannah's notched steel spoon. The red band under the elk sigil on his sleeve marked him as an Antler captain. Cropped dark hair, square face, clearly Ferish.

"Marcot Cièntus," Iannah said after we left. "My new captain. From the academy year below me. He took my spoon."

"Natzo would let you keep it if you like it that much—"

"It means Cièntus is watching me. And wants me to know." She glanced back down the street. "He saw me leave with Airedain last week. Lectured me later on 'associating with civilians.' He can suspend me from duty if he thinks I'm seeing someone. I wanted to make damned sure he knows Airedain's courting you. Like I'd ever have a secret romance with a—"

"If you say 'viirelei,' we're not friends anymore."

"—with a man." Iannah cut through an alley and climbed a snowbank. "Why are you in Caladheâ?"

"To see Falwen. Can you get me in?"

"Falwen's not here. Sailed north to — which nation lives on the coast? Beru? His aide's scheduling people for when he's expected back."

Odd. Something must've come up suddenly if neither Fendul nor Tokoda knew he'd left.

Iannah told me the latest on the food shortages. Meat and fish prices had shot up. The Council intervened by forcing prices lower, yet they were still high enough that farmers and fishermen didn't seek better money outside Eremur. They set a famine tax, bought rye and flax in bulk, and gave a grain allotment to everyone in poverty. All fish were purchased by the port authority to be rationed out.

"I admit, I'm impressed how the Council's handling this," I said.

"Don't be. It's political. Nothing scares my people more than the famine that drove them out of Ferland."

"Does it matter why councillors act, as long as they do?"

Iannah looked at me. "Think about Parr and ask yourself that."

The day of my appointment, an Antler told me it was delayed. Worried, I went to the fish market to ask Jonalin if he'd heard anything from other sailors about Falwen's ship. Grey-armoured Elkhounds were everywhere. Before giving up and returning to Toel Ginu, I decided to ask Iannah on her next day off. Again, Cièntus was at Natzo's reading a newspaper.

"He has other guards watching me," Iannah said outside. "On duty, in the mess hall, during combat practice. He knows I looked Cattil up in the naval records. Maybe he thinks I'm resentful enough about losing the captaincy to defect."

I looked up from thawing my gloves. "So if he wasn't watching you for a secret romance, why lecture you about Airedain? Not a single Iyo has joined Suriel."

"Don't know. He might've discovered Airedain's training as

a warrior. I can't find out, though. Can't even look into Falwen without drawing attention."

I'd been gone eight days. Fendul would wonder what kept me. I asked Airedain and Jonalin to drop me off at Toel Ginu while they fished, but in the dim hour before sunrise, Elkhounds stopped us at the Iyo docks. Their armour, embroidered with rearing red elk, had become too familiar. "No viirelei leave until further notice," one said.

Jonalin raised his hands in the start of a protest. Airedain, making good on his promise to avoid pointless fights, pulled Jonalin away. Which left me stuck in Caladheå. Fendul would realize something was wrong when Iyo stopped returning to Toel Ginu, but I wasn't sure he could get me out.

I woke the next day to banging. I sat up on the floor rubbing my eyes. Stripes of light fell through the shutters. Jonalin tumbled out of bed, brown hair sticking up like ryegrass, and flung the door open.

Segowa pushed inside. "Up. Hurry. You too, Kateiko." She tossed Airedain's jerkin at him.

Airedain yawned. "Tema, what's going on——"

"Elkhounds are rounding up Aikoto. Bring your weapons, but keep them hidden."

We clattered downstairs. Snowbanks blocked each end of the street, guarded by Elkhounds whose spears winked in the sunlight. They directed us into the gathering place. Two hundred Iyo stood among the brick pillars, soothing sleepy children. Guards pushed another hundred in along with a few Kae and Yula.

A captain spoke to a grey-braided woman, a cousin of Tokoda and Wotelem. She led him outside to the food storage sheds. Guards moved through the crowd questioning everyone. Nearly every question was about fish. Who'd caught salmon or whitefish, how much, where, when, how it was preserved. If it was sold, for what price, and who bought it.

An Elkhound with a thick Ferish accent took our identification cards. "Kateiko Sohikoehl of the Iyo nation." His pronunciation sounded like he was chewing rocks. "You live in Caladheå?"

"Nei. Toel Ginu. I'm just here to see the Officer of the Viirelei."

"Why?"

"To hire a schoolteacher for the Rin-jouyen. It says so on my Colonnium form."

He left it at that and looked again at his page of notes. "Airedain Kiyorem. You're employed at your mother's embroidery shop?"

"Yes." Airedain jammed his hands in his pockets. Officially, he didn't work at the Knox Arms anymore.

"We have records of you leaving Caladheå's docks up to four days a week. Quite the risk considering the weather."

He shrugged. "Fishing's what we do."

"Anyone offered to pay you extra for fish?"

"Nei."

"Care to explain why you've sold nothing to the port authority for rationing?"

"My cousin here sells our catch, and we split the money. No point in both waiting in line."

"Somewhere more important to be? You don't even trade off days?"

Jonalin elbowed Airedain. "My cousin's a jerk. Makes me wait in line so he can hang out with girls." He pointed at me. "*This* girl when she's in town. He doesn't want her to know about the others."

The Elkhound smirked. "Good luck, boy." He passed our identification back. "We'll be watching."

*

The day was a long smudge of waiting. Four Iyo were taken away for more questioning. Wotelem and Hiyua arrived at night, summoned from Toel Ginu, and got the Elkhounds to let us out of the gathering place. Hiyua kissed my hair and said Fendul felt awful for sending me away, that no one knew Falwen wasn't here. Drained, I went to sleep on Airedain's floor.

Voices drifted into my dreams, rising from whispers into sharp jabs. Then the door shut, and there was just the thump of boots and creak of floorboards near my head. I rubbed my eyes. Shadows muddled everything. The shutters were open, showing a strip of pale pink sky. Ice crusted the windowsill. Airedain paced the room, a few steps each way.

"Where's Jonalin?" I asked, yawning.

"Ai — you're awake." Airedain stopped. "Jona went to see if we can leave the city yet. Bad time to be in Caladheå."

"Why?"

"Huge fucking scandal." He tossed a soggy newspaper at me. "Two Ferish councillors got caught buying lamb on the black market. Elkhounds raided their homes and found stockpiled salmon. That's why they locked us down."

I jerked upright, my grizzly pelt blanket sliding off. "Our salmon?"

"Can't be. It's frozen, not smoked. Northern jouyen's way."

"Beru and Haka—" My sleepy mind dragged. "Did raiders hit that far north?"

"Dunno. Bet Falwen went to find out." Airedain twirled his daggers, brimming with restlessness. "I have a favour to ask. But you can say no."

"What is it?"

"Teach me to fight like a Rin. The newspaper's calling for a protest, and we saw how fast those got violent last year. If we're stuck here, I gotta be ready to defend my people."

I wasn't thrilled about fighting him, even for practice, but he was right. We set up sparring mats in the gathering place. His technique needed work, but he was quick, strong, and his height gave him a long reach. Every so often he managed to flip me onto the floor. Once he pulled me back up and right against him. We stood panting, my hand on his damp chest, until I drew back with a hot flush.

Jonalin returned with more news. The four Iyo taken for questioning had been released, but we couldn't leave Caladheå. Wotelem and Hiyua had gone to deal with the Council. Itherans protested at the Colonnium, demanding the resignation of the councillors involved in the scandal. All we could do was wait. Airedain and I took shifts guarding our street along with Iyo warriors.

With every day, I grew more restless. We were in a tinderbox ready to ignite. Word came in that the councillors refused to resign because it'd force an election. Hiyua mentioned seeing Iannah on duty at the protests, so, desperate to learn more, I decided to track her down.

She wasn't at the front gates as Hiyua had said. Another Antler said she'd gone around the north wall. Airedain and I found her and four others at a timber gate crossed with iron bars.

"Did Cièntus send you here?" I asked.

"I requested to move." Iannah's expression was brittle. "Someone read my mail. When I reported it, Cièntus said I should have nothing to hide."

I glanced at the gate. "Why are you outside the wall? There are no protesters here."

"Watch." Iannah pointed downhill. "Food for five hundred soldiers, politicians, and clerks comes through this gate."

A workhorse came into sight, straining to pull a heavy sledge. A few people who had drifted away from the protest tossed snowballs at the Elkhounds guarding the load. One struck the horse's flank. The animal shied, tipping the sledge. Grain sacks slid off into the snow.

"Hold," Iannah called to her comrades.

"Shouldn't we help?" asked a boy with a moustache thin as berry fuzz.

"Cièntus said hold the gate."

The Elkhounds held off protesters while the driver reloaded the sledge. They were nearly up the hill when another snowball hit the horse, which tossed its head and backed up. The sledge went sideways and ran into deep unpacked snow. The white wall collapsed, burying half the sledge. People ran at it, dodging the Elkhounds.

Iannah swore in Ferish. "Go," she told Airedain and me, then beckoned to the other Antlers.

We turned back the way we came — only to see Cièntus round the corner of the outer wall. The footpath led right to us. "In here," I said, noticing an abandoned hay wagon by the path. I stood on a wheel spoke and vaulted inside. Airedain jumped in behind me.

The wagon was full of snow. We lay in a bed of it, staring up at wispy clouds. A horn shrilled. Cièntus crunched past. Airedain drew one of his daggers but stayed with me.

Voices snapped like thin ice. Wood cracked, the horse shrieked, a man groaned. I dug snow away from a sideboard until I could peer between the slats. Grain speckled the snow around the broken sledge. The Elkhounds and four Antlers held people at spearpoint. The sledge driver was on the ground. A Ferish man in a patched coat dove at him, knife in hand.

Iannah wrested the blade away. She kicked the man's stomach, sending him sprawling, and pressed her spearpoint to his chest.

"Take them inside," Cièntus said from out of sight. "Except that one."

Every guard except Iannah forced their captives toward the Colonnium, passing a few paces away from us. The sledge driver followed with the snorting horse, leaving the torn grain sacks for lost. The gate scraped open and thudded shut.

"Pelennus," Cièntus said. "That spear better be sharp."

Iannah didn't move. "Everyone heard the alarm. Protesters will swarm this gate in a few minutes. If they find a corpse, we'll have a riot."

"Those protesters are unarmed."

"Then it'll be a slaughter."

The man in the patched coat squirmed under Iannah's spear. Airedain's breathing was ragged next to me.

"Pelennus. You already defied orders by leaving the gate. Kill him or I will."

Iannah's expression cracked. "You *want* a riot. That's why you volunteered our unit for the protest? To get your moment of glory as a captain?"

Cièntus stepped into view. His square face was blank, spear straight at his side. "Question me again, and you're suspended."

Iannah looked down at her captive. He'd die either way. Faint voices sounded from the protest.

"The moment she does it, we run," I whispered.

"You're gonna let her murder a man?" Airedain hissed.

"*He* was about to murder someone. And being a warrior isn't all about fighting battles. It's about surviving until the battles you can win."

He scowled, but sheathed his dagger.

Then Iannah said, "Kill this man, and I'll tell our commander the truth, Cièntus. You covered up the scandal. You tried to stop me talking to Airedain Kiyorem *before* he was questioned about illegally selling salmon. Colonnium guards shouldn't know details of that investigation. Was it you who read my letters? Worried I found a way into the black market? That *I* reported the councillors?"

Cièntus paced around her. "Our former captain considered you as his replacement. I talked him out of it. Not because you're a woman — that was his reasoning — but because you ask too many questions." He tilted his spear at Iannah. "Ruin my career and I'll ruin yours."

"You can't." She dropped her spear.

Cièntus put his boot on the man's throat before he could escape. "Of course I can—"

"No." Iannah unbuttoned her coat and tossed it on the snow, copper elk pin and all. "You can't."

14.

CLEARS

We reached the streets of Bronnoi Ridge before Iannah stopped —
abrupt, like hitting a wall. She went through a dozen expressions
with her brows alone, the realization her life as she'd known it was
gone. No job, no home, no future.

She punched a fence. The whitewashed board cracked down the
middle. She cursed, shaking out her fingers. Splinters stuck from
her leather glove.

"Ia." I grabbed her wrist. Her teeth chattered as I hugged her.
All she'd been wearing under her thick coat was a white sleeveless shirt.

Airedain draped his cloak over her shoulders. He led us downtown through crowds that no longer parted for Iannah. Without the
elk sigil, no one knew she was a soldier.

Segowa's shop was closed. Airedain unlocked the folding
door and rammed his shoulder into it, shattering a seal of ice. He

went into the back and returned carrying a hooded deerskin cloak trimmed with brown fur. "The woman who ordered this never paid. Keep it if you want." He traded Iannah for his cloak, then kissed my cheek, so deliberate she couldn't miss it. "I'm gonna go report to the Iyo. See ya, Rin-girl."

"Does he have to do that?" she asked after he left.

"He's being nice. Take what you can get." I filled mugs with steaming water and pulled out crates to sit on.

Iannah tugged at the cloak, trying to cover her shirt. "Nine years of that coat. I expected to die wearing it."

"You've had it longer than I've had my tattoos." I tilted my head. "What else do you need? Food, money, somewhere to sleep?"

"A weapon. At least until I get my sword from the barracks."

I held out my hunting knife. Kohekai, the blood bringer.

Iannah shook her head. "I can't take your father's knife."

"I've got Nurivel and Antalei. My temal would rather know my friends are safe."

She tucked the bone blade into her belt. "We were only allowed spears on duty, ever since a rioter took a guard's dagger and killed a Colonnium clerk. I hate spears. Flimsy things. Should've stuck mine up Cièntus's behind. Not that there's room with his head there."

I choked on my water. She didn't notice.

"My wages are in the bank," she said. "That'll cover an inn until my military discharge is complete. Dishonourable, probably."

Without Iannah in the Colonnium, we couldn't use her military resources to track the Corvittai. Hollowness pulled at my ribs like waves eroding a cliff. "What happens after you're discharged? Will you go home to Laca vi Miero?"

"Only if I have to. Can't decide which is worse, living with my parents or my siblings."

We held hands as we walked the snowy streets. The grey sky

felt thick and low, the buildings too close. We were being crushed by this city.

The bank was an old sandstone structure on the edge of Bronnoi Ridge. While she went in, I found a bakery, bought crusty wheat buns sprinkled with seeds, then waited on the bank's icy steps. The Colonnium's spires cut the sky in the east. Cièntus must not have caused a riot, or we'd know from here. Still, I was glad when Iannah came outside, pocket clinking with coins.

She stretched out her legs as we ate on the steps. "I should replace my breeches. Time for a different colour."

"Don't you have any others?"

"Just my summer uniform. Moved to Caladheå at fourteen, remember. Outgrew everything I brought."

We went to a tailor next. A girl wearing a sprigged dress gaped at us and called out in Ferish. A man emerged from a back room and spoke with Iannah briefly. She gestured at her breeches. He shook his head.

"*Porqués?*" she demanded.

Yesterday, he might've shrunk back. Instead he smiled like it hurt, picked up a book from the counter, and flipped through pages showing corseted women in gold-buttoned dresses. Iannah's face flushed. Her hand went to Kohekai, then she strode out.

I ran after her. "What happened?"

"He only has patterns for men's breeches." Her nostrils flared. "What am I now, Koehl? Not a soldier, not a proper woman. My sisters have children, houses, lace curtains. My brothers are black-smiths. Twenty-three years old and I'm nothing—"

"*Ia.*" I held her shoulders. "Look at me. *Look*. You think I'm nothing? I'm not a warrior if I take off my weapons? I'm not a woman because I wear leggings and can't sew as well as Nili?"

Iannah took a deep breath.

"I'd sooner have you at my back than anyone else in Caladheå." I pulled her south toward Ashtown. "Come on. I'll get you breeches."

Airedain answered the door of Segowa's flat. He leaned against the doorframe, thread and bone needle in hand. They were working here until Segowa reopened her shop. "Couldn't stay away, Rin-girl?"

I elbowed him. "I need your tema, not you."

"Hang on." He shut the door, leaving us in the building's cramped entry.

Segowa's muffled voice was followed by rustling. Iannah's eyes roved over the ashy, leaky stairway to the second-level flats. Airedain reopened the door and sat at the workbench, one boot resting on his stool's cross-brace. Segowa rose from her embroidery to greet us.

Her flat was like Airedain's, with furs hung on the brick walls and stone makiri over the stove, but her mattress was on the ground instead of a bedstead. The fishy aroma of smelt oil lingered. It took me a moment to realize what had changed. They'd put the woven bark mats away, leaving the floorboards exposed. Iannah could enter but not stay.

I explained what we needed. Iannah took off her cloak and boots so Segowa could examine her breeches. The fawn-coloured wool fit snug over her muscular legs, laced up her calves.

"I should be able to make something similar," Segowa said. "You'll be easier to measure if you undress."

Iannah looked pointedly at Airedain, who went on basting a glove. He wouldn't leave her with his mother, even with me in the room.

I sighed. "Just measure over her clothes."

After they finished, Segowa showed us swatches of dyed wool. Iannah picked moss green for breeches and cream for a new shirt. She paid for the deerskin cloak at the same time. Segowa looked happier as we left. Maybe one day, all the parts of my life would fit together as smooth as her careful seams.

I saw Iannah to an inn, then went to the gathering place to wait for Hiyua's return from the Colonnium. She'd been sleeping in a flat set aside for visiting Aikoto leaders, but preferred eating with the Iyo. When I eventually got to Airedain's flat, Jonalin was out, his sleep habits unsettled from years of working dockhand shifts.

We started with tea and moved on to the whisky I'd given Airedain on the autumn equinox. It smelled sweet and warm like burnt wood. Ingdanrad's distillery aged it in maple barrels from over the mountains. I sat by the stove in sock feet as I rubbed deer tallow into my boots, making the leather supple and waterproof, then sealed the cracks with resin.

Airedain leaned his chair back on two legs. "We coulda left this morning, soon as those protesters went for the sledge. Were you testing me? Seeing if I'd join the fight?"

"You passed." I capped the resin jar and finished my whisky. Cloudiness had settled in my head. "I should switch to something else. I didn't know anyone made liquor stronger than brånnvin."

He got up, letting his chair thump down. "Wasn't sure you'd ever drink with me again."

"Yeah, well. Nothing to do tomorrow. Iannah's going to the Colonnium to get discharged, and I'm not going near there again."

He clanked around his liquor shelf. "Ai, Rin-girl. Ever played clears? One person asks a question, the other gives a clear answer or takes a clear drink. Liam and I play with straight vodka, but I've got fennel brånnvin, the way you like it."

I chewed my lip. "I can ask anything?"

"Anything." He grabbed a bottle made of kelp-green glass, kicked off his boots, and draped across his bed. "You wanna know me better, right?"

"Fine. Have you ever been arrested?"

Airedain winced. "Straight for the throat. Twice. First for breaking an itheran's jaw at school — self-defense, I promise. Spent a week in prison. Second time was for 'drunkenness and public indecency.' Fucking prude pigeons. I don't see how anything me and a girl do together is a crime if our clothes are still on."

I covered my mouth, giggling. "I expected worse."

"Sorry to disappoint ya." He drummed his fingers on the bottle. "My turn. What do you have nightmares about?"

"Bears."

"*Bears?* Your cousin attunes to a grizzly."

"Have you seen Dunehein mad? I've killed three people with a throwing dagger. If an angry grizzly's in range, I'm already dead."

"There's something else. A man. You talk in your sleep."

Parr. I still heard his voice every night. Saw him bleeding, felt his weight on my body until I couldn't breathe. I grabbed the bottle, took a swig, and flumped next to Airedain, our elbows brushing. The woody scent of fennel mixed with pine resin in his hair. "Have you ever been in love?"

"Other than you?"

Three words like a canoe to the face. "Other than me," I choked out.

He took a long pull of brännvin.

"You can't drop that on me and not answer!" I protested.

"Sure I can. It's part of the game. What's the first thing you think in the morning?"

"Usually, 'Kaid, I need to pee.'"

Airedain snorted. "Okay, that doesn't count. Lemme try again."

146

He drank without seeming to notice. "What's the furthest you've gone with an itheran?"

I drank. "How many people have you tapped?"

"Four. Ilani, a Gallnach, Britte — you saw her at the Knox last winter, remember — and another Sverbian. Not Viviwen."

"You got *four* women to take bloodweed for you?"

"Does that bother you?"

"Nei, just hope it was worth it." I still remembered the pain and tremors from the poisonous herb that induced my bloodflow. I jerked up from slouching. "Wait. *Did* they take it? This isn't part of the game, Iyo-boy. You don't have any kids, right?"

He flinched. "None. I swear."

"Then it doesn't matter."

Airedain stretched out his long legs on the mattress. "So . . . you just wondered if tapping me is worth it?"

I drank.

He threw his head back in laughter, his spiked hair crumpling against the wall. Then he slid his arm around my waist, curving his body into mine. "Kateiko. Can I kiss you?"

My reasons for waiting seemed distant, like pebbles at the bottom of a swamp. I couldn't get over Parr when his voice was always with me. I needed to block him out. Even if it meant drowning in the mire.

I straddled Airedain's hips and tipped sideways. He caught me. We were the same height this way, though the bricks behind him didn't stay in place. He knotted his fingers into my hair, kissing me hard. Prickles shot through my body, but his mouth, hands, body heat felt dulled.

I fumbled his jerkin off his shoulders. He pulled his tunic off in one smooth motion. Combat training had left bruises over his taut muscles. A scruff of hair, almost invisible, grew over the pointed drummer tattoo in the centre of his chest. The ink blurred.

Drown. I took a swig of liquor and moved his hand under my shirt, wiping clean the feel of Parr.

Airedain gave a soft groan — then swore and pulled back. "Rin-girl. Wait. It kills me to say this, but . . . we're both trashed. Seriously, I was a fucking wreck my first time. Barely remembered it. No girl deserves that."

My first time was too clear. *Darling girl.* It'd take far more alcohol to make Parr fade. I climbed off Airedain and slumped next to him.

He cupped my jaw. "Ai. You okay?"

"Yeah. I mean . . ." The words felt blocky in my throat. "I don't know. I can't think right."

"Then we definitely ain't going further." Airedain bundled me up in his arms. "Tomorrow, if you want. Tonight, holding you is the second-best thing I can imagine."

Rap-rap-rap.

I groaned. My head was a block of wood, the noise a chisel. "If Elkhounds round us up again . . ."

Rap-rap-rap.

"Probably one of Jona's friends." Airedain heaved his caribou blanket aside and thumped out of bed, swearing at the cold. The door creaked. "Jona ain't ho— *oh.* 'Bout time you turned up."

I forced my eyes open. Falwen stood in the doorway, snow on his grey coat. He looked from Airedain, shirtless and shivering, to me in bed. I snapped upright.

"Sohikoehl. Good. The Okoreni-Rin said you were staying here," Falwen said. It was impossible to place which jouyen his accent was from. He stepped past Airedain, opened the shutters, and sat at the table.

I grabbed my herb pouch and collapsed into the chair opposite him. "My okorebai sent me to talk to you, but you weren't in town. Then we weren't allowed to leave."

"The Beru-jouyen requested help dealing with raids. I boarded the first ship sailing north. Eremur's navy had driven the raiders there, and they were stealing salmon to sell on the black market here. I am heading to the Colonnium to testify that no Aikoto participated in illegal trade. This lockdown should be lifted soon. However, we have a more pressing issue."

I looked up from trying to remember which vial in my herb pouch was willowcloak.

"Eight Beru antayul were taken during raids on their fishing camps. They have not been found."

A vial slid from my hand and rolled across the floor. "Raiders tried to kidnap me during the salmon run. Why would they want antayul?"

"To sell," Falwen said. "My educated guess is that Iollan och Cormic, unable to open a rift alone, has decided to force others to help. Somehow antayul are necessary, and he will pay to get them."

Something pulled inside me, like snare wire hooked into my navel. All the layers of the world had to be torn open to make a rift. Iollan was an earth druid. Suriel controlled air. The Corvittai didn't have a jinrayul since Nonil died, but they'd already torched places. Water-callers were the last they needed.

"Given the Beru's proximity to Anwen Bel, the Okorebai-Rin should hear about this," Falwen told me. "Hiyua wants you to carry the message to Toel Ginu while she deals with the Council."

"I'm coming," Airedain said immediately.

"No doubt you were." Falwen glanced at the rumpled bed, ignoring my embarrassed splutter. "However, your arrest record complicates things, Kiyorem. I was only able to arrange for a few to pass the lockdown."

"It's fine," I told Airedain. "Look after Iannah. Even if she complains."

Falwen rose, his chair scraping back. "Oh — Sohikoehl, please tell the Okorebai-Rin I will find your jouyen a Kae schoolteacher once this is dealt with."

I nodded. With a click of the latch, he was gone.

"Odd that Falwen went to Beru territory himself," I said. "He usually sends messengers."

Airedain shrugged, turning logs in the stove. Sparks hissed through the air. "Maybe he was checking on family up north. I think he's from the Haka-jouyen."

"You think?"

"Falwen's lived in Caladheå longer than I've been alive. What's odd is he came here to my flat. Guess an okoreni's daughter gets personal visits." He kicked the grate closed. "You don't have to go. An Iyo can tell Fendul."

"My tema asked me to. And I've been gone half a month."

He hooked his thumbs on his belt. "Every time you walk out this door, I'm scared you won't come back."

The wire in my navel pulled tighter. If I had to choose, I'd stay with the Rin — but the closer that decision got, the more painful it became.

15.

MOVING ON

I'd just entered the Rin stockade when a thought struck me. I turned as Aliko barred the gate. "Weren't you on the night shift?"

Her eyes widened. "The okorebai switched me to day," she squeaked. "So, umm, my weaving apprentices aren't alone at night."

I shrugged. Didn't matter to me.

Everyone had been driven inside by the cold. I waded through snow into a covered walkway and along to my plank house. Nili, Yironem, and Rikuja besieged me with questions but exchanged awkward looks when I mentioned Fendul.

"What?" I asked with dread.

"I can't keep secrets from you, Kako," Nili wailed. "Just go talk to him."

Muttering, I trudged back outside and across the stockade. Fendul and a few Rin were by the far gate, gutting the catch from an ice fishing trip. The creek trout in their buckets were thin and dull-scaled.

Fendul leapt up and hugged me. "Kako, thank the aeldu—"

"Ew. You're getting fish blood in my hair."

"Sorry." He wiped his hands in the snow. "Let's talk alone. The woodshop's empty."

The scent of cut timber met us inside. We sat on rioden chests ready to be waterproofed. I filled in what Fendul hadn't heard about the lockdown and repeated Falwen's news about kidnapped Beru. "You know what this means, Fen," I said. "We're running out of time to find Iollan."

He sighed. "I'll talk to Tokoda."

"What's happened here? Nili sent me to talk to you."

"Nothing," he said too fast. "The jouyen's fine. No news."

My eyes narrowed. "Remember, no secrets, no lies."

"This — it's not important."

"*Fen*. I'll pry it out of Nili eventually."

Fendul paced across the workshop, crunching on woodchips. "I . . . slept with Aliko while you were gone."

I stared. Laughter stuttered out of me until I was cracking up. "You changed Aliko's shift to tap her? Aeldu save me—"

"She asked to change," he snapped. "I didn't realize why until — you know—"

"*Aliko*? Really? You said she's dumb as a rock!"

"That's what I thought, but . . ." Fendul pinched his temples. "It turns out she acted like a blissful idiot all these years so I'd help her with everything. I'm not sure if that makes her smart for knowing I would or dumb for thinking it'd make me like her."

I swallowed my laughter. Suddenly I realized how closely she'd been watching us our whole lives. Every time I got mad at Fendul for correcting my combat stance or fixing my snares, she'd been there, asking for his help. Making him feel useful. Respected. Desired. "Why'd you do it?"

"Because I *wanted* to. Aliko's kind and brave and hard-working, and, well, she's attractive. For one night, I didn't want to be the okorebai. I just turned twenty-two, and I've never been with a girl. You're hooking up with Airedain—"

"Nei. I'm not."

It was his turn to stare. "You've been sleeping at his flat."

"On his floor."

Fendul slumped onto a stack of split wood. "I thought . . . you couldn't be upset if you already . . ."

"Fen," I said softly and sat next to him. "Don't you know I understand? Tiernan bled my heart, but Parr wanted me. I wanted to be happy for once. To step outside my life. I slept with the man who sent Nonil to slaughter us. I can't be mad about Aliko."

So much was changing. Old certainties cracking like thin ice under my feet.

That evening, Nili asked me to visit the Rin burial ground with her. Yironem's stockade confinement was over, so he came along and sat by his friend's grave while Nili and I moved on, snowshoeing over waist-high drifts. I paused at Isu's grave to tell her I was back safe.

Nili crouched where Taworen was buried. She trailed her hand over the whiteness. "I keep thinking about Bódhain. I saw that guised figure on the pier, *felt* it, like the air moved differently around it, yet my arrow went right through. I believe you that it was someone in another world, but . . . I didn't understand why I could see it when I never had before. Eventually, I realized it's because of Taworen."

"You were looking for him," I said.

She nodded. "Losing my temal and sister in the Dona war — well, we saw it coming. The Blackbird Battle was so sudden. I hardly had time to talk to Tawo. He thought I was just tapping him for fun, but . . . after all those months, I loved him. And after he died, I wanted so bad to tell him that your story about Folk bringing people back from Aeldu-yan got in my head."

I crouched next to her. "Taworen figured it out. You've never been able to hide when you're happy. He didn't bother fending off other boys because he knew they didn't stand a chance."

Nili choked with laughter, tears seeping from her eyes. "*I* should've fended them off. I was scared to admit it. You know, after breaking up with Orelein and swearing to never marry a Rin."

"So . . . are you here to say goodbye?"

"Yeah." She took the black drummer wristbands, embroidered with Taworen's rioden needle crest, from her purse. "It's time."

We dug through the snow over his grave. I thawed the earth and Nili used her hunting knife to scoop out a hole. She laid the wristbands inside and packed dirt overtop. In the spring, the cottonspun would decay, joining with his body to nourish the rioden growing at the head of his grave.

"Everyone's moving on," she said as we traipsed back to Yironem. "Barolein asked Mereku to marry him. She said yes."

"*Really*? So soon after his wife's blood met the ground?"

"Akiga's right about one thing. We need to rebuild our numbers. Mereku can't fight well missing an arm, but she'll make a good mother. Barolein, well, he's an antayul and a healer. The more Rin he trains, the better. They may as well have kids with a partner they like."

Tokoda sent a fleet of Iyo warriors north to search for the missing Beru. Our canoe carver and his brother went along, leaving their workshop empty and their apprentices with Orelein. The tattooist's sister flew north to tell the Tamu. Our jouyen was scattering over the rainforest, a cloud breaking into drops.

During gate duty, I went through ways to track Iollan, each more dangerous than the last. Return to Ingdanrad to find Tiernan. Stow away on a ship heading north. Climb Suriel's mountain. Enlist the help of another surviving saidu. It was all pointless. Fendul couldn't spare more Rin, nor did I want to leave, no matter how awkward it was eyeing Aliko's hands for bloodweed tremors.

"Ai!" a voice boomed through the frost-trimmed forest one afternoon. "Little help here!"

I unbarred the gate and ran outside. Dunehein pulled two sledges, one with each hand. Three Tamu followed with more sledges, all loaded with bundles of furs. Dunehein scooped me into a crushing hug and tossed me into a snowbank.

"Jerk!" I spluttered. "Where's everyone else?"

"They're fine," he said through his laughter. "Still trapping in Anwen Bel."

The tattooist took over gate duty so I could help haul the furs in. Rikuja dropped onto a bed in relief when she saw Dunehein. People from the other plank house crowded into ours for news. Dunehein sat on the floor with baby Sihaja in his arms and a throng of kids around him.

"Us trappers are camped onshore, ready to paddle back," he told them, "worried about travelling with hundreds of sovs' worth of fur. When we hear about the missing Beru antayul, we realize we're even bigger targets, but we've gotta get these to Toel before winter hits in full. Then we see a ship sail our way. We're thinking, do we fight? Run? Take the furs or leave 'em? And who do ya think it is?"

"Itherans!" a boy shouted.

"Pirates!" yelled a girl.

"Itheran pirates!"

"Wrong!" Dunehein grinned. "Tamu warriors on an itheran ship! Remember they agreed to guard our borders while we live here nice and snug? Sailing's faster than paddling, so they learned how. And they say to me, 'We'll get you to Toel Ginu. Raiders won't look for antayul on a Sverbian ship!'"

We pulled apart the fur bundles. Shaggy black bear, sleek cloud weasel, plush marsh rat, rusty fox, grey elk, tawny mountain cat. Nili and her apprentices chattered about everything they could sew.

"I'd forgotten what it's like to trap on good land," Dunehein said. "Game everywhere. Tamu trappers have barely made a dent compared to what itherans did here. Feel how thick those pelts are though. The animals know winter's gonna get worse. I'll rest a day and head back."

Rikuja frowned. "That soon?"

He kissed her hair. "Sorry, love. The Tamu don't wanna wait, and I ain't canoeing alone."

"I could attune and carry you," Yironem said.

"Then *you'd* have to come back alone," I said.

"Not if I stay with Dunehein."

We turned to look at Yironem. He shrank back.

"It's just," he said hastily, "I was confined to the stockade for a month. I want to get out and be useful. I've helped with your trapline, Kateiko. I know how."

Fendul frowned. "Even if you're legally an adult, Yironem, I'm not letting you leave without your mother's knowledge."

Hiyua returned from Caladheå that night. The lockdown had been lifted. The two councillors caught buying illegal salmon had resigned, forcing an election. It was set to happen in a month.

Hiyua wasn't happy about Yironem leaving, but agreed it'd be good for him to have time away. She knew some Rin called him a spirit traitor. Nili and I told her what else we'd heard — *pigeon-fucker*, accusations he snuck out to tap Viviwen, mutters that he got his kinaru body through loyalty to Suriel. Akiga kept silent, shamed, but we feared what else she might do to him.

Yironem and Dunehein stayed long enough for Barolein and Mereku's wedding. It was simple and sweet — the tattooing ceremony in our plank house, a feast with meat Dunehein had brought, and snowball fights in the stockade. Mereku was still getting used to throwing with her remaining arm, but Barolein vowed revenge on anyone who hit his new wife.

Well after dark, he carried her into our plank house away from his apprentices' teasing. The rest of us stayed outside drinking pine needle tea around the firepits. Orelein, looking lost without his brother, sat next to Nili. She blinked like she was seeing into another world. Dunehein sat with Sihaja sleeping in one arm and Rikuja in the other. I shared a mock grimace with Yironem when we realized Fendul and Aliko were missing.

Two days later, as I fought the urge to feel sorry for my loneliness, a wiry figure slid over a snowbank. Airedain didn't return my smile as I opened the gate.

"I dunno if this is good or bad news," he said. "Someone asked Iannah to join the Corvittai."

16.

LEGACIES

"Why are we here?" I asked as we approached the Knox Arms. "Iannah doesn't drink."

"You'll see," Airedain said.

He led me through the pub and down a side hall where he knocked on a door. Iannah opened it, showing a cramped room with a straw mattress. She wore her new clothes from Segowa, but still had her auburn hair in a tight bun. Airedain nodded at her and headed to the kitchen.

I ducked under the door frame. Freshly whitewashed walls gleamed in the light from a frosty window, hung with lace curtains like her sisters' houses. A bundle of letters and the kinaru makiri I'd given Iannah were the only objects on the scrubbed shelves. "You live here now?"

"Thanks to Airedain," Iannah said. "Working here, too, as a night guard. People have been rummaging through the alley for scraps. Emílie's worried someone will break into her cellar."

"You must hate that. From guarding councillors to cabbage."

"I still carry a weapon." She patted her sword. "This was a storage room. Don't know if I'll be here long enough to bother getting a bedstead."

She only had one stool, so we kicked off our boots and sat on her mattress. Emílie had lent her red knitted blankets and a sheepskin. After sharing a room with her sisters, going to boarding school, then living in the barracks, this was probably the first time Iannah had ever slept alone.

"Tell me about the Corvittai," I said.

"It happened yesterday," she said. "I went to the post office to get my mail redirected. A Ferish man stopped me on the way. He knew everything about me. My name, resignation from the Colonnium, that Cièntus spied on me. Someone's still leaking military info. He didn't name the Corvittai directly but said if I want to 'put my skills to use again,' a mercenary commander called Arril has personal interest in me. Supposedly Arril's fed up with military corruption, too."

Like Cattil offering Gallnach mercenaries exactly what they wanted — revenge or escape. I shuddered. "I thought we killed all the Ferish Corvittai. No one's seen any in months."

"Arril probably kept a small force separate from Nonil's. Bodyguards and stewards like this man."

"What'd you tell him?"

"I'd consider it." Iannah stared at the ceiling. "It's a better opportunity than anything we imagined. If I earn their trust, maybe I can find Iollan. Or Suriel."

"I tried working with the Corvittai. I got Maika killed."

"That's why I didn't agree yet. Tried following the man, but I lost him downtown. I'm supposed to meet him in three days if I want in."

My head swirled with names. *Peimil. Cattil. Arril. Quinil.* I'd focused on Cattil, figuring that since her mercenaries were protecting Iollan, she was the way to him. But she was too clever, too hidden. Now we had a way straight to their heart. It just meant putting another of my friends in danger.

"Arril must've been an Eremur soldier once," I mused. "Why'd Parr's son leave the military?"

Iannah shrugged. "Ask ten people and you'll get ten answers."

I pulled my knees close to my chest. Five months since I'd killed Parr, and his legacy was still here. Not even death could get his taint off me.

"Ai, what happened to Cièntus?" I asked to distract myself.

She allowed the hint of a smile. "I reported him for covering up the black market and trying to instigate a riot. I threatened to go to the newspaper, too. He got thrown out of the military. Whoever replaces him will be just as bad, but damned if it didn't feel good watching him crumble."

While Iannah was on duty, I sat in the kitchen talking to Emílie's daughter, Orla. Whenever the Rin got our Kae schoolteacher, it'd fall on me to help. Orla showed me her tattered spelling book. She'd lived in Caladheå since she was three, going to Sverbian school and only learning Gallnach history at home.

"Your writing's beautiful," I said, admiring her gentle chalk curves. "You could be a scribe."

"I'd like that." Orla wiped her slate clean and started over. "Better than waking at three o'clock to bake bread. I can teach when I turn sixteen, but when Viviwen worked here, she said the schools—" She cut herself off.

"What?"

"Ma says not to talk about her. Or Magnå. Or anyone else Airedain—"

"Orla!" Maeve cried.

I stifled a laugh. Airedain dropped a bowl into the sink, splashing up soapy water, and lurched through the swinging half doors to the pub.

"Don't worry, lass," Emílie told me. "The lad's head over rump for you. He wouldn't have asked me to hire a Ferish soldier otherwise."

"Why did you?" I asked. "Iannah's a bit out of place here."

"So are we. If Ferish Elkhounds come sniffing, I want someone who can translate, maybe talk 'em down. And she's the only soldier in Caladheå who knows you're not Iyo. If anyone will keep our secret about being Gallnach, it's her."

After the dinner rush, Airedain and I walked back to his flat. I sat on a corner of his bed. "Iyo-boy. Can we talk?"

He pulled up a chair, looking wary.

"I wasn't ready to, you know, be together last time. Drunk Kateiko kissed you, not wise Kateiko. So thanks for stopping me. I'm still sorting myself out, and . . . there are still things I don't know about you. Like Magnå, apparently."

"Shit." He ran a hand over his crest of hair. "You don't wanna hear about her."

"Nei, *you* don't want to tell me."

"Why does it matter?"

"Tiernan didn't tell me he loved Maika. After they got married, I wound up here." I gestured at the room. "If some girl comes back into your life, what happens to me? Where do I go? Iannah and I are talking about dealing with the Corvittai again. I need one thing stable in Caladheå."

Airedain sighed, resting his elbows on his chair back. He was quiet awhile. "I met Magnå three years ago. She's Gallnach but took a Sverbian name to blend in. She was starting a midwife apprenticeship in Caladheå. I thought she came to the Knox to visit Maeve. Liam finally pointed out she was coming to see me, but . . . I was a wreck at the time. Didn't want anything to do with girls.

"Magnå was patient, one of those people so good you sorta hate them. She came by my tema's shop and asked about the embroidery. Wanted to know the meaning of all the designs. And, well, we wound up together. I brought her to Liwa's wedding. Liwa liked her, and my sister doesn't like anyone. My tema was just glad I quit drinking myself to death.

"After a year together, I wanted to ask Magnå to marry me, but I was freaking out. We were nineteen, same age my temal was when he married my tema, and . . . I thought it'd never work with an itheran. It'd be too hard dealing with the shit that mixed-blood families go through. So I went to the spring equinox alone in Toel. And I fucked it all up.

"Ilani and I got drunk together. She wanted to 'cure' me of loving an itheran. Maybe I wanted her to. Like a bludgehead, I admitted I'd never tapped an Iyo girl, and, well, I have now. Worst fucking mistake of my life. I confessed to Magnå, and that was the end with her. She left Caladheå a couple months later when she finished her apprenticeship. We write letters, but I haven't seen her since."

My mind felt like swamp sludge. I'd heard gossip about Airedain's itheran lovers, but never knew it went that far. Magnå had probably slept in his bed where I sat now, used the mirror where I cut my hair for the first time, kissed him against the door. She was still in this room the way Tiernan was in the scar on my neck.

Airedain picked up the poker and stabbed crackling logs in the stove. "Told ya you didn't wanna hear it."

"Nei, it's just . . . what would you do if Magnå came back?"

"She won't. She's a midwife now in the southern colonies. Married a Gallnach farmer." He flipped over some charred wood, spraying out sparks. "I found out before this year's spring equinox. S'why I almost hooked up with Ilani again. Vodka and spite. But I couldn't do it, not with her. We got into a huge fight after you left the shrine. First time Ilani ever called me a pigeonfucker."

"So . . . every time you got involved with a girl since Magnå, were you just trying to get over her?"

"Yeah. Nice to feel wanted."

I bit my lip. "Then what am I?"

"You, Rin-girl . . ." Airedain slumped forward onto the table. "You're like looking into a shattered mirror, all the parts of me broken up and put together different. We've lost lovers, family, friends, homes, even our second names. But you don't look out from that mirror and just see the past. You see a future for our people. I wanna build that with you. You're the first girl it feels like I could have that with.

"Know what else? Liwa likes you. My tema adores you. And don't tell Iannah, but I respect her. We fit into each other's lives, and I spent so long missing Magnå, I didn't find you 'til I almost lost you. I promise I'll be here, whenever, whatever you need. But I'm fucking scared, 'cause I dunno if you want me or if you're just using me to get over someone."

"I'm not. Well — not the way you think—"

"Don't try to explain. This ain't politics. Tell me what you *want*."

"You." My answer spilled out. "I want to kiss you, and — aeldu save me, you have no idea. I missed you in Toel. I wish you'd move back there, as awful and selfish as that is. I . . . I think I'm falling for you. But *that* scares me for so many reasons."

✳

Segowa had reopened her shop. I helped out to keep my hands and mind busy. Her work occupied the back room, so Airedain and I sat on crates in the front, sewing goatskin. The shop was a nest of colour — salmon pink, barley yellow, moss green, huckleberry purple. Segowa had adapted to the market, using itheran dyes alongside Iyo ones.

Two women in high-necked dresses browsed the goods, loudly discussing the quality of stitching and materials. It was a quirk of certain Ferish to speak to each other in Coast Trader instead of their native language. Jonalin, who used to work with Ferish dockhands, had explained that it separated old immigrants from new. Some flaunted their family's bravery in being first to 'settle' a new land.

"My granddaughter needs a handkerchief for next month's social," one woman said. "Something lively to stand out against her black muslin gown."

"How's this?" The other held up a pattern of pale orange berries. "So exotic."

I rolled my eyes, earning a snicker from Airedain. They were salmonberries, common as weeds in the rainforest. Even though the women had grown up here, they clearly never left the city. I watched gold earrings sway among the first woman's tight grey curls, imagining how it'd feel to wear that much money. Painful, probably. Gold was heavy.

"I saw him this morning at the bank," one woman was saying. "Poor dear. I suppose he returned from fighting in Ferland to manage the estate."

"Was he there? I heard he was in the southern colonies working as a missionary."

"They weren't the most pious family, were they, the Parrs? Though that *would* explain why the boy left on poor terms with his father."

My needle slipped, jabbing my finger. The women ignored my yelp. Airedain stared at me over a half-stitched slipper.

He was here. Antoch Parr's son was in Caladheå.

*

"People have been claiming to see Nerio Parr for years," Iannah said in her room. "The estranged son of a councillor attracts gossip like flies. Especially a murdered councillor."

"Right when Arril contacts you?" I said. "It's too much of a coincidence."

"Visiting the bank, though?" She frowned, picking over our dinner. She was fine with mutton stew and barley loaf, but didn't touch the fermented cabbage Emílie made for Sverbian customers. "Not what you'd expect from the most wanted mercenary in the province."

"Speaking of Arril, you're not thinking of going, are you?"

"Might be better to get it over with. When Marijka missed her meeting with Suriel, the Corvittai went looking for her. They know where I sleep."

"It could be a trap."

"What's the point? I'm a soldier. No political power, no ransom value, no use dead. And if they want to bait you, they'll also get an Iyo with dual-wield daggers and anger issues." Iannah buckled on her scabbard. "I'd better get to work. Don't do anything stupid, Koehl."

I shivered as I left with Airedain, pulling up my hood. Dunehein had brought furs just in time. Nili and Hiyua would be sewing now, working by lamplight with aching fingers.

"Listen," Airedain said suddenly, staring at the sky.

We stopped. I heard lots of things. A banging window shutter, whistling drainpipes, icicles cracking loose and shattering on brick doorsteps. This side of Ashtown was always windy, so close to the ocean. Then, like icy water down my back, I realized the gusts weren't from the bay.

Airedain looked east. Beyond the city, the Roannveldt sprawled toward the distant mountains. "I heard — a voice, I think."

I scuttered up a snowbank and stood on a windowsill. Using iron bars over the glass as footholds, I climbed past the second floor onto the slanted roof. Wind knocked me back. I scrabbled through the snow until my gloves gripped on shingles.

"What in Aeldu-yan are you doing?" Airedain called.

"Listening!"

Caladheå spread out around me, veiled by night — silhouettes of tall buildings downtown, winking ship lights in the harbour, fires burning among refugee shacks at the city edge. My hood blew off. Snowflakes swirled up from the roof and stung my eyes.

I heard the voice. Voices, maybe. Crashing together, shredding into fibres of sound. They grew louder. Closer. White light split the sky, streaking toward us straight as an arrow. The clouds were tearing apart, letting moonlight pour through.

The screams hit. Shrieking, wailing, howling. Drawn-out cries soared to a crescendo and whooshed past, chilling the deepest parts of my spirit. No words, just raw pain and fury, the language of something that always was and always would be.

Suriel was back.

17.

BLIZZARD

"Suriel!" I shouted. "Remember me? Kateiko Rin? Come talk to me!"

Just screaming wind. I latched onto a chimney, coughing from smoke billowing out of it. Suriel had said my devotion to tel-saidu stopped him from killing Tiernan. I'd proven myself accidentally, but I was Rin, a child of kinaru. If I could get Suriel's attention, talk him down from destroying a city—

"Kateiko!" Airedain yelled. "Get the fuck down here!"

"I have to find him!" I shot a beacon of water into the sky. It wrenched out of my control, minced into thousands of icy shards. "Suriel! You want antayul! I'm right here!"

The squall raged on, ripping my breath away. Shingles tore loose and sailed past. I shielded my eyes, listening for Suriel's voice in the howls. It had to be him—

Airedain scrambled over the gutter and grabbed me. We hit the roof hard. A sledge slammed into the chimney where I'd been a second before, sending splinters everywhere.

"Come on!" he cried.

I shimmied down a rattling drainpipe and jumped into a snowbank. We tumbled through the streets, leaning into the wind, falling on ice and scrambling up again. White rose around us, scoured from every surface. As we neared the Iyo street, fresh snow dropped from the sky like a waterfall, so thick I couldn't see Airedain. I grabbed his hand.

We collided with the row of Iyo flats and worked our way along, counting doors. Every one looked the same. When we found Airedain's, he fumbled his key out and tried jamming it into the lock. It was frozen solid. I shoved my mind into the tiny space, feeling out the iron pins, willing the ice to melt. I was too cold, teeth chattering, legs shaking—

The door swung open, blinding me with firelight. Jonalin yanked us into the entryway and slammed the door. We collapsed on the stairs. White eddies settled around us.

Jonalin held up a tin lantern. "Good timing. Just about to go look for you."

We shook off as much snow as possible and tromped upstairs. The Iyo woman from across the hall was in Airedain and Jonalin's flat, nailing down the shutters. Her husband went to bar the outer door now that everyone in their building was back. Airedain's hair stuck out in frosty spikes. My braid was so brittle that loose strands snapped off. Our faces were scraped and bleeding wherever the wind had touched us.

"Your tema's fine," Jonalin told Airedain. "We were in the gathering place when we heard it coming. She's gonna wait it out there."

"Suriel must be pissed," Airedain said. "Fucking tel-saidu. Just disappears in summer and comes back like this?"

I knocked snow out of my boots. "The worst part is what comes next. People only survive by fleeing wherever Suriel's storms hit. We can't evacuate the entire capital. This is where refugees fled *to*."

There was nothing to do until it ended. We wrapped ourselves in pelts from the walls and huddled by the stove, playing card games Airedain and Jonalin had learned from itherans. Hours later, with no sign of it calming, we blew out the lamp to conserve oil and passed brånnvin around in the dark. Iannah was safe at the Knox Arms, at least. She and Emílie's family were probably in the kitchen with anyone else in the area who needed shelter.

Cold seeped through the brick. Snow came down the stovepipe and hissed on the flames. Our firewood stack shrank, but no one wanted to go to the woodshed in the dark. We relieved ourselves in a ceramic pot and threw it on the fire. Sleep was impossible.

The only hint of morning was a faint lightening at the window. We unbarred the building's back door to a world of swirling blue-grey. Airedain tied a rope to the door and the other end around his waist before going to haul firewood. If he got swept into the field behind the flats, he'd never find his way back. When he got too cold, Jonalin took over. Every time they tromped inside, I melted ice from their eyelashes and the shawls wrapped around their faces. They brought wood for all four flats, then stacked more in the hallways.

Eventually, I fell asleep in Airedain's bed. When I opened my eyes, he was seated at the table with his frame drum, watching me as though it ached. I smiled, hoping to ease whatever it was. He dropped his mallet and swore.

Jonalin thumped up from his chair. "I'm gonna visit the downstairs neighbours. Can't deal with you two."

After the door shut, a laugh slipped out of me. "I don't think Jonalin likes me."

"If he didn't, you'd know about it." Then, almost lost to the storm, Airedain said softly, "But sometimes I don't like you."

My brow furrowed. "Why?"

"Never mind."

"You can't just back out of that—"

"Why not? You do. All the time."

I sat up. "What in Aeldu-yan does that mean?"

Airedain set down his drum. The coyote painted on the drumskin eyed me. "I've done everything you asked, Rin-girl. Answered your questions, let you meet my family, told you my mistakes. I'll keep waiting, but I dunno what for. You didn't tell me anything when we played clears. Some man scares the shit outta you, so much you gotta be drunk to kiss me, and you won't talk about it."

"I can't."

"Why? Who's in your nightmares? If it's Tiernan, I *get* it. If it's me, tell me how to make you feel safe." He waved at the shutters. "Everything's gonna turn upside down after this storm. The more I know, the easier it'll be."

I swallowed. It was like inhaling a sea urchin. "I can't tell you because you'd hate me."

He laughed. "I'll never hate you. Any sane person woulda left you on that roof last night. Let you die yelling at Suriel. But nei, I went after you, 'cause I love you too much to lose you. There it is, in case I didn't say it clear enough before. And I — I don't expect you to love me back. But you can't demand honesty and give none in return."

I couldn't breathe. Not from his confession, because I knew that, but because I knew he was right. Trust went both ways. Nerio Parr was in Caladheå, and I hadn't told Airedain what happened with Nerio's father.

170

I held out my hand. "Give me your blades."

Airedain passed his daggers and fan knife over. I threw them and my weapons under the stove, hard to retrieve without burning ourselves. I took several slow breaths, digging my fingernails into his caribou blanket. There was no coming back from this.

"I . . . slept with Antoch Parr. Two days before the Blackbird Battle."

Airedain looked like he didn't recognize me. "Seventeen Iyo died in that battle. Warriors I'd been training with."

"I didn't know he'd send Nonil after us. He helped me with Suriel, and — I trusted him. I needed someone to trust. I didn't know he killed Maika—"

"You knew what he was. Not just a fucking brown pigeon, but a councillor. Ex-military."

"I thought Parr was different! He was kind to me. He was so good at twisting the truth—"

"Why *him*?" Airedain struck the table. "Of everyone in this province, why him?"

"Because I was lonely. And terrified." My voice cracked. "Maika was dead, Tiernan wanted to kill me, I thought Suriel was coming, and I had nowhere else to go. Parr was gentle. He felt safe."

"You coulda come here."

"I did," I whispered over the shrieking gusts. "You were out with Viviwen."

"*Yan taku.*" He got up, hands clenched. He paced the room, jaw working, then kicked the water pail. It hit the stove and rang like a bell. He slammed his fist into the door. "Fuck. Fuck!"

I slid onto the floorboards, arms over my head. Nothing else in my body would move. My head was full of screaming, raging, feral wind.

Airedain turned. Saw me shaking. His anger cracked, splintered. The pieces warped into horror.

"Shit. Kateiko, nei—" He froze, a moment held like a painting, then dropped to his knees. "Nei, nei, nei. I'm so sorry. Please don't be scared—"

"I knew you'd be mad," I gasped.

"Not at you. At me. At every aeldu-cursed takuran who made you like this." He kissed my hair. "I love you. Ya hear me? I won't hurt you. Ever."

I curled into him. Airedain picked me up, a firework exploding in his arms. He murmured into my ear until my sobbing slowed, then pulled back his blankets and laid me on his mattress.

"I can't escape Parr," I choked out. "I killed him, and he's still here. In my dreams, in the voices I hear. Now his son's in Caladheå."

"That's why you wanna know everything about me? In case I'm like Parr?"

I nodded.

"Trust me, I'd kill that scum myself if you hadn't." He wiped my tears with his thumb. His knuckles were bleeding, studded with splinters from the door. "What should I do? Right now. I can leave you alone, get the Iyo woman across the hall—"

I held out my arms. Airedain crawled into bed and wrapped himself around me, warm and solid. He tapped a rhythm on my back, singing an Iyo song of the ocean, murky depths where nothing could touch us. I sank into his voice, an anchor keeping me safe. For now.

The blizzard kept beating icy fists against us. We gathered downstairs with all the neighbours so we only had to heat one flat, spreading blankets and pelts on the floor like wolves in a den.

After the fifth night, I woke confused. It wasn't until I heard a seagull squawk that I realized the wind had stopped. Upstairs, we pulled nails from the shutters. Rippling snow filled the street, so deep I could only see second-storey windows and peaked roofs.

Jonalin took to the sky in his osprey form to scout. I borrowed his snowshoes and squeezed through the window into cold, clear air. It felt like hatching from an egg, waking to a new world. I didn't know how long we had until the Corvittai came. In past attacks, they'd waited a day after Suriel's storm, and there were a hundred thousand people here who couldn't escape this in one day.

Up and down the street, people trickled from windows. Jonalin returned and said all of Caladheä was snowed in. The Iyo were the only ones outside besides a few itherans on skis. No one else could move through the mess.

One building was missing its roof, torn off like a flower from its stem. Airedain boosted me up to peer over the wall. The rooms were full of snow. I let my mind sink through the packed layers, searching for warm spots where people might've burrowed. Nothing. They'd either fled or frozen to death.

The snow was disturbed around the Knox, flattened in barrel-sized hollows. I frowned until it clicked. Giant webbed footprints. A kinaru had landed here and stomped around to mask its tracks.

"Rin-girl," Airedain said. He pulled an envelope from a nail in a windowsill and tore it open. "It's in Ferish. Must be for Iannah."

I banged on a window shutter, then again. "Hello?"

"Hold on!" came a muffled voice. Moments later, the shutter popped open. Maeve stuck her head out. "Goodness, you're both alive! Come in! We're still digging out the doors."

I pulled off my snowshoes and crawled inside. Leaning over the balcony railing, I saw Emílie, Liam, and several patrons below, hauling buckets of snow and dumping it in wash basins, old ale casks, whatever they could find. Maeve returned with Iannah and mugs of steaming tea, then bustled off again.

Iannah skimmed the note. "It says, 'Two weeks today. Same time and place. Arril.'" She looked up. "I don't think the Corvittai knew this blizzard was coming."

My breath caught. "So they're not planning an attack?"

"It'd be idiotic. This is the best-defended city in Eremur, and viirelei and Sverbians are better in the snow. They're probably scrambling more than us right now."

"I don't want to count on that. Where can we get news in a city that's shut down?"

"The Colonnium, but I can't get inside anymore."

"The docklands," Airedain suggested. "Only boats will be moving for a while."

Iannah glanced at his snowshoes. "Mind if I borrow those? The military's more likely to talk to me."

Airedain snickered. "Good luck. I'd pay to watch you walk on these things."

He had a point. Iannah could knock me down on solid ground, but on snowshoes, she had the grace of a waddling goose. She kept stepping on the long back of whichever foot was in front. I gave her a few minutes to practise in the street.

The docklands reminded me too much of Rutnaast — capsized ships, splintered wood, Eremur's elk flag fluttering at half-mast. Here, though, voices drifted from inside the Customs House. A few people shovelled snow off piers into the water. The deaf Sverbian fish-monger was among them, her golden braid slung over one shoulder.

I waved and worked my way closer so she could read my lips. "Were you in the city during that storm?"

She turned to her constant companion, the man with anchor tattoos on his wrists. They exchanged a few complex hand motions.

"We were on the water," he told us. "Escaped the worst of it.

But now we got a drifter full of frozen fish and nowhere to unload, so we'll stick around, see how we can help."

Iannah spoke in rapid Ferish to an Elkhound on skis, who said the navy had been commandeered to bring supplies. I spoke to a Sverbian who'd just arrived with a team of yowling sled dogs. He was going to circle the city and look for stranded people. An Iyo scout who flew from Toel Ginu said they got hit by the blizzard's edge, but they were fine, Rin included.

Everyone was nervous. What went unspoken was how many people had already died. I'd stood in a battlefield drenched with blood, and I was afraid to see the refugee shacks where people had no food or warm clothes.

In the empty fish market, I saw someone familiar. Black hair pulled away from his face, green cloak, longbow strapped to his back — and snowshoes like ours. If any itheran knew how to get around, it was a ranger. He was digging through snow with an arrow.

Iannah caught my wary look. "Who's that?"

"Rhonos Arquiere."

She arched an eyebrow. Rhonos had warned me about Nonil, but also marked an arrow for my death. Spending months since then with Tiernan probably hadn't done much for his opinion of me.

"Kateiko," he called, coming closer. "Of all times to run into an old . . . acquaintance."

Iannah's eyes locked on Rhonos, her flat expression mirroring his. "You said he's a mercenary." She pointed at a brass tag on a cord around his neck. "He's military."

I gaped at him. "Really?"

Rhonos tucked the tag under his cloak. "Ex-military. Eighteen months with Eremur's mounted archers." He and Iannah looked ready to take each other down.

"Quit it," I said. "Rhonos, meet Iannah Pelennus, also ex-military. If you're not planning to kill me today, can we talk somewhere warm?"

Grudgingly, Rhonos led us to a shipyard and picked a workshop lock. Inside the massive hall, a ship frame loomed like a whale skeleton, set on logs so the whole thing could be slid into the water. We unlaced our snowshoes, Iannah rubbing her legs. Rhonos lit a fire in a coal stove used for steaming timber.

"Last I heard, you got turned away from Ingdanrad," I said. "Where'd you go after?"

"All over the Turquoise Mountains," Rhonos said. "Tiernan sent me with knowledge of Iollan och Cormic's magic that we hoped would aid in finding him. It did not. What I did find was an abrupt upswing in windstorms. I returned to Caladheå to warn my old military contacts that Suriel is active again. I stopped at the Blackened Oak and asked Nhys to pass the news on to you, Kateiko, but I was too late. The blizzard hit that night."

I dropped onto a coil of anchor rope thicker than my waist. "I . . . hoped for something more useful."

"Have you done any better?"

Iannah and I exchanged a look. Rhonos had marked an arrow for me because of Marijka. He was angry I hadn't asked for help dealing with Suriel, despite that neither he nor Tiernan had been around. I couldn't pass up his help now.

"Iannah has an invitation to join the Corvittai," I said. "From Arril, their commander. We think he's Antoch Parr's son."

Rhonos shook his head. "Nerio Parr would never serve Suriel."

"How do you—" My eyes widened. "You were in the military at the same time. You knew Nerio."

"Well enough to be sure he is not Corvittai."

"He's here in Caladheå. Someone saw him the morning before

the blizzard. And Parr was protecting a source high in the Corvittai, remember. He killed Maika for demanding to know who it was."

Rhonos folded his hands in front of his face. "What would you do if you met Nerio?"

I bit my lip. "If he's here to finish what Parr started, I'll kill him. If not, it doesn't matter. We have nothing to do with each other."

Rhonos wavered, then removed the cord around his neck and handed it to me. The brass tag was warm from his body. I studied the etched symbols.

Nerio Rhonos Parr. 5th Royal Eremur Mounted Archers.

I jerked up, dropping the tag. That's why the portrait of the young soldier in Parr Manor looked familiar. I saw Parr in the angle of Rhonos's jaw, the shape of his brows, that proud posture. A ghost watched me through brown eyes.

I scrambled away through the workshop, knocking into stacked crates, ignoring Iannah's calls. Panic thrashed in my chest like fish in a net. I'd always wondered if I would recognize Parr's son. I never dreamed it was the ranger I stood with at Tiernan's wedding, who lifted Marijka's body from her kitchen floor, who fell asleep beside me on a creek bank. One of two Ferish people I trusted.

He carried the blood of the man I let touch me in a way no one else had. Parr's voice screamed across my skin like so many days of wind.

"Kaid!" I shoved a barrel, sending it clattering into the wall.

"Kateiko." Rhonos stepped into view. His accent flowed through my name the way Parr's had. "We are on the same side."

"I thought that about Antoch Parr." I stared past him at the ribs of the unfinished ship. "That's how you knew Nonil was coming? Through your father?"

"I wanted to stop it. The Corvittai were already on their way. As soon as he told me, I left to warn the Rin."

"Then you *left me*. You said they'd torture you for warning us, but Parr would've protected you. You left me to die there!"

Rhonos winced. "I could not kill my father if I met him in battle. Allow me that."

"Forty-nine Rin are dead because of him. My aunt, my oko-rebai, my sister's lover. I don't have to allow shit—"

Iannah swung forward and gripped my elbow. "Let him explain before you tear his throat out."

I folded my arms, teeth clenched.

Rhonos bowed to her. "I know better than anyone what my father was like. He only spoke openly at home. Yes, he was brutal, his good intentions twisted by years on the battlefield. He grew so desperate to stem the bloodshed that he dealt with anyone useful, from petty criminals to Ferish holy extremists. Tiernan — still friends with my father then — mentored me, helped me make sense of the complexities of war. Yet only I knew my father's deepest feelings.

"When he ran for Council, I feared what he might do under pressure. I could no longer play the loyal son. So I gave him an ultimatum — drop out of the election, or I would leave. He won a seat. At sixteen I gave up my home, military career, even my name. My father spun two stories, one that I left to serve in Ferland's military, the other that I went south to become a religious missionary. Patriotism or devoutness, whichever the public preferred to believe."

"You're a coward," I spat. "You could've destroyed Parr's reputation. Kept him off the Council."

"Who would listen? He was a decorated captain, and Eremur still suffers from the Elken Wars. People want strong leaders. Councillor Montès enacted laws that let soldiers kill viirelei, and he kept getting elected."

Iannah snorted. "Montès also got an arrow in the heart."

"So why'd you go back to Parr?" I demanded.

"To learn how Marijka died. After I realized traitors in the military were helping the Corvittai, I suspected my father was more involved than he had told you. I feigned a change of heart and coaxed him into admitting it. I sincerely believe he did not intend to kill her. Years of dangerous alliances made him paranoid and quick to draw a blade."

"You're defending him? Maika was unarmed!"

Rhonos lifted his chin. "Do not pretend you are beyond reproach. You led him to her."

"You never warned me about him! He thought we were too dangerous to live, but he was the violent one, a racist fucking takuran who doesn't deserve to be buried in dirt—"

"He *is* buried, because of *your* people. Viirelei murdered him in our home."

"Because he wanted us dead!" Fury seared through my vision. I thrust Nurivel at him. "If you ever threaten us—"

Iannah wrenched my dagger away and flung it across the workshop. "We don't need more corpses."

Rhonos stepped back, crunching on the frozen dirt. "Kateiko. You came to me when Tiernan decided to fight Suriel. Why?"

I unclenched my aching teeth. "Tiernan listens to you."

"He knows who I am. He ended his friendship with my father after I explained why I disowned my family. Would he have asked me to be his *stjolvind* at his wedding if he did not trust me around Marijka? Would he let me anywhere near you if there was the slightest chance I might harm you?"

"How should I know? Tiernan wanted to kill me!"

"He *held back*. Our enemies are out there." Rhonos spread his arms. "You need me. My father told me things about the Corvittai. My name goes far in this province."

I scowled.

"If that is not enough," Rhonos added, "I have your horse."

"What?"

"You left Anwea in Tiernan's care this summer. I took her when we travelled to Ingdanrad. She will not survive alone in this weather. If you wish her to live, I advise not stabbing me."

18.

SOFTER THINGS

As we walked back to the Knox Arms, Iannah filled Rhonos in on all we knew, pausing to talk with people who leaned out second-storey windows. At the pub, they'd finished digging a tunnel to the surface. A hastily written sign said anyone who needed food or lodging was welcome. We slid down the tunnel and clattered inside.

"Mother of mountains," Emílie said. "Two Ferish soldiers in my pub who aren't arresting anyone. That's a first."

Iannah led Rhonos toward her room. I held Airedain back in the dim hallway and put my hands on his chest, hoping my touch might calm his anger.

"Please don't freak out," I whispered. "Arril isn't Parr's son. Rhonos is."

Airedain tensed, a ripple spreading through his body. "Lying bastard. Why'd you bring him here? To slit his throat?"

"We need his help. I don't like it either."

"Does he know you killed his father?"

"Nei. Or . . . what else I did with Parr."

He closed his eyes, jaw taut, drumming his fingers on my waist. His knuckles still had a purplish flush from punching his door.

Airedain pulled me into Iannah's room. He put an arm tight around my shoulders, glaring at Rhonos. "If you or anyone in your fucking bloodline touches a hair on Kateiko's head, I'll tear out your beating heart, feed it to the wolves, and bait my fishing line with your guts. When I die, I'll find your spirit and rip it into shreds so tiny no one will know what you were."

Rhonos glanced at Airedain's daggers. "Not the most intimidating weapons."

"You're looking in the wrong place." Airedain drew back his lips, showing sharp coyote teeth. A spasm crossed Rhonos's face.

Iannah slammed her palm onto the table. "Enough. Arquiere, start talking."

Rhonos and Airedain took the stools, eyeing each other. Iannah and I sat on her mattress with the sheepskin over our laps. She'd lit candles since snow blocked all light from the window.

"Bear in mind, I spoke to my father for an hour at most this summer," Rhonos said. "He only mentioned Arril in passing, and Peimil not at all. Cattil seems to have had little influence until Nonil's death, when she became the sole military hand. I can, however, tell you about the fifth captain."

"Quinil," Iannah said.

"He is their spymaster. If we consider the emperor constellation, as you are suggesting, Quinil being the feet, my guess is he took that name because he remains at a distance from other Corvittai. He would be in great danger if his identity got out. My father, skeptical of my change in allegiance, would not tell me who Quinil is."

"Parr knew," I breathed. "That's the source he was protecting?"

"They were close friends. My father trusted very few people besides Tiernan and me. He vented frustrations with the military to Quinil, believing they would never be repeated, but these secrets were passed to Arril. That is how the Corvittai kept an advantage throughout the war. Quinil may have even manipulated my father's actions in government.

"This past summer, he confessed everything in hopes of getting Parr to recruit Tiernan. Quinil claimed he was loyal to Eremur, and joined the Corvittai to learn Suriel's plans. That was nearly the end of their friendship, but my father decided the betrayal was justified, since Quinil had indeed gained Suriel's trust. Parr struck plenty of similar deals in his career.

"I suspect Quinil has a Colonnium position. It would explain how they were in frequent contact and how the Corvittai knew about your resignation, Pelennus." Rhonos folded his hands, thumbs parallel, exactly like Parr used to. "You worked near my father for years. Who was he close to?"

Iannah looked at the shadowed ceiling as she thought. "Not any Gallnach. They don't work in government. Draws too much attention. Quinil must be Ferish, but Parr made a show of knowing everyone so you'd never guess who he was dealing with."

Rhonos nodded. "Regardless, we should assume Quinil has seen you and Kateiko together. We can use that."

"How?" I asked.

"The Corvittai need antayul to open a rift. Go with Pelennus to this meeting and offer yourself to Arril."

Airedain jerked up, knocking into the table. "Nei. Not happening."

"Two spies are twice as effective as one." Rhonos looked at me like I was the only person in the room. "You want to atone for Marijka's death, do you not?"

"They'll never accept Koehl," Iannah said.

"They believed once she wanted to help Suriel."

"Before they massacred the Rin," Airedain snapped. "She ain't going near them again—"

"I'll do it," I said.

Everyone fell silent.

"I've realized something. Suriel disappeared before the Blackbird Battle, so maybe he had no idea it happened. Five months later, he's returned and found out Nonil slaughtered almost fifty Rin. Children of the kinaru, the only people Suriel refuses to kill.

"He was furious at his *own captains*. They didn't stop Nonil, they haven't opened a rift, their army's dead, and their navy's in shambles. Arril, Quinil, and Cattil are probably all in Caladheå. This blizzard was punishment. Five nights for five months of failure. If I'm right, the Corvittai will do everything possible to appease Suriel, which includes not harming another Rin. I'm untouchable."

✳

We spent the day helping however we could — digging out homes, sharing food and medicine, hauling firewood, carrying messages. Iyo returned from the refugee shacks with a look I knew from the battlefield, like they'd been scraped hollow. They'd found bodies gaunt with starvation and black with frostbite. They warmed up and went back to searching.

Several itherans had spent the early hours of the blizzard guiding refugees to better shelter. In Ashtown, they wound up in the Iyo gathering place, the Customs House, or workshops housing the brick-making kilns. In northern Caladheå, they fled from shacks along the river to the Shawnaast stavehall and old town hall, the waterfront hotel, or the Ferish holy *sancte*. Thousands survived because of a few people's bravery. Hundreds still died.

Caladheå woke up over the next few days. News trickled in. Suriel had swept from the mountains all the way over the Roannveldt. Caladheå got the brunt of his wrath, but villages across the plain were snowed in, too. Uncounted farmers and goatherds had gotten lost in the storm. Eremur's election was delayed while the province recovered.

Rhonos took me to the Blackened Oak, where Anwea was stabled. Letting her freeze had been an empty threat. She recognized me and nickered, rubbing her nose into my cloak in search of food. I couldn't stop stroking her glossy brown coat long enough to fetch sugar lumps from the pub, so Rhonos went for me.

"You may have her back," he said. "She belonged to one of my father's men, but . . . she did become yours."

"You need a horse more than I do," I said. "Take care of her."

On the winter solstice, every Iyo and I returned to Toel Ginu. Our two jouyen wove together for a night, snowshoeing into the depths of South Iyun Bel where we climbed the tallest trees and threw blazing torches into the canopy. Nili lit a beacon for Taworen, Fendul for his father, I for Isu and Marijka. Airedain shared our tree and lit one for Nokohin.

Last Yanben, near Tiernan's cabin, I'd looked across the bay and seen flickering orange on the horizon. Now, looking back from the opposite side, North Iyun Bel was dark. My family and friends were scattered — Dunehein and Yironem trapping in Anwen Bel, Tiernan in Ingdanrad, Iannah and Rhonos in Caladheå.

Late that night, warming up by our hearth, I told Fendul and my family about our plan to infiltrate the Corvittai. They hated it but couldn't deny we had to do something. The Rin and Iyo searching for the Beru antayul hadn't come back.

"We'll do it better this time," I said. "Not like when I tried with Maika. We're not alone now."

I stayed in Toel Ginu only a day before returning to Caladheå. We had too much preparation to do. In Iannah's room at the Knox Arms, she studied me, arms crossed.

"You know how to fight," she said. "You need to learn how not to fight."

"What's that mean?"

"You're like Airedain. Quick to anger." She raised a hand, cutting off my protest. "Like that. Whatever happens at this meeting, you need to stay in control. Quinil knows everything about me and possibly about you. He has a lot to use against us. Do you trust me?"

"Of course, Ia."

She passed me a knife. "Bite down on that. Hands at your sides. This is how we taught restraint to Colonnium recruits. Show no fear, no surprise, no emotion."

I made a face but did as she said.

"Don't let the knife fall. Pretend it's made of the finest glass, an heirloom from my great-grandmother in Ferland, and I'll gut you if it breaks. Got it?"

I nodded.

Iannah lunged. I reeled back, crashing into her shelves. The knife clattered onto the floor.

She slapped my stomach with the flat of the blade. "Gutted." She handed it back and replaced her fallen kinaru makiri. "Again."

I dusted the knife off and bit down. Iannah smacked her hands next to my ear, making a loud *crack*. I flinched, but held onto the knife. She nodded. Then she grabbed my throat. I shrieked. The blade sliced my lip as it fell.

The door swung open. "Everything okay?" Emílie asked.

Iannah stepped back. "Military training."

"It's fine," I gasped, wiping blood from my mouth.

"Carry on, then." Emílie went back to the kitchen.

"Let's try something quieter. I'm used to doing this in the barracks." Iannah kicked the knife at me. "Oh, speaking of the Colonnium. You're not the first viirelei Antoch Parr slept with."

I spat the knife out. "*What?*"

She slapped my stomach. "Gutted."

"Ai — you're lying, right? It's part of the game?"

"Yes." When I was ready again she said, "The first person I killed was Iyo."

I caught myself in time. After she nodded, I took the knife out to speak. "Is that true?"

"Maybe. The first person I stabbed was Iyo. Not sure if he died."

I shuddered at how blank her face stayed. Nine years of this training would do that to someone.

"Again." Iannah beckoned. "I kissed Rhonos Arquiere while you were at Yanben."

The knife hit the floor as I laughed. "That's a lie."

"Your guts are spilling out and you care who I kissed?"

We went on that way until my lips prickled with cuts. Rubbing my jaw, I went to the kitchen and came back with smoked herring and half a loaf of rye sourbread. Emílie had told us to eat whenever we were here and forget about the money. Fair price for fighting Corvittai, she said.

When I had a mouthful of bread, Iannah said, "I've slept with a woman."

I chewed. Swallowed. "Are we still training?"

She gave me an odd look. "You're meant to be shocked."

"Why? When Cièntus was spying on you and Airedain, you said you'd never have a secret romance with a man. I've seen you eye that milkmaid in the Bronnoi Ridge market, but every time I point out a lush boy you look appalled."

"Because you have terrible taste in men."

I elbowed her. She allowed the hint of a smile.

"I do like some men," Iannah said. "But in the military, I wasn't allowed to be with any. Women being together was overlooked because it kept us content. Less likely to get pregnant. It didn't bother me much since I've always preferred females."

"I'm the other way," I said. "I prefer boys, but sometimes a girl catches my eye. I kissed a Sverbian goatherd girl once, on a trading trip up north, though it didn't go past that. Next summer, I wound up with her older brother."

"Did your aunt pressure you to choose him? Since you're expected to have children."

"Nei. I just liked him better. Isu would've let me marry a girl as long as my wife and I had kids by surrogate fathers."

Iannah's brows furrowed. "You're lucky. I couldn't walk into the sancte holding my lover's hand without priests proclaiming we'll burn alive."

I mulled over that. For the past year, she'd held my hand when I needed comforting, even wrestled me in public parks for combat training. She did care what people thought, considering her humiliation over a tailor refusing to make her breeches, but lived how she wanted anyway.

"Was it another Antler?" I asked. "Your lover?"

Iannah nodded. "Pia Rossius. She was sixteen when she joined my unit. I was seventeen. Pia was . . . there's no one like her. Bouncing black curls, the grace of a sabre dancer, a smile like mint water. We were together two years, but she couldn't handle Colonnium life and resigned." She looked up at her letters on the shelf. "Most of those are from Pia. I hate that Cièntus read them. Worse yet if Quinil knows."

"That's why you told me? In case Arril uses it against you?"

"You and Fendul have your deal. No secrets, no lies. Figured we'd better do the same."

"Did you get too close to Airedain's fangs?" Rhonos asked in the pub, looking at my cut lips.

"Shut up." I pushed him toward two padded chairs along the wall.

When we were seated, I said, "You told me to offer myself to Arril in atonement. Fine, but you have to atone, too. You knew what your father was like and did nothing. I don't care what your reasons were — fear, pride, whatever. Parr was on the Council for six years unchecked. He sent Nonil to butcher my jouyen, and you *weren't here*."

"I am truly sorry, Kateiko—"

"I need help, not an apology. The Okorebai-Rin and Okorebai-Iyo sent me with a proposal." I leaned forward, elbows on my knees. "The provincial election's coming. Run for Parr's Council seat. Work with the Aikoto Confederacy and fix the damage your people have done."

Rhonos folded his hands in front of his face. "I would never win. I am twenty-two, barely old enough to vote."

"All I know about Council elections is candidates need status and money. You have that."

"Less than you think."

I raised my eyebrows.

He sighed. "My family made our fortune from natural resources, but we lost a great deal in the Elken Wars. By the time I was born, our mines had run low and game was trapped to nothing. Storms took our lumber camps. We sold off land, then our belongings. When my father won a Council seat, he moved heirlooms into his

Colonnium office to maintain appearances of wealth. He stopped hosting company at home."

My memories of Parr Manor surfaced clear as winter sunlight. Empty rooms, the last pieces of furniture covered in white sheets. In Rhonos's bedroom, someone had taken his military uniform out of storage. I wondered if it was him or Parr, nostalgic during Rhonos's brief return home. Only Parr's bedroom and the dusty front room still had their old fineries.

"Maybe you can do it without money," I said. "Iannah thinks if you announce your return, the newspaper will do the rest, spinning the tale of a loyal young soldier coming home to take up his dead father's duties. I heard women gossip about seeing you at the bank. They felt bad for you."

"Sycophants," he muttered. "I was at the bank to list Parr Manor for sale. It was a military hospital during the Elken Wars. I hoped it could be put to use again. The delay is only because proving my identity and claim to the estate has been an ordeal."

"It'd look better to keep the manor. Even if you don't live there."

"Still, I would need to 'donate' to the appropriate causes." Rhonos crossed and uncrossed his legs, like he'd forgotten how to sit in a chair after six years of living on the road. "The funds would have to come from sources your leaders do not likely approve of."

"Like what?"

"The sancte, perhaps, if I could garner the priests' support. Supposedly, I have been down south working as a missionary."

"If I get my elders to agree, will you do it?"

Rhonos rubbed the bridge of his nose. For a moment, with his Sverbian jerkin and a bit of hay in his hair, he looked more like Tiernan than like his father.

"I know it's asking a lot. To give up being a ranger, to return to the life you fled. But Iannah can't spy in the Colonnium anymore. You might be able to find out who Quinil is."

"Give me time to consider it. I am not even used to hearing my real name again."

Nerio Parr. It felt off. He was Rhonos to me. "What's Arquiere mean, anyway?"

He smirked. "You never guessed? It is Ferish for 'archer.'"

I sent word to Toel Ginu with an Iyo. The reply came a day later. Rhonos could ask the sancte for funds, but Tokoda and Fendul wanted to know every demand the priests made in exchange. He had, in fact, spent several winters down south among the Kowichelk Confederacy, and a Kowichelk who'd recently married into the Iyo agreed to back his story of doing missionary work there. Iannah instructed Rhonos on which of Parr's recent contacts he could wheedle for support.

Between Iannah's guard shifts at the Knox Arms, she drilled me on negotiation strategies, how to read threats on people's faces, mental exercises to keep my focus. She condensed years of training from the military academy and reading she'd done in hopes of becoming a captain. I fell asleep every night feeling like she'd been rooting through my skull.

"How'd you stay calm at the Colonnium?" I asked on the last day before meeting Arril. "The things you saw must've been infuriating."

"I vent in my downtime," Iannah said. "Screaming at the war memorial outside town helps. So did hitting other guards in combat practice. Though sometimes it's better to do . . . softer things."

"Like Pia?"

She stomped on my foot.

"Ow!" I cried.

Iannah slapped my stomach. "Gutted."

That evening, I curled up on Airedain's bed, too tense to sleep. He sat at the table tapping scraps of music on his frame drum. Jonalin had gone out, promising he'd be back for the meeting.

We'd scouted the site and found nothing. Likely Iannah and I would be taken somewhere else. Jonalin would follow from the sky, Rhonos and Airedain from the ground. Between a ranger and an ex-convict who knew the city's back routes from years of dodging Elkhounds, they could track us anywhere. A band of Iyo warriors would be on hand to intervene if needed.

"Nervous?" Airedain asked.

I realized I was pulling hairs from his caribou fur blanket. "Sorry. Can't stay still."

"Then don't try." He shifted into a lively beat. "Show me a dance, Rin-girl."

Laughing, I pulled my cloak on and held it out like wings. Nili and Yironem had taught me simple shawl dances. I spun in the cramped room, cloak brushing the furniture, hair flowing around me. My feet thumped the floorboards. From the flat below came muffled singing, then from across the hall, the thin notes of a wooden flute.

When I slowed, Airedain got up and took my hands. The dancing faded into just swaying together in the lamplight. My gaze kept drifting to the curve of his mouth. He'd grown familiar. The scent of pine resin, the deep brown of his eyes, all the ways he laughed, vibrations from him always drumming on something. One thing I didn't know well was how he tasted.

"Kiss me," I said.

Airedain tilted his mouth down to mine. He pulled my hair over my shoulder, pressing it to his leather jerkin over his heart. There, that flutter in my chest, the stirring of frozen sap. His lips were chapped, mine laced with cuts, but it felt . . . right. My head wasn't clouded by brånnvin. The faint music from other flats drowned out Parr's voice. Everything else was beautifully clear.

19.

ARRIL & QUINIL

At the Knox Arms the next morning, I put water bands on Airedain, Jonalin, and Rhonos, hoping they'd be easier to maintain than the ones at Bódhain. Iannah and I walked ahead with the others trailing out of sight. Crews had cleared the main roads down to the original layer of snow packed flat for sleighs. We waited inside the meeting place, an abandoned cabinetmaker's shop with boarded-up windows. The dim room reeked of mildew.

My nerves splintered like a frozen pond, cracking further the longer we waited. Finally, the door swung open. Two Ferish men wearing swords stomped snow off their boots. From the way Iannah nodded at one, slender with a black beard, I guessed he was the steward who invited her.

"Kateiko Rin?" he asked me. "We were told you might come."

I bit down, imagining the knife between my teeth. Not many itherans knew I wasn't Iyo.

The stockier man, a bodyguard from his looks, held out a sack. "Weapons, please."

Iannah put her sword and a dagger in. I dropped my flail and knives on top, the metal clanking. The men patted us for hidden weapons. Then the steward snapped something cold around my wrist — an iron cuff etched with glowing white symbols.

Numbness swept over me. In horror I realized what it was. Ingdanrad had used runes to neutralize Iollan's magic in prison. My water bands were erased. I couldn't sense Airedain or the others, couldn't call anything, as if my own hand wouldn't respond to me telling it to make a fist. I tugged on the cuff. It was locked.

"A necessary precaution," he said. "Your magic will return once it's removed."

Iannah had said as long as they weren't stabbing anyone, we should go along with everything. They led us into an alley where a cart and driver waited. The steward offered his hand to help me up. I accepted, gritting my teeth. Once we were settled, the men blindfolded Iannah and I with wool scarves. At least we'd be easy to follow.

Iannah's gloved hand found mine as the cart jolted forward. I tried mentally mapping our route, but the driver took so many turns, I lost track. Normally, it would've been easy to sense the ocean, or the Stengar if we crossed a bridge into Shawnaast. Instead, there was a blank spot in my mind. All I could tell was we stayed on level ground awhile, then went uphill toward the outer edges of Caladheä.

When we stopped, the men helped us onto snowy ground and guided us indoors. Only then did they remove our blindfolds. We were in a log cabin with two more guards, armed and wearing steel plate. The steward opened a trap door and went down with a lantern. The bodyguard indicated for Iannah and me to go next.

I climbed down a ladder into a dirt passageway. The air was warm and still. As we followed the bobbing lantern, I saw low rooms with casks, crates, and bins of turnip and squash. We were in a massive root cellar.

The passageway opened into a wide room, its deep corners hidden in shadow. Rows of wooden posts held up the dirt ceiling. On the far wall hung a black flag with Suriel's kinaru sigil in white. In front of a crackling fireplace stood a figure wearing leather armour, a concealing black muslin veil, and a curved sword. The men bowed to the figure and moved off to each side. "Iannah Pelennus and Kateiko Rin," came a clear voice from under the veil. Female. Gliding Ferish accent. Her dark hair was pulled into a tight bun, matching Iannah's. "Pleasure to meet you at last. I am Arril. No doubt you've figured out who I represent."

"Nice to meet *another* captain who's had me watched," Iannah said dryly.

"Consider it a testament to your value," Arril said. "It's rare I can recruit Colonnium guards. Most are blindly loyal. When I heard the circumstances of your resignation, blackmailing Marcot Cièntus to prevent a riot, I was fascinated. That's the sort of ethics I seek."

"Ethics? You've sanctioned hundreds of deaths."

"Fewer than you think. It was my idea to follow Suriel's windstorms with small attacks. Training people, so when a storm hit they would flee, and we could avoid more bloodshed."

"Explain Rutnaast. That was a massacre."

"I didn't sanction that. My naval captain, Cattil, is a wildcard. She defied me and paid the price. Fifty lashes, and I stripped her of naval command until she regained my trust."

"What about the Blackbird Battle?" I asked, fighting to keep my voice level.

Arril sank to one knee. "On behalf of the Corvittai, I offer my deepest apologies to the Rin nation. Nonil betrayed us more gravely than I could've imagined. I lost a hundred comrades that day. Your side and mine were never meant to clash. We share the kinaru crest, after all."

I stared at her veil. She could be smiling as she lied. The iron cuff felt cold around my wrist, resisting my body heat. Arril had taken everything I could use from a distance. Her men would put a knife in my heart before I got close enough to snap her neck.

Bite down. Don't speak.

"An effective commander controls her captains," Iannah said.

Arril rose again, dusting off her knee. "An effective commander rectifies her mistakes. I would've executed Nonil for mutiny if he hadn't fallen in combat. That's why I invited you, Pelennus. I need soldiers who understand there's more to war than swinging swords. Your intimate knowledge of Council Hall is a bonus. There are parts of government even my spymaster can't reach."

"What do you offer for my help?"

"The usual mercenary price. Silver and spoils of battle. But that's not enough, is it?" Arril drew closer. She was tall for a Ferish woman, well-muscled, and she moved with a slight limp. "I fought in Eremur's military for ten years. Female soldiers are rarer there than in the Colonnium, yet you wouldn't recognize my true name. I was passed over for captaincy again and again. So I left and formed a mercenary band.

"Suriel offered the greatest contract of all. To fight for the most powerful entity in this land, a god incarnate. He lets me command how I see fit. What more can we soldiers dream of? Freedom from corruption and interference, the chance to do a task well.

"Nonil isn't a name. It's a title given to my army captain, my favoured hand. I now find myself without one. What I offer, Pelennus, is that title. Rise above the foul, stinking morass of the military we left behind. Rise above a Sverbian pub in the slums, a devastating waste of your skills. Gain my trust and become my new Nonil."

Iannah tilted her head. That was more than we expected.

Our plan held, though. She had to refuse at first, or they'd think her too eager and realize she was spying. "As a Colonnium guard, I outranked you," Iannah said. "I'm only at the Knox Arms while I decide which warlord in the southern colonies I'd rather work for. They have armies, gold, the chance to set up a decent government. I've got no interest in being hand of a commander who hasn't proven herself worthy."

"Give me time. Consider this a standing offer." Arril clapped her hands. "Now, Kateiko. Tell me why you've come."

"For Suriel." I raised my iron cuff. "He needs antayul to open a rift, right? I want to help him again."

"Yes, you offered him a mage, then disappeared. Strange we heard nothing more from you."

I began my practiced story. "I found the mage murdered in her home. Suriel went missing before I could tell him."

"You profess devotion but never came looking for him?"

"I've been protecting the Rin-jouyen, children of the kinaru. Suriel doesn't want us harmed. That's why he sent the blizzard, isn't it? Punishing you for failing to stop Nonil."

"Very astute." Arril tapped her veiled chin. "One gap in your story. Three weeks passed between your disappearance and your reunion with the Rin nation. What did you do in that time?"

Looked after Tiernan. Tracked down Rhonos. Slept with Parr. "I had lung sickness. I was coughing, starving, and couldn't leave my campsite."

"Is that so? You claimed to have betrayed the man you love to serve Suriel. That man had to be Tiernan Heilind, who you offered your life to protect. So when my spymaster couldn't locate you, I sent soldiers to Heilind's cabin. They saw you there. Forgive me for questioning where your devotion lies."

I swore internally. I'd been careless, too distraught over Marijka's death to notice anyone spying.

"As I thought." Arril clicked her tongue. "Pity. A willing water mage would've been useful. Well, if that's all, we'll return you to Ashtown—"

"Wait," said a man. "I vouch for Kateiko Rin."

I froze. Only Aikoto pronounced my name perfectly.

Arril gave a clipped laugh. "Of course you'd get involved, Quinil."

Iannah tensed next to me. The marks of falling knives stung my lips. *Bite down.*

A man stepped out from the shadowy corner. Tall and wiry, veiled like Arril, with cropped brown hair and a grey Ferish-style coat and breeches.

"Young love is fleeting." Quinil's rapid speech sounded familiar. "Kateiko has not seen Heilind in months. Moreover, she is the daughter of the new Okoreni-Rin, granting her respect in our confederacy. She is far more useful than you realize. Let me deal with her."

Arril flicked her fingers. "Fine. Maybe I can sway Pelennus while you're busy."

Quinil picked up the lantern we'd brought in. "Come."

I cast a stunned look back at Iannah. Quinil led me down a narrow passage, opened a plank door, and ushered me in. The dirt room was cramped, with a desk, two rough chairs, and a stack of wood by a hearth. A carved kinaru watched from the mantelpiece.

"Be calm," Quinil said as soon as the door closed. "I am your ally." He slipped off his veil.

Falwen.

Rhonos said Quinil was Parr's close friend. The first time I met Parr properly, he'd just left Falwen's office. They'd worked together throughout the inquiry into Suriel, but a Ferish councillor and the Officer of the Viirelei were such an unlikely pair, I never realized how close they were. Then again, here I was with Iannah.

Falwen began building a fire. "You were followed, I assume? By Airedain Kiyorem and others? Let us hope they were careful. My influence has limits."

He reminded me of a Sverbian folk tale about a creature with a thousand eyes and a thousand ears. He knew everything about the Aikoto Confederacy. Everything about *me*. I might as well have gone naked to his office. Which is where we stood now, I realized. An office like his in the Colonnium, but without cabinets of files. He must have everything memorized.

I stayed near the door, ready to run. "You better have a good explanation."

"I became Quinil to protect our people. Suriel is erratic, and his shield for the Rin does not protect other jouyen. Like you, I feigned devotion to find out what he was doing. Now I pass Arril enough information to keep her trust and steer things in our favour."

Exactly what he told Parr to justify leaking military secrets. "How long have you been with them?"

"A while. *I* sent Parr to destroy the Corvittai cache at his family's lumber camp, just as you arrived in the south. Unsurprisingly, he never told me he broke your leg on the way." Falwen brushed woodchips off his hands and stepped back from the budding fire. "I kept Arril away from the Iyo. I made Cattil hold off attacking Rutnaast until all our people were away at the Okoreni-Yula's wedding. The Toel Ginu shrine was a necessary sacrifice."

"*You* told Suriel to raze it? Rikuja was inside!"

"It was meant to be empty. She was there finishing work delayed by your arrival. I offered the aeldu's sacred ground to prove Suriel is the only spirit I care about. Compromises must be made."

"Is that what you call working with Parr? Compromise?"

"That was a mistake." Falwen gestured at a chair. "Sit. We have much to discuss, Sohikoehl."

I didn't move.

He leaned against his desk, legs crossed. "I trusted Parr. Not fully, but he was the only councillor who took my advice. After your meeting fell through with Suriel, I sent Parr to look for you, hoping to keep you from Arril's grasp. Instead he killed Marijka Riekkanehl."

"To protect you." Bitterness stained my voice. "She wanted to know who his source was."

"I should have realized how unstable he was. Paranoid, conflicted, still living the horrors of the war with the Sverbian Rúonbattai." Falwen twisted his discarded veil. "I balanced many factions. The scales tipped. All at once, Peimil broke out of prison, Arril left me to manage Nonil, Suriel went quiet, and the Rin came south. I slipped up."

"How?"

"I confessed to Parr how difficult it was managing the Rin-jouyen's arrival."

The realization trickled down my body like wet paint. "He didn't know we were here until then."

He tossed the veil aside. "I tried to backtrack. Parr guessed my evasiveness was linked to Suriel. He sought Arril for answers but instead found Nonil, who told him what I was desperate to hide — that Suriel massacred the Rúonbattai but spared their Rin allies. Parr would have done anything to destroy the last of that alliance. He traded my friendship for his vendetta. All he had to do was goad Nonil."

"So you're claiming you had *nothing* to do with the Blackbird Battle? Parr found Nili's necklace on the battlefield and gave it to you!"

"He lied about its origin. I swear to the aeldu I had no idea the battle took place until you and the Okorebai-Rin came to my office bleeding. I realized then that Parr had crossed a line he could never return from. I gave the necklace to you, trusting you to figure out how he got it. Yes, I sent you to kill my closest friend. I do not regret it."

I stared at him, wondering if he knew what Parr was to me. Something didn't fit. "What was so bad about the Rin arriving?"

Falwen paced in a tight circle. He was usually quick to answer, his mind darting like a sparrow.

"We're the only Aikoto here. If you want me to trust you, you'd better talk."

He smiled wryly. "We are more connected than you realize."

I paused. Airedain thought Falwen was Haka, but his accent sounded Rin sometimes.

"Few people know. My lineage is not carved on any plank houses. I am equal parts Rin, Iyo, Haka, and Ferish, born forty-four years ago into a jouyen of mixed-blood nomads." Falwen tossed his coat on the desk and rolled up his sleeve.

A black seagull marked his upper arm. Dona-jouyen.

I reeled back into the wall, painfully aware Arril's steward had taken my weapons. I'd never seen that crest on a living person. Only corpses, young and old. "I didn't think there were any Dona left—"

"A few of us refused to fight our Rin relatives." Falwen tapped the rioden needles inked under the seagull. "From my grandfather. Look familiar?"

My throat tightened. Rioden needles were Taworen's crest. If he'd lived, Nili might've married into that family.

He pulled his sleeve back down. "In one month of war, my entire family's blood met the ground except my youngest nieces and nephews. I had them adopted into the Yula-jouyen and vowed our confederacy would never suffer like that again. So when Suriel became a threat, I became Quinil. Did Parr ever tell you that phrase he liked so much? 'A wise man keeps one eye on his enemies and one on his friends?' I taught him that."

I sank into the chair he'd offered, as uncomfortable as the one in his other office. "So what now? You told Arril I was useful."

"Now we make amends for trusting Parr." Falwen took the other chair. "I have a task for you."

"I'm listening."

"Cattil has the kidnapped Beru antayul on a remote island called Innisbán. My real reason for sailing north was to check on them. If Parr was a river, Cattil is the raging ocean. Arril should have hanged her long ago. I can send you on the premise of being an intermediary, an antayul familiar with rift magic who will convince the Beru to cooperate. In truth, you will be going to kill Cattil."

I closed my eyes. Another death. "Cattil's just a title, isn't it? Someone will take her place."

"Her first mate Láchlan, who is more sympathetic to us. More rational. The Beru will be safer in his hands until we can free them — which will be difficult. The island is heavily defended."

"Isn't it easier to ambush Cattil somewhere?"

Falwen rubbed the gap between his eyebrows. "She is the best smuggler on this coast. You will not find her unless she wants to be found. Besides, if you earn Láchlan's trust, you can protect the Beru while I find a way to get them out. If it helps, you may bring Pelennus. Arril wants to test her."

I gazed at his coat and veil on the desk. We didn't find him until he wanted it, either. "You can't expect me to keep this secret."

"Tell your jouyen that Arril is sending you. Do not mention me. I cannot protect you if I am dead."

"If everything you say is true, you can defend yourself to Fendul and Tokoda."

"For being the Corvittai spymaster *and* being Dona? My ancestors were Rin and Iyo deserters who struck peace treaties with Arril's and Nonil's ancestors. My jouyen killed your okorebai's mother in battle. I am not willing to test the bounds of his trust when the lives of eight Beru are at stake."

We eyed each other over his desk. Everything was stamped onto the vast blackness of my mind where my water-calling should be. Aeldu knew how Iollan dealt with his magic being numbed for years.

"You caught my attention the moment we met," Falwen said. "A lone Rin here without permission. When you asked Parr to invite the Iyo-jouyen to testify about Suriel, I realized you would be difficult to manage. I had good reason not to involve the Iyo in that inquiry."

"Because Wotelem's testimony made the Council declare war on Suriel?"

"Because bringing any part of our confederacy into public view endangers us all. I had no idea what you might do next, so I arranged leverage. I sent you to Parr with a plea letter to spare Baliad Iyo from being hanged. Sealed in that envelope were plans for assassinating Councillor Montès."

"You were behind *that* too?"

No wonder Parr seemed distraught when I delivered the envelope. Talking about his dead wife and estranged son, questioning his decision to join the Council. He'd become what Rhonos feared. Maybe that set him down the path toward betraying Falwen.

"Leverage," I repeated. "So if I out your identity, you'll accuse me of being an accomplice in the murder of a councillor."

Disgust pulsed through my body. If Falwen blamed me and I implicated Parr, I'd take Rhonos down with me. He'd never get voted to the Council. And my people would lose our only protection in Eremur's government.

Falwen rose and perched on the edge of his desk. "This is not how I want it to be, Sohikoehl. You, me, and everyone we are trying to save would die. Believe it or not, I have always looked out for you. We both came to Caladheå alone at a young age. I know what it is like."

I bit down on my retort. He had no idea what it was like to be used as someone's personal assassin.

"One question," I said. "If we free the Beru antayul, Suriel will find other people to open a rift. Are you trying to help him or stop him?"

Falwen's smile didn't reach his eyes. "I could ask you the same."

20.

DEEP NORTH

Iannah and I met up with Airedain, Rhonos, and Jonalin at the Knox Arms. They'd followed us to and from a log cabin on the edge of Shawnaast. Iannah said there were hidden tunnels everywhere in Caladheå, dug out during the Elken Wars.

Falwen's threat couldn't keep me from telling my friends. Rhonos was shocked his father was close friends with a viirelei. Iannah said she'd help no matter who I chose to kill, Cattil or Falwen. Airedain restrained his rage to swearing and stabbing vegetables with his fan knife. Even Jonalin looked silently livid.

I left for Toel Ginu straight away. Nili seized me in a hug at our stockade gate, wailing that she thought I'd died. The droplets in her necklace had dissipated when Arril's steward numbed my water-calling.

Fendul looked disgusted. "I trusted him," he kept muttering. We stayed up into the night with Nili, Hiyua, and Rikuja, sorting through everything. Fendul pressed me for my opinion on what to do, but relented after I kept refusing to offer one.

Every okorebai relied on Falwen as an emissary and a source of knowledge. Outing him would cut the axle from the wheel of the Aikoto Confederacy. The Council would put an itheran in the Office of the Viirelei and execute Falwen for treason, if a Rin didn't murder him for being Dona first. In the end, Hiyua gently reminded Fendul that consequences were easier to face with allies.

The next morning, we met with Tokoda and Wotelem in Toel Ginu's gathering place. They couldn't hide their fury that Falwen hid being Quinil, but they admitted to knowing he was Dona. Tokoda had approved his appointment in the city because she believed his mixed blood made him impartial. Wotelem, who dealt with Falwen the most, advised keeping quiet while we watched him.

Fendul pointed out we had an opportunity to do more than just kill Cattil. A heavily defended island in the remote north had to be where Iollan was hiding. The Corvittai didn't have enough manpower to guard anywhere else. A few hours and several mugs of tea later, we had a strategy.

Falwen wanted to put Iannah and me on the next of Cattil's supply smuggling ships. Unknown to Falwen, our scouts would follow and study Innisbán's defenses. A few weeks later, smelt would start spawning, swimming upriver under the ice. Rin and Iyo "fishing groups" would paddle north. They'd pick up Dunehein, Yironem, the other trappers in Anwen Bel, the search party looking for the Beru antayul, and any others they found. Ingdanrad was sure to help. The fleet would descend on Innisbán, catch or kill Iollan and Cattil, and rescue Iannah, me, and the antayul.

Cold clamped down on Toel Ginu, followed by boatloads of snow. On the first decent day, Falwen brought our new school-teacher. The Kae man was in his mid-twenties, spoke fluent

Sverbian, Gallnach, and Coast Trader, had his own books, and wrote beautifully with willow charcoal. Nili bet ten pann he was spying for Falwen. I refused to take the bet. Privately, Falwen told me everything was arranged. We'd sail in two weeks.

While I waited to leave, Airedain arrived with the news that Rhonos had managed to get into the military records and found a female soldier who matched what we'd told him of Arril. Sofia Mazzina, born in a Ferish farming village in southern Eremur, two medals for being wounded in combat, honourable discharge. Suspected of illegal mercenary work, never caught. She'd be forty-five now. Arril was right — none of us recognized her real name.

Later, Airedain and I slipped off to the canoe workshop and lay in the sawdust trading kisses. Quick ones, long ones, knocking noses, learning each other. Whenever I tensed up, hearing Parr on the breeze, he drummed on my arms to distract me.

"I made you something," he said into the curve of my neck. He held out a purple linen flower with four blossoms. Sewed onto it were triangular green leaves. Fireweed and arrowhead, our family crests. "They'll be together when we're not. Hang onto 'em until we meet again on Innisbán."

"You're coming with the rescue? You mean you passed your combat test already?"

"Took it today." He beamed. "Iannah's been drilling me."

I laughed in amazement. He'd come so far, from getting stabbed by an Antler to training with one.

"I used to dream about becoming a warrior." He ran his hand over his crest of hair. "This is a warrior's hairstyle in a confederacy far southeast. I started wearing it after I got out of prison. Made me feel braver."

It worked. He was brave in so many ways. Not just killing a raider or tailing me to Arril's base, but accepting his father's abandonment and making a new life for himself in Caladheå. Trusting itherans after all they'd done to us. Confessing it all to me. Letting me leave for Innisbán without him. I understood what he meant about seeing each other in a shattered mirror. Tonight, it was my turn to reach through it and draw on his strength.

I'd never touched his hair. Since I met him, I'd been curious in a tactile way, wondering how the strands felt with pine resin stiffening them, but it meant touching his spirit. Admitting I wanted to. Admitting I needed him.

I reached up, trembling. My fingertips grazed the cropped hair on the side of his head, soft as leaf fuzz. Airedain inhaled sharply. His dark lashes fluttered. I slid my fingers up to the crest shaped into a shark fin. The thin brown spikes were crunchy, sharp at the tips, smooth from linseed oil in the resin paste.

"Kako," he said breathlessly.

He tilted his head down, lowering the shark fin. The ends tickled my nose and lips. I pressed my palms to each side of his head and breathed the scent of pine. He smelled like home. "Bring me back here," I whispered.

The day before we sailed, a Sverbian woman with darting blue eyes came to the Knox Arms. I'd met Janekke when I went to Ingdanrad. She'd been Marijka's friend at the mage school. Marijka had gone on to herbalism, but Janekke specialized in cutting people up and putting them back together. She'd come with a ship of mages who'd answered our call for aid.

In Iannah's room, Janekke showed us two fingernail-sized stones etched with delicate marks. "These are magnets amplified for distance. You carry one, and the scout carrying its match can track you anywhere. Our best runic mage created them. Even that nulli-fying cuff Arril made you wear can't break their bond."

I held a stone in each hand. They pulled toward each other, drawn together like lovers. "Wouldn't it be better to mark the runes on me?"

"Gods no. One, you're not magnetic. Two, Ingdanrad law for-bids putting runes on other people. Only the mage who inscribes a rune can safely remove it, so if they refuse, or die, you're stuck with it."

"Then how do I get this past Cattil? How do I out-smuggle a smuggler?"

Janekke opened a worn satchel, showing rows of shiny tools bound in place. "The trick is Cattil can't out-surge a surgeon. I'll put the stone in your arm. Worst-case scenario, you can tear it out with your teeth. However, Tiernan Heilind insisted you be fully informed before consenting to get cut open. Pelennus, you've got no connection to Eremur's military anymore, correct?"

"None," Iannah replied, examining Janekke's tools.

"Good. They already think mages are uncontrollable fanatics, given our work in depraved subjects like terraforming and breeding woollier sheep. What I'm about to say must stay quiet." Janekke smoothed her apron. "Iollan och Cormic was imprisoned for carving amplification runes into his acolyte's chest. The boy died of a seizure."

I cringed. "I've only heard of standing on amp runes. That's how Tiernan tested my water-calling."

"Bodily inscription is far more powerful, and that increased power can help the rune-wearer tear a rift in the world. It's also far riskier. Och Cormic should've been hanged for murder, but he claims the acolyte inscribed himself to enhance his earth magic, and we couldn't prove the runes killed the boy."

"Suriel must've paid them well," Iannah muttered, opening and closing a pair of clamps.

Janekke shook her head. "Och Cormic's research was always an ethical peat bog. My guess is they wanted to work with Suriel. A three-thousand-year-old air spirit is a treasure trove for scholars."

"Hang on," I said, realizing I'd never seen Tiernan barechested. "Did Tiernan do this body stuff when he was Iollan's acolyte?"

"No. That's where it gets interesting. Our linguists solved the cipher och Cormic used to code his research, but it covers intensely complex magic across multiple disciplines — theology, anatomy, ecomancy. Heilind has spent the past few months working through it. The first mention of bodily inscription is dated five years ago. It's a sheet of amp runes designed for a fire mage with, theoretically, enough stamina to withstand the effects."

"A soldier." I felt sick. "Iollan designed them for Tiernan."

"Exactly, but Heilind had left Ingdanrad and refused to return, so och Cormic adapted them for earth magic and carved them on a teenage acolyte." Janekke paused while footsteps thumped past in the pub hall. "We suspect Nonil, or Alesso Spariere as I knew him, later carved the fire designs on himself. Did you see inscriptions on his body?"

"I crushed his ribcage. I didn't look too close."

She grimaced sympathetically. "Spariere was a poor acolyte — inexperienced, arrogant, and not especially clever — but strong enough to survive. I assume the offer of enhanced magic is why he defected to the Corvittai. We taught him how to set things on fire and och Cormic taught him how to do it better."

Iannah squinted at a steel hook in Janekke's tools. "What are the odds Iollan adapted these runes for water mages?"

"Extremely high. Kateiko, if he insists on inscribing you, pick whichever body part you value least." Janekke held up a bone saw. "I'll remove the problem."

"He won't get close enough," Iannah said firmly.

Janekke smiled. "Optimism. Lovely. Well then, ready to get cut open?"

I passed her a tracking stone. "Let's get it over with."

She gave me a small dose of evergreen-scented needlemint. When my limbs felt tingly, she cut my forearm with a scalpel, pushed the stone into the gash, and sealed it magically. My flesh knitting itself back together stung more than getting cut. Afterward, smooth skin covered the hard lump of the stone. Even Marijka couldn't heal people without leaving scars.

"If all goes well," Janekke said, "I'll remove that in a month or so after stepping on och Cormic's corpse."

A day later, Iannah and I walked to the abandoned cabinetmaker's shop. Neither of us brought weapons. Arril's cart driver searched us and again put the runed iron cuff on my wrist. We drove along the coast to a cove sheltered by dense forest. A sleek two-masted schooner bobbed in the water, its long bowsprit jutting forward like a needle.

The four sailors were immigrants from Gallun. We could only communicate in patchy Sverbian. I translated for Iannah, leaving out their cruder comments, though she could guess from their leers. The driver snapped something about Cattil. The sailors' laughter broke off like twigs.

They sent us below decks. I slept and when I woke, we were sailing up a channel between a snowy island and the mainland. All day and the next the landscape looked the same, winding along the splintered coast of Anwen Bel. It was the first time I'd seen my home in more than a year, and I'd never seen it from this vantage point. Fog rolled in and snuck damp fingers under my hooded cloak, then it was just misty whiteness and the bowsprit plunging into endless waves.

Somewhere behind us, a ship carried Ingdanrad mages and three of our scouts. One Iyo attuned to a dolphin, one to a seal, and the Rin to a heron, but they wouldn't get close enough to be seen. I felt the constant pull of the tracking stone in my arm calling to its match.

We ate stale flatbread for every meal, with salt pork at dinner that was probably stolen. The sailors drank watery ale. Iannah switched between throwing up and cursing in Ferish. The tinctures Barolein had given me for seasickness were slushy in their vials. I had to tuck them into my shirt to thaw them.

The men refused to remove my cuff even when I offered to dry their clothes or thaw their ale. It gave me a headache that grew worse by the hour. Willowcloak and needlemint did nothing. The pain was fused to my skull. I felt bad that Iollan had endured this for years, until I remembered he'd been thrown in prison for killing his acolyte.

"Can't you see it's hurting her?" Iannah demanded, but the sailors didn't understand or care.

One icy morning, an Eremur navy patrol boarded our ship and searched the hold. I showed them paperwork forged by Falwen that said I was delivering food to a famine-stricken Beru village. I'd hired Gallnach immigrants for my crew and a Ferish mercenary for my guard. The gaunt naval soldiers left with a crate of elk jerky as a bribe to not verify the paperwork.

We waited until night to sail past inhabited areas. Tamun Dael, the Tamu settlement where a hundred Rin died in the First Elken War. Caladsten, a city of Sverbian immigrants, street lamps twinkling. Beru whaling villages in Nokun Bel, scattered amid a long stretch of towering mountains and rainforest. Then we left the Aikoto Confederacy's territory and were in Nuthalha lands.

A front of indigo clouds appeared, and there was nowhere to make port. The coast was a breakwall of cloudy blue-green ice. The men shoved Iannah and me below decks while they reefed the sails. Rain struck first, followed by rattling hail. I was pressing my linen fireweed and arrowhead leaves to my lips, muttering to the aeldu, when a sailor toppled through the hatch and unlocked my cuff.

The storm hit my mind like a collapsing roof. My scream was drowned out by howling wind. The man dragged me outside. Hailstones bounced off the deck and struck our legs. The foresail's ropes had snapped. Soaked canvas billowed out to the side, straining to tear free of the mast. Our ship pitched nearly out of control toward an iceberg that would smash us to splinters. The man mimed climbing, then shielded his eyes. He couldn't see to fix the ropes.

I wove a cocoon around him, blocking out hail and sea spray. He climbed the rigging, swinging through the sky with the plunging ship. He was fixing the last rope when a wave struck the hull. The craft tipped. Icy seawater spilled past me. A sailor grabbed my hand before I fell over the bulwark into the roiling depths.

After the storm, they didn't put my cuff back on.

We veered northwest into open ocean. The sailors hauled caribou furs out of the hold — long hooded coats, trousers that fit over my leggings and Iannah's breeches, thick mittens that made our hands clumsy as dolphin flippers. Clothing only the Nuthalha Confederacy made.

For days, we saw only vast, glittering icebergs. I was a northerner to everyone in Eremur, but this was true north, deep north. The rigging grew spiky with frost. Normally, I'd hear voices in the waves. Here, the world was empty. Even birds and whales had migrated south.

Finally, a sailor pointed at a smear on the horizon. Innisbán. The white island.

21.

INNISBÁN

A dogsled convoy waited ashore, the only living thing in an expanse of treeless snow. Half a dozen itheran men in furs caught the thrown ropes and hauled our ship alongside a jut of ice. Strapped on their backs were metal-capped wooden rods.

"What are those?" I whispered.

Iannah looked grim. "Muskets. They're not used in the rainforest because it's too wet. Blackpowder won't ignite and the mechanisms rust. But they win wars in the old countries."

They'd work here. Crackling cold stripped all moisture from the air.

A sailor replaced my cuff, blanketing me with familiar numbness. He threatened to gut me if Cattil found out they removed it. I rode with a gruff man behind yapping, heavily furred dogs. Our convoy followed a trail inland, gliding over packed snow. Innisbán rose slowly in elevation and then flattened into a vast whiteness. Snowflakes swirled past, and the darkening sky swallowed the coast.

The trail dipped down and ended at whitewashed doors set into a valley wall. Wisps of smoke rose in the distance. Iollan must've dug the Corvittai base with earth-calling in the same way the druids had hollowed a mountain to build Ingdanrad. No one would spot it until they got close, and no one had followed him here. Until now.

A sled driver fit a square stone into a rune etched on the doors. Light flashed across it. The doors grated open, showing a tunnel that disappeared into blackness. I shuddered, reminded of Innisburren's tombs. Iannah and I followed the sailors in, leaving the drivers to tend their dogs. The tracking stone flared hot in my arm, reacting to some magical ward, then resumed its gentle tug.

Our torches cast shadows like faces on the jagged walls. The tunnel sloped down, winding around slabs of rock and narrowing to single file. Bone supports held up the roof. Under our crunching footsteps, everything sounded intensely still.

Deep underground, the air warmed. Guards holding muskets showed Iannah and me into a dirt room where we shed our bulky furs. A man with flecked scars on his face dumped my purse out on the floor. He ignored my linen fireweed and hardly glanced at my identification card — I doubted he could read Coast Trader. He said I'd get my herbalism supplies back if their medic approved them, and then moved on to Iannah. He examined her kinaru makiri, which she'd gone back to wearing as a pendant, and returned it.

Then we waited.

There was no mistaking the woman who swaggered in, filling more of the room than her small frame took up. Cattil moved with her arms loose like she was ready to hit something. Her thick golden braid draped over one shoulder. A man with anchor tattoos on his wrists followed.

The deaf fishmonger and her translator.

Now, instead of a white dress and fish knife, Cattil had a black woolwrap and skirt with a coiled whip on her belt. "Kateiko Rin, eh?" she said with a voice like gravel. "And our future Nonil."

"You can *talk*?" I demanded.

"In four languages. I could hear once." Cattil spoke too loud, not realizing or not caring. "But in some places a Gallnach accent can get one killed. No one questions a deaf mute."

I forced myself to slow down so she could read my lips. "That's why you gave me a Sverbian coin at the fish market? So I'd think you're from Sverba?"

"Did it work?" She smiled coldly and nodded at her translator. "Láchlan, my first mate. *He* grew up in Sverba. I got him out."

Her replacement if she died. I'd have to watch him.

"Welcome to the Wolf Den," Láchlan said as they led us through a tunnel. "You'll get used to the sled dogs' barking. Rations are two meals and two whisky shots a day. You start work with the water mages tomorrow. I'd say 'at first light' if we saw any down here."

The tunnel opened into a low room with jumbled iron and bone supports. A red-and-black Gallun flag hung over a dirt hearth. Men slouched around plank tables, eating, drinking, and eyeing each others' playing cards. A few glanced at Iannah and me and snapped their heads away. I didn't know why until I saw Cattil's hand on her whip.

Cattil left down another tunnel. Láchlan spoke to a sullen woman in a white dress and stained bodice. When she answered in perfect but listless Sverbian, I realized she'd been captured like the Beru. She brought two bowls from an adjoining kitchen. The stew was grey and sludgy with a few gristly bits of caribou, but it was the first hot food we'd eaten in half a month.

Most of the men were probably off-duty guards. Emílie had

told me how to get the trust of any Gallnach mercenary. Fitting that most would only understand if I spoke in Sverbian.

I stood on a bench and held up a copper coin. "Quarter-sov to whoever tells the best story of killing a Sverb bastard."

Láchlan and a few others chuckled. More people eyed the coin.

"You first, lassie," said a mud-splattered man next to me. He reeked of wet dog. "Give us somethin' to beat."

"Easy." I tapped my neck scar and funnelled my disgust at Parr into my voice. "A Sverb tried to slit my throat for poaching on 'his' land, even though it's my nation's by treaty. So my lover and I gutted the man and his wife while they slept. Then we rolled the bodies onto the floor and fucked in their bed."

A roar of laughter went up. I forced a smirk.

"How 'bout the Ferlander?" the muddy sled driver said. "Looks like a stick's rammed so far up her arse she can pick her teeth."

I translated as Iannah spoke, telling how a Sverbian farmer came to her family's smithy claiming her father cheated him. The farmer got her sister by the hair with a knife to her throat. Twelve-year-old Iannah put an axe in his heart, then used a shovel hot from the forge to cauterize the wound so he stopped bleeding on the floor. She kept her flat Antler expression through the whole story.

The mercenaries raised their drinks in respect. One called to the serving woman, who brought whisky in clay cups. I downed mine to cheers. Iannah added hers to the prize. The men told stories of strangling, drowning, and knifing Sverbian soldiers in Gallun. I gave the prize to Láchlan, who'd burned eight soldiers alive, then used the soot to tattoo himself. He showed us the faded knotwork band around his muscular arm.

Afterward I said, "Cattil must have good stories. I heard she's wanted for war crimes."

"Fíannula ó Brennen, woman of my dreams and nightmares," someone said, rousing a few sniggers.

"Aye, we called her Lady Black in the old country," said a red-haired man. "Reckon she's killed more Sverbs than any of us. Their clerics made us attend rites to get purified or some sheepshit, so Cattil destroyed the stavehall with the clerics inside."

"What'd she do, raze it?" I asked.

"Worse. Smuggled in twenty kegs of blackpowder and blew the place apart. You ever seen blackpowder explode, lass? Fire birthed from the mother of mountains herself."

"She and I lit up a ship loaded with it," said a man with an eye-patch. "Flattened a Sverb navy port. We were too close, didn't realize how big it'd blow. I got a shard of wood in the eye. Cattil's eardrums burst like steppin' on a jellyfish. She says blackpowder explosions are all she can hear now, like six centuries of dead Gallnach howling in triumph."

Iannah's hand found mine under the table. She didn't know what they were saying, but she felt me tremble. I'd seen Rutnaast's stavehall. Shattered windows, charred timbers, a bloody cleric's robe nailed to the door. Cattil's work.

Láchlan showed Iannah and me to a tiny room near the barracks. It was one of the few rooms with a door, but that wasn't much comfort. Rin didn't live underground. We were children of the kinaru, meant for mountaintops and open skies. Down here, everything was dark and smoke-stained. I washed my hair in a basin of murky water and felt no cleaner.

"Nicer than the floor," Iannah said about the thin mattresses filled with musty tundra grass.

I woke repeatedly, feeling like the ground was our ship rolling on the ocean. One time, the dirt *did* shudder. An earthquake. I was still awake when someone rapped on the door. We ate barley porridge in the common room, then Cattil, Láchlan, and their musketmen led us through the tunnels and past a sailcloth curtain.

We stepped into a hall with stone pillars supporting the roof. Six dark-eyed people with runed cuffs clustered together, three male and three female. They were too short to be Aikoto. The moment they saw me, they burst into a stream of unfamiliar words.

"What is this?" I asked Cattil. "Quinil sent me to work with Beru antayul."

She shrugged. "My trading partners pick up lots of people. These came from farther north."

"They're Nuthalha? That's a different confederacy! We don't speak the same language!"

"Exactly. Mother of mountains knows what you'd say to your own people. Quinil trusts you, but I don't."

Bite down. Keep control. Inside, I panicked. Maybe Iollan inscribed the Beru with runes and they didn't survive. Maybe Falwen had lied, and they were never here. Iannah had on her blank Antler look. *Go with it*, that meant.

I could introduce myself, at least. We'd sent emissaries after the Blackbird Battle, affirming shaky peace with neighbouring confederacies. I pushed up my sleeve to show them my kinaru tattoo, then traced where an okorebai band would go, hoping they understood I was in line. "Kateiko," I said, tapping my chest. I said Iannah's name as I tapped her arm, then my heart. Friend, lover. It didn't matter how they took it.

A gaunt Nuthalha woman with short black hair patted her chest. "Uqiat." She looked about twenty, probably in a position of authority, since her elders allowed her to introduce them.

Láchlan pointed at white lines painted on the floor. "Your first task — get 'em to stand on that and control water."

I walked around the rune. It was similar to a design Tiernan had me use, but not exact. Maybe this was the Gallnach way of drawing it. Or those slight alterations changed everything. *Ku* just meant "this" in Aikoto, but *ko* was the basis of everything — the flow of time, blood, and water.

"It's an amp rune, right?" I asked. "Why won't they use it?"

"One did," Cattil said. "She realized it made her stronger and tried to drown us, so we shot her. Now the others act like touching it will kill them."

I closed my eyes, needing a moment to steady myself. "Nuthalha believe in spirit possession. They probably think the rune takes over people's minds and turns them suicidally violent. Didn't Quinil mention that?"

Láchlan translated with a flurry of his hands. Cattil's face flickered with annoyance.

"It's your problem now," she told me. "Suriel needs their magic."

A guard seized a Nuthalha boy around Yironem's age and dragged him kicking toward the rune. Uqiat yelled and tried to pull him back. The boy squirmed, twisting awkwardly to keep his feet off the lines.

"Wait—" I began.

The guard slammed a musket into the boy's skull, knocking him to the floor. Shouts went up from the Nuthalha. The boy screamed as his nose broke under the guard's foot.

"Enough!" Iannah wrenched the guard's musket away and pinned his arms behind him.

A Nuthalha man dashed forward and pressed his sleeve to the boy's bloody nose. I stood over them, daring anyone to get close. Iannah and Cattil stared each other down.

"Here are my terms," Iannah said. "If you harm any captives, Arril's chances of getting me as Nonil are gone."

Cattil folded her arms. "Your Rin friend better get to work, then."

I held out my runed cuff. "Let me demonstrate. They won't cooperate until they believe it's safe."

Cattil and Láchlan's hands flew, debating. He won and unlocked my cuff. My awareness returned with a faint pulse. Uqiat watched through narrowed eyes. I couldn't blame her for distrusting me, someone who could be freed by simply asking.

I sensed a reservoir behind a wall. I could pull water through and it'd drain back out via trenches leading to slits in the wall, never flooding this room unless I unbalanced the cycle. Probably how the Nuthalha woman tried to drown Cattil. I stood with my toes at the edge of the rune. For all I knew, it *would* possess me.

I raised my hand and paced my breathing. Water fell from my palm, a steady stream like when Tiernan measured my control for his research. I stepped forward.

The rune flared. My stream erupted into a torrent, casting glints of runelight everywhere. I'd forgotten amp runes felt so good. I could throw an ice shard into Cattil's heart and raise a water wall to shield myself. It felt like the dead antayul woman stood inside me. If that boy with the broken nose were Yironem, I'd kill every guard here to get him out.

I stumbled off the rune, twitching. Iannah caught me. The light faded. Muddy water gushed into the trenches and flowed into the reservoir.

The Nuthalha whispered among themselves. Uqiat looked skeptical. They watched as I went through experiments I'd done with Tiernan, testing ice and steam on the rune. Iannah stood on it and nothing happened. Eventually a Nuthalha man with crow's feet around his eyes edged forward.

"*Akesida*," he told me, pointing at the rune, then himself.

"What'd he say?" Cattil asked.

"I don't know," I said, but I did.

Young woman. He'd learned some Aikoto in his long life. It wasn't until he was on the rune repeating my tests that it hit me. The dead antayul was his young woman, maybe daughter or niece or granddaughter. He might go on believing she died because runic magic compelled her to attack their captors, just as Emílie believed her father drowned by Folk hands instead of by choice — but he took the risk first so another young Nuthalha didn't have to.

That evening, Iannah and I wandered the maze-like Wolf Den, seeing how far we could go. Brawny men used pickaxes to clear a tunnel that had caved in. Heat lured us to a forge where a sweaty blacksmith hammered a bent shovel back into shape. In the kennels, sled dogs gnawed the reeking remains of a seal and barked when we got close. Guards blocked the route beyond. Iannah guessed it was a second entrance for the sleds.

Down one long tunnel were workshops and storage. Each room was grouped by purpose. Muskets, blackpowder, lead shot. Tools and lumber. Sailcloth, tar pitch, anchor chain links. One room held only bones — caribou and seal mostly, a few from tundra bears, none human. The quartermaster shooed us away from the cellars. By accident, we wound up outside the rune hall. A guard stood by the curtain-door picking his teeth with a knife.

Next morning, an itheran woman waited in the rune hall. She introduced herself as Peimil's acolyte. A red wool pendant looped into the diamond-shaped druidic knot rested on her burlap robes. She took over the experiments, working from papers covered in Gallnach writing, painting runes on the floor for us to test. I demonstrated mindless tasks of water-calling, and the Nuthalha repeated them.

Uqiat and I pulled down our collars to compare antayul tattoos. Instead of a fan-shaped mark, she had a wave pattern, free of rune carvings. In exchange for my and Iannah's whisky rations, a guard told us that Quinil forbade anyone to inscribe captives, not expecting them to survive it. He guessed the acolyte didn't inscribe me because I was too likely to survive. Nothing could get him to talk about Iollan or the Beru.

From then on, we lived a cycle. Barley porridge, water-calling, caribou stew, sleep. An exhausted ache settled in my muscles. We never saw the acolyte or the other antayul outside the rune hall. I tried asking the elderly Nuthalha man where he slept, but Cattil cracked her whip whenever I spoke in Aikoto.

Earthquakes shook the Wolf Den several times a day, raining down dust and pebbles. One morning, a boulder came loose and crushed a rune, sending sparks everywhere. The acolyte gave some explanation about geological faults. Uqiat only said one word. *Marmar*.

Every sacred animal on the coast was related to water. Aikoto territory had kinaru, huge waterfowl that dominated the skies, so we used to revere tel-saidu. Nuthalha revered edim-saidu, the earth spirits, because here in their land, giant otter-like creatures roamed the tundra. I'd seen enough not to question the existence of the marmar, though I doubted we could feel them stomping about this far underground.

The tracking stone's tug in my arm faded. Our scouts had finished their spying and left Innisbán, hopefully to return in a few weeks with our rescue.

We spent longer in the rune hall each day. Cattil, seeming bored, stopped coming. Láchlan joked with the guards and winked at

Iannah, earning a roll of her eyes. When the middle-aged Nuthalha man spent too long on a rune and passed out, Láchlan sent for the medic. I helped get the man's shirt off to check him over and found white scars crossing his back like scattered hay. Later I saw Láchlan argue with the acolyte.

Cattil, her mercenaries, and the serving woman were the only people we saw in the common room. Láchlan was always at Cattil's side during meals, their hands flickering in conversation. They didn't seem like family or lovers. He only touched her to get her attention.

"How'd you wind up with Cattil?" I asked him one evening as we left the rune hall.

Láchlan shrugged. "I was seventeen, a Gallnach raised in Sverba, about to be hung for arson. Fíannula swapped a cask of brånnvin for my life. She needed someone to be her ears. Said I smelled less like sheepshit than other street rats did."

"Just arson?" Iannah asked.

"Thinking of this?" He chuckled and pushed up his sleeve to show his knotwork tattoo. "Aye, that's soot from a Sverbian fort in my arm. Wasn't no one in it, though. Fíannula's the only sailor whose stories are all true."

"So you're here to repay Cattil?" I said. "I mean, this place is . . ."

"Godsawful, I know. We're meant to go in the dirt *after* we die." He glanced at me. "I can guess why you're here."

My stomach dropped into the earth.

"Quinil sent you to look after the water mages, right? You're too sane to be Suriel's fanatic. But Peimil, Arril, they keep pushin' for this rune stuff to work, and it's gonna come down on somebody."

At dinner a few days later, the quartermaster hauled in a sled driver and spoke to Cattil. Her laughter died. She set down her whisky and shrugged off her leather jerkin, revealing a sleeveless shirt. Láchlan addressed the room in Gallnach. Looking resigned, he stripped the sled driver to his tattooed chest and bound the man's hands to an iron support post. Mercenaries shoved the tables back.

"What happened?" I murmured.

The sailor next to me shook his head. "Dumb bastard. He went topside to hunt and kept some game. We're all on rations, even Lady Black."

Cattil uncoiled her whip and rolled her shoulders. Her history was written on her sun-starved skin. Speckled scars from black-powder explosions, shiny twisted skin on her wrist where she burned away the smuggler brand, raised white lines on the bit of her back that was visible. Arril had whipped her for the Rutnaast massacre. Suddenly I knew what the Nuthalha man's scars were.

Cattil circled the sled driver. She flicked her golden braid aside. Silence pressed down.

Her whip cracked. The sled driver groaned. Blood ran from the deep cut across his back. Iannah held my elbow, knowing me too well.

Crack. The man's spine twisted. *Crack.* He sagged to his knees, held upright by his bound hands. Glistening red streaks laced his back.

"*Saigh sa,*" Cattil snarled. Her skirt whirled with every blow. "*Saigh sa. Saigh sa!*"

"'Get up,' she says," muttered the sailor next to me.

Cattil yelled something else, making everyone flinch. I looked to the nearby sailor.

"She's taunting him," he whispered. "Said 'Gallnach bleed on our feet.'"

Crack. The man's screams didn't sound human. Cattil couldn't hear them. Sled dogs yowled from the kennels, smelling blood.

Iannah opened the door to our room — and thrust out an arm to stop me. A figure stood in shadow inside. She kicked the person's legs and had them face down in the dirt before I was through the doorway.

"Why are you here?" Iannah said through gritted teeth.

I held up our whale-oil lantern. The girl's skin was so tight over her cheekbones I hardly recognized her. "*Ilani?*"

"I had to see you," Ilani gasped.

"And do what? Beat the shit out of me like you did my brother?"

"Mako — they have Makoril—"

My insides wrenched. I shut the door. "Let her go, Ia."

Iannah took her knee off Ilani's back. "She's the Iyo who got exiled up here?"

"Who are you to ask?" Ilani snapped.

"Iannah's a friend," I said. "Just tell us what happened. And be quiet, for aeldu's sake. You want Cattil to find you?"

Ilani slumped against the wall. Her hair was stringy, her cloak and leggings torn. "Makoril, Ganiam, and I joined up with a family of Nuthalha seal hunters. Itherans attacked our camp two months ago. They sold us to Cattil's men, who brought us here and took the antayul away. I haven't seen Mako since, but we cook rations for fifteen more prisoners than we get locked up with."

Six Nuthalha, one Iyo, and the eight missing Beru. All still alive. I let out a slow breath. "How'd you know I was here?"

"I've been watching from the kitchen, wondering whose side you're on. I still don't know, but after that whipping . . ." Ilani grimaced. "I bribed a guard to let me into your room. Don't ask what I did for him."

"How much of this place have you seen?"

"Barely any, but Ganiam's done repairs all over." Ilani dragged her fingernail through the dirt, drawing three squares in a V formation. "This left square's the living area. Barracks, kitchen, common room, and the forge to keep it warm. Our cells are beyond the kennels. No one can sneak in or out, because the dogs bark when anyone passes. The middle square is workshops and storage. It has ladders to the surface to move supplies up and down. The right square's where the antayul got taken, but the route there is . . . gone. Solid dirt."

I peered at the map. The design seemed familiar. I was missing something. I marked the centre where the rune hall would be — then it clicked. *Dirt*. I laughed at the simplicity.

"Druidism has everything in fours. Four sacred days in the year, four directions, four elements." I drew another square, turning the V into a diamond. "Look at it sideways, like a compass where the kitchen and forge are in the south. They heat the fire quarter, the east air quarter connects to the surface, and the antayul are held in the north water quarter. That leaves earth in the west. There's another section behind the rune hall. *That's* where Iollan is."

Iannah began marking curved lines for tunnels. "Explains the bizarre layout. This entire damned place is a druidic knot."

I sat back on my heels. "Ilani, if you learned about itheran religions instead of attacking people who do, you'd have figured it out."

She scowled. "Then why's no one seen that section?"

"Iollan's an edimyul, remember. He can make tunnels anywhere. I bet that causes the earthquakes. The earth and water sections are only open long enough to move people in and out. Iollan probably does experiments with Makoril and the Beru there while I got the group I can't talk to."

"So how do we reach the antayul?"

I hesitated. Cattil could've sent her to pry secrets from us, but Ilani was the last person who'd side with itherans. Airedain had once trusted her enough to sleep with her. "We can't yet," I said. "Pretty soon Aikoto warriors and Ingdanrad mages will break this place open."

Ilani's eyebrows shot up. "How soon?"

"I don't know exactly. Half a month at most."

She stared at me. Her face had always been thin, but now her eyes looked too big. "You haven't seen the cellars. They're empty. Cattil's ships haven't been getting through."

I stared back.

Iannah ran a hand over her dusty hair. "How long do we have?"

"Half a month of barley, less of meat. These itherans are useless at hunting in deep snow. The sled dogs were stolen from Nuthalha, you know. At this rate, they'll either eat us or the dogs."

"Kaid," I swore, sinking onto my mattress.

"Hold on," Iannah said. "Cattil can't kill the antayul. They're too valuable to Suriel. How many other captives are there?"

"Seven," Ilani said. "Ganiam, me, the Sverbian serving woman, and four Nuthalha."

"Killing seven captives won't stretch forty Gallnach's rations much. You're more useful alive. You can hunt." Iannah cracked her knuckles. "I'll either talk sense into Cattil or beat it in."

I flashed her a grateful smile. To Ilani, I said, "You have to keep quiet. If you see any Aikoto outside, attuned or not, don't acknowledge them. They *will* find us."

"So I do nothing? Just wait for my friends to die in this filthy pit?"

"We won't let that happen." I tossed her my linen fireweed. "There's your proof. I have an Iyo lover, so I have to protect his jouyen."

Ilani uncrumpled the fabric and froze, recognizing the sewn-on arrowhead leaves as Airedain's crest. She nodded, dropped the fireweed in my lap, and left.

"You didn't tell her Cattil already shot an antayul," I said.

"She'll find out soon enough," Iannah said.

22.

ESCAPE

The amp runes heightened my awareness as well as my strength. Now that I knew to look, I sensed empty spaces beyond the rune hall, lower water density where frozen dirt gave way to dry air. Two sealed tunnels led to what must be the earth and water quarters. Earthquakes had damaged the walls so badly I'd never noticed the tunnels' rough seals.

Ilani, the other hunters, and their guard returned a few days later with a fresh-killed walrus and left again. That night, I woke sweating from my dreams. The tracking stone tugged in my arm. Our rescue was close.

We were eating when warning runes flared on the ceiling. I threw an arm over my eyes, squinting. When I lowered it, Cattil and Láchlan were on their feet giving orders. Men ran to lock down the entrances. The blacksmith hustled in with boxes of musketshot.

Mercenaries downed their whisky and started measuring black-powder into paper cartridges.

Cattil, skirt swishing, snapped her fingers at the man with the eyepatch. "Deal with them," she said, pointing at Iannah and me.

"We can help," I said. "We'll fight."

"On whose side?" she retorted.

Iannah let the man bind her wrists. I grudgingly followed. He put my runed cuff on, tied us to iron support posts, hauled the Sverbian serving woman from the kitchen, and bound her, too. Cattil and her men dispersed, leaving the common room empty except for we three captives.

I tried undoing the rope around my wrists, but couldn't get my fingers in the right place. I tried shifting my hands into paws so they'd be small enough to get free, but couldn't focus with the cuff numbing my mind and an itheran stranger watching. The itch of attuning prickled all over my body. With my arms behind me, shifting fully into a wolf would dislocate my shoulders.

Underground, the only measure of time was the dimming fire. Sled dogs bayed. Tremors shook the Wolf Den, loosing dust that sent us coughing. One distant rumble made dishes rattle on the tables. The tracking stone throbbed, then stung, pulling toward the hearth.

Rustles came down the chimney. A black-feathered ball hurtled out over the coals and shifted in midair. Fendul landed on his feet, streaked with soot. I laughed in disbelief. A falcon shot out, then a waxwing, shifting into Orelein and Aliko. Of course Aliko would follow Fendul. The Sverbian woman gawked.

"Kako," Fendul said. "Thank the aeldu."

They untied us, a tangle of chatter, talking over each other. I hugged Fendul, feeling the chill of outdoors on his bulky furs. He and Iannah greeted each other with nods.

"Where's everyone else?" I asked, stretching my stiff joints.

Fendul grimaced. "Bad news. Suriel sent a blizzard at Ingdanrad as their mages sailed out. Two of four ships sank. We found this place easily enough" — he lifted his crow amulet with the second tracking stone looped onto its cord — "but we counted on more help getting past Iollan's defenses. He has fire that burns on snow, powder that chokes people, things I've never seen. Airedain and Dunehein are with our army trying to break through. Nili's hunting Corvittai scouts."

Aliko sniffed her sleeve and wrinkled her nose. "We found a hole in the ground and went for it."

"That's burnt dung you smell," said the Sverbian. She peered into the kitchen. "No weapons. They took the knives."

Iannah beckoned. "We'll make do." She led us into a tunnel, checking for guards.

In the smithy, she found a pair of long-handled clamps and cut through my cuff with a wrench of metal. Sparks showered from the runes. I'd never been so glad she was a blacksmith's daughter. I tucked the clamps and a hammer into my belt, the Sverbian took a wrench, and Iannah took a thick iron chain.

"We don't have a hope of catching Iollan ourselves," I said, "but we can free the captives. Ia, check the cells in case Ilani's back. Fen, go with her since you and I can track each other. We'll get the antayul."

Too late I remembered I wasn't meant to command my oko-rebai, but Fendul was already leaving. The Sverbian followed me. We grabbed shovels from an abandoned cave-in and headed for the rune hall. Aliko's javelin downed the guard before he could fire his musket. Orelein finished him with two arrows in the chest.

Inside, I showed them the sealed route to the water quarter. The dirt barrier crumbled under our onslaught. Runelight blazed on the ceiling all the way down a winding tunnel, into a wide room where Uqiat stared out from behind iron bars. A runed cuff hung from her bony wrist. Haggard faces loomed behind her.

Four slouching guards jerked up and raised their muskets. I formed an ice wall just as loud bangs tore through the room. My ice shattered. Aliko staggered. Orelein's arrow thudded into a guard's shoulder.

"Hold!" one guard said. "It's the Rin lass."

"We don't have to fight," I said breathlessly. "Let the antayul go."

"Not happening," another scoffed, loading his next shot.

"An army's coming! Is Peimil worth dying for? Is *Cattil*?"

An earthquake rocked the room. The cell bars groaned. Rocks slammed down, cracking the ground. The guards exchanged looks, then ran down a side tunnel.

The furs were turning red on Aliko's thigh. Coughing from musket smoke, I used her hunting knife to cut her snow trousers and leggings away. Blood flowed from a round hole.

"Let me," the Sverbian said, taking the bogmoss from my herb pouch. "Free your mages."

I counted faces in the cell. Uqiat and the five other Nuthalha I'd worked with, eight Beru with whale tattoos on their neck, and Makoril. Everyone was here.

"Kateiko Rin," Makoril said in his soft voice. Dusty black hair hung in his eyes. "Last time we met, you cut me up something good. Now you're rescuing us?"

"We don't have to," Orelein said acidly, standing watch with an arrow nocked.

I ignored them. The bars had no lock, no handle, just smooth metal. Glowing lines webbed across them. I reached out.

"Don't!" a Beru woman cried.

I yanked my hand back. Heat radiated off the bars. "How do these open?"

233

"Magic," said a voice behind us.

I spun. An itheran stepped out of the tunnel we'd come from, his hands raised. Every bit of him was filthy, like he'd burrowed nose-first from the surface. Ash flaked off his scorched furs. Behind him followed another burnt, dirty figure, looking backward to guard their rear. Bloody daggers in hand, hair spiked into a rumpled warrior's crest.

Airedain turned. He saw the cell, his face twisting in disgust. Then he saw me. He shoved past the others and kissed me so hard my tooth went through my lip. He smelled like smoke. As quick as we collided, he pulled away again.

"What happened?" I asked, wiping blood from my mouth.

He scoured the room, thrumming with tension. "We were with the vanguard. Got past runed doors into a tunnel, thought our mages broke all the wards, then the whole place blew. Flames everywhere. *People* everywhere, bits of 'em."

A lump rose in my throat. "Cattil. Blackpowder."

"Your Ferish friend sent us to help you," the itheran said, examining the cell. He tapped a bar. His mitten sizzled. "Wish I was a fire mage. This will hurt."

"What are you?"

"A metallurgist. Stand back."

He wrapped his hands around two bars. Glowing orange shot through the metal, then sideways through the crossbars. The musty smell of burning leather filled the room, followed by the stench of seared flesh. A grunt tore through his clenched teeth. The webbed lines swelled and burst, spitting out molten iron.

The metallurgist stumbled backward, cursing violently in Sverbian. The bars melted like wax and clumped on the floor. Orelein gave a low whistle.

Uqiat helped older antayul over the smoking sludge. I sliced through their cuffs with the clamps, nicking a few wrists in my haste. They were in no shape to fight, starving and exhausted, but they might not have a choice. The Sverbian finished bandaging Aliko's leg with scraps of her dress. I heaved Aliko up and swung her arm over my shoulders. Airedain led us back down the tunnel, spinning his daggers.

"Where's Ilani and Ganiam?" Makoril asked.

"Fendul's looking," I said. "If they're not here, they're hunting. Probably safer than us."

In the rune hall, a sooty itheran pressed her palm to the seal over the tunnel to the earth quarter. The dirt bowed, then sprang back into place. "It's like sawing a tree with my fingernails," she told us. "The island's working against us. It's not earth spirits, either. They're dormant here."

"This room's the centre of a druidic knot," I said. "Does that matter?"

She rounded on me, speechless.

"*Någvakt bøkkhem,*" the metallurgist swore. "Druidic knots were the earliest form of runic magic. This whole complex is under och Cormic's control. That brilliant, godsforsaken Gall."

I swallowed my panic. "So you can't reach him?"

"Not the easy way." The earth mage grabbed a shovel.

The metallurgist looked at his palms, red and peeling under the holes in his mittens. He groaned. "Och Cormic's our mess to clean up. Get out while you can."

The rest of us were hurrying down the long tunnel to the air quarter when a quake struck. Aliko and I toppled over. My teeth vibrated. Uqiat jerked her leg aside just in time to avoid a falling boulder.

"Run!" I cried.

Orelein scooped Aliko up. Antayul grabbed their elders. We bolted. The roof collapsed behind us, billowing dust. When I looked back, the way was blocked by a jumble of rock sparking with broken runes.

I followed the tracking stone's insistent tug through the storage maze. The cellars were empty like Ilani said, only a few sacks of barley left, as well as the quartermaster, whose guts spilled on the floor. The Sverbian gave him a contemptuous two-hand salute. I'd seen his hands on her when Cattil wasn't around.

In a cramped tunnel, Fendul cut down a mercenary. Iannah had her chain around a man's neck. He scrabbled, his face purpling. She wrenched it tighter until he slumped. Airedain shoved his daggers into another man's chest and pulled them out with a spray of blood.

"No sign of the other captives," Fendul said, wiping his sword on a mercenary's woolwrap.

Makoril grabbed my wrist. "You sure they're hunting?"

Airedain slammed him into a wall. "I don't care how long you've been trapped down here. Don't ever touch Kateiko again."

I pulled Airedain away. Fendul frowned. He'd seen it, too, a shadow in Airedain's eyes.

Iannah waved everyone into a storage room. Furs were piled on the ground. We sorted through coats, trousers, mittens, pulling on whatever fit. Orelein eased Aliko down onto a cape of white tundra bear. Uqiat made sure all the Nuthalha were dressed before finding clothes for herself.

"There's a ladder two rooms over," Fendul said. "Someone needs to climb up and make sure the surface is safe."

"I'll go," I said. "Maybe I can talk any guards out of fighting."

He nodded. "Take Airedain. You might need a translator. And hurry. I'm not sure how long we can defend a room without a door."

Airedain and I crept back into the tunnel. The man Iannah had choked twitched on the ground, unconscious. Her motto was *Stab as few people as possible.*

I raised my hammer, then lowered it. He was the guard we'd bribed with whisky. "He helped us. I know his name." And his voice, which meant I'd hear him forever. "I can't do it."

Airedain scraped his daggers together. "I can."

I held his arm. "Leave this one. Please."

"He ain't innocent, Rin-girl. They had our people in fucking cages. Have you been in prison? 'Cause I have—"

"I know. But right now, he's not the one scaring me. *You* are."

He flinched. The shadow didn't fully lift from his eyes, but he let a few Beru tie the man up while we went to the room Fendul mentioned. A rope ladder rose into darkness beyond reach of the warning runelight. Dry tundra grass crunched under our boots. The mercenaries must've pitched it down to use as fuel and bedding.

I started climbing, swinging in the stillness. The ladder pulled as Airedain grabbed on below. Dirt closed in, narrowing until my elbows bumped the walls. *Imagine it's a hollow log*, I told myself.

My head thumped on something solid. I reached up and pushed. A trap door swung open, showering me with ice. Turquoise light flooded in. I climbed another rung, breaking free of the Wolf Den. My nostrils crackled in the sudden frost.

Snow spread around me, rising and falling in ridges, dyed by shimmering veils across the night sky. The streaked bands looked like glowing silhouettes of forested mountains, backed by green darker than stormy seas. They rustled in the silence.

"What do you see?" Airedain said, hanging below me.

"The house of the dead." Or the aurora, as itherans called it.

I hauled myself up. Someone had shovelled a wide circle around the trapdoor, pushing the snow into a steep bank. In the other direction was an abandoned dogsled. Bodies lay draped on top. I edged close and rolled one over.

Ganiam's eyes stared up through a layer of ice. I pulled back another hood. A round-cheeked Nuthalha woman, throat slashed. I moved her arm and found Ilani's windburnt face.

"Nei," I said. "Nei, nei, nei . . ."

Airedain swore. He shifted into his coyote body, sniffed the air, and bounded up the snowbank.

Iannah's training prickled my skull. *Think*. Their furs were bloody. The snow wasn't. They'd been killed somewhere else and left here. *Why?*

I raised my mittens to the light. Glittering blackpowder dusted the furs.

A trap.

Airedain howled. Muskets boomed. A mercenary crawled out from behind the snowbank, flailing at the coyote tearing at his throat. I shrieked.

"Get back!" came a distant shout.

I ran. A grizzly bear plowed toward me, churning up clouds of snow. Its left ear was gone. Dunehein. Riding on his back was a man whose face I'd never forget. *Tiernan*.

The world exploded. Searing air flung me forward. Blinding orange light flickered into darkness.

I woke face down in a swamp of melted snow and mud. My head throbbed. Smoke clogged my lungs. A severed arm oozed into the muck nearby. I coughed mud, then started throwing up. The rotten grass under me blurred.

A musket barrel flashed. The riderless grizzly roared. My ears rang too loud to hear. Dunehein swatted his attacker with massive claws, shredding the man's coat. The sled was gone. So was the snowbank.

I scrambled up, searching for Airedain. Instead I saw Cattil, golden braid swinging, dressed hood-to-boot in white caribou furs.

No one would've seen her hiding in the snow. Now she stood out like ghostblossom against the blackened tundra.

Cattil stepped on someone's neck. Someone with damp brown hair, clutching a dagger. She put a musket to his head and fired.

I felt myself scream. Cattil wiped blood off her face and loaded another shot. She looked up, saw me, and aimed.

A falcon flew at me. Orelein had come up from below. I dropped into my wolf body and bolted. Every time I tried turning to go after the others, Orelein raked his talons across my hide. I howled in pain and rage. He screeched back, driving me away from the battle. Dunehein charged after us.

Scorched grass gave way to snow. I stumbled over the frozen surface, my paws barely leaving dents. The shivering turquoise light made my stomach wrench with nausea.

The burnt odour of blackpowder faded, replaced by seaweed and wet dog. A sled pursued us. I arced away from it. Orelein swooped, steering me back straight. I crested a ridge and realized his plan. An ocean channel stretched out to either side. The dog-sled couldn't cross it.

Neither could I, like this. I shifted to human and collapsed. I felt cold, so cold. Orelein banked back around. Dunehein caught up a moment later, sides heaving, tongue lolling.

"I can't," I panted. My voice sounded like I'd spoken into a bottle. At least my hearing was returning. "I can't even see straight. I'll drown."

Dunehein crouched low and nudged me with his snout. I climbed on his back, clinging to his singed fur. He slid onto greenish ice bordering the channel. It bowed under his weight. His nose twitched, ear turned.

He growled and backed onto land.

An enormous shape darted underwater. It was too early for whales to migrate north, but Uqiat said there were marmar here. When I was a child, Dunehein had told me stories, pointing at otters and telling me to imagine ones that drank ponds in a single gulp.

Faintly, I heard barking. The sled skidded to a stop. A musket boomed. Lead shot streaked past my hood, ruffling the fur trim. Out in the channel, an iceberg cracked.

An idea struck me. I thrust my mind out and lashed at the iceberg. A chunk split off and plummeted into the channel. Nearby, the marmar surfaced with an upward rush of water. It glared at us, twitching its whiskers. It would've been cute if I knew it wouldn't swallow me whole.

The sled driver gaped. The mercenary riding with him rammed a cartridge into his musket, aimed at the marmar's head, and fired.

The marmar roared. Its reeking breath rolled over us. It crashed onto the ice, grabbed the mercenary in its jaws, and flung him into the water.

"Yan taku," I said.

Like a surging mountain, the marmar bounded onto shore. Seaweed trailed off its brown pelt. Its dripping body stretched on and on into a sleek tail that thrashed the air. It sniffed Dunehein and cocked its head. He kept still. I stared up at its round black eyes and raised my hands.

The marmar swung back to the sled. The dogs howled, yanking at their ganglines. The marmar snarled. The dogs whined and hunkered down.

"Call off your monster!" the driver shouted.

"It's smart!" I shouted back. "Drop your weapon!"

He tossed his musket aside. The marmar slammed down a paw, crumpling the barrel.

Another dogsled pulled up, spraying snow. Cattil jumped off. Wisely, she left her musket. Láchlan stayed on, ready to drive away.

For the first time since landing on Innisbán, I had the chance to kill Cattil and survive. I sat astride a growling grizzly with a falcon circling overhead and an impossibly large otter pacing around us. My runed cuff was gone, and I had the ocean behind me. I could do what Falwen sent me to do.

"Kateiko Rin," Cattil called. Her swagger was chipped. "This doesn't have to end badly for you."

"You tried to blow me up! By *baiting* me with murdered Iyo!"

"I can't let you leave. You know too much." She held out a mittened hand as if for me to take it. "If you're as devoted to Suriel as you claim, you'll come back."

Thoughts flickered in and out with the aurora. Iannah would say to take a strategic approach, but I couldn't think. Airedain might be dead. Ilani was. Tiernan — I had no idea.

The sled driver slunk backward. I recognized him as the one Cattil whipped for stealing food. She ignored him, her eyes darting from Dunehein to the marmar. The driver circled, creeping up behind her.

Láchlan saw. He stayed intensely still. It was too quiet to hear with my ringing ears, but I could imagine the man's boots crunching on the snow, his shallow breath, the rasp as he drew a knife. Cattil couldn't hear it, either.

The sled driver grabbed her jaw. His knife whipped up and sliced her throat open.

Her eyes flew wide. She clutched her gushing neck. He shoved her into the snow. She thrashed, her furs turning red.

"*Saigh sa,*" he spat. I knew the rest. *Gallnach bleed on our feet. Get up. Get up!*

Cattil's face twisted. She grabbed at his ankle. He stomped on her wrist. Blood bloomed around her, then she stilled.

The marmar ran a huge pink tongue across her. It snorted in disgust. Blackpowder residue, I realized. It curled around and leapt into the ocean with a colossal splash. Its silhouette slithered away up the channel.

Láchlan closed Cattil's eyes and fished a keyring from her pocket. "So ends Fíannula ó Brennen, Lady Black. I called her friend and lover once. Not sure if she changed or I did."

The sled driver wavered. Waiting.

"As the new Cattil, I reckon I owe you an apology," Láchlan told him. "A guard admitted you were smuggling food to our captives. Bloody brave to try under Fíannula's nose. Worthy of my new first mate."

The man dropped to his knees, too relieved to speak.

Láchlan turned to me, swinging the keys. "We don't have much time, lass, and it don't look good. This invasion was lost afore it started. You know what happens if they get near Peimil?"

I shook my head.

"He'll cave in every bit of the Wolf Den 'cept where he is. Your people and mine will be crushed under ten thousand tons of rock. Those water mages you came here to protect will die. My brothers from the old country will die. This whole godsforsaken island will be a mass grave."

My throat felt tight. Fendul and Iannah were still down there with Aliko, Makoril, and the rest. The metallurgist and earth mage were digging toward everyone's deaths. "So what do we do?"

"Declare a ceasefire. Call off our soldiers."

"If you free the antayul."

Láchlan chuckled dryly. "Sorry. Arril would throw me outta the Corvittai, and mother of mountains knows who she'd replace me with. But I'll protect 'em from Peimil best I can."

I slid off Dunehein's back. He rose onto his hind legs and returned to human, still a head taller than me. Orelein dropped from the sky, shifted, and landed on my other side. We faced Láchlan and his first mate over Cattil's body.

"I can't make that decision," I said. "Let me take you to the Okorebai-Rin."

"With respect, I've never met him," Láchlan said. "And if he led this invasion, I ain't keen on dealing with him. No, lass, it's gotta be you, and now."

"I don't have that authority."

Dunehein gripped my shoulder. "Only you know what it's like down there, Kako. Fendul trusts you."

Even when I didn't trust myself. I looked at Orelein, desperate.

"Nili trusts you, too," he said.

That ruled him out. He loved Nili enough to follow her blindly.

I lifted my eyes to the iridescent sky. In the rainforest, the house of the dead was a place of safety for our aeldu. Gallnach buried their dead where druids could guide them home at Bódhain. This wasn't home to any of us. We weren't meant to die here.

I pulled the hammer from my belt and tossed it in the bloody snow. "Call off your men."

23.

GOING HOME

I didn't remember how I got to the runed doors in the valley. I only recalled flashes of what happened there — me shouting at the first Aikoto I saw to fall back, Láchlan carrying Cattil's body, Dunehein's face as he repeated my name. Later, he'd tell me I was shivering and slurring too much to be understood. The Okoreni-Beru, Fendul's second-in-command on this mission, ordered that I be brought to the healers. I went on Dunehein's promise that he'd find Airedain.

Below deck on an anchored ship, an Ingdanrad medic flitted in and out of view, snapping Sverbian words I barely understood. *Concussion, smoke inhalation, hypothermia.* The explosion had scorched holes in my furs. The back of my body was a mess of burns, frostbite, splinters, and cuts from Orelein's talons. My braid only survived because it'd been tucked in my hood. I was given hot broth, a blanket, and willowcloak for the pain. The warriors being carried in needed more help.

Dazed, I lay on my stomach, my cheek pressed to rough timber. Turquoise light filtered through a porthole. Through the constant ringing, I heard voices, creaking wood, gentle waves. Images rippled through my mind. Ganiam's frozen eyes. Cattil's mittens clutching her throat. The dark-haired man bleeding from a hole in his skull.

Grief struck like the explosion all over again. I couldn't cry. Instead, I curled up gasping, ignoring the dull throb everywhere. Maybe it was all a hallucination. Some magic Iollan created to drive attackers into insanity. "He's not dead," I muttered. "He's not dead."

An Iyo woman with a bandaged stump for a leg touched my shuddering ribs. A grey braid draped over her shoulder. If I let my eyes unfocus, she looked like Isu. "Who's not dead?" she rasped.

"Airedain. Airedain Iyo."

"Ah — you're his Rin-girl. I helped with his warrior training." She smiled faintly. "No one's dead until you see the body, *akesida*."

I pressed my linen fireweed and arrowhead leaves to my mouth. *Together when we're not.*

The Iyo woman was asleep when I heard a familiar voice. "Where is she? Where's Kateiko?"

I tried to roll over and yelped. Airedain shoved past healers, snapping his head back and forth until he saw me. He dropped to his knees and reached for my face, then hooked his hand around his neck like it'd taken a detour.

"You're alive," he said. "You're really alive."

I half-laughed, half-sobbed. His hair was burnt away on one side, but there was no hole in his skull. "You . . . I saw Cattil shoot someone in the head."

"A Beru warrior. I got knocked out by the explosion, so Cattil figured I was dead already." Airedain pulled a bloody splinter from his arm and crushed it with his boot. "Fucking psychotic, that

245

woman. How do we get Ilani and Ganiam home? How do we bury someone in pieces?"

"At least the Rin all survived," Dunehein said, coming over. "Guess the aeldu decided we were due for a break."

"How'd you find us so fast?" I asked him.

"We were already coming. A scout sent us to deal with the trap. Gotta say, never expected to let an itheran ride me, but . . . I know what Tiernan was to you, and it was the fastest way to get there. We woulda been too late except for your Iyo-boy here. The Corvittai were about to light it up when he started tearing their throats out."

"Too late? They *did* light it up."

Dunehein tugged on his singed braid. "There's something you'd better see."

He helped me up. I draped my blanket over myself like a shawl and waited for Airedain, but he didn't move.

"Ain't my place to be there," he said.

Confused and annoyed about getting separated, I followed Dunehein around canvas hammocks of groaning warriors. A Nuthalha man with bandaged eyes was likely blind. Aliko waved, her leg propped on a box. Orelein held a mage down while a healer dug musketshot from the mage's shoulder. An itheran woman sat in the centre of it all, glowing orange, heating the room.

In a hammock at the far end was Tiernan. He lay still, his eyes closed. Sooty skin peeled off his face. I sank down next to him. "Is he . . ."

"Sedated." Janekke, the surgeon, stepped over. "While he recovers."

"Tiernan deflected the explosion," Dunehein said. "You'd be dead otherwise, little cousin."

I shook my head. "He's not *that* strong a jinrayul."

"He is now." Janekke pulled back his blanket.

His jerkin and tunic had been cut open. Jagged scars radiated from the centre of his pale chest. The blistered skin around them was shot through with black veins.

"Oh, Tiernan," I murmured.

Janekke sighed, straightening her apron. "It's the amp rune och Cormic designed for him. Heilind carved it on himself before we set sail. He said we'd need every advantage we could get. I think he feels responsible for not realizing what och Cormic would become."

"What will it do to him?"

"Truthfully? We don't know." She replaced the blanket and left to attend someone else.

I touched his cheek. He was cold. "Did he know it was me at the sled?"

Dunehein shrugged.

My fingertips lingered on Tiernan's face. It'd be so easy to brush his hair aside, to cup his bearded jaw. But he'd never been mine to touch that way.

A delicate gold chain looped around his neck, half-hidden in the folds of his tunic. I tugged on it and found a ring attached like a pendant. I knew the etched knotwork. Marijka's wedding ring.

"What's this pattern mean?" I asked a passing woman in a woolwrap.

She bent close to see. "I couldn't tell you. It looks Gallnach, but it's nothing I recognize."

One more secret he only trusted Marijka with. It didn't bother me like it used to. I kissed his burnt forehead. "Thank you," I whispered.

Dunehein left me alone with Airedain. I managed to sit upright by leaning on him so my injured back didn't touch anything. We shared a flask of whisky someone had found in the Wolf Den. It burned my split lip, but numbness would kick in soon enough.

"So . . ." Airedain ventured.

I'd spent a month thinking about what to say when we reunited, kneading my sentences like dough. Now they fell apart in my hands. I just showed him my fireweed and arrowhead leaves — filthy, wrinkled, but together. He smiled, though the shadow still lingered in his eyes.

"I'm sorry," he said.

"What for?"

He touched my lip. "Of all your wounds, I keep thinkin', I caused this one. After promising to never hurt you."

"Oh, Aire." I leaned my head on his shoulder. "Things are different in battle."

"Maybe. Maybe not." He ran his tongue over his teeth, shuddered, and took a swig of whisky. "I still taste human blood. Part of those itherans' spirits is in me now. I don't regret killing 'em to save you and avenge my people, but there's a stain on my coyote body that ain't ever gonna come out."

Through my haze came a word — *bjørnbattai*, legendary Sverbian warriors who shapeshifted into bears and went mad with bloodlust. Today I'd seen Airedain on the edge of something dark. But after everything that happened on this island, I understood.

I kissed him gently, accepting my split lip and the blood in his mouth. There was an odd solace in having survived together. I'd never find the right words to describe this day, but with Airedain, I wouldn't have to.

Nili and Yironem came below deck, shivering and slumped with exhaustion. Yironem had flown around Innisbán carrying Nili to find the dead and injured. His toes were tinged with frostbite from landing in the snow. I heated a bucket of water to warm his feet, and we huddled together in a blanket nest.

Fendul and Iannah returned before dawn. The leaders of every group, including the Nuthalha who'd joined the invasion in search of their missing seal hunters, had agreed on terms. The Beru and Nuthalha could each choose one person to live in the Wolf Den, look after their antayul, and act on behalf of their people. In exchange, the Aikoto and Nuthalha confederacies would provide food. Makoril and the Sverbian had been released to appease the Iyo-jouyen and Ingdanrad.

"Are you mad at me?" I asked Fendul quietly.

He squeezed my hand. "No. I would've made the same decision." Then he admitted, "Ingdanrad's mages are livid. They would've let their own soldiers die to put Iollan's head on a stake. But I won't let them touch you."

At least Janekke wasn't angry. She cut the tracking stone from my arm and sealed my skin. Yironem got the matched stone from Fendul and used one to drag the other across the floor. If they got too close, they snapped together. *Clack*. He pulled them apart and dragged one again. *Clack*.

When daylight came, Iannah and I braved the cold to meet Láchlan on the tundra. Snow billowed past in sheets. He promised to boil ale next Bódhain to feed our dead. We exchanged a Gallnach peace gesture, gripping each other's forearms, then returned to our tiny fleet.

Ingdanrad's ships were four-masted galleons, slower and bigger than the Corvittai schooner we arrived on, but cramped with so many people. Healers tripped over the wounded in the crew quarters. The dead were preserved on ice and laid in the captain's quarters. The galley stove blazed, heating broth that got devoured as fast as it was made. We shuffled around to put Rin on each ship as a safeguard against Suriel. My family, friends, and I went on the one Tiernan wasn't on.

As we prepared to set sail, Nili left our quarters below deck and didn't return. I found her on deck, puking over the bulwark. "You okay?" I asked.

She wiped her mouth on her fur sleeve. "Yeah. I'm used to it."

"What, seasickness? We're still anchored."

Nili, who always had at least two ways to say everything, hesitated. "You probably wondered why I went chasing Corvittai scouts instead of rescuing you."

I leaned on the bulwark. "Sort of, yeah. You promised you'd be here."

"Then I promised our tema I'd avoid the battle. Because . . . well . . . I have someone else to protect now."

"Who?"

She tapped her stomach. "It's Orelein's. Surprise."

My eyes widened. "Nili — do you *want* this?"

"I guess I don't mind?" She retched and spat into the ocean. "The Rin blather so much about rebuilding the jouyen, I decided to skip taking bloodweed and see what happened. Ore agreed to it."

"So he knows."

Nili nodded. "He promised to help raise the kid no matter what happens between us. I've seen him with his woodworking apprentices. He'll be a good temal."

I hugged her. It was the only thing to do.

When we separated, I said, "Aeldu save us. Everything's going to change."

She rested her chin in her hand. "I think . . . I'm okay with that. Remember we always talked about travelling? Meeting people? I crossed a wasteland, hiked back home through tunnels with Marijka, carved canoes with the Tamu-jouyen. I left Caladheå's shit-lined streets on a herring drifter and watched druids open tombs at Bódhain. I flew over the tundra on a kinaru. How many Rin can say that?"

"Fendul could've died last night. Then if something happens to Tema, I become Okorebai-Rin. Imagine *me* leading the jouyen. I won't force it onto you or Yiro, so I'd better start taking it seriously. Commit to the Rin, raise my kid and my embroidery apprentices, pay attention to all this political stuff. It's time for things to change."

After the things I'd seen on Innisbán, having a baby felt unthinkable. I didn't live in the same world anymore. I couldn't risk my child ending up somewhere like this.

"My sister should've done all this first," Nili said softly. "Aoreli was twenty when her blood met the ground in the Dona war. Same age I am now."

Her words yanked at my guts, reminding me I wasn't her blood sister. But the moment I thought it, she flung her arms around me. I kissed strands of brown hair peeking from under her hood.

Nili sniffled into my shoulder. "You know, Orelein wanted to come with me last night. *Insisted.* I said if he let you die, I'd sew his breeches shut and never speak to him again."

I laughed. We stayed like that as itheran sailors leaned on the long-handled capstan, turning it in a circle, and the anchor rose rattling and dripping from the ocean. A seabird squalled overhead, maybe a wandering Nuthalha, maybe a real bird returning north. It seemed to be saying goodbye.

Half a month after leaving Innisbán, Ferish farmhouses appeared in the fog, marking the northern reaches of Eremur. Aikoto messengers flew ahead to bring the news. Our first glimpse of Toel Ginu was dark masses of people waiting on the docks and clifftops, desperate to see their loved ones.

Hiyua spent a second deciding who to hug first, then grabbed Nili, Yironem, and me at once. Dunehein clung to Rikuja, who had Sihaja in a sling on her chest. I lost Airedain to a crowd of his family. Iannah hung back with the itherans. The relief of every Rin returning alive was numbed by the wails of Iyo seeing their dead.

Ilani's mother kept her composure until the crate holding pieces of her daughter was opened. She fell to her knees, screaming like her heart had been torn out. Both children killed in half a year, both by Gallnach. She screeched at an itheran sailor until another Iyo dragged her away. There'd be a new grave next to Esiad's.

Falwen waited on the cliffs, his grey coat dusted with snow-flakes. Tokoda had held off arresting him to not tip our hand until we got home safe, and doing it now would violate the ceasefire. Our antayul stayed captive, and the traitor who put them there walked free.

He snagged my sleeve. "Idiot girl," he hissed so only I could hear. "How could you do this?"

I glared back. "Cattil's dead. You got what you asked for."

"How many Aikoto went with her? I told you I was working on plans to get our antayul out safely—"

"There wasn't time for your plans. The antayul were dying in that prison. You must've known!"

"Of course. That is why I told you to kill Cattil. Láchlan would have stopped the abuse and sent more hunters out for food, which would have bought us time. Instead, you orchestrated a blindingly stupid invasion behind my back."

I dug my fingernails into my legs. Punching a Corvittai captain *would* be blindingly stupid. "Don't pin this on me. Tokoda and Fendul planned the raid."

"Then I suppose that they also know I am Quinil?"

"I told who needed to know, no one else, or your head would already be on our stakewall."

Something flashed across Falwen's face. He reined it in. "I gave you instructions. You disobeyed. I wanted to trust you, but I no longer can."

"Fine," I snapped. "Quit relying on a nineteen-year-old girl. You can't stay hidden forever. Now you'll have to get people killed on your own."

"Bitterness does not suit you, Sohikoehl." He pushed me toward the others. "Go. We are done."

The mages stayed just long enough to restock supplies. I saw a man with shoulder-length brown hair on deck, looking toward the old shrine island, but from a distance I couldn't tell if it was Tiernan. By sunset, the ships were gone.

It was too late to take Iannah to Caladheå, so I spread a mattress on the floor between my bed and Fendul's. Ferish were rarer in Toel Ginu than crow teeth, but I didn't need to worry about her safety, of all people.

Airedain came back late at night. On the voyage home, we'd often spasmed awake as if the explosion was hitting us again. Seeing each other's faces always brought us back to reality, so we'd taken to sleeping side by side. He curled up next to me in bed and pulled my mother's blanket over us, a cocoon of embroidered fir branches.

Fendul gave me a tired smile as I blew out my vellum lantern with the painted ladder pines. Iannah shuffled on the floor. Dunehein snored next to Rikuja with Sihaja nestled between them. Nili, Hiyua, and Yironem slept farther down.

For one beautiful night, all the people I loved were under one roof.

24.

FAMINE

We'd missed the smelt spawn by going to Innisbán, so several Iyo families shared their catch. We had no room for pride. Our meat and flour had run out. The Rin had been living on foraged roots, seeds, and bark. Akiga, still bitter, resurrected her mutters about Fendul selling our salmon to itherans. Hiyua silenced her with a pointed look at Akiga's cropped hair.

At breakfast, I handed Iannah lichen dripping with oil. Skimmed from rotten boiled smelt, the oil reeked like nothing else, but was packed with nutrients. She ate it valiantly, covering her gagging with a hand. To me, eating smelt usually felt like waking after winter, but spring was nowhere in sight.

"Ai, I forgot," Airedain said as we ate. He tossed a wad of inky paper on my bed. "Jona brought that from Caladheä yesterday. Your ranger friend won a seat in the election. Scraped through."

Iannah uncrumpled the newspaper. "'Nerio Parr, youngest councillor in Eremur history,'" she read. "And he thought he couldn't do it."

Nili peered over Iannah's shoulder, chewing. "Do I really have to learn to read?"

"Yes," Fendul and I said.

"You're lucky," Airedain said. "I saw your Kae schoolteacher. He's lush enough to make me swing that way."

I elbowed him. He laughed. At least reading lessons would go smoother now that Hiyua had decided the teacher wasn't Falwen's spy.

Airedain, Jonalin, and I paddled Iannah back to Caladheå. Emílie gladly offered her lodging and guard work again. People had broken into the Knox Arms cellar twice while we were gone, making off with sacks of barley and tins of smoked herring. They'd avoided the mutton, because Jonalin had protected it with drops of smelt oil.

By afternoon, Rhonos would be done attending weekly rites at the sancte, part of his campaign to act as a devout former missionary. Iannah came with me to the Colonnium. Jonalin had given us stiff cards bearing Rhonos's tightly looped signature and Eremur's red elk sigil. The guards inspected them and swung open the creaking iron gates. Across the lawn on the Colonnium's stone steps, Iannah pushed the heavy doors open.

Nothing had changed on the surface. The marble lobby was as cold and white as ever. Council Hall was silent behind its finely carved doors. But beneath, like water rushing under a river's frozen surface, everything was different. Gélus, the clerk, droned out his welcome spiel and took our weapons, looking through Iannah like he hadn't seen her daily for nine years. We entered the gallery of armoured statues and climbed the stairs. I knew the right door without reading the engraved nameplate.

Rhonos answered my knock. His hair was pulled back with a ribbon. He'd traded his Sverbian travelling clothes for a green silk waistcoat and high-collared shirt, and black hair grew over his top lip.

I laughed. "You have a caterpillar on your face."

He glowered. "It is the style in Ferish high society. I am told it makes me look older."

"And weighs down any chance of a smile."

"Hush," he snapped. "You put me up to this."

My laughter faded. Antoch Parr's office was as I remembered — the wall-sized map with gold script, paintings in gilt frames, misty glass doors to the outside loggia. A black Council robe hung on a hook. Rhonos had only changed a few things. I crouched to peer at a jade turtle on his desk. Whaleskin turtles were a jouyen crest from the Kowichelk Confederacy where Rhonos supposedly did missionary work.

"My Kowichelk supporter lent it to me," Rhonos said, pushing aside ribbon-bound scrolls. "She assures me it is acceptable for public display."

Iannah studied a metal three-blossom flower, the Ferish holy symbol, newly hanging on the wall. "Eremur-wrought iron. Good. Parr always supported local tradesmen."

"You can identify its origin?" he asked.

"My father's a blacksmith. I know the brands of every smithy in the province." She glanced at him. "Do you actually follow Ferish religion or is this just to keep the priests' support?"

He stopped shuffling papers. "That is a highly personal question."

"You're a public figure."

Their eyes locked. I knew who'd win.

Rhonos dropped his gaze. "I believe in our god. Faith gave me strength when I had nothing else. I have never attempted to convert anyone, nor do I agree with all the doctrines. Now, if you are done scrutinizing my office . . ." He indicated two padded benches.

Iannah sat next to me, her spine not touching the brocade back. She'd always stood in this room. As we spoke, Rhonos took notes on our trip to Innisbán. He was especially interested in Cattil and her blackpowder. At the mention of Tiernan inscribing himself, he set down his quill and sighed.

"I wish Tiernan had returned to Caladheå," he said. "He still has people who care for him here, and god knows I could use his guidance again."

"Janekke wants to monitor him," I said. "Most people don't survive bodily inscription this long."

Rhonos seemed to debate with himself. "The lack of inscribed water mages on Innisbán makes me suspect Iollan's pre-arrest notes were outdated. I hesitate to go this route, but . . . what you *did* see sounds worryingly familiar. In autumn, Tiernan wrote down all he remembered of his research. Nhys has the documents in a vault at the Blackened Oak."

A new copy of the notes Tiernan had destroyed. I still remembered the smell of burning paper.

"There are things in there you haven't told us?" Iannah asked.

Wearily, Rhonos said, "They contain grounds for serious accusations against Tiernan. Ingdanrad would have held him for questioning and prevented him from going with you to Innisbán. Now . . . we may not be able to consult him again. Give me time to go through the papers before we release them."

"I'll help," Iannah said. It was an order, not an offer.

Things hadn't been much better in Caladheå than at home. Winter had taken its toll. Itherans protested the ongoing famine tax while thousands more begged on the streets. Rhonos had initiated a program that sent the unemployed out on naval ships to fish, which angered fishermen who now had more competition for the catch.

"Damned for going left, damned for going right," Iannah said. "And so the Council goes ever on."

Rhonos quirked an eyebrow in agreement. "I gained Council permission to purchase food from the Iyo nation, but they say they have none to spare. Is that true?"

I tapped the bench, thinking. "From what Airedain says, yeah. They're already helping the Rin. Plus, it's tradition to feed everyone who comes on the spring equinox, and there'll be a lot of visitors this year. The two most influential okorebai living in Toel Ginu is a big deal."

Iannah got up to study the wall map. "What about Innisburren? It's close, and Koehl said they had plenty of food at Bódhain. Shepherds might butcher their flocks for the right price."

Rhonos followed her. "To feed a province that arrests their kinsmen for druidism? It would require considerable persuasion, and our Gallnach emissaries fled when people accused them of helping raiders."

Their sleeves brushed. Iannah shifted away, focused on the map. Rhonos's face sank. I smirked. They had plenty in common.

"Emílie might help," I said. "She's planning to import food for the Knox again. She'll want immunity, though. A promise Elkhounds won't storm the pub once the Council knows she's Gallnach."

Rhonos nodded. "I will see what I can do."

That night, I helped wash dishes while Iannah was on guard duty. Liam and the other drummers played in the pub, vibrating the pots on the kitchen walls. Aikoto were still banned from performing in public, and Airedain had stopped risking it after Elkhounds investigated him, but for once he didn't cast moody looks over the half doors. Instead he nipped my ear or grazed my waist like I'd fade away if he went too long without touching me.

"I don't believe for a second my immunity will last," Emílie said, tenderizing the last bit of mutton with a hammer. "So be it, though. I won't let my neighbours starve, even Sverbs. We've got a long, hungry slog until spring."

A knock came from the half doors. Jonalin leaned in, broad shoulders filling the gap. "Ai, Kateiko. You busy?"

He'd never come searching for me. Airedain waved us on. We went out to the terrace and leaned over the railing, looking down at the ash-blackened street. The tipsy patrons ignored us.

"I'm leaving tomorrow," Jonalin said. "Got into that unemployment program that Councillor Parr — the new one, your friend — set up."

"Where are you going?"

"Nord—" He squinted one eye like Airedain did sometimes. "Nordfyskar. Gotta work on that. A Sverbian fishery on Algard Island. Every ship heading north is gonna operate out of there, and a few Kae are gonna teach itherans to build clam gardens."

"You've been fishing here all winter. Why leave?"

"*Lis otrès lingues.* Got hired as a translator."

I laughed, then caught myself when he looked offended. "Sorry, it's just — you barely talk. I had no idea you spoke Ferish that well."

"Seven years working with immigrant dockhands." He took a scrap of cord from his breeches pocket and knotted a sailor's hitch without looking. "Anyway, figured you should know since you're at our flat so often."

"Yeah, sorry about that." I scratched at peeling paint on the railing. "You didn't have to avoid us."

"I'm used to Aire bringing girls home. Uh—" Jonalin coughed, undid his knot, and started another. "That came out wrong. I'm glad it's you these days. He's gonna need you."

"What do you mean?"

"He was doing real good in his warrior training, trying to get sober. But what happened in the north . . . it fucked him up. He's hiding it, but I know my cousin."

I frowned. "If you're asking me to fix him . . ."

"Nei. Just be good to him."

I nodded. It was strange having my first serious conversation with Jonalin right before he left. The fishing program ran until next winter, and the Rin might not be here when he returned.

We woke early to see Jonalin off. Afterward, I meant to return to Toel Ginu, but Airedain asked a favour first.

"Sorry, Rin-girl," he said. "Aeldu knows you've got enough to worry about. But Maeve and Orla know this Sverbian family. Six kids. None of 'em have been at school, so Orla went by their house, and . . . well, they can't afford a medic."

"I'm not a healer," I protested.

"You've worked with Barolein and Marijka. If you could just try."

He looked so hopeful, I gave in. Anything to keep him with me in the light.

Maeve took me to a flat near the brick-making kilns. She knocked, and her mitten came away dark with coal ash. A woman holding a crying baby scrutinized me before letting us in. Three children dozed in the only bed. Two older kids shivered on a cot, wrapped in thin blankets. The fire was low. A bin by the stove had only a few lumps of glistening coal. Ash stuck between the floorboards, to the table, in hair and clothes.

Maeve explained in fluid Sverbian that I'd worked with a herbalist, leaving out that Marijka trained in Ingdanrad as a mage. I wished I'd worn my white dress rather than my shirt and leggings. The mother eyed my braid. Her pale hair was hastily pinned up.

"It's this air," she said, wiping her baby's brow with a filthy rag. "We were fine in Rutnaast. Good clean mountain air. Halskander, come here."

The oldest boy, fourteen or fifteen, heaved himself up. His skin had a yellowish tinge, and his feet were too swollen for shoes. He pulled back his lips to reveal bloody gums, then pushed his teeth with his tongue. Every one was loose. That wasn't from breathing coal ash. Airedain had lived in Ashtown for ten years and was fine.

"What have they been eating?" I asked.

The mother scoffed. "I can feed my family. Look — Hal's not that thin."

"We know," Maeve said gently.

"Sourbread and porridge," the mother said, rocking her wailing baby. "There's nothing but rye at the market. Our root cellar's been empty for months."

A lump rose in my throat. She was killing her family and didn't realize. "I think I know what's wrong. We'll be back in an hour."

Outside, Maeve gave me a confused look. "How can you tell from that?"

"It's called scurvy," I said. "Sailors' plague. Tiernan got sick on the voyage here from Sverba, but he got better on land. My jouyen's healer, Barolein, says it's because itheran sailors live on grain for months. My people never get sick from it."

Even Marijka hadn't known that. It was so easy to fix, it was unbelievable anyone could die of it. I spent so little time worrying about scurvy — I wouldn't have remembered if Jonalin hadn't set sail with itherans that morning.

Maeve and I got sacks from the Knox and trudged to a slushy park. We hacked off clusters of pine needles and filled the sacks, then stuffed more in my pockets and her apron. I gathered an armful of kindling and built a fire back at the Sverbian family's house, where I boiled water and steeped the needles into an infusion.

"It's bitter, but make it strong," I told the mother. "Your kids should be better in a couple of weeks. Keep drinking it, you and your husband and everyone you know, until you can get meat or vegetables."

After we left, Maeve said, "You should be a medic."

I half-smiled. Maybe in another life, another world. If I was wrong, pine needle tea wouldn't hurt anyone, but I wouldn't always be so lucky. I couldn't deal with more spirits blaming me for their deaths.

25.

BREATH

"Well?" Nili demanded when I stepped into our plank house. "Did you tap Iyo-boy now that you're not stuck on a ship?"

"Nei." I brushed snow off my hood into the sizzling hearth, glad Fendul was outside.

"Her hands would be shaking if she took bloodweed." Rikuja shifted Sihaja against her chest. "You will take it, right, Kako? I don't care what Akiga says about rebuilding our numbers. One of you girls having a baby is enough."

Hiyua just gave me a look.

"Aeldu save me." I grabbed Yironem, who'd covered his ears. "We're going outside to train."

With nothing else to do on the voyage home from Innisbán, we'd spent our days on antayul lessons. It hadn't helped. Yironem still couldn't move water, stuck at the level of a six-year-old. He wasn't the only one. Another Rin antayul said his kids had more trouble than when they began learning. My water-calling had been messed up all winter, from visions into the shoirdryge to the runed cuff, but I felt it, too. Sleepiness in the water, like it was always on the brink of freezing. The world was breaking down drop by drop.

I had an idea knocking around, a way to see if Iollan opening a rift would be as bad as everyone said. For once, I didn't ask Nili for help. She had enough to deal with — her apprentices, Orelein, preparing to be okoreni one day. I was waiting for someone else. Someone whose teasing laugh I couldn't get out of my head.

Halfway through meditation, Yironem flicked slush at me. I was too slow to dodge. He snickered. "Distracted?"

"Brat." I wrestled him into a snowdrift.

Neither of us were as strong as we once were. He'd spent a winter not eating enough when he should've been growing. I wondered if he was taller in the shoirdryge.

Visitors swarmed Toel Ginu in the days before the equinox. The northern Tamu, Beru, and Haka packed into our plank houses, still officially visitors' houses. We shoved everything aside in our workshops to make room for the southern Yula and Kae. Sverbians and a few Kowichelk and Nuthalha slept in the Iyo gathering place.

Airedain came on the equinox with news. Láchlan's messenger had told Arril we had nothing to do with Cattil's death, but it wasn't enough. Arril had made a show of being disappointed she couldn't trust Iannah to become Nonil. Both our ways into the Corvittai were gone.

"Kill Arril and be done with her," one Rin said, but Fendul shut that down. It wouldn't get our antayul back or Iollan's blood in the ground.

I put my idea to Airedain while we gutted trout I'd caught ice fishing. His fingers glided over the iridescent scales, unfolding pale orange flesh. A man good with a fish knife was said to be good at handling other things. Mentally, I kicked myself. *No distractions.*

Skeptical, he brought his frame drum painted with a coyote. What I was about to do was offensive to both Rin and Iyo aeldu. Fendul, sighing, said if they hadn't cursed me yet, they wouldn't bother now.

Airedain and I crossed the stone bridge to the old shrine island, passing under the rioden gate carved with leaping dolphins. The snow was free of tracks, the burnt stumps crystallized with frost. We climbed crumbling steps into the shrine's husk. The blackened pillars looked like scratch marks against the clouds. I shoved aside collapsed timbers to clear a space. A few crests were intact, remnants of the Iyo-jouyen's history recorded on the walls.

"I loved this place when I was a kid," Airedain said as he helped. "I'd watch my uncle Ranelin from the top balcony, longing for the day I was old enough to drum with him. Not even fighting with my temal could take that joy away."

"What changed?"

"Life, I guess. I haven't been in this shrine sober since I was seventeen. Blamed vodka for my vision last year, until you started talking about other worlds."

A year ago today, on this island, I'd seen into the shoirdryge. So had Airedain. "Tell me again what you saw," I said.

He pointed at chunks of stone appearing and disappearing under foamy waves. "That rock pillar collapsed. The echo off the cliffs sounded wrong though. Too thin and quiet. When I looked closer, it was still standing."

I chewed my lip. "Makes sense. I see that world through water. Fog, humidity, snow, sometimes my own water-calling. You grew up learning music, plus four different languages, so you *heard* that world first. Nili grew up as a dancer, and she felt that guised figure at Bódhain before she saw it. Like it moved wrong."

"So you're going for all three?"

"Yeah. Something's got to work."

The guised figure had seen me, too. If I could maintain a vision, maybe I could communicate with the other Toel Ginu. Find out if the Suriel there also wanted to open a rift into the void, tearing another hole for natural elements to vanish into. And if he did, I wanted to know what horrors from that world — more Cattils and Nonils and Parrs — might be able to travel through the void into ours.

I put on the kinaru shawl Nili had given me when we left Anwen Bel. Only dancers were allowed to wear them, a way of communicating with the aeldu, but I wasn't looking for Aeldu-yan. Airedain tied the laces around my wrists. When I spread my arms I had wings, black outside and white inside.

He sat cross-legged and began to drum. I closed my eyes, absorbing sound into my muscles. *Breathe.* Cool, salty air. *Feel.* Humidity brushing my skin. *Extend.* Like a map, I sensed the shrine around me. Icicle-draped holes in the floorboards, frosty debris, snowdrifts against the walls. I knew where to step without looking.

I spun. My wings billowed around me. Airedain's voice rose in wailing song, cries to a world beyond. I dipped and soared, remembering the boundless grace of riding a kinaru over glacial mountains. Every thump of my boots sent snowflakes billowing into the sky. A blizzard fell upward. Tingling crept into my skull.

I swirled to a stop and opened my eyes. The shrine stood intact around me. Carved walls, tiered balconies, the roof three storeys up. Snow hung in midair, drifting like dust in afternoon light from the windows. Three Iyo men in sleeveless shirts carried casks for the equinox festival, oblivious to winter invading their shrine.

Airedain was gone. I stepped sideways. There he was, shimmering, his coyote drum in his lap. He'd promised to keep playing until I asked him to stop or something went wrong. By the way his brows drew together, he knew I was seeing it.

I tried stepping on a staircase that'd been burned away in our world. It looked solid, but my foot went through it. I walked the ground floor instead. A woman shouldered open a door, letting sunlight spill in. She had bark cord in her braid and a chisel tucked in her belt. *Rikuja*. She'd always intended to become a shrine carver. Sleeves covered her arms. I couldn't see if she had tattoos for marriage or children. In that world, Sihaja might never have been born.

I called out, spread my wings, pushed floating snow at her. Rikuja didn't look my way. As much as I wanted to stay with her, I needed someone to notice me. I turned back to the central shrine.

A lanky boy with shaved brown hair backed out of a storage room, carrying a bulky drum. His face was angled away from me.

The drifting snow locked in place. I ran Airedain's life path in my mind. Prison and shark-fin hair at fifteen, making a home in Caladheå, meeting me, becoming a warrior. If that first point never happened, maybe the rest didn't, either. My ribs felt hollow.

"Kateiko."

The voice sounded distant. Disembodied. The lanky boy paused, freeing a snagged drum strap from the doorframe.

"C'mon, Rin-girl. Wake up!"

The boy turned. I spun away—

"*Kako!*"

The floating snow dropped. The shrine vanished. I inhaled, choking. My Airedain's face sagged with relief, framed by the open sky. He eased me down and held me.

My throat scraped. "What happened?"

"You stopped breathing." He kissed the cropped hair over my forehead. "Don't ever do this again, Kako. Please."

"But it was working—"

"*Nei.*" It came out like a growl. "Promise you won't. It's too dangerous."

I nodded. He was right for more reasons than he knew.

Spring equinox or not, the remembered ache of hypothermia kept me in my winter leggings and shirt. Nili, enduring my complaints about being unable to show some skin, folded my neckline down and added some stitches to hold it. She lent me a black-and-teal bead necklace. "At least *you'll* look nice," she huffed, tugging her shirt over her stomach.

"Your baby's not even showing," I said, tying her dark hair back with red ribbons.

Besides, it didn't deter some of her admirers. The Rin canoe carver eyed her as we stepped outside into crisp night air. Orelein's glare sent him scrambling.

Airedain met us at our stockade gate. His eyes dropped to my chest. "Nice necklace."

I spared him my usual shove. There was still an off note in his voice. He wore drummer regalia with painted blue lines curling out from under his collar and sleeves. His tunic and breeches were properly black for once, not smudged with ash and mud.

The new shrine was a short hike down the coast, overlooking a gorge where waves funnelled in and broke with a torrent of sea spray. Tonight would be the first time non-Iyo were allowed past the gate onto sacred ground. Airedain and I passed through it hand in hand.

Beyond lilac saplings that awaited warm weather to bloom, the shrine's rioden timbers were rich auburn, not yet storm-faded. Tinkling ropes of seashells hung from its eaves. Tokoda stood on the stairs, arms folded. She nodded as we passed. Dunehein opened the doors and released a wave of drumbeats.

It'd take centuries for the walls to fill with carvings again, but flickering torchlight and shadows masked the blankness. Yironem disappeared into the thrumming mass of bodies, Fendul headed for Aliko, and Dunehein went off with Rikuja. Her parents had Sihaja for the night. A Yula boy pulled Nili into the throng. Beaming, she waved goodbye, ribbons swinging.

Iyo drummers were trading off all night, so Airedain wouldn't perform until later. I headed for the ale casks, but he grabbed my arm.

"Rin-girl." He wavered. "Don't let me drink tonight, okay? I wanna try . . . getting through an equinox without it."

"Sure," I said, surprised. "Then I won't, either."

He kissed my cheek. But when he moved toward the crowd, my feet wouldn't budge. I hadn't planned on spending the night sober. Memories of last year scraped at me. My back against Tiernan's chest, now carved with that awful rune. Airedain's hands on Ilani. I wondered if her spirit had made it back here.

"What's wrong?" he asked.

"Last spring," I mumbled.

He frowned. "You miss him?"

I shook my head. Seeing Tiernan again had felt like closure, but Innisbán had ripped something from me and left a fistful of ice in its place. Heat from the hearths skirted around me. I couldn't celebrate the end of winter when it was still here.

"Come upstairs," Airedain said. "It's quieter there."

We climbed to the third-storey balconies. The floor vibrated. In a knot of teenage Rin and Iyo, Yironem danced with Airedain's youngest cousin, Tamiwa. Taking after that side of the family, she was a palm taller than Yironem. One good thing about him not growing any more was he'd settled into his height, moving with grace from years of shawl dancing. They curved around each other like fish swimming opposite directions — until she stepped on his foot and they both went sprawling. Airedain and I snorted.

That was the chisel that cracked the ice. Our jouyen were together. I slid my arms around Airedain, letting him guide our motion. Yironem, not to be shown up, grabbed Tamiwa's waist. She blinked like she wasn't sure his hands were real. People jostled around us, snagging on my unbraided hair, but tonight, it didn't matter.

We weren't upstairs only for my sake. All the ale casks were on the ground floor. A few of Airedain's friends showed up and offered us mugs, but nodded in understanding when he refused. Sometimes he cocked his head, listening to something I couldn't hear. I left for a bit to talk with Fendul, came back, and gently took a mug from Airedain's hands.

When I saw Nili again, her arms were draped around Orelein. He couldn't look away from her. She stared back through narrowed eyes, smiling like she knew it was a bad idea to encourage him and didn't care.

Airedain and I scraped snow off a windowsill and flicked it over the balcony onto the crowd. Faces snapped up to catch us. We ducked back laughing. I grabbed another handful of snow and put it down his tunic. He swore and kissed me. I clung to him, forgetting for a moment anyone else was around.

When it was time for him to perform, we went downstairs and I slid into a gap near the stage. He stripped off his tunic to show the painted lines and four-pointed drummer tattoo on his chest. His elk-skin drum hung from straps around his narrow hips. Its buckles glinted as he whirled across the stage. He never strayed for long, always returning with a wink or a spin of a mallet. I smiled up at him, clapping along.

He was lush. I'd never questioned that, with ridged muscles over his stomach and a jaw sharp enough to cut myself on. But this was so much more. It'd been months since he drummed this way. His mallets bounded through the air like dolphins leaping from the ocean.

By the time Airedain swung offstage, I was strung tight as a fiddle. His hands found my waist as the next drummers started. The beat thudded through us. I pressed my back against him, my hair rubbing against his skin. His tongue grazed my ear. Our hips moved in time. Suddenly, I knew why he was determined to stay sober tonight.

"Let's go somewhere," I said.

He led me through the crowd, grabbing a candle, and into a dark, chilly side room. I kicked the door shut, muffling the music. In an instant, his mouth was on mine. We folded together, a tangle of lips and hands and tongues.

An odd feeling tugged at me. I broke away gasping. "Hang on. Where are we?"

He yanked back a tarp to show drums stacked along a wall. "Storage. Ain't much, but no one will come in."

The old and new shrines had the same layout. This was the room I saw the lanky boy with shaved hair emerge from.

Airedain lit a tiny vellum lantern hanging from the ceiling. As I wondered why it was there, he lit another, and another, like embers swaying overhead. The frosty window shutters glittered orange. With the gloom pushed back, I saw blankets spread over a grizzly pelt on the floor.

I laughed. "Sleaze. You planned this."

"Planned? Nei. Hoped?" He scrunched one eye shut. "Ya got me there. But only if you're ready—"

"Shut up and kiss me again."

He came at me so fast, we staggered into the wall. My hair snagged on the planks. I dug my nails into his bare chest, feeling his muscles flex.

"Wait," I cried when he pulled at my shirt. "It's too cold!"

"Fuck the cold." He kissed my neck and grinned. "Fuck Suriel and his blizzards and this aeldu-cursed winter."

He wrestled me into the makeshift bed. I yanked off my shirt, tearing the neckline's new stitches. Blue paint smudged across us as we scrabbled at each other. His lips landed everywhere — my scars, tattoos, burns from the explosion. Parr's voice couldn't reach me through the faint drumbeats from the shrine.

No matter how close I got to Airedain, it wasn't enough. Every fibre of me trembled. I wanted to meld together in that warm cocoon, interweaving each other's spirits, and emerge as something more beautiful than we were separate. Here on sacred ground, we could become one.

My hand found the laces on his breeches. His eyebrows twitched up. Daring me.

A moment of scrambling later, our clothes lay rumpled on the floor. He knelt above me, supporting himself on his elbows, his breath misting on my cheek.

"Kako," he whispered. "Please say yes."

"Yes." I wove my fingers into his tousled hair. "Yes, yes, yes."

He settled his weight onto my body. The sap that'd been frozen in my veins for so long burst and flowed free — and I seized up.

I couldn't breathe. My lungs didn't work. I grabbed his shoulders and shoved.

Airedain jerked off me, cursing in Aikoto, Sverbian, Gallnach. "Sorry, Kako, I'm so sorry—"

I jammed my fists into my mouth. A muffled scream tore through my clenched teeth. It wasn't *fair*. I was in the safest place possible. He'd chosen it for me. Parr's spirit could never get into a place guarded by Iyo aeldu — unless this was their curse for me messing around in their torched shrine. Furious tears leaked out. I pulled my knees to my chest and rocked.

Airedain stroked my back. "What is it? Parr?"

I nodded. I'd bawl if I spoke.

Slowly enough that I could stop him, he curled around me and kissed my hair. "If you can tell me what happened just now, maybe we can fix it."

I wiped my eyes. *Breathe. You have to.* "With Parr, that's how we . . . him, on top. He was heavy. It was . . . hard to breathe, but I didn't ask him to move. I couldn't make myself talk."

"Okay. Here." He rolled onto his back. "If you're still up for it, get on top of me. Then you're in control. You can stop whenever you want."

"You're sure? That's twice today I stopped breathing. I thought you wouldn't even touch me now."

He gave a husky laugh. "You don't realize how bad I want you, Rin-girl."

Biting my lip, I straddled his thighs, sitting upright. He draped the blankets around my shoulders. I went through my meditation exercises, extending outward to trace the blood coursing through his body. Warm. Alive. When air flowed steadily through my chest, I eased onto him.

Water dripped off the window shutters. I hadn't meant to melt the frost, not wanting to trigger another vision, but this time, I saw only this world. Only my Airedain.

❋

Exhausted, we snuggled together in our cozy den. Half the lanterns had gone out. Muted murmurs came through the door. Airedain propped himself up on one elbow, trailing calloused fingers over me. One of his black drummer's wristbands had come unknotted. He lingered on the forehead scar I'd covered by cutting my hair.

I touched his temple. The Innisbán explosions had left a burn that continued onto his scalp, making a streak where hair would never grow again. "Ai, we match."

He smirked. "Mine came from a battle, not a bar fight."

My jaw dropped. "Ass."

I stretched out into the frigid air and fumbled through the pocket of my discarded leggings. I'd taken to carrying bloodweed everywhere, figuring it'd ease Airedain's mind to see me take it. I swallowed a dark green tablet and called enough water into my cupped hand to rinse away the mossy taste.

Partly I was delaying what I had to say. "This afternoon . . ." I murmured. "In the other world, someone came out of this room. It looked like you."

His smile faded.

"I'm not sure, though, and . . . I don't want to know. It doesn't matter who you are there." I brushed my fingertips over the leaf-fuzz hair above his ear. "I want *you*. This you, everything that's come before and everything after. I — I love you, Airedain Iyo."

He stared, as if he, the one who could hear other worlds, didn't trust his own hearing. So I kissed him, weaving my fingers into his crest of hair.

"Kateiko," he whispered. Every sound was perfect, lilting with his accent. He knew what my name meant like he knew the resonance of a drum. In his breath was truth.

26.

SACRIFICE

"Wake up, sleepies!" Nili flopped across my bed, crushing my legs.

I groaned. I'd stumbled back to my plank house in the dark, shaky with bloodweed poisoning, since non-Iyo had to be out of the shrine by dawn. It was light now. "How are you so cheerful?"

"'Cause *I* didn't have to take bloodweed. Can't get pregnant again." She pulled back my blanket and grabbed my elbow. "Good, your rash is gone."

Airedain sat up next to me, bleary-eyed. His hair looked more like a sea urchin than a shark fin. "Talk louder, ai? The Nuthalha didn't hear up north."

I wrapped my arms around him, keeping him in bed. I'd woken several times during the night, wracked with nausea, and smiled every time to find him there. I balled up my hands to keep them from wandering. Plenty of times I'd seen or heard couples be intimate in a plank house, but I wasn't ready to be *that* public.

"Who'd Nili tap last night?" I asked over breakfast. "Five pann on Orelein."

"No bet," Rikuja said, bouncing Sihaja on her knee. "He walked out of here earlier whistling."

Airedain stopped humming. Dunehein burst out laughing and choked on a mouthful of smelt.

We spent the day in Airedain's plank house with Segowa and their family. Yironem and Tamiwa went off alone, supposedly for him to teach her archery. I fully expected them to return with as many arrows as they left with.

That afternoon, Rhonos and Iannah arrived through grey sheets of rain. Rhonos rode my old horse, Anwea. I helped Iannah down from a borrowed mare. I was realizing her combat skills were limited to when she was on foot, although next to an ex-member of Eremur's mounted archers, anyone would look bad at riding.

People sidled out of their plank houses, pointing at Rhonos's fur-trimmed coat and the scarlet ribbon wound into Anwea's mane. Ferish politicians rarely came to Toel Ginu and never with only one bodyguard. The whispers that it was Parr's son were followed by mutters about using his hair for fishing line. Segowa sharply reminded them he'd turned on his father to warn us about Nonil.

Fendul met us at the Iyo gathering place and showed us into a room set aside for diplomatic meetings. Tapestries of curling dolphins hung on the walls. Hiyua had embroidered a panel of soaring kinaru that covered the ceiling. We sat on woven bark mats, Rhonos and Iannah next to each other, Fendul, Airedain, and I facing them. Airedain had earned Fendul's approval as an Iyo advisor.

Rhonos opened a waterproof elk bladder and eased out a thick roll of paper. "Pelennus and I combed through Tiernan's research. It is as I thought. Iollan och Cormic seems to have shifted strategies." He passed me the top sheet.

I smoothed it out. Airedain peered over my shoulder. He read faster than me.

"Yan taku," he muttered.

"Tiernan long suspected humans are not powerful enough to open a rift," Rhonos explained. "Our hearts give out first. However, there is no such danger with inorganic processes. His theory is that an amplified firebomb, strategically placed, can displace enough water, earth, and air to tear through every layer of the world."

My eyes widened. "An explosion."

"Precisely. It would be magnitudes stronger than anything Cattil produced. The only labour besides making the amplification runes is that of water mages, who must keep large amounts of black-powder dry enough to ignite."

Fendul ran a hand over his face. "Aeldu save us. That's why the Corvittai took our antayul."

I sifted through the sheets, spreading them across the floor. Diagrams, cramped text, notes jotted in the margins, all in Tiernan's fine handwriting. "You're sure it's not a coincidence? Cattil has a history of using blackpowder."

"There are too many similarities. These papers are very much the sign of mentor and acolyte continuing the same research threads independently."

Iannah nudged Rhonos. "There's more."

"Tell us," Fendul said with an edge.

Rhonos glanced up at the kinaru tapestry, a reminder of who held power here. He handed me a circular design, the strongest amp rune Tiernan had gotten me to stand on. On the back of the sheet was my height, weight, resting heart rate, notes about my water-calling, and more. Tiernan had measured so many things, I'd quit trying to make sense of it. I hadn't expected him to remember it all perfectly when he rewrote this, months after burning his notes.

"Kateiko..." Rhonos couldn't meet my eyes. "Tiernan designed that rune specifically for you. When he told you to stay here in Toel Ginu last spring, it was because his desire to see his friends alive in the shoirdryge was consuming him. Every day you spent at his cabin, he was tempted to coerce you into helping him."

I sat in stunned silence. "Maika knew," I said finally. "She read his notes."

"She let it go because he vowed to abandon his research, but it came up again when they discussed helping Suriel. It is one of many things they argued about before her death." His voice softened. "He does truly feel ashamed."

It was hard to be mad at Tiernan for something he'd resisted. Still, every new thing I learned about him made me glad he was gone from my life. More than ever, I wanted to tangle myself up with Airedain and never let go.

Airedain spun his fan knife. The man he wanted to stab was several days' sailing away and already dying of a rune carved into his chest. But instead of lashing out, something surfaced in his mind. I saw the change on his face. He ran his thumb down a list of dates.

"Every day relating to other worlds, from every religion Tiernan studied," Iannah said. "Matches your guess about Iollan trying to open a rift on Bódhain."

"I guessed wrong," he said. "Sacred days in druidism have linked elements. Fire at Bódhain when Gallnach burn crops for the dead, earth in winter when the rites are underground, water at Abhain when farmers pray for rain for the crops, air in summer when they do rites up in the mountains. Water's the most important part of Iollan's plan. Without water-calling, the explosion won't go off. He'll think antayul are strongest on Abhain."

Rhonos cleared his throat. "As a councillor, I must point out you are suspiciously familiar with a banned religion."

Airedain flicked his wrist, snapping out his fan knife. "Do I look like a fuckin' druid?"

"Council laws don't apply here," Fendul said.

"Wait," I said with dawning alarm. "Abhain is only six weeks away."

"Iollan has been working for Suriel for years," Rhonos said. "They may not be aiming for this Abhain."

"Nei, listen. After the battle on Innisbán, Láchlan told us the only blessing to burying his mercenaries was he didn't have to pay them anymore. I'm not sure he can afford to keep the Corvittai together another year."

Fendul rose and paced the room, holding his crow amulet at his throat. "Then we need a plan. Soon. We need to know where Iollan will trigger an explosion and how to stop him."

I pressed my fingers to my lips. "I might have a way back into the Corvittai. But it'll have a price."

The next evening, my footsteps echoing in the empty Colonnium, I rapped on Falwen's office door. He answered immediately. His lip curled, but he stepped aside. His office never changed in appearance, though I imagined the cabinets grew more packed with files. Beyond the glass doors to the loggia, rain gusted under the arched stone roof.

I draped myself across a hard-backed chair and propped my dripping boots on his desk. *Be cocky*, Iannah had said, deciding I'd pull it off better than she would with her Antler-style restraint. Cocky was easy now that we had an edge. I just had to channel Airedain.

"I know what Peimil's doing with blackpowder," I said. "I know he's running out of time. Councillor Nerio Parr will defend me if you accuse me of anything, but *I* still have leverage. If I out you as the Corvittai spymaster, you'll be executed for treason."

Falwen sat on the edge of his desk and pushed my feet off. "What do you want, Sohikoehl?"

"The truth, first. Why does Suriel want to reach the void?"

"What will you do with that knowledge?"

I shrugged.

"Youths," he grumbled, drying his desk with a handkerchief. "I hope you enjoy history. Suriel came into existence three thousand years ago, recently by saidu standards. He collected human followers like a child trapping insects. As older saidu went dormant, Suriel grew closer to us. A change was happening.

"He began developing emotion, a concept unknown to saidu. They think, argue, scuffle over territory, but they do not feel. Imagine you grew up underground in pure darkness. The first glimpse of a glowing mushroom would be disorienting. A sliver of sunlight would be unearthly. Disturbed, Suriel retreated to his mountain and drove his followers away with windstorms. He was all but forgotten for centuries."

"Until Imarein Rin climbed Se Ji Ainu in a blizzard," I said. It was one of our jouyen's lesser-known stories. Imarein lost all his family in the First Elken War, so instead of going back to an empty home, he ran away to find Suriel.

Falwen nodded. "They were as alike as a human and tel-saidu could be. Brash, moody adolescents in self-imposed exile. Imarein lived on Se Ji Ainu, sleeping alongside kinaru in their nests and subsisting on raw fish. He shaved his head and inked over his family crest as a show of devotion to Suriel. When he visited the Rin-jouyen ten years later, no one recognized him."

"He'd gone crazy," I said. "He wore a cloak of crow feathers and spoke in bird calls. People weren't sure he was fully human anymore."

"Yet he was surprisingly well-informed. He visited the Rin because Eremur had just established its military. Imarein, fearing another war, tried persuading Rin to take sanctuary at Se Ji Ainu. He insisted that Suriel wanted followers again and would protect anyone who swore devotion. No one believed it. Bitter at their refusal, Imarein returned to Se Ji Ainu alone.

"Suriel shared Imarein's anger, to whatever degree he could feel it, but having his most loyal follower back made up for it. Over many decades, they grew closer. Imarein's attuned form changed to a kinaru. He learned to call air and became the first known telyul. The first human Suriel respected. Cared for. Then, after eighty years together, Imarein died.

"Imagine your underground cave collapses. You *drown* in sunlight. It burns. Blinds you. Suriel was stunned to feel grief. Loss does not exist for saidu, who see the world as infinite and cyclical. He could not understand his pain. Had no idea how to mourn. Suriel believed he ceased to be a true saidu. How do you escape burning light when it is everywhere?"

I swallowed a lump in my throat. "The void's not just escape to him. He's committing suicide."

"Essentially." Falwen glanced through the doors at the sodden fields. Somewhere beyond them was Suriel. "He sees himself as an abomination. He has tried to kill himself and to let other saidu kill him. Self-preservation kicks in. Saidu are not meant to die before their natural end. Arril agreed to help him out of compassion."

"Okay, a few problems. How do you even know opening a rift is safe? That it won't annihilate everything?"

"Because one already exists. Well, existed."

"*What?* Where?"

"Across the ocean. Peimil says Tiernan Heilind discovered it back when he lived in Sverba. No one can find it anymore."

I stared at Falwen.

"Arril and I have gone through this all, so I can guess your other concerns. First, that Suriel's suicide means losing another saidu and having our world swing farther out of balance. Second, if we can seal a rift without the help of saidu or if we will be connected to other worlds forever. Both issues may have the same solution.

"I believe we are leaving the era of spirits and entering the era of humans. Aikoto have antayul, itherans have jinrayul and edimyul. Imarein proved that people can become telyul. With practice and innovation, we could do the work of saidu. Thus, demanding that one lives when he wants to die seems needlessly cruel — not to mention dangerous."

"Dangerous how?"

"Suriel's grief is not fading. In fact, it worsens. When he disappeared this summer, it was ten years to the day since Imarein's death. He returned from mourning, discovered his army killed half the remaining Rin, and sent a blizzard at Caladheå to punish his captains — not caring that Iyo were in the firing line and not considering that Rin could be. His rage blinds him. I refuse to sit idle while his myopia grows."

I flicked my braid over my shoulder, trying to regain my arrogant pretense. "And you think blowing up the barrier between worlds is safer?"

Falwen looked down at me from his seat on his desk. "Remember the saying 'the wind dies a thousand deaths'? Saidu live fifty millenia on average. A thousand generations from now, Suriel could still be here, more erratic than ever. How long do you think we will survive? We have much better odds of learning to do his work in his absence. Yes, I will take that future over our complete destruction."

Maybe he believed his words, but I wouldn't make that trade. I had to get close enough to stop the Corvittai. "I want back in," I said.

Falwen snorted. "I want a seaside cottage with a butler. Too bad for us."

"You can't do this alone. You tried and accidentally sent Parr and Nonil after the Rin. What happens next time you crack under pressure?"

"*You* have been trying to stop Peimil since you found out about him. I highly doubt I have changed your mind."

"Nei. Innisbán changed it." I held aside my braid to show faded burns on my neck. "Ilani and countless others didn't make it. Tiernan's dying. Only striking a deal with Láchlan kept everyone else alive — my lover, my okorebai, my family. I don't want to fight anymore. When I found out my sister's pregnant . . . I started thinking about the future."

I steadied my breathing. Time to lie to the best liar I'd ever met. Rhonos had given me advice on appearing sincere — eyes straight ahead, hands away from my face, no fidgeting — gained from years of pretending to be someone he wasn't. As quick as sweat formed on my body, I dried it up.

"For the first time in my life, there's someone I want to start a family with. My kids with Airedain will be half Rin. Our grandkids might be a quarter. When will Suriel decide our descendants are no longer children of kinaru? When will he stop protecting them? I don't know the best way to deal with him, but we can't keep out-manouevring each other. We have to pick a way and stick with it."

"Too late, Sohikoehl. You destroyed my trust."

I stood up, scraping my chair against the floor. "I never had your trust. You wanted to control me, and I'm sick of it. So let me back in. I know something that'll help Peimil. Something from Tiernan."

Falwen arched an eyebrow. "Arril thinks you got Cattil killed. I can do nothing now."

"Go over Arril's head. Help me lie to Suriel. Say I'm abandoning everyone else and going back to him. If he likes moody Rin teen-agers, he can't get better than me."

His hand twitched like he wanted to hit something. "Get out. I have work to do."

"Fine. Whatever." I turned away. "But you should know my brother's flying me to Se Ji Ainu tonight. Your choice if you come."

I was at the door when Falwen said, thick with aggravation, "Wait."

Under cover of night, Yironem and I hiked to the edge of North Iyun Bel, away from prying eyes. A crow and coyote trailed after us. Fendul and Airedain shifted back in the shelter of dripping conifers to say goodbye. Where Yironem and I were going, there was no way to follow unseen.

Airedain looped his arms around my waist. "It might not be so bad. Half that stuff about Imarein sounds like an old wives' tale."

"So did kinaru until I saw one for myself." I leaned into him. "Imarein was a different person after giving himself to Suriel. I don't know how I'll change, or how fast, but it'll happen."

"It's killin' me that I can't help you," he muttered.

"Maybe you can." With a deep breath, I pulled a long strand of hair from my head. "Keep this safe. Hide it from Suriel. Then a tiny part of me will still exist."

Airedain's face crinkled. "You trust me that much? Not even married couples keep each other's hair."

"I know. But I'll feel better if you have it."

I coiled the strand and wrapped it in my linen fireweed. He touched the bundle to his lips and tucked it into an inner pocket of his jerkin.

"You understand why I'm going to Suriel, right?" I asked.

"Yeah." He kissed me, slow and tender. "I think I always knew you'd do something like this. That's why I fell in love with you."

Fendul spoke quietly to Yironem, who nodded along. Speech seemed to be beyond him. A kinaru in Suriel's presence would be the safest living thing in the land, but meeting a saidu was far more complicated than that.

I felt bad for taking Yironem away from Tamiwa just as they were getting to know each other. He'd agreed without hesitation, though, as I knew he would. Always going to battle even when he was too young to fight, helping however he could. I had a feeling that was one of the reasons Tamiwa liked him.

"I can't protect you after this, Kako," Fendul said for the hundredth time.

I didn't want him to try. Suriel would never believe the Okorebai-Rin turned to his side after leading an attack on Innisbán. It had to look like Yironem and I were acting alone.

Fendul and Airedain waited hidden in a spruce copse, blades ready in case Falwen decided to off me instead. I braided the rest of my hair in preparation for the journey. The rain drizzled out. Soon after, a kinaru rustled the canopy and circled overhead. Yironem stepped into a slushy clearing and spread his arms. They shifted into wings, black outside, white inside. Within a breath he was a kinaru. He hunkered low to the forest floor. I climbed onto his back and wrapped my arms around his neck, clinging to his feathers.

"Today we fly," I whispered. Our Rin battle cry.

Yironem lurched forward, running on webbed feet to pick up speed. With a jolt, he launched into the air. The rainforest fell away, smoothing into immense waves. My braid streamed out behind me. The rush of air made my eyes water.

The other kinaru arced toward us. Falwen, riding with an ease I hadn't mastered, led us northeast toward Tømmbrind Creek. Even in the darkness, I knew what was below — Marijka's home on the bank, Tiernan's cabin nestled in the trees. An hour or two along the creek, the forest opened into the abandoned lumber camp. An hour or two past that were the lights of Crieknaast.

We cut a line over Tømmbrind Creek, a ribbon of reflected moonlight doing breakneck turns through mountain valleys. Over Dúnravn Pass, the last resting place of so many soldiers. Up, up, up toward a spine of jagged peaks. This time I knew what to look for — four stone columns surrounding a platform on the highest precipice. Se Ji Ainu, the Pillared Mountain.

This last stretch was why I brought Falwen. Not because I expected to get his approval, but so it looked like I already had it, so Suriel didn't send a blizzard to test my determination.

Dawn glowed deep blue in front of us. We sailed over a glacial lake overflowing in waterfalls and landed with thumps on the pillared platform. I slid off Yironem and staggered. Falwen did the same next to me. I felt a flash of spiteful pleasure that he wasn't immune to the pains of flying.

My ears rang after so many hours of air streaming past. Fog covered the far end of the platform. If Suriel was there, I couldn't see him. Yironem clacked his bill. His head swivelled on its long neck. I stroked his side, willing him strength.

Wind rustled his feathers. A hollow voice surrounded us. *Not one of mine.*

Maybe Suriel felt emotion, but I couldn't sense it in his words. I wished Airedain were here. He heard things I never could.

"Suriel, this is my brother, Yironem Rin," I said. "He attuned to one of your kinaru."

Show me.

Yironem shifted back to human. We knelt side by side, shivering in our cloaks and fur mantles. Snowflakes skidded across the scoured stone. Falwen looked on with folded arms.

How did you get that form?

Yironem turned to me, panicking. I held his hand. Fendul had told him to be honest and leave the half-truths and lies to me.

"I killed one of your soldiers who mutinied," he told Suriel. "Then I saw your kinaru, and . . . I couldn't bring myself to harm them. I thought there had to be a way out of battle, to get my sisters to safety. Suddenly I was a kinaru. That's all I know."

Another young Rin fled war once. He came to me.

As the platform brightened with the coming sun, I saw a glimmer of Suriel's humanesque form in the fog — translucent, hooded, colossal enough to pick me up in one hand. I realized this form was like attuning for him. If I could lift that misty hood, I wondered if I'd see Imarein's face.

The snowflakes spiralled closer. *Kateiko Rin. You came. Then you left.*

I bowed my head. "Please, let me explain."

Speak.

"I thought you broke our deal and ordered Marijka Riekkanehl's death. I thought you didn't want me anymore. By the time I found out Antoch Parr killed her, you were gone. I did all I could in your absence, though. I protected the Rin and killed Nonil for betraying you. I sailed to Ingdanrad in search of you. That didn't work, so I devoted myself to finding your captains.

"When you returned, I called to you during your blizzard. Did you hear? I would've stayed on that rooftop, but an Iyo pulled me down. I was ecstatic when Quinil asked me for help. Finally, I could serve you again. I led warriors to Innisbán to stop Cattil from harming your antayul."

Falwen's hood rippled. After a moment, he nodded. He and Suriel were speaking privately, their voices directed away from me by the breeze.

Quinil says I should not trust you, Kateiko Rin.

"I came to prove you can. To prove my devotion." I slid my shoulder bag off and took out the pieces of my ladder-pine lantern. I'd unhinged the frame and folded it flat, but now I put it back together on the ground. "This was a gift from my Iyo lover. He won't be my lover anymore. He doesn't revere saidu like he should."

I opened a flask of fish oil, drizzled it over the vellum panels, and struck my flint against Nurivel's steel edge. Sparks flew off and ignited the oil, bright orange in the dawn. The vellum curled and disintegrated. Airedain's careful brush strokes crumbled into ash. Never again would I gaze at the lantern's warm flush before falling asleep.

Imarein hadn't had a lover, but he'd sacrificed everything else for Suriel. I didn't have enough patience for his methods. I unclasped my cloak and mantle and pushed up my sleeve. Goosebumps swarmed over my skin. I set Nurivel in the blazing lantern. While the steel grew hot, I drew Kohekai, the blood bringer — and sliced into my fireweed tattoo.

Blood pulsed down my arm. I seized Nurivel and pressed the glowing red blade to the wound, cauterizing it shut. A scream pushed against my teeth. My skin erupted with white blisters. The fireweed, one of the last traces of my family, was gone. All that remained was my kinaru tattoo.

The reek of burning flesh made me want to vomit. Falwen covered his nose. Suriel was solidifying, growing sharper around the edges. I had him on the edge of a chasm. Yironem cringed, knowing what was next.

I pulled my braid over my shoulder. Giving Airedain a strand of hair had been hard enough. Cutting it all meant hacking off a connection to my memories, the pride of my ancestors, all that made me who I was.

That much I could live with. I'd keep going forward. Even if I forgot what I used to be, Airedain held a tiny piece of my old self.

I sliced through my braid at chin level. It came away in my hand, a brown plait the length of my arm. It didn't look real. My head felt lighter, like the weightless sense of soaring through the sky. Wind stirred loose strands at the back of my neck.

Heart, blood, hair. The sacred triad of the body. Love, life, spirit. Every part was meant to return to the earth when I died.

I set my braid on the ground. "Suriel, this is my gift to you. You can lock it up somewhere it'll never decay, keep my spirit stuck between this world and Aeldu-yan if it pleases you. This is my devotion."

Yironem shifted back to his kinaru form. He spread his wings behind me and lifted his head. His call shuddered across the mountain, answered by other kinaru hidden in the fog. We stood there like one creature, human and bird, female and male, stronger together.

Suriel drifted forward. He was clearer than I'd ever seen. Yet if I let my eyes shift out of focus, like switching from seeing this world to a shoirdryge, the peak of his hood became a kinaru bill. The folds of a cloak became feathers.

My heart pounded. This had to work. I had nothing left to give.

Sunrise broke in the east. Se Ji Ainu glittered in its radiance. Light sparked off the scudding snowflakes and breathed life into the mist. All around us, mountain peaks basked in yellow. Part of me saw, truly, why Imarein stayed. Everything else that mattered in the world was distant.

Suriel floated over my burnt lantern, spattered blood, and disembodied braid, stirring the stray ends. Icy, translucent wingtip fingers grazed my kinaru tattoo. His touch was everything at once — the wildness of the sky, the embrace of a loved one, the murmur of things lost. His hollow voice echoed in my head.

I accept.

27.

GIFTS

Suriel told Yironem and me to wait in a forested valley at the foot of Se Ji Ainu. He didn't say how long.

I knew what was meant to happen. Falwen would go to Toel Ginu to verify my story. Airedain would act distraught, "admitting" I had made veiled comments about fixing things so we could start a family. Tamiwa, blushing to her ears, had agreed to say she and Yironem were together. It'd look like I bullied him into helping me, now that he, too, was with an Iyo and only a few years off marrying age. It was the only lie we'd thought of that Falwen might believe.

Meanwhile, Iannah would track down Arril and tell her the same story I told atop Se Ji Ainu — that I genuinely abandoned everyone, went full Imarein, and swore devotion to Suriel. As proof of my loyalty, she'd give Arril the amp rune Tiernan designed for me. Even if Falwen told the other Corvittai captains I was lying, it'd be his word against Suriel's.

For now, we just had to survive. My shoulder bag had food for several days, the most Fendul could spare from the Rin's limited stores. I set snares near a frozen stream, wincing at my burned arm. Yironem and I bent springy hemlock saplings over and roped them together, then wove in evergreen boughs to make a crude shelter, one side open for a fire.

Every motion kept me aware of my missing braid. No weight when I turned my head, little friction against my hood. The ends were itchy on my neck. Whenever I bent down, a wave of brown hair fell into my face instead a thick braid sliding over my shoulder. I felt things physically, but that was it. There was nothing left inside.

When Aikoto boys cut their hair, they burned it afterward. *They* were always fine. Even people like Akiga who had their braids taken by force didn't seem as hollow as I felt. Something about gifting my hair to Suriel and him accepting made this different. Makiri came to life when a person accepted them. This felt like a death instead.

Yironem eyed me suspiciously, but he had problems, too. He kept looking around, twitching whenever a bird rustled through the trees. He tried to toss kindling on the fire. It sailed past into a cluster of leafless salmonberry bushes.

"You okay?" I asked.

He stared at the fallen kindling. I waited. We'd developed a way of communicating, understanding one another. I hoped I could keep that much going.

Snowflakes were steaming on the flames when he spoke. "I heard voices up on the mountain."

"What'd they say?"

"Nothing. They sounded like kinaru, but . . . different. Whispering. They were everywhere."

I'd always wondered if kinaru went to Aeldu-yan. Their spirits must've been drawn here like aeldu were to shrines. All those years

Yironem spent learning the kinaru shawl dance, hoping to hear his father's voice, and he heard dead kinaru first.

"When Imarein came home, he sometimes spoke in bird calls," I said. "Maybe one of the voices up there is *him*."

If Suriel heard them, too, then every day he spent on Se Ji Ainu, Imarein's voice haunted him. A constant reminder of his loss. He'd fled twice that I knew of, during the saidu war and on the ten-year anniversary of Imarein's death, but he returned both times. I'd fled Aeti Ginu because everything reminded me of the dead, and I know better than most how strong the call of home was.

Yironem wrapped his arms around his knees. "My kinaru body's meant to be a gift from the aeldu. Do you think . . . Imarein's spirit gave it to me?"

"Makes more sense than anything else we've thought of." Though that raised more questions, ones I didn't dare voice in case Suriel heard. Like if the gift was so Yironem could rescue Nili and me, or if aeldu-Imarein had something permanent in mind. Perhaps he wanted Yironem to become a telyul, too, part of the new era of humans Falwen talked about.

We slept bunched up in our shelter. My dreams were full of flames sweeping across alpine forests. We woke in the afternoon to snow dusting our eyebrows like flour and melting on our skin. I set to weaving branches into a door for our shelter. Yironem wandered into the forest to gather firewood.

I mulled over things while he was gone. Imarein had learned to call air when no other human had managed it. I doubted Suriel was a patient teacher, so Imarein must've used everything available, adapting his years of water-calling lessons. I no longer felt attached to my family's rigid way of teaching. A whole range of possibilities had opened up.

Yironem returned with an armful of soggy branches. He dropped them in the snow and held one out for me to dry. "Not yet," I said, banking ashes over our fire. "I want to try something."

We hiked along the stream until the foliage opened into a clearing. I swept my arm in arcs, pushing away snow to reach the bottom layer, packed solid enough to stand on. Water-calling didn't work on top of Se Ji Ainu, a show of Suriel's dominance, but it worked down here.

"I've been teaching you wrong," I said. "Trying to make you move water when you're barely moving. I ignored all that time you spent dancing."

Yironem craned his neck. Se Ji Ainu loomed overhead, its craggy peak dwarfing other mountains. "You want me to dance here?"

"Remember, the shawl dance was for tel-saidu before it was for aeldu." I stepped back. "I did something like this two days ago in the burnt shrine. I'll talk you through it."

"I don't have my kinaru shawl."

"You of all people don't need it. Start with meditation."

He closed his eyes. I watched him go through the steps. *Breathe.* Thin white puffs streamed from his nostrils. *Feel.* His fingertips grazed his snowy breeches. *Extend.* His mouth puckered in concentration as he pushed his mind outward, sensing snow around him.

"Hold your thoughts like that," I said. "Keep your eyes closed. I'll stop you if you're about to fall into the stream."

Yironem spread his cloak like wings. He spun, sinking and soaring, arms tilting with the grace of flight. His boots hardly touched the ground. He didn't need drums or singing. The music lived in him.

"There. Your cloak catches snowflakes and pulls them with you. When you move the air, it sends the snow around you swirling. Do you feel it?"

"Yes," he breathed.

"Now push farther out. Think of being a kinaru. Think how much space that body takes up. Sweep the snow up in your wings."

Yironem's eyes snapped open. A thin trail of crystal flakes spiralled after him and rose into the air. He whooped with joy. His control broke, and they drifted to the ground, but for a second, he'd done it.

Yironem kept practising while we foraged. I wanted to stretch the smelt we'd brought as long as possible. We peeled back cottonwood bark and cut strips of frozen inner bark, which we chewed while gathering whatever else had survived the winter — frost-blackened mushrooms high on trees, seeds on dead brown plants, bearberries hidden under the snow.

No one came. My snares stayed empty. Wildlife hadn't returned to the deep mountains yet. We had to go farther to gather firewood and food, breaking paths through deep white drifts. We had no sinew to make snowshoes. If we stayed still to conserve energy, we'd freeze to death. Better to keep moving. Keep busy or go crazy fretting about what was happening outside this valley.

After half a month, our smelt ran out. I still felt hunger, so I knew Yironem suffered, too, but him wasting away didn't bother me like it used to. That's when I started to realize how much I'd lost. I knew I needed to keep my little brother alive — if Falwen was right, Yironem was our best hope of producing a telyul to manage the wind and repair the world — but this was a calculation, not borne of love.

I stood in the clearing by the stream and called into the mountains. "Suriel, can you hear me? Please let my brother leave to search for food. Look how thin he is after this long winter. He's not growing anymore. I'll stay here, I promise."

I waited, shivering. Moments later, a breeze ruffled my cut hair. *He may go.*

Yironem returned an hour later, sinking from the sky with an enormous limp fish clamped in his bill. He beat his wings hard, straining under its weight, and dropped it at my feet. A pebbly grey sturgeon, whiskered, spiked from head to tail, longer than I was tall.

"I followed another kinaru," he explained as we gutted it. "I wondered what they ate with the lakes frozen over. Turns out they fish the inland stretches of Burren Inlet. The north arm's a couple valleys away."

"How'd you catch it?" I asked. "Sturgeon are bottom-feeders."

"Yeah, but know how they jump? This one wouldn't stop. Like something scared it. The other kinaru helped me carry it to land until it stopped wriggling."

"Thank you," I said to the sky. "Thank you, thank you."

The fish's belly was full of roe, thousands of barley-sized black eggs caked together like berry mash. Any other time, I would've salted them to make caviar and sold them for a hefty bag of sovereigns. Instead we ate them plain by the fingerful. We cut the pale flesh away in chunks, packed some in snow, and left some out in offering. That night, kinaru wailed in the woods. The next morning, the offering was gone.

Every day from then on, warm wind filled the valley. Slush dripped off trees and pitted the snow in honeycomb patterns. Suriel seemed to be fighting this little section of the world's slide into ruin. It was an odd gesture considering he'd ignored me during the Caladheä blizzard. I wondered if owning my spirit affected him, too, granting him a sliver of my lost compassion.

There was no way to know if something had gone wrong or if this was a test. Leaving without permission would sever Suriel's trust forever, and I would've sacrificed my spirit for nothing. I notched a hemlock, counting the days. Yironem and I occupied ourselves with antayul lessons. Teaching him seemed more and more important as time passed, my original reason for coming here slipping away.

"Look at your reflection," Yironem said one morning.

I called up a glassy pool and peered into it, parting my hair to see the roots. They were coming in white. Pretty, I thought, but the look on Yironem's face told me not to admit that.

After a month in the valley, a kinaru called in the distance. We dashed to the clearing for a better look. I thought its rider was Arril — black leather armour, curved sword, hair in a severe bun — until they thumped down on the soggy bank. Iannah sat astride the bird.

"Suriel sent me to get you," she said. "You've got new orders."

Strong wind bore us back west, making the trip far faster than when we'd come. Iannah didn't speak when we rested, just tilted her head at her kinaru. I didn't know if it understood Coast Trader and didn't want to find out. It warbled at Yironem a few times, but he stayed quiet.

We arced around Caladheå and over the bay to an island so small I'd never seen it on maps. A schooner with rust-red sails was moored in a sheltered cove, only visible from the air. We landed on the muddy shore. Iannah's kinaru took off again, dipping into the waves in search of food.

"Snowshoes, ships, horses, and giant waterfowl," Iannah said, rubbing her calves. "Give me solid ground any day."

"What's going on?" I asked. "Whose ship is that?"

"Láchlan's. This is an old smuggling hideout. I'll explain on the way." She nodded at my hair. "The white — was that meant to happen?"

"I don't know. Imarein kept his head shaved."

Iannah squeezed my hand. For Yironem, she managed a smile. She began walking down the shore. "Arril dragged her feet about taking you back, Koehl. She said keeping Suriel company counts as serving him. So Arquiere and I tried another plan. He started rumours about a resurgence in the black market and got the Council to search the Shawnaast district near Arril's base.

"Arril fled, of course. I followed her to a fishing shack outside Caladheå. Said I wanted back in, too. That if they're going to cause an explosion, I want it done right. No casualties. Pointed out they had two weeks until Abhain, no army, and barely any ships or money. Reminded her I can move freely through Caladheå. Arril didn't listen. Insisted she had it under control.

"Two days later, Láchlan arrived with an extra freight ship and tried to buy a load of blackpowder from Gallnach smugglers. Thing is, Arquiere's rumours sent the navy scrambling. They're watching every craft in these waters. They stormed the sale and seized everything — blackpowder, money, smugglers, the freight ship, and two of Láchlan's sailors."

I looked up from navigating the driftwood-strewn beach. "And the Corvittai got desperate enough to take you?"

"Yeah. Láchlan rampaged at Arril. Said he wished he'd had the guts to challenge Cattil. That we had every right to invade Innisbán to rescue starving prisoners. That Cattil invited her death by abusing her mercenaries and murdering viirelei captives, and if we *had* killed her, he couldn't have complained. He said that if Arril had used my military connections instead of relying on Falwen, they might've dodged the naval raid."

"So which captain do you work for?"

"I am one. You're looking at the new Nonil." Iannah unbuckled her breastplate. Embroidered on her black shirt was Suriel's kinaru, its head turned aside.

I whistled.

"They won't tell me much about Iollan, but Falwen took me to meet Suriel. Bloody hell. Don't know how you did it, Yironem. At fourteen, I was scared of my academy captains."

He beamed. Before my sacrifice, I would've felt grateful to Iannah for encouraging him.

"Anyway," she said, "my first mission is joint with Láchlan. He wants to steal the blackpowder back."

"Should we? Or . . ." I eyed the overcast sky. I couldn't say *sabotage*.

She dropped her voice. "I think we have to. There's a chance the Corvittai are hiding something big. If we interfere, best result is we delay them, and we're out forever. If we help, we're in for good. That's the only way to get near Iollan."

Near the schooner, we turned and headed into the forest. Patches of rotten leaves and spruce needles showed through the snow. Láchlan and four other itherans drank from tin cups around a smoky fire. I recognized them all, but didn't see Láchlan's first mate, the dogsled driver who'd killed Cattil. Wise to keep him away from Arril.

Láchlan rose and thumped my back. He was coated with dirt, masking the anchor tattoos on his wrists. "Good to see you again, Kateiko. That old windsack ran you through the mill, eh? Lads, get our friends a drink."

A man with a hoop earring poured two cups from a flask and handed them to Yironem and me. I knew the peaty smell right away. Whisky. Another man passed Iannah a cup of water.

I raised my drink. "To getting off one godsawful island and onto another."

The men laughed. Yironem, following my lead, choked his whisky down. They nodded their respect and made space for us by the fire.

"Our blackpowder's still on the *Róg Sál*, moored in Caladheå," Iannah said. "The Council wants to sell it to the highest bidder. They're low on money after funding famine programs, and warlords in the southern colonies have started training musketmen."

Láchlan grimaced. "Then we better work fast. Gold greases tough deals."

"What's your plan?" I asked. "We can't fight the entire navy."

"No. And it'll take all my spare men to crew the ship." He fixed me with a hard look. "I'll be straight with you, Kateiko Rin. Our new Nonil here says you gave up everyone for Suriel, Quinil says you didn't, and Arril isn't sure, but I don't give a sheep's woolly arse either way. We need hands and weapons. So bring whatever help you can get."

I blinked. "You trust me that much?"

"I trust you to see sense, lass. You did on Innisbán when you backed off to stop a massacre. That much powder can supply an army. The only reason I ain't bailed on Peimil is 'cause he won't use it on people. I seen enough of that being around the last Cattil."

"Suriel gave me permission to recruit viirelei," Iannah said. "We can't plan from here, though. We need eyes on that ship."

Láchlan thumped his leg. "Agreed. Let's heave anchor. We can be in Caladheå by dusk, get a good sleep on land, and start scouting in the morning."

We separated at the docks. Yironem and I went first to Segowa's flat. I kept my hood up to avoid her reaction to my hair.

"I need two favours," I said. "One, I need somewhere for Yiro to sleep. Two, can you ask an Iyo to carry a message to Toel Ginu? I don't want Suriel to think we're returning to the Rin."

Segowa nodded. "My brother Ranelin is in town. He'll go."

While she pulled her spare mattress from behind her workbench, I sifted through my memories. They were fragmented, the emotions stripped out. I needed a parting message for Yironem, something the old me would've said, so he'd stop worrying about me. So he wouldn't question me.

I settled on teasing him and whispered, "Ask Segowa to show you her nieces' embroidery. Word will get back to Tamiwa. Girls like it when you care about their work."

Yironem rolled his eyes. "I know how to deal with girls."

"Says the kid who was too scared to talk to her all winter."

He shoved me.

After giving Segowa a message asking Fendul to send everyone willing, I headed back outside and stood in spitting rain. Airedain's building was down the street. Lamplight glowed in his window, luring me close. The air was still. Even if I stretched my mind up into the clouds, the raindrops fell straight.

"Suriel," I called. "Are you there?"

If he was too far away to hear, he couldn't see me, either. Probably. Maybe. Did he know Airedain was the lover I swore to have left? I was allowed to recruit Aikoto, but of all people to return to . . .

"Suriel, I need you. Please. If you're there, answer me."

Just darkness and rain. I strolled casually toward Airedain's building, splashing through puddles. The outer door was unlocked.

Inside, free of Suriel's sight, I took the stairs two at a time and banged on his door.

It swung open. Airedain gawked at me. "You're alive." He pushed back my hood and froze. "Your *hair*."

"Yeah."

He reached for my white roots but lowered his hand to feel the cropped brown ends instead. Then he kissed me so hard we thumped into the corridor wall. "It ain't so bad. Maybe it'll grow normal now that you're away from Suriel."

I tried to smile. He pulled me into his flat and shut the door. We didn't speak for a while, our mouths busy. His breath was sour with alcohol. I didn't care. He was here, real, mine — more than I could say for myself.

A vodka bottle sat open on the table. When we broke away, he corked it, trying to block it from view. The bin under his liquor shelf was full of empty bottles to be taken to the glassware-seller.

I touched his elbow. "You don't have to hide that. I don't blame you."

He ran a hand across his crest of hair, flattening it from back to front. "Kako . . . I wanna be a man you're proud of. I've been doin' whatever I can here to hold off the famine, volunteering at stave-hall food banks, keeping people alive like you would. But staying put was fuckin' hard when you were out there with Suriel suffering aeldu knows what. Even as a warrior, all I could do to help you was protect the hair you gave me."

"You still have it, then?"

"Right here." Airedain held up his wrist, circled by a rope bracelet. "I wove it in. No one has noticed it."

Among the dull fibres was the tiniest shimmer of glossy brown. I ran my fingertip over it. Like with Suriel, I'd given the strand to

Airedain willingly. Maybe that gave it power, too. I looked up and realized he was watching me strangely.

I lowered my hand. "There's another way you can help me. I need to steal a shipload of blackpowder."

Airedain frowned. "You're serious."

"Yes. You know how to move through this city better than any of us. Even Iannah admits it."

"The Corvittai won't trust me. I fought 'em on Innisbán. Unless you want me to cut off my hair, too—"

"Nei!" I said too fast. "We can lie. Claim that even after my sacrifice, you love me enough to do anything for me."

"It ain't a lie."

I remembered how it felt physically when he said such things — weight in my stomach, tightness in my throat. I needed time to process my memories and figure out how to keep up this façade. Unflinching as his love may be, it'd be easier if he didn't know how far gone I was.

"Um . . ." I dropped my eyes. "Can I bathe? I've been sleeping on the ground. I feel like I'm made of mud."

"Ai, yeah. Sorry." Airedain got a pail for me to fill, then set it on the stove to heat.

He dropped into a chair and pulled me into his lap. I distracted him by talking about the valley, Suriel's gift of sturgeon, the meeting with Láchlan. When he started kissing my neck, I let him. It felt nice. We moved only to dump hot water into the wooden wash basin, refill the pail, and set it to heat again.

When the basin was half-full he said, "Want me to leave?"

"Don't be ridiculous. You've seen me naked." I stripped off my dusty clothes and stepped into the basin, letting my feet adjust to the temperature.

Airedain watched me hungrily. "You're still lush with short hair, Rin-girl."

I laughed. It sounded strange. "You're drunk."

"Doesn' mean I'm wrong."

I eased into the steaming water, knees to my chest so I fit. Dirt was layered onto me like the rings of a tree. I scrubbed slimy brown lye soap over my skin, washing away all traces of the valley. If only I could wash the scar from my fireweed tattoo, the white from my hair.

He knelt next to me, resting his arms on the basin. "One day, I'll have money to buy you nice soap. White and scented with lilac."

"Nei. Pine, so I can smell like you." I flicked murky droplets at him.

I lifted my arms to wash my hair and winced. My muscles ached from clinging to Yironem's back for hours, trying not to plunge to my death.

Airedain rolled up his sleeves. "Close your eyes."

He cupped his hands into the water, poured it over my head, and lathered soap into my hair. After rinsing away the suds, he tucked my linen fireweed and arrowhead leaves behind my ear. He'd kept them safe, too.

I wondered what would happen if I touched his hair. If I could reach through the shattered mirror once more and draw on the spirit of a warrior who loved fiercely and gently at once. But my hands wouldn't move. I couldn't tell if it felt like betraying my vow to Suriel or if the fragment of my spirit Airedain held was afraid to know the answer.

Yet I hadn't lost everything. My body could still feel. Maybe that, along with the bracelet, would be enough to hold onto traces of my old self. I rose dripping and shivering, dried myself with a few flicks of my hand, and stepped into Airedain's arms. He wrapped a wool blanket around my shoulders, scooped me up, and dropped me onto his bed.

"Wait," I said hastily. "I can't take bloodweed. I can't afford to be sick tomorrow."

"There's other things we can do." He knelt over me. "I wanna make you feel good, Kako. Let me give you that."

28.

FATHER'S DAUGHTER

The next morning, Nili and Dunehein arrived bleary-eyed at the Iyo gathering place. They'd travelled overnight from Toel Ginu. Nili switched between hugging Yironem and wailing over my missing braid. Dunehein just ruffled my hair, white roots and all. Airedain handed out breakfast while we caught up on news.

"It's just us," Dunehein said, soaking up smelt oil with a wedge of brassroot flatbread. "Not many Rin support this. They'd rather attack the Corvittai now than play the long con. Aliko's staying neutral so she doesn't cause Fendul trouble for being with her. Rija wants to help, but she's gotta look after Sihaja."

"What'd my okorebai say?" Airedain asked.

"No," Nili said. "Emphatically, even after Ranelin argued it's your choice. But Tokoda knows you'll do it anyway, and she can't interfere without violating the ceasefire."

"Tokoda's no fool, though," Dunehein added. "You can bet she'll have scouts following that ship."

Nili watched me while we ate. I had a chance of deceiving Airedain while he was hungover, but not my sister, who knew me better than anyone. After I collected our dishes, she followed me to the side room with the wash basins.

"All right," she said, hands on her hips. "Something's going on. You sacrificed yourself to protect the Rin, and now you're asking for our help. For *mine* when I'm pregnant."

"I'll keep you and Yiro out of combat—"

"Bearshit. This isn't you. The old Kako would've thrown me in a canoe back to Toel."

"Then why are you here?" I asked, filling a basin.

"To help you, bludgehead. Whatever's wrong, you gotta fake it better. We're your family, we love you no matter what, but if another Aikoto realizes you made a deal with Suriel . . ."

I sighed. "Fine. How do I fake it?"

"First, we cover that." Nili jabbed at my white hair. "Charcoal will have to do for now. Second, keep away from other people. Third, I'm the future okoreni, so I'm in charge of every Rin pulling this heist. Got it?"

I raised my hands, not protesting.

"Good." She paused. "And if you can't smile, try to look annoyed or something. That blankness is creepy."

Following Iannah's instructions, we crossed the bridge over the Stengar into Shawnaast. The *Róg Sál*, an unremarkable white-sailed schooner, was moored at the old docks safely away from the shipping district. Its name had been painted over, but it was clear we had the right ship. Ten men in naval uniform — red cloth over leather breastplates — lounged on the dock. A few held a spitting contest into the ocean.

Nili, Dunehein, and Yironem left to scout. Several figures, hooded against the rain, fished off piers. Even from shore, I knew Iannah was the one fumbling with a rod. Airedain and I set up next to her with long-handled nets. It was perfect for spying, with a view all along the bay. If Láchlan recognized Airedain from the Innisbán battle, he said nothing.

"Took you long enough," Iannah said. "I saw Rhonos before Council started. He had news. A warlord just bought the black-powder."

"Good news," Láchlan clarified. "They'll load the ship with supplies to sail south. When they heave anchor, we make our move."

"Which is?" I asked.

"Remove guards, board ship, escape." He lifted a squirming minnow from the water, slid it off his hook, and tossed it into a bucket. "Easy, right?"

Airedain snorted.

Quietly, never looking at the ship, Láchlan and Iannah explained their plan. They'd cobbled it together from his knowledge of the navy and hers of the city guard. "The main problem is if more guards show up," Iannah added. "Fire's a good distraction, but razing anywhere near the ocean will wind up with a bucket brigade in the middle of our heist."

"Shawnaast's old town hall," Airedain said immediately. "It's all wood and close to the river. And it's ruined, so no one will be inside."

"Spent time in this district, eh?" Láchlan said.

"I used to see an itheran girl who went to boarding school here. Got arrested while visiting her. Learned to dodge Elkhounds pretty fast after that."

Láchlan chuckled. "I like you, lad."

Iannah coughed. A fisherman was approaching. Láchlan began rambling in fluent Sverbian about endless winter and bad catches. Airedain joined in, tipping our bucket upside down. All that fell out was rainwater. The fisherman peered at Láchlan's bucket of minnows and left. Airedain muttered something in Gallnach, earning a laugh from Láchlan.

"The other big problem," Láchlan said, "is sailing out of the bay. Last thing we need's the navy on our arses. I know a few officers who'd look the other way, but we don't have the coin to grease their gambling debts."

I exchanged a look with Airedain. We'd known this might come up. "Would a purse of silver be enough?"

"Aye, if you could get it—"

"I've got it," Airedain said. "We took it from one of your mercenaries last year at Bódhain. My cousin said I can use his half."

He held back words about the cost of not spending that silver, stained with the blood of Rutnaast townsfolk. Instead, he and Jonalin had chosen to work. Airedain's payment was getting falsely linked to the black market and having to stop drumming to evade arrest. Jonalin's was leaving home for the Algard Island fishery, set up because of this famine. Cattil and Láchlan had had their hands in it all.

Láchlan could tell something went unsaid. "I can't fault you for whatever you did to my men. Just hope they didn't suffer."

"We let those ones go," I said. "Sent them to the southern colonies."

He looked surprised. "Then you saved their lives. They wouldn't have survived this winter in jail. Rations ain't good for Gallnach immigrants."

Wotelem had taken Gallnach captives from Rutnaast and the salmon raid to prison. We hadn't known there'd be a famine. I sifted through my memories for the right feeling. Guilt? Yes, better not try to show that one.

Láchlan pulled up his fishing rod. "Enough grief for one morning. C'mon, lad. Show me this town hall and I'll show you how to torch it."

That evening, Iannah and I went to meet Rhonos. It'd look odd to visit his Colonnium office too often, so he'd agreed to come to Natzo's. I was surprised Iannah told him about it. Then again, it had stopped being our secret haven when Cièntus started watching her.

"Are you still living at the Knox?" I asked, sidestepping a puddle.

"My mail goes there," Iannah said. "I'm only around to eat and sleep. Too busy to work. Though word got 'round that Emílie hired an ex-Colonnium guard. No one's tried breaking into the cellar since."

"If only they knew who you are now." I couldn't get used to her being Nonil. "You really think Rhonos will go through with this plan?"

"I'll convince Arquiere. I'm his advisor, after all."

I looked sideways at her. "You must be seeing a lot of him."

"Is that a problem?"

I shrugged. Not *my* problem.

Iannah pushed open the door to Natzo's. She froze. "*That* might be a problem."

I peered into the candlelit room. Rhonos and Falwen faced each other, deep in conversation in rapid Ferish. Their bowls were down to a few drops of soup. Falwen's hands spun through the air, punctuating his words. Under the table, Rhonos tapped his leg with measured irritation.

Falwen noticed us and beckoned. We wound through tables and chairs toward them.

"What a coincidence," Falwen said. "Sohikoehl, I had no idea you were back in Caladheå."

Something prickled deep inside me. I realized I was gritting my teeth. "I had no idea you ate here," I said.

"Conveniently near the Colonnium, as you know." He gave Iannah a clipped bow. "Care to join us?"

I had nothing to fear from him. Suriel wanted me alive. "I'll find you later," I told Iannah and grabbed Falwen's arm. "Let's go."

He rose without argument. "Forgive me, Councillor Parr." He dropped an iron five-pann on the counter for Natzo and followed me outside.

I whirled on him. "What are you doing?"

"Discussing politics with a colleague—"

"The son of your dead friend," I hissed.

"This is not a discussion to have here. Come."

He strode off. I thought we were going to the Colonnium, but he turned down a street where leafless alders arched overhead to form a tunnel. Wet cobblestones gleamed under street lamps. Falwen opened a wrought-iron gate and unlocked a brick flat.

His home. Not only was Bronnoi Ridge the government district, but he could hide his business from us here. He wiped his boots on a mat and glared at me until I did the same. The place smelled like mothballs and spice.

Falwen cracked the shutters to let in street light and nodded at a chair with an ornate scalloped back. "I only have one. Take it."

I stayed standing. He had a fondness for uncomfortable furniture. The chair matched a desk and bookshelf, the book titles masked by shadows. Unlike the Iyo flats, his place had more than one room. A narrow staircase zigzagged up. A closed door likely led to a kitchen.

He tossed split logs onto coals in the fireplace. "Antoch Parr betrayed us both. I want to know if his son will, too."

As firelight illuminated the room, I saw three makiri on the mantelpiece. Haka grizzly, Iyo dolphin, Rin kinaru. Nothing for the Ferish quarter of his bloodline. On a shelf above was a seagull with its wings spread, the Dona-jouyen that combined them all. I wondered who'd visited Falwen in the thirty years he'd lived in Caladheå. He wouldn't have let many people see those.

He held out a hand for my cloak. I didn't move. He shrugged and hung his grey coat on a hook. His waistcoat underneath was tailored to his wiry frame, his high-collared shirt thick enough so his tattoos didn't show.

"A story for you," he said, hanging a copper kettle over the flames. "It begins last summer. The day after Parr took you to Suriel, he came to my office. He seemed uncomfortable. Unlike himself. He wanted to know of specific customs among our people — age of consent, contraception, intimacy out of wedlock.

"Apprehensive, I told him the truth. It broke no laws nor spiritual taboos. I figured nothing came of it, as you returned to Heilind soon after. Three weeks later, Parr told me you visited his home again, but he implied nothing happened. I did not know what to believe. Until recently.

"Gossip abounds in Toel Ginu. Your nightmares of an anonymous man. You and Airedain Kiyorem on the spring equinox, reportedly your first time. I have seen you alone together at his flat, so why use the shrine unless you needed to feel safe? My guess is Kiyorem was not your first. An Iyo herbalist recalls selling you bloodweed around the time you returned to Parr Manor."

"And when did that become your business?" I asked.

Falwen cast me a look of strained patience. "When Parr tried to commit genocide on the Rin-jouyen. Obviously."

As much as I disliked it, he was the only person I might get answers from. No one else truly knew Parr except Rhonos, and I'd never tell him this secret. "Parr claimed he . . . didn't know I was Rin. He didn't know what my tattoo meant."

"I believe that. For decades I have let itheran politicians remain ignorant about the meaning of our crests. They would look on me less kindly if they knew I was once an illiterate Dona nomad."

"How could you call Parr your closest friend while you lied to him? What kind of friendship is that?"

"A safe one." He took his kinaru makiri from the mantel and balanced it on his fingertips. "To him, I was the ideal viirelei, proof we can be 'civilized.' Itherans choose what is acceptable from our culture. It changes. Kiyorem has drummed for thousands of itherans to great acclaim, yet now it is grounds for arrest. Hide what is sacred, and they cannot take it away. Parr and I cared for the parts of each other we revealed. I presume it was the same for you."

Cared. Parr had used a stronger word for me.

Falwen put the makiri back. "Ferland black or Haka herbal. Choose."

"What?"

"Tea, Sohikoehl. What is Hiyua's phrase? 'Shared food for shared hurts'? If tea does not suffice, I have *pérossetto* rolls. Parr mentioned you liked them."

I stared.

"Herbal it is." He took a ball of dried leaves from a tin and set it by the teapot, waiting for the kettle to whistle. "I admit, I am offended you trust Parr's son over me. Did he not also hide their connection?"

"Rhonos left years ago. You didn't turn on Parr until he sent Nonil to butcher us. I don't believe for a second you care what he did to me."

Falwen slumped into his scallop-backed chair and rested his forehead in his hands. His fingernails were clean and trimmed, but one thumb bore a deep scar that might've come from a fish knife. We were alike once.

"I have no children. Only nieces and nephews I have not seen since they were small. Yet . . ." He rubbed his eyes. "After so long watching over you, one who shares my Rin blood, I understand the trouble of raising teenagers. Aggravation at your obstinance, trumped by disgust at a man who violated you. Fury at myself for failing you. This must be how it feels to have a daughter."

My jaw went slack. I was on my third mother, but I hadn't had a father in years.

For a second, it was a beautiful thought. Falwen wasn't mad at me for sleeping with Parr. He knew enough about everything, everyone, to protect me. I imagined him standing next to Hiyua at my wedding.

But it was a false thought. A vision of a world that never existed. The prickling sensation from before grew stronger. Anger, I realized distantly. I *did* have an emotion left — the only one Suriel had ever expressed.

"Nei," I said. "You don't get to play fucking mind games, bringing me here to make me feel sorry for your loneliness. It won't work. Whatever you want, you're not getting it."

"Sohikoehl. Wait."

I turned back at the door. It was petty, but with a flick of my hand, the steam faded from the kettle. "Enjoy your tea."

29.

HEIST

In the misty dawn near Shawnaast's stavehall, I said goodbye to my family. Nili and Yironem carried their bows and skins of oil. Dunehein had knives up his sleeves in case things went sour. Airedain drummed impatiently on his legs. He was to guide them to the old town hall and back. I couldn't kiss him where Suriel could see, so we just smiled.

I flexed my cold fingers and started climbing the stavehall, hauling myself onto the shingle roofs of its tiers and gables. After years of scaling trees, the height didn't bother me. What worried me was some early riser sounding an alarm, but the city was as sleepy as ever when I reached the top platform of the bell tower. An engraving of a leafless nine-branched tree adorned the huge bronze bell overhead.

Fog veiled the streets. Only the peaks of Shawnaast showed through — steep roofs, brick chimneys, weather vanes lazily turning. In the distance, the town hall's clock tower looked like a mossy island, its copper roof turned green by age. I knelt down and marked chalk lines across the timber platform, meticulously copying the amp rune Tiernan designed for me. Then I hid by a pillar as the eastern sky turned bright.

CLANG.

I snapped out of dozing. The bell rope plunged up and down as someone downstairs pulled it, signalling sunrise. My teeth vibrated. I threw my arms over my ears until the bronze clapper stopped swinging.

Sunlight thinned the fog, revealing murky waves in the bay. Tiny figures scurried across the docks, loading the *Róg Sál* with supplies. Rhonos was down there somewhere with an agent of the warlord who'd bought the blackpowder. As the only ex-military councillor, he'd had no trouble arranging to oversee the deal. When sailors on deck began turning the capstan to raise the anchor, it was time.

I stretched my mind across rows of buildings to the old town hall and slashed frost on its clock tower. Once Airedain and Dunehein saw my signal, they'd drench the hall in oil and run. Nili and Yironem, hiding on a nearby roof, would shoot flaming arrows at it. As I watched, black smoke billowed into the sky. Ant-like people darted up the streets toward it.

That was my next cue. I stepped onto my chalk rune. Energy surged through me. It was tuned perfectly to my body, far stronger than the ones Iollan's acolyte made on Innisbán. I closed my eyes and sank into meditation. The remaining fog gave me something to start with. I swept my mind across Shawnaast and pulled every airborne droplet to shore. The harbour vanished under a cloud.

Deep within that cloud, everything solid felt like darkness where my water couldn't go. It let me "see" silhouettes. Sailors paused at the *Róg Sál*'s capstan. Dockhands turned in confusion. I called water from the ocean and dispersed it into more mist. My muscles twitched under the strain. As long as I didn't open my eyes, I couldn't see the shoirdryge.

Out in the bay, a ship ghosted toward land. I knew the shape of its hull — not one of Láchlan's swift smuggling ships, but the sturdy herring drifter he used when pretending to be a fishmonger. He and his crew would land at the *Róg Sál*'s dock, pretending they got lost in the fog. Like they'd intended to reach the fish market.

CLANG.

I stumbled. My eyes flew wide. I grabbed a pillar, catching myself a second before toppling off the platform into the sky. Cobblestones swung far below.

CLANG. I reeled back from the tower edge.

Through the ringing, I heard shouts about fire. Someone had raised an alarm. Yet the bell was motionless — rope, clapper, and all. I spun toward the old town hall. Its clock tower rose unburnt from weather-worn walls. The smoke was gone.

"Kaid," I cursed. The snowy hills beyond Shawnaast were suddenly green with spring. My cloud remained in the harbour, but it'd drift apart if I didn't get ahold of it. If anybody saw Láchlan at the docks and called Elkhounds for backup, his chance of escape was gone.

Airedain trusted sound over vision. I clung to the bell's clear resonance, riding back to where I belonged. My world, where the ringing had summoned people to douse the blazing town hall. I blinked. Still smokeless spring. *Focus*, I berated myself.

"—trespassing street rat," I heard between clangs.

I moved to the trap door leading down into the tower. It flipped open and a man stuck his head up. Without guessing which world he was in, I swung Antalei's chain around his neck.

He scrabbled, grabbing the flail's spiked head. His yelp of pain was choked. Slowly, face turning blue, eyes bulging, he went limp.

His fingers slipped from the ladder rung. I caught him and hauled him onto the platform.

"Thank you, Ia," I muttered. She'd drilled disarming techniques into me.

The man wore an iron pendant of the nine-branched tree. Likely a stavehall attendant, he must've been calling to someone below. I doused the platform timbers. My chalk rune dissolved and its power with it. I yanked my hood low, scampered down the ladder, and jumped off into a wood-walled room. A cleric in white robes goggled at me. I bolted past him into the bright street.

Hands yanked me into an alley. I stumbled into a brick wall. Airedain steadied me.

"Got caught," I gasped. "Knocked him out."

His fingers curled into my arm. "Can you hold the fog without the rune?"

"Not from here. It's too far."

"Go on, then." He shoved me. "We'll catch up."

I ran. I didn't know the route, only the direction. Everyone streamed the other way, heading for plumes of smoke from the old town hall. Elkhounds yelled instructions about hauling water from the Stengar. I kept going away from the river and plowed into a world of mist. It slipped into my clothes and coalesced on my eyelashes.

Shouting led me up the shore. Láchlan's herring drifter, loaded with crates, was moored near the *Róg Sál*. While he argued with red-uniformed guards, his crew threw off the crate lids. Five veiled Corvittai burst out and swarmed onto the dock. The guards gaped. Leading Arril's men was Iannah, sword raised. She slammed the hilt into one man's elbow, dislocating it, and twirled out of reach.

The guards rallied. Metal rang against metal. The dockhands fled. Láchlan and his crew dashed for the *Róg Sál*, scaled the ropes, and swung onto its deck. The sailors raised their hands in surrender. They weren't paid for combat.

Rhonos emerged through the swirling haze, dressed in his black Council robe with a scarlet hem. The warlord's agent, a Ferish man with his hands balled into fists, followed at a safe distance. I dove behind a cluster of barrels. I couldn't get caught again.

Near the dock, Rhonos seized a sword from a fallen guard. He skewered one of Arril's men, yanked the sword out with a spray of blood, and kicked him into the ocean. The warlord's agent looked impressed.

Then Rhonos met Iannah.

Their blades sang like sleigh bells. His robe billowed. Her veil fluttered. At every blow, I flinched like it was a death strike. They weren't supposed to hurt each other, but maybe Rhonos changed his mind.

It didn't matter. An Antler would beat an archer in hand-to-hand combat any day. Iannah's sword kissed Rhonos's throat. He surrendered his blade. She dragged him down the dock toward the gangplank. This was our plan to stop the navy from sinking the *Róg Sál* or torching it if they were desperate enough to cause an explosion. Councillor Nerio Parr was too valuable to kill.

Our silver bribe would keep away some ships. Láchlan could dodge the rest if I kept his cover up, but the fog was vastly more water than I usually handled. I tried to slow my breathing and keep control. I didn't have time to draw another rune.

This time, I saw an attacker coming.

I leapt off the dock. A shock of icy water enveloped me. I sank through clouds of seaweed, holding my breath. Seconds later, a guard toppled into the ocean, an arrow in his eye. Blood whorled past flecks of algae.

Only lifelong archers aimed that well. Rhonos wouldn't kill a naval soldier, which meant Nili or Yironem had caught up. I kicked hard and surfaced. The warlord's agent was shouting for help. Iannah turned. Saw me. She shoved Rhonos at one of Arril's mercenaries and strode back down the dock.

"Hide," she said, passing me. "I'll protect the others."

I swam under the dock and grabbed a post, cutting my palms on barnacles. My teeth chattered. I forced myself to close my eyes. Yironem was too young by law to be in battle, and I'd sworn to keep Nili out of it, but they'd be safe with Iannah. I had my own task.

The ocean gave me a conduit straight to the *Róg Sál*. I felt its anchor rise dripping into the air. Its hull drifted away from the dock, a shadow on the surface. I packed fog up to its mast tip. Across the harbour, a navy cutter veered toward them. I pushed back with the ocean, slowing its approach.

I hung on until the *Róg Sál* was a fleck in my mind, then I let the fog go. Now that they'd reached open ocean, Suriel would speed them along. I pushed out from under the dock and floated on my back. Sunlight dazzled my eyes. Bodies in red uniforms lay everywhere. One of Arril's men sprawled off the dock, bleeding into the water.

"Ai!" a voice called.

Dunehein stood on shore, the only living person in sight. I swam toward him. My limbs ached with cold. When my feet hit earth, I ran, splashing through the shallows and onto muddy beach. The smell of burnt wood wafted off him.

Yironem met us in the streets. Dunehein shouldered open a door and pushed us into an abandoned tailor's shop, the meeting point Airedain had showed us. Nili sat on the dusty floor rubbing her bad leg. Her other hand held her middle.

I dropped into a crouch. "Nili. Are you okay? Your baby?"

"Just sore," she said, grimacing. "Elkhounds followed us toward the docks, so Airedain lured them back into town. I sent Iannah to get him."

"I have to go, too."

Dunehein grabbed my arm. "It ain't safe——"

I yanked free and ran outside. Brick walls and iron fences flew past. I snapped my head left and right, looking for coyote prints or the glint of daggers. Water flowed through the gutters. I followed its path backward and found snowbanks melting around the old town hall. The courtyard was an ashy lake. Soot-smeared people tossed buckets of water onto the flames. Steam billowed over the rooftops.

Iannah prowled the courtyard. No one paid attention to her. She'd left her veil, sword, and bloodstained armour somewhere.

I grabbed her sleeve. "Where's Airedain?"

Her always blank expression was wrong. "Koehl——"

"Where. Is. He?"

"Keep your voice down——"

I slammed her into a hitching post. "*Where is he?!*"

Iannah wheezed. She dragged me down a cobblestone lane. "I don't know. We tried to escape through a lumberyard and got separated."

"You said you'd protect him!" I pushed her into a brick wall.

She flipped me onto the ground. Dirty water splashed everywhere. I groaned, seeing flashes of light, and scrambled back up. She spun me around and pinned me to the wall.

"Listen." She breathed hard. "I looked everywhere. So did the Iyo who were here. I'm sorry, Koehl. Airedain's gone."

30.

TEN YEARS

I paced in circles in the Iyo gathering place. "It's Falwen. It must be. He couldn't control me, so he took my lover."

Nili sat on a bark mat, stretching her legs. "He's creepy, but would he go that far?"

"Yes!" I smashed the wall. Pain seared through my fist.

"You've gotten Suriel's temper," Nili muttered, then cringed when she realized I'd heard.

She'd insisted on keeping me here while the chaos died down. Dunehein had gone to find Segowa. Yironem had flown to Toel Ginu to tell them Airedain was missing. Iannah, seeming glad to get away from me, was reporting to Arril. I busied myself with replacing the charcoal that had washed out of my hair.

Dunehein wasn't gone long. Segowa returned with him. She looked at me and then away, a silent accusation on her face. Tokoda had banned Airedain from helping with the heist, and he'd done it anyway. For me.

"You've been through this before, right?" Dunehein asked her. "When Airedain got arrested."

She nodded. "The first time, his classmates only knew he got dragged out of school, not where he went. The Elkhounds told Falwen before they told me. The second time, Airedain went out to see an itheran girl and didn't come home until the next morning. I had no idea he'd spent the night locked up."

I had to find Falwen. Dunehein and two Iyo came with me as far as the rearing elk statues at the Colonnium gate since only I had an entry card. Slush melted as I crossed the courtyard. The fountain boiled. I dropped my weapons on the front desk, strode past the startled clerk into the south gallery, took the stairs two at a time, and flung open Falwen's office door.

He sat across from a Ferish man in fine clothes. Not a councillor, since they'd be surrounded by bodyguards now that Rhonos had been "kidnapped," but someone else important. They rose at the sight of me.

"My niece," Falwen told him. "She forgets social graces like knocking. May we continue later?"

The man chuckled. He glided out, shutting the door.

I shoved aside his abandoned chair and thumped my palms onto Falwen's desk. "What'd you do?"

"Today? This month?"

"Don't play dumb!" I yanked him forward by the collar. "Airedain's gone!"

Falwen gazed at me, unblinking. "Perhaps he chose to leave you."

"He loves me, spirit or no spirit. That's why he helped us. You know that."

"I am well-connected, not omniscient. Tell me what happened."

"I don't know! He was near Shawnaast's old town hall with Iannah, then he wasn't!"

He muttered under his breath. "I need to make some inquiries. Stay here." He cut off my protest. "If you want to see Kiyorem again, let me handle this."

Seething, I stepped aside. After he left, I locked the doors and shoved his cabinets into a blockade. I wouldn't be caught in a trap. A wren fluttered past the loggia, an Iyo keeping watch. She'd tell Dunehein if anything happened. A raging grizzly would tear through the guards before anyone broke in here.

I tried reading papers from Falwen's cabinets. Not all were in his flowing handwriting. Some were dated decades ago, the time of the last Officer of the Viirelei. Useless. I slammed a drawer shut. The wren outside ruffled its wings. I was juddering around like a trapped bee when Falwen returned.

"I am truly sorry, Sohikoehl," he said. "This was not meant to happen. Kiyorem was arrested for arson. He is in prison. Again."

After all I'd seen — Ingdanrad's dungeon, magic-numbing cuffs, the heat-runed cell on Innisbán — Caladheä's prison seemed too mundane. Too simple. "Prove it," I said. "I want to see him."

"Only family can visit prisoners." Falwen dragged one of his cabinets back into place. It grated across the stone floor. "I sent Segowa, but—"

"I'll lie. You always tell me to. I'll say we're related."

"Do you know how much information is in these drawers? The first time Kiyorem was arrested, I had to hand over everything with his name, including a family tree so extensive it includes his half-siblings in the Kowichelk Confederacy. You are not on it. Thankfully, for your future children."

I grabbed his neck. "We'll never *have* children if Airedain dies in there!"

Falwen's throat worked under my palm. "Sohikoehl, we must handle this delicately. I can get you in, but it will take time."

"Nei. You've done enough." I stalked out. If Airedain was in prison, Segowa would know soon.

Airedain was in prison.

Segowa's eyes were red with crying. Their family arrived from Toel Ginu late at night. Within minutes, his sister Lituwa had blamed me, my family, everyone else in the heist, and everyone in Shawnaast. When she started railing that Airedain was a mudskull to ever have gone near me, their uncle Ranelin hushed her.

Wotelem and Hiyua had come too. Hiyua kissed my hair and held me. "Fendul wants to be here," she murmured. "One of us has to stay with the Rin though, and I might be able to help Airedain. I spent enough time with the Council during the black-market scandal."

Our hushed discussion with Wotelem went in circles. Falwen was right. The situation was delicate, and we had no argument for Airedain's innocence. Once the Elkhounds pieced everything together, they might charge him with bribing naval captains and conspiring to steal blackpowder. Which was treason. Which meant hanging.

Maybe Suriel knew I'd given a strand of hair to Airedain and this was punishment. Arril might've ordered Iannah to lead him into a trap, steal his rope bracelet, and abandon him. If Iannah thought he was unreliable, still a deadbeat alcoholic . . .

I couldn't think that way. Falwen wanted it. If he drove us apart, he could control us.

He'd braided himself into my life, always getting back in. We were forever clawing at each other. I'd threatened him with execution for treason, so he spun it around onto Airedain, the easiest target and the most disposable. Iannah was too valuable, and Suriel wouldn't risk the death of a Rin, but an Iyo death was acceptable.

Lituwa was right. Airedain shouldn't have trusted me.

Around sunrise, as rain beat the roof, Nili shook me awake. "Yironem brought Rhonos back."

"What?" I sat up, rubbing my eyes.

She crouched on her heels. "Iyo scouts saw Láchlan drop Rhonos on land, so Yiro went and picked him up. They're heading to the Colonnium to see what they can do for your Iyo-boy."

Scouts returned with more news. The *Róg Sál* was moored at Láchlan's island hideout. It was still raining when Rhonos arrived riding Anwea, Yironem behind him in the saddle. Rhonos wrung out his Council robe, a spare from his office. He'd ditched his old one to support a story of jumping overboard and swimming to freedom. His face was bruised enough to make the capture look real.

He produced two stiff white cards from a waterproof bladder. "A gift. I persuaded Falwen to forge new identification saying you and Airedain are married. I need to return to the Colonnium and finish reporting to the military, but I can take you to Airedain first."

I swung up on Anwea behind Rhonos and held his waist. He knew to pull his hair over his shoulder so it didn't touch me. We cantered past the southeast edge of the city where farmhouses were scattered among soggy pastures. On the shore of a lagoon was a vast sandstone structure. Barred windows made a grid across its pale walls.

Elkhounds opened a spiked iron gate into the muddy grounds. Caged dogs howled as we hitched Anwea. When we entered the iron-braced doors, the temperature dropped like we'd entered a cave. Four itherans in grey armour lazed around a table, picking over a lunch of bread and cheese. One had a black eye swollen shut.

A man with a captain's band on his sleeve leapt up. "Councillor Parr. Good to see you back safe. What can we do for you?"

Rhonos passed him the cards. "Missus Kiyorem would like to see her husband."

The captain peered at a thick ledger. "Kiyorem, Kiyorem . . . oh, him. Real brawler. Gave Corderus here quite the shiner." He looked up. "Kiyorem is listed as unmarried."

"Their wedding was last week. They had not filed with Falwen yet. Missus Kiyorem is my personal acquaintance, and I assure you they are married."

The captain wavered. "Falwen usually accompanies Iyo visitors. It's all very . . . irregular. Does the missus have any other proof? Don't viirelei get marriage tattoos?"

I tensed. I didn't have Airedain's arrowhead leaves or a dolphin.

Rhonos levelled his best withering gaze at the captain. "You would force a young lady to bare her arms for strange men? In *this* place? My father would never have stood for such disrespect to a companion of his. Should I take this to your superior?"

The man hustled back, bumping into another guard. "No, no, of course not. Apologies, Councillor. Please go ahead."

Corderus grabbed a torch and led the way. A maze of hallways led off in every direction, but we didn't go far. He unlocked a heavy door with a sign that said *Temporary Holding*. Inside, a wall split the room into halves. The right said *Standard* and had one large, communal cell with filthy rain-streaked windows. All I could see was a man passed out in his own vomit.

The left said *Dangerous Prisoners and Viirelei*. Corderus went that way. No windows here, and the stone walls separating each cell meant I couldn't see inside one until I passed it. Every cell had a stained straw mat and a bucket. The smell was horrific. An itheran with a mouth of black teeth leered at me. Another wearing only torn breeches hollered after Corderus in broken Coast Trader.

The middle cells were empty. At the far end, Airedain was slumped on the floor. He scrambled up and cracked his head on the ceiling. Soot and dust lined his skin. To my immense relief, he still wore the rope bracelet.

"Kako. You came." He reached through the bars and gripped my arm tight enough to bruise, but didn't touch me otherwise. He'd been here enough to know only family could visit.

Rhonos coughed. "Corderus, allow a bride her privacy."

Airedain swiftly turned his surprise into a look of longing. Corderus scrutinized me. I glared back. Cowed, he lit a torch in its bracket and retreated past the still-hollering prisoner into the hallway.

Rhonos stepped forward. "This must be quick. I spoke with the head of the city guard. Airedain, you were seen soaking Shawnaast's old town hall with oil before it caught fire. We cannot disprove that. The primary concern is avoiding treason charges, so I spun a story that I supposedly heard during my capture. A man offered you money to raze the hall. You agreed in order to pay off debts and ease your new marriage. You knew nothing about the blackpowder heist. Since Láchlan arranged the actual bribes, there is no evidence you supplied the silver.

"This trial will be very public, and the famine works in our favour. Many people owe you and your 'wife.' You fed itherans after the blizzard, Kateiko cured a neighbourhood of scurvy, and you have recently been seen volunteering at stavehall food banks. It will look bad to hang you. Political backlash aside, the last execution of an Iyo provoked an assassination. Wotelem, Hiyua, and I struck a deal with the Council. You will only be charged with arson, and the Iyo nation will not protest."

"What's the sentence for arson?" Airedain asked.

"For a viirelei with prior arrests for violence and aggression . . . ten years imprisonment."

Ten years. I could hardly imagine our lives then if we survived what was to come. I'd be twenty-nine. Airedain would be thirty-one. The shoirdryge had split off around ten years ago, and it looked completely different in my visions.

Rhonos bowed his head. "I apologize. That is the best we could do. I must return to the Colonnium now."

As soon as we were alone, Airedain pulled me close and kissed me. The cell bars pressed into my cheeks. His bottom lip was split.

"I'm not leaving you here," I said.

"Kako . . ."

"Cattil broke Iollan out of a magical dungeon." I examined his cell. Its bars and lock were ordinary metal. "This one can't be that hard—"

"*Kako.*" Airedain grabbed my wrist. "Where's Iollan now?"

"What?"

"No one knows, right? He's been on the run since he escaped." His eyes dropped. "I've been in this cell for a day, thinking. My tema and I talked last night. I don't wanna be a fugitive."

I stared at him. Segowa, one of the strongest women I knew, had cried all night after visiting him. "What are you saying?"

"Iyun Bel is my home. If I run, I can't come back."

"Come north with the Rin. Anwen Bel can be your home."

"I ain't sure *you* can go north. Now that Suriel has your spirit, you can only travel where he allows. If he makes you stay here in the south, you'll need a new jouyen. A new family. I can give you mine."

I sank onto the cold stone. Airedain slid down with me. Water dripped onto the floor, flowing through the prison from the roof.

"Are you asking me to marry you?" I said faintly.

He winced. "Nei. Not yet. So much can change in ten years, and . . . I dunno how much of you will be left by then. If you'll feel anything for me. The Rin didn't recognize Imarein after ten years of being with Suriel. But I won't ever give up hope of getting you back from him. I *want* to marry you, Kateiko, and I'll wait for the chance."

"You could die in here. Starvation, riots, another influenza epidemic—"

"I could die outside, too. Almost did a few times." He pulled up his tunic to show numerous scars from the Innisbán explosions. "So could you. That's our life every day, living with itherans and fighting Suriel."

His hands shook. He was brittle as baked clay. He'd come in throwing punches, but now his struggle was to not fight, not give the guards any excuse to mistreat him or extend his sentence. If he was to survive, I had to give him something to hope for — and I needed him to survive, to guard the last scrap of my spirit.

"My parents said a warrior isn't measured by how many lives they take," I said. "It's how many they save. You've rescued me time and time again. When you lured the Elkhounds away, you saved my family, Iannah, Láchlan, and their mercenaries. That's the kind of man I want to marry."

He grinned. Iron bars couldn't keep our hands or mouths apart. I didn't care if the prisoners in the far cells overheard our ragged breath, if Corderus returned and saw Airedain's breeches unlaced or his hand down my leggings. This might be our only chance for years. I wanted to fix every part of him in my memory, his pine scent and the roughness of his skin. All the emotions that belonged with this moment would soak into that strand of hair around his wrist, and maybe one day I could reclaim them.

After we slumped to the floor, panting, I said, "I have something for you." I tore my linen fireweed down the middle, two petals and two arrowhead leaves each. I pressed one half into his hand.

"I've got things for you, too." Airedain fumbled through his pocket and gave me two iron keys. "For my flat and the building. You said once you want somewhere stable in Caladheå. The flat's yours until Jona comes back next winter."

I nodded. I couldn't imagine being in his home without him, but I might need refuge in the weeks to come.

"And . . ." He squinted one eye as if steeling himself, then pulled a dark brown hair from his head. "It's only fair."

"I can't accept that. I can't protect it—"

"Kako, I love you. If you die, part of my spirit dies, too. It should go with you."

He looked so determined that I gave in. I took the hair gingerly, not knowing what my touch might condemn him to, and placed it in an empty vial from my herb pouch.

"Together when we're not," he said.

And so ten years began.

31.

SINKING

My family and I crammed into the flat for visiting Aikoto leaders. We woke the next morning to a knock. Half-asleep on the floor, I ignored Hiyua's conversation with a Rin woman until I heard my name. Fendul had summoned us back to Toel Ginu.

I was wary of doing anything else without Suriel's permission, but he wasn't around to ask, away guarding the *Róg Sál*. Successfully stealing it seemed like good evidence of my and Yironem's loyalty though, and anyway, Imarein had been allowed to visit the Rin.

We canoed south through a grey deluge and arrived at the stockade soaking wet. It was a good excuse to keep a hood over my hair. Fendul and Akiga came to meet us, Akiga wielding a smug look I hadn't seen in a long time.

"I always suspected you were more than just a deserter," Akiga said. "A traitor, too, it seems."

"What are you talking about?" I said. "The blackpowder heist? It wasn't a secret."

"Not that." Fendul's shoulders slumped. "She knows you slept with Parr."

I didn't need to ask who told her. He'd goaded me into admitting it. Knew I'd be desperate for answers about Parr. While I was trying to save Airedain, Falwen had torn apart the rest of my life.

More Rin flooded outside, forming a circle around us, blocking the gate. I tried to read their faces. Disbelief. Disgust. Akiga had had a perfect chance to rally support with Hiyua away in Caladheå.

"You can't blame Kako," Nili said incredulously. "Parr manipulated her. It was a stupid fling. How many of us have had those?"

"Decent people don't have them with murderous warmongers," Akiga said.

"She didn't know! What is this, a trial?" Nili swept her arm at the circle. "Kako *killed* Parr!"

"So she and the Okorebai-Rin claim. He has always shown Kateiko favour, defending her disappearances and having private meetings with her itheran friends. No one else saw Parr's murder."

Dunehein moved beside me. "It was last year. We've all seen Kako and Airedain together since. Show me one person who doesn't believe they're head over rump in love."

"Then where is he now?" someone asked.

"Prison." My voice sounded hollow.

"See," Akiga crowed. "No one is safe around Kateiko, now more than ever. Go on, girl. Show them your hair."

"Don't," Nili hissed at me.

But I couldn't hide it any longer. The circle was closing in, and I didn't have enough family to fend them all off. I pulled back my hood.

Gasps went up. My severed locks hung damp and tangled to my chin. Rain washed any remaining charcoal away from my roots.

Akiga spread her arms to the gathered Rin. "Look on her mutilation. How does such a thing happen? Where have Kateiko and Yironem been for the last month? What else is being kept from us?"

Nili and Dunehein snapped back at the same time. Rain crackled on the verge of freezing. I thought of when we stood here in the first snowstorm six months ago. Akiga wouldn't challenge Fendul again in her disgraced state, but she could've groomed someone else to do it.

I pictured the jouyen splitting again. Only my family and Aliko, Fendul's always-loyal lover, were guaranteed to take our side. Barolein had been the deciding vote before. Now he looked at me with loathing. I'd slept with the man who caused his first wife's death. If Barolein turned against us, his new wife, Mereku, might, too and maybe even his brother Orelein.

"What do you want?" I asked.

Akiga looked nonplussed, like she'd expected me to argue.

"You can't take a braid I don't have. You can't execute me for treason, or you'd look like an itheran politician, aeldu forbid. So what do you want?"

She drew herself up. "An infection must be cut out. It has spread too far already. Yironem can stay in hopes we can cleanse him, but you repeatedly show an alarming level of disloyalty. I demand your exile from the Rin-jouyen."

I fell to my knees. My fingers slid into the mud. Even through my numbness, I felt this — because Suriel had, too, shunned by other saidu for turning from their ways, shunned by the Rin when Imarein invited them to live at Se Ji Ainu. Everyone spoke over one another, their voices a terraced hill rising to the sky.

"No," Hiyua said loudly. "Kateiko's my daughter. No one can send her away."

"The okorebai can," Akiga said.

Fendul and I locked gazes. He looked bone-weary. The arguing faded from my ears. We spoke silently of years together, arguments, amends, promises. We both knew he wouldn't exile me. Then he'd lose the okorebai challenge, and his supporters would never follow Akiga. The Rin-jouyen would crack like an egg, our lifeblood spilling onto the stockade ground.

I saw the future in Fendul's dark eyes. Devastation at his failure, facing his ancestors in shame. Yironem separated from dozens of Rin that Imarein's spirit told him to protect. Dunehein and Rikuja cut off from the jouyen they chose to raise their daughter in. Nili with no chance to make up with Orelein. Her child growing up without its father.

We wouldn't have enough people to protect ourselves. If Akiga claimed Aeti Ginu, we wouldn't have a home. We'd be nomads like the Dona-jouyen. Yironem, brave but frail after the long winter, would die in battle. Nili, Dunehein, and Rikuja would have to choose between fleeing with their children or fighting. Fendul wouldn't have a baby with Aliko while he needed her as a warrior. Our half of the Rin would die out, just like the Dona.

So would the other half. They'd followed Fendul out of respect and turned to Akiga out of fear. It wouldn't last. She'd betray dissenters the way she let Iyo assault Yironem. When she inevitably pushed itherans too far, her supporters would die in combat. I couldn't condemn my jouyen to extinction.

Fendul shook his head. *Don't, Kako*, he begged.

We'd been on this course since I broke our engagement. I wouldn't let my choices keep dragging him down. It was time to accept my consequences. Time to let go and sink alone.

My hearing roared back into existence. Dunehein shouted at Akiga. Rikuja held him back, but it was like restraining a storm. Sihaja squalled in her arms. Nili shook Orelein, shrieking that if he loved her, he'd fight against this. A kinaru's screech vibrated the buds of hemlock trees. Yironem's wings cast a shadow over me, blocking the rain.

No matter where I went or what I became, they'd always love me. I'd never doubt that.

I threw Antalei at Akiga's feet. It sent mud splattering across her boots. "I'll leave."

Nili gaped in horror.

The voices trickled off. Akiga plucked my flail from the ground and held it above her head. Maybe she expected people to cheer, but everyone stayed silent. I couldn't care anymore. I lifted my face and let rain wash over me.

I was allowed to get my things from our plank house. I tucked my mother's fir branch blanket and my kinaru shawl into my carry-frame. Now that I'd burned my lantern from Airedain, there wasn't much left in this place except memories. No longer would I see Fendul moonlit in the next bed, sit gossiping with Nili and Rikuja over chores, or smell Hiyua frying flatbread at sunrise.

Nili stood with her hands on her hips, feet apart, a short glowering wall. "I won't let you go."

I looked around, gauging how much I could trust everyone in hearing range. "Fendul didn't command it, so it's not binding. Akiga's forty years older than me. She won't live forever."

"You're gonna come back when she *dies*? That could be decades!"

I sank onto my bed. "I . . . learned from Airedain. I want a family to come back to. Maybe Falwen will quit messing with my life after Abhain, maybe he won't, but I can't ask my loved ones to keep paying for my mistakes. Maika and Airedain already did."

"You're my *sister*," Nili wailed. "You're supposed to be here when I have my baby. Trap furs to swaddle it, help me pick a name, tell me when I'm being a stupid mother."

We couldn't get a word out of Yironem. I flooded him with every bit of advice I could think of, from water-calling to girls to fur trapping. He stared at his feet, then interrupted by flinging his arms around me.

"Love you," he mumbled. Never had I wanted a little brother so much as the day I was losing mine.

Hiyua hugged us all together, even with her weak, scarred arm. It'd taken time, but she understood. I had a feeling she and Segowa had talked in Caladheå. When she let go, Rikuja nestled Sihaja in my lap. At nine months, she was a dark-haired fountain of babbling and cooing. Her little hands latched onto mine.

"She'll be talking soon enough," Rikuja said. "Dune and I will make sure she knows Aunt Kako's name."

Dunehein came inside and dropped his battle axe. He flumped onto my mattress, making the dry grass crackle. "I followed Akiga around the stockade. Think that scared her straight." He looped a hefty arm around my head. "It ain't much comfort now, but exiles can join other jouyen. You can marry Airedain when he gets outta prison, become Iyo for real."

Fendul came last, with Antalei cleaned of mud. He tucked it into the sheath on my belt. "Your parents gave this to you. No one can take it away."

Nili grabbed his arm. "Fendul, make Kako stay. Order her."

"I tried to make her stay in Anwen Bel once. Remember how that went?" He pinched his temples. "There's one thing I can do. The spring equinox is a day for all visitors. I decree right now that it includes exiled Rin. Kako, that's as strong an order as I'll give. Come back once a year. Please."

I pressed my fingers to my lips. "Will Akiga accept that?"

"She already did. She seems oddly worried."

Dunehein yanked my blanket over his battle axe. Rikuja smothered a laugh.

Hiyua shepherded everyone outside, leaving Fendul and me alone. He sank onto his bed, covered with his kinaru blanket. Even the newly carved makiri over the hearth seemed to avert their gazes.

Fendul handed me one of the runed tracking stones from Janekke. "Take it with you. I'll wear its match with my crow amulet so you can always find your way back."

I nodded. "You think this is the last time we'll see each other here?"

"Probably. The Rin have to back out of this war. It's tearing us apart. I'll keep us in the Aikoto alliance, but once the ocean seems safe enough to travel, I'm taking everyone home." He rubbed his okorebai tattoo through his sleeve and asked softly, "What will you do?"

I shrugged. "Stop Iollan och Cormic. Then . . ."

Fendul moved next to me. His arm was warm against mine. I fixed that sensation in my memory, marking it with a thought — there were people who believed I could come back from all this. I curled into him, searching for comfort I could no longer feel.

32.

SPIRITS

I climbed the stairs of Airedain's building and unlocked his flat. Mine now until Jonalin returned. I opened the vial holding Airedain's hair and breathed the lingering scent of pine. His laugh ghosted along my skin. I wanted it to fill the room like it used to, bold and vibrant and careless, and flow into some lively song backed by his pounding drum. My footsteps weren't loud enough to bring life into this sepulchre. I set the vial safely on his makiri shelf and threw open the shutters to let in the downpour. Raindrops gusted inside, thrumming in the cool air.

I clanked around on his liquor shelf. Vodka, cranberry wine, a dusty flask of spirits with a label I couldn't read. Jonalin had won it in a bet with a Ferish sailor, something involving a stray chicken. I passed over the whisky I'd given Airedain. Maybe I could smuggle it into prison, and we could finish it together. Instead I took down a bottle of fennel brännvin, bit the cork, and yanked.

Savouring the familiar burn, I slumped onto the floor. Well into the bottle and the night, I realized I felt vaguely cold, but I didn't trust myself to light the stove without setting something on fire. I dug through Airedain's rioden chest and pulled on his spare jerkin. It was the closest I could get to his embrace.

The floor swayed like the ocean. Brånnvin in hand, I trailed my fingers over the walls, navigating by touch. Plush marsh rat pelt by the door. Scratchy fishing net hung where it wouldn't tangle. Cracked mirror over the washstand. I unscrewed the pot of paste Airedain used on his hair, dipped my finger in, and marked a streak down my throat. How was I to live like this, clinging to whatever scraps of love I could touch? How was I to go on fighting Suriel while starting to understand how he got this way?

Someone knocked. My hand jerked, hitting the pot. It clattered into the wash basin.

"Koehl?" came Iannah's voice. "Is that you?"

I fumbled through the dark and locked the door. She'd get pissed off if she saw me drunk.

"I know someone's in there. I'll bring the Elkhounds if I have to."

"Go 'way."

The latch rattled. "Bloody hell, Koehl, open the door."

I leaned against the door and took a swig from my bottle. I heard mutters, then footsteps, retreating.

The heist had been her plan. She'd let Elkhounds catch Airedain. I hurled Nurivel across the room. Something shattered.

Brånnvin wasn't strong enough. I found the dusty flask, chugged, and doubled over choking. Once I recovered, I hung out the window and breathed damp air. Whispers fell with the rain. At least the aeldu were here — Isu, my cousins, what might've been Behadul. Their voices soothed me, suppressing Suriel's hold.

I was spread-eagle on the floor when another knock sounded. And another.

"Fuck off!" I yelled.

"Kateiko?" came a crisp voice. "Pelennus sent me."

For a terrifying second, I thought Iannah *had* brought Elkhounds. But they wouldn't call me by my first name.

"Kateiko, I can pick locks, you know."

Rhonos. I tried to sit up and instantly changed my mind. The room spun like I was a flail whipping through the air. Metal rattled. Lamplight poured across me, chasing away precious darkness. I flung an arm over my face.

He pulled my flask away. "How on earth did you get mezcale?"

I opened my mouth to say something sarcastic, and instead threw up on the floor.

"Good god." Rhonos hauled me upright, leaned me against a bed, and wiped my chin with a handkerchief. He closed the shutters. "Are you trying to get hypothermia?"

I ignored him. In the sudden stillness, there was . . . nothing. The voices had vanished with the rain. "Open 'em again," I demanded.

"The room is flooding. The people downstairs complained of their ceiling leaking."

"Give 'm back!" I grabbed the bedframe and tried to drag myself up. "Give my family back!"

Rhonos pushed me down. "Stay still. You will hurt yourself—"

I screamed. I screamed and screamed to block out the ringing silence, to fill the void that pushed my ribs outward until they felt ready to crack. Hands grabbed me. Thrashing, I saw Iannah's auburn bun, heard her sharp voice. Something struck my head. My eyes rolled back and I slid into blackness.

I came to in Airedain's bed, feet bare, wet hair stuck to my cheek. My memory was hazy as pond scum. My clothes hung by the crackling stove. I peeked under the caribou fur blanket. An unbleached linen chemise covered my body.

"Why . . ." I muttered.

Rhonos, reading at the table, looked up. He tapped my carry-frame where the chemise had been bundled with my other Sverbian clothes. "Pelennus dressed you. You and the room were soaked."

I jerked around, bringing on a wave of dizziness. Airedain's drums were safe in their waterproof boxes. The vial was still on the makiri shelf. I swung back to Rhonos. "How'd you get in? And where's Iannah?"

"You made it clear she was unwanted." He handed me a mug and a wheat bun.

My stomach growled. I downed the lukewarm tea, tore into the soft bread, and waved at my hair. The water in it ignored me. Still drunk, then. I tapped my face. It was numb.

Rhonos refilled my mug from the well bucket. "An Iyo neighbour said you exiled yourself from the Rin nation."

I chewed, mute.

"Kateiko, if that is true, I am one of the last people you have left. I cannot help you unless I know what happened."

"Don' need help."

"Would you rather sleep in your own vomit?" He leaned back in his chair. "I exiled myself too, remember. In the days after, mezcale was also my undoing. I picked a fight in a Ferish inn with one of my father's supporters. The innkeeper threw me out, so I went to the Blackened Oak. Nhys tied me to a bench until Tiernan arrived to look after me."

I wondered if he was lying. My vision was too blurred to read his face. I changed the topic. "What're you reading?"

Rhonos held up the book, bound in worn brown leather. "My mother's diary. I found it at Parr Manor."

"What was she like?"

"By all accounts, spirited but flawlessly mannered. I never knew her. She contracted influenza when I was an infant and was not allowed near me lest I caught it. I grew up hearing of her sacrifice. It comforted me that perhaps I inherited more of her traits than my father's."

"Did you?"

He arched his brows. "If I answer that, will you tell me what happened?"

I shrugged. Probably not, but listening to his misery was better than dwelling on mine. Rhonos folded his hands as if preparing for a story. I sat up and draped the caribou fur over my shoulders.

"My mother was born into Ferland's aristocracy. Her parents wanted a foothold in the new world, so they arranged her marriage to my father. Their first meeting was when she stepped off a ship at the Caladheå docks. Their wedding was within the month. She was older, seventeen while he was fifteen, but she was charmed by her dashing soldier husband and excited to be in a new land.

"My paternal family and other military wives adored her. When Parr was deployed in the Third Elken War, she volunteered with the ladies' society collecting supplies for soldiers. I always wondered how someone so gentle-hearted could care about my father. I assumed they were not married long enough for her to realize his nature. Or perhaps he was different then. People say her death changed him.

"Her diary explains it." Rhonos flipped to a random page and read aloud. "'Saw a soldier in hospital die from an arrow wound. He was of an age with my darling Antoch. O, so many brave souls claimed by Savages, wilder and crueller than even Sverbians. The viirelei have fled Caladheå and good riddance. God willing, this war will cleanse the land of them so we may begin settling it in a civilized fashion.'"

I recoiled. "She was as bad as Parr."

"Worse. That passage is from early in the war, and her hatred only grew. I shudder to think what she would write about her son sitting with a barely dressed Rin girl in the home of an Iyo criminal."

"Yet you're still here."

"I ended my exile to atone for my family's mistakes, not repeat them." He closed the book. "Your turn. Why did you leave the Rin?"

I huddled under the fur blanket. *No secrets, no lies.* I'd confessed to Airedain in this room.

Rhonos's waistcoat and breeches seemed more fitting without his Council robe. Even with his ridiculous moustache, he looked more like himself than he had in a while, like when we sat by the creek near Marijka's house and I admitted my role in her death. He'd find out this mistake soon enough.

"I slept with your father," I said.

His face twisted like a wrung rag.

"Yeah. S'what my jouyen thought, too." I thrust out my hand. "Now give back my liquor."

"As disturbing as this has suddenly become, I will not let you drink yourself to death."

"*Disturbing?* If Parr knocked me up, he might've killed our child, your half-sibling. S'way past disturbing. It's fucked up."

Rhonos cleared his throat. "When were you, ah, with him?"

"Two days before I — before he died."

He paced the cramped room, hands clasped, muttering. Finally, he stopped. "I have something that might interest you." He reached into his breast pocket and passed me a silk bag.

I loosed the drawstring. A gold ring slid onto my palm. Firelight made the smoky brown gemstone look like a glass lantern, flickering with orange and amber sparks. Its filigree band suited Parr's tastes, but it was too small for a man.

"A family heirloom," Rhonos said. "It was on a table by an empty wine bottle when I returned home last year. My father said the quartz matched his lady interest's eyes, but she was not likely to accept it."

"Is . . ." I dropped the ring onto the mattress. "Is that a *wedding* ring?"

"I have been trying to identify the lady for months, searching, of course, among Ferish high society. Even from the grave my father surprises me."

"Nei. You're lying. Or Parr lied. He wasn't even sure he loved me."

"He did not marry for love the first time, either." Rhonos sank onto the floor at the foot of the bed. "I suspect marrying you would have been his safeguard. After I disowned him, he could not bear losing another child. I do not know what he felt for you, but if you'd had a baby, he would not have harmed it."

"That s'pposed to comfort me?"

"It is the truth. After all we have been through together, you deserve that."

I picked the ring up with a fold of my chemise and tossed it at him. "Keep it. Sell it. I don't care."

We lapsed into silence while I sobered up. He retrieved his book, then sighed and put it away. Rain battered the shutters. A pigeon warbled outside under the eaves. Clearly Rhonos was serious about not leaving me alone to drink, which left me with nothing to do but talk.

"Airedain wants to marry me," I said abruptly.

Rhonos looked up. "Do you share his feelings?"

"I did. Until this." I swatted my cut hair. "Falwen said that for Suriel, discovering emotion was like seeing the sun after growing up underground. Me, I plunged into the dark. Gutted myself. Cut out all my feelings, good and bad. Airedain's stuck in a damp cell waiting for a life with me, but I'm in a prison of my own. And I don't think I can get out."

"Your outburst tonight says otherwise."

"Is that anger mine, though? Or is it Suriel's anger about losing Imarein?"

Rhonos's eyes widened.

"I didn't just give my spirit to Suriel. I'm getting his in return. In Toel today . . . a Rin elder called me an infection. That's how Suriel sees himself, too, the corruption that caused other saidu to kill each other. He has all this confusing pain and rage without love to temper him. I think Falwen honestly believes letting Suriel vanish into the void is the safest option."

"Then have you changed your mind about helping them?"

"I know that before all this, we decided opening a rift is too big a risk. But . . ." I peered into the cracked mirror. My roots had grown into a white band where my hair parted. "I'm losing myself. Suriel's getting more erratic, so I will, too. I have no idea what comes next and no family left to help me through it."

Rhonos put a hand on my arm. "As long as Pelennus and I are alive, you will have help."

33.

HAIR OF THE DOG

I awoke to a thump and muffled Ferish cursing. Rhonos sat on Jonalin's bed holding the toe he'd just stubbed. He'd slept there in breeches and a tunic borrowed from Airedain, rolled up at the cuffs, so his day clothes stayed neat enough to wear again. I squeezed my eyes shut as he got changed.

When I woke again, squinting in the midday sun, Rhonos was gone. A note explained that he'd gone to the Colonnium, but I should wait for instructions. And, *Do not be angry at Pelennus. She was responsible for none of this.*

My head ached as if a gaggle of kids had played leatherball with it. I downed my last vial of willowcloak. An hour later, I was no better. Emílie's hangover advice was to "swallow the hair of the dog that bit you." I was finishing my brånnvin bottle when a knock sounded.

I flung open the door. Falwen put a hand against it before I could slam it in his face. We stared at each other. Then I punched him.

He reeled, clutching his mouth. I shook out my fist. I had better aim sober. I'd wanted to break his nose.

Falwen licked blood off his lip. "The heist persuaded Arril. She wants you and Yironem back."

"Yiro stays with the Rin." I took a swig of brånnvin, distracting him while my other hand went to Kohekai's sheath. "*You* can tell Suriel why."

"Sohikoehl—"

"You ruined my life. I won't let you ruin my brother's, too. You knew what'd happen, and you told the Rin about Parr anyway. *And* about my hair, which of course I couldn't explain."

"Yes," Falwen said coolly. "I also told Suriel not to accept your sacrifice. I knew it would break you. My only choice left was taking away your power in the Rin-jouyen so you could not endanger them again."

I slammed him into the wall. I arced Kohekai forward, stopping it just over his heart. He was the same height as me, with the slight build of one who spent his days inside. I'd killed stronger men than him.

He raised his hands in surrender. His breath was hot on my cheek. "I did not abandon you. I showed you a refuge beforehand."

"What, your house?" I laughed. "I learned from Parr. I was desperate once and went to the wrong person. I'll never, ever go to you."

"I am not the monster you believe I am. I will gladly tell Arril to leave Yironem alone. Furthermore, Kiyorem's arrest was not my doing, and I am trying to make arrangements for him. More visits, better food, a drier cell. Once we have dealt with Suriel, I will help restore your place in the Rin."

My blade pressed into the threads of his coat. There was a chance he was being honest, and I'd never killed one of my own people. Today wasn't the day to start. Before I left Toel Ginu,

Fendul had asked me to trust him with handling Falwen. To wait. I yanked Kohekai away.

Falwen straightened his coat. "Find Pelennus tonight. She will give you the details."

I was sober by the time I left the flat. Cobblestones formed islands among the puddles, an endless archipelago through the streets. I looped behind the Knox Arms to the back-alley entrance. Liam was dumping soapy water into the gutter. Instead of his usual joking hello, he jammed the dish tub under his arm and went inside. That was what I was owed for sending his friend to prison.

I followed him in, dodging Emílie in the kitchen, and headed down the hall to Iannah's room. Muffled voices came from within. I paused long enough to identify Rhonos. He must've come straight here after Council ended. I pushed open the door.

Rhonos knocked a mug off the table. It hit the floorboards and rolled, leaving a trail of water. He hastily mopped it up with a handkerchief. Iannah, sitting nearby, was flushed pink. It wasn't easy to embarrass an ex-Antler. *Still not my problem*, I thought.

"Falwen sent me," I said to fill the silence.

"Right." Iannah shut the door and blocked it with a brick. "If all's on schedule, Iollan and everyone else have left Innisbán and are sailing south. Arril wants you to manage the antayul again."

I peered at her map, held flat on the table with splintered firewood. "What's the plan?"

She tapped the tip of South Iyun Bel's peninsula. "Arril said to be at another smuggling hideout in five days. We'll join my men from the heist. Láchlan will pick us up on the *Róg Sál* and take us to Ile vi Pumèze." Her finger slid west, callouses scratching the map, to an island in the open ocean. "It's covered in pumice. The Ferish explorer who named it wasn't very creative. Good spot for a rift, though. Uninhabited, isolated, and damaged from volcanoes. Tiernan had listed it in his notes as a potential spot to open a rift.

"Iollan will be vulnerable on the way there, but so will the antayul. It's too risky to attack until we can separate them on land. We could set an ambush on the island, but Iollan's probably been there before. He could've left traps. Only mages would find them, and we don't have the time or resources to contact Ingdanrad. Better to take our safe route in and get as close as possible before breaking the ceasefire."

"You are not invincible," Rhonos scolded her. "Nor are you the only ones involved. Let Kateiko ask the Iyo nation for help."

"We're not causing another massacre like Innisbán. Koehl's people have lost enough."

"It's not our decision," I said. "I'll get a message to Tokoda."

"I could come," Rhonos said. "I was a ranger not so long ago—"

"You stay here," Iannah snapped. "We need you in Council Hall. And don't send the navy looking for Iollan. They'll sink the ship and everyone on it."

"And we just wait?" I asked.

She rubbed her face. Twists of hair hung loose from her bun, usually a sign she'd slept on it. "Doesn't give much leeway before Abhain. But I don't know what else to do."

Rhonos watched her like he was in pain. I didn't want to be there between whatever was happening with them. All I wanted was to drink myself into blindness. If they couldn't come up with a better plan with all their military experience, I couldn't, either.

I raised Airedain's keys. "You know where to find me."

*

The next morning, I was on the floor naked, brånnvin in one hand and Kohekai in the other, when the door swung open. I shrieked. Maeve shrieked louder. Flinging an arm over her eyes, she said Liam lent her a spare key, she didn't want to wake me by knocking, she just brought breakfast, she was so, so sorry—

"Can you do surgery?" I interrupted.

She stuttered into silence.

I showed her my tracking stone. Since I couldn't seal wounds like Janekke, I planned to insert it into my thigh where Corvittai wouldn't dare look. The brånnvin was for disinfection and courage.

Maeve looked green, but refused to let me do it myself. Grit-teethed, she slit my skin, pushed in the stone, and stitched me up with Airedain's embroidery needle. I soaked up the blood with sawdust. Neither of us could stomach the barley bread she'd brought, so we talked over tea. About what, I couldn't remember, but at least she didn't hate me like her brother did now.

My other problem was how to safely bring Airedain's hair. It was too short to weave into anything. I wound up dying ropeweed fibres dark brown, gluing the hair on with pine resin, and twisting it all into a bracelet. Once I rubbed soot on it, it was rough enough to look like I'd had it long before meeting Airedain.

Of the remaining days, I was sober for one. I spent it mud-dling through Segowa's shop's paperwork, puzzling out legal terms and adding up sovereigns earned and spent. The other days she put me to work stewing bark and lichen into dyes. Her warmth had cooled. She'd lost her son and then got an exiled Rin as a daughter-in-law in exchange. Shitty trade. On my last day in Caladheå, she said, "Airedain sacrificed his freedom to give you this chance. Make it count."

Segowa was right, of course. I should've trained with Iannah, but she was never around. Before the market closed for the day, I sold my marsh rat mantle to a furrier, then took the sovs to Emílie asking for the strongest liquor she had. She gave me two flasks of Sverbian jenever that tasted like pine sap on fire. I used the rest of the money to restock my herb pouches.

Maeve helped me sweep, scrub, and polish every surface of Airedain's flat. If I didn't come back, at least it'd be clean for Jonalin. I sewed my linen fireweed and arrowhead leaves into the lining of my purse. That and my bracelet were all I dared take beyond travel gear. I packed everything else — my kinaru shawl, my mother's blanket, the wire wolf I'd once given Fendul — into a rioden chest.

Early the next day, I headed to the Knox Arms and dissipated the fog on Iannah's window to check if Falwen was lurking. Through a gap in the curtains I saw Iannah with her arms folded. Rhonos faced her, his words muted by the glass. As I stood wondering if he skipped Council or if it wasn't in session, if I got the right day, he touched her chin.

Oh no, I thought.

I watched with bated breath. She deserved privacy, but I had reason to be wary of Parr men. He spoke into her ear, brushed away a stray hair, then kissed her cheek.

She pulled back. Her mouth twitched in a stumbled reply. Rhonos went red, awkwardness dripping from his apologies. I winced. Now that he was a councillor, I sometimes forgot he was twenty-three, prone to stupid young love — though Iannah was twenty-four and seemed immune.

Or not.

She grabbed his wrist. She, who'd bested him with a sword and without, looked unsure. Iannah had explained once why Parr was shocked that I kissed him. In Ferish culture, women didn't make the first move. Ever. Unless it was two women, in which case . . . well, she'd never explained that.

Rhonos tipped her face up. His lips brushed hers.

I jerked away. I'd wait in the kitchen with Maeve.

Iannah had two horses in the Knox stables. I didn't ask where they came from. Elkhounds at the guard post waved us out of town, bored by a registered Iyo taking a friend home. Instead, once we were out of sight, we veered southeast to skirt Toel Ginu. The Roannveldt plain had become a swamp. Workhorses dragged plows through fields of rotten winter rye. Abhain usually marked the end of sowing season, but everything was late this year.

I took a swig from my waterskin, laced with jenever, before speaking. "I saw Rhonos kiss you."

Iannah frowned. "You were spying?"

"Close your curtains better."

"I wasn't expecting things to go that way. And since when you do care?"

"I don't. But what if Falwen saw? He had me kill Parr, his closest friend. You think he won't hurt Parr's son in order to control you? He already took everyone *I* love."

Iannah shifted in her saddle. "Rhonos won't be near us on Abhain. I made sure. And if the Corvittai wanted to use someone against me, they'd go after Pia. Arril knows about her. We spent a while discussing it."

I choked on my water. My horse whinnied in surprise. "When? Why?"

"She interrogated me before accepting me as Nonil. Better to be honest. Pia can handle whatever they throw at her."

"If you still care so much for Pia, what are you doing kissing Rhonos?"

Her mouth tightened with exasperation. "Look — I promised Pia if I left the Colonnium, I'd find her again. Instead, I got recruited as a Corvittai. Rhonos is all I've had for months. You of all people can't criticize me for taking comfort where I can find it."

"That's messy as shit, Ia. I thought you'd learn from my mistakes, but he doesn't know how you feel, does he? You didn't deal with it before you left."

"Fine. Let's talk about dealing with things." She grabbed my waterskin and sniffed it. "What's in here, hellseed?"

I yanked it back. "Piss off. Not like you've been around to help. Too busy gossiping with Arril, apparently."

Iannah snorted. "You have no idea, do you? The night I found you drunk in Airedain's flat, you said some awful things. I won't repeat them, but — you threw me out, Koehl."

I swallowed. "Sorry."

"Forget it. We have other problems."

"Yeah. Like we're being followed."

Her hands tensed on the reins. "By?"

I glanced at the sky. "Something white. Maybe a gull, maybe a snow bird. It's flying above the cloud cover and dipping down to track us."

"You told the Iyo to go to Ile vi Pumèze, right?"

"I passed on your news. I don't know if they went. It's not like they're sharing war plans with an exiled Rin."

Our horses couldn't outrun a bird through the boggy plain. There was nothing to do but let it come. Once we reached South Iyun Bel, it had to follow closer through the dense foliage. I glimpsed a delicate orange bill and feet. A northern tern. With their migration range, people from all jouyen could attune to them. When we made camp for the night, it flew up into the canopy to wait.

*

In a brief respite from rain, we coaxed our horses up a steep trail sheltered by budding alders. Someone had hacked the underbrush back with a machete. We emerged high above an oval of clear blue water ringed by cliffs, connected to Burren Inlet by a gorge. The gorge walls met at the top like wizened men bowing to each other. Sea spray masked the opening below. Approaching sailors would think they were about to sail into a rock face.

We looped around the cliffs to a lookout. Iannah's surviving Corvittai greeted her with nods, but searched my saddlebags and patted me down, eyeing my white hair. Her glare kept them from the tracking stone in my thigh. They examined my bracelet and seemed to decide it was plain rope. They were hard, flinty men, one in his twenties and one in his forties, ex-soldiers from Ferland who hadn't learned Coast Trader. I couldn't talk to them even if I wanted to.

They'd made camp amid a ring of thick salt spruce. Their dye-mottled tent blended with the underbrush. Snowdrifts lay thick in the shadows, melting away in creeks that plummeted down the cliffs into the sea. I was wiping sweat off my horse when an arrow whirred. A tern shot into the air squawking.

Iannah snapped at the younger Corvittai. He lowered his bow and answered flatly. She whipped out a dagger and sliced through his bowstring. By the time she finished lecturing, he was staring into his stew bowl, ears red with shame.

"Thinks he can get away with things when Arril's away," she muttered. "The ceasefire won't last if we're shooting at enemy scouts."

"Enemy?" I repeated.

"You know what I mean."

Later, searching for level ground to pitch our tent, I found a pit of decaying animals, every kind and size, from a hummingbird torn apart by an arrow to a buck growing new antlers. All but the smallest birds had been stripped of meat. Attuned people shifted back to human form when they died, so the men hadn't committed cannibalism, but I felt ill wondering if they knew or cared.

My mind felt fuzzier than expected after drinking diluted jenever. The older man flipped over a stone to show me softly glowing runes. They radiated a weak magical haze for a league around us — not enough to stop my water-calling or the expertly made tracking stone, but it might throw off a mage long enough for us to escape. The last Nonil had made it when hiding in Dúnravn Pass.

At dusk, the temperature dropped, but we couldn't risk a fire being seen. I wished I hadn't sold my fur mantle. Iannah refused to snuggle in our tent like Nili and I always did. I swigged jenever for warmth instead. That had the added benefit of knocking me out. Halfway through the night, the men roused us to trade watches. At the lookout, my teeth chattered hard enough to break. Iannah brought venison from the food cache, but I couldn't eat game after seeing the carrion pit.

The forest was eerily still. Suriel had left days ago, protecting Iollan's ship on the voyage south. Faintly, I hoped other saidu might stop him from opening a rift, since it was their nature to hold the world together, but the island was so far from Aikoto territory that the Rin hadn't woken the saidu there.

Just past dawn, something surfaced in the harbour. I squinted down. The wriggling thing looked like a dolphin. Only one, not a real animal in a pod.

Iannah spat out a chunk of gristle. "I know what you're thinking. Don't."

"It's probably an Iyo. Maybe they'll talk to me."

"My men could wake any minute. If they see you with a scout, I can't defend you."

"Then distract them. You're their captain." I got up, ignoring her sigh.

A dirt track did hairpin turns down a cliff. I went straight down instead, gripping roots and branches, leaping to the next level of track to steady myself before moving on again. At the bottom strip of sand, I hung my cloak, boots, and weapons on a shrub and stepped into the icy water. The shock hit with the memory of hypothermia.

When it got too deep to walk, I dove under and swam. The dolphin was a pale blur ahead. Twice my length, it darted in the glassy blue depths. I drifted long enough for it to see my face, then went up for air and swam back to land. A slender young man came after me, wet clothes clinging to his skin. He dried them with a flick of his hand. His black hair was shaved short.

Makoril. I'd heard the gossip. His wife didn't want a violent former exile for a husband, so when we'd returned from Innisbán, she did the closest thing Aikoto had to divorce and made him shave his head. He couldn't grow it out again until she took him back.

He leered at the cut strands stuck to my cheek. "Finally on equal ground," he said in his irritatingly soft way. "Two cast-outs face to face."

"Why are *you* here?" I asked. "We got in a knife fight. You're the last person the Okorebai-Iyo would send."

"She doesn't know I came." He shifted his feet. "We're not supposed to tell you anything, either."

"So you came to make dolphin screeches at me? We'll get caught soon. Talk or go."

Reluctantly, Makoril beckoned me into the shadow of the cliffs. "Tokoda got Ingdanrad to check that volcanic island. They found signs that humans were there a while ago, but there were no traps, so our warriors went. Mostly north and south jouyen, since only a few Iyo could leave Toel without tipping off Falwen. They're waiting with the mages to ambush Iollan. But — I don't know. It doesn't sit right. Too easy."

I scoffed. "We'll be facing Suriel, the Corvittai, and the best rift mage on this coast. That's easy?"

"Compared to the Wolf Den on Innisbán? Yeah. You saw it, too. So I can't help but think you're leading us astray."

"I passed on what I got told. I can't guarantee it's true."

He seized my wrist. I tensed. His hand had landed on my bracelet.

"Kateiko." His voice crackled like reeds. "Those Nuthalha seal hunters, they took us in, me and Ilani and Ganiam. Five are dead now, along with my friends. Six are stuck with the Corvittai. I got out as a bargaining chip, something to appease a jouyen that doesn't want me. I — I know that's my fault, but those Nuthalha don't deserve this. Neither do those Beru."

I glanced at the sun glowing behind clouds. We didn't have long before the mercenaries woke. There was only one way to prove my loyalty.

"Come with me," I said. "Suriel can't touch you underwater. Are you fast enough to follow a ship?"

"I can swim circles around one."

"Then come with me, no matter where I get taken. Help me save the antayul."

Makoril's brow crinkled. He probably thought I was leading him back to capture, but he wasn't so unlike me now. Cut off from his lover and jouyen — and bad at taking orders from his okorebai.

34.

PURSUIT

Two more nights of trading watches later, nothing had entered the harbour. According to Rhonos, the average speed of a Gallnach schooner in good wind was eight knots. It'd take a day and night to reach Ile vi Pumèze, then hours more to unload and set up the blackpowder. That gave one day leeway before Abhain ended and the window was shut.

There was no better prospect than ruining Iollan's plans by arriving late. Increasingly, though, I suspected the other Corvittai weren't coming for us. That they were keeping us out of the way again. I paced the lookout, wearing a path into the muck. I couldn't search for Aikoto scouts while Iannah's men were awake. I wasn't even sure Makoril had stuck around. I'd told him to hide in our blind spot on the far side of the gorge.

Finally, during an afternoon drizzle, a white-sailed schooner appeared in the mist. Iannah and I passed a spyglass back and forth.

The sailors looked like an ordinary crew in Sverbian tunics and trousers, but the flag had an anchor in each bottom corner, matching Láchlan's wrist tattoos. The *Róg Sál.*

"Remember what I taught you about controlling anger?" Iannah asked. "Use it now. We're not sailing to Ile vi Pumèze."

I turned slowly. "Where are we going, Ia?"

"The opposite direction. Up Burren Inlet into the mountains, where the inlet's four arms meet."

I'd canoed through that spot on the way to Ingdanrad. For Gallnach, just like the centres of diamond-shaped druidic knots were sites of power, so were the centres of crosses. Everything in fours. Burren Inlet, a hundred leagues from end to end, was the largest natural cross on the coast. Tiernan had listed its crux in his notes, but no one expected Iollan to sail back toward the place where he'd been imprisoned.

"You knew all along," I said.

"I figured you'd ignore my warning and tell the Iyo. Now they're safe on a remote island. If we live through this, you'll have a jouyen to marry into one day." She ran a hand over her dripping bun and flicked rain off her fingers. "I won't apologize for that."

"We had a deal. 'No secrets, no lies.'"

"That was before you gave your soul to Suriel. You told Rhonos you're losing yourself, then almost killed Falwen in a rage. You only think of Rhonos as something for the Corvittai to use against me. I'm not sure you care how dangerous a battle would be for your confederacy."

"You sentenced us to death instead. We can't survive this alone."

"No. You and I probably can't." Iannah folded up the spyglass and slid it into her pocket. "But if we play it right, wait for the right moment, the captive antayul might get out alive. *If* you trust me to keep you on track."

"Trust?" I laughed. "My trust in you got Airedain arrested. Who turned you into a liar? Falwen? Or maybe Arril? I bet that's where you've been lately, swapping military stories with her and learning to backstab your friends. Who *are* you?"

"I'm still your friend."

"Nei. You're Nonil. You like it, don't you? Finally, soldiers bow to you. Kaid, you even look like Arril." I shoved her black leather breastplate. "The commander's loyal hand. Do you want to be her or fuck her? That's how women do it, right, with their hands?"

For all her Antler training, she looked like I'd slapped her. "That's low."

"Am I wrong? Maybe you kissed Rhonos to hide it—"

Iannah kneed me in the gut. I crumpled. On all fours in the mud, I threw up into a puddle, spattering my reflection.

"You're drunk," she said. "That cleared out any alcohol in your stomach, and I'll pretend you never said those things. Arril's a war criminal. I feel nothing but disgust for her."

I slumped over, gasping. Rain rolled into my eyes. Iannah took the waterskin from my belt and dumped it out, jenever and all.

As she reached down to help me up, I grabbed a black cord around her neck and yanked. It snapped. The kinaru makiri I'd given her came away in my hand. I hurled it over the cliff into the ocean. Never again would the Rin-jouyen protect her.

As the *Róg Sál* sailed through the mist curtain into the harbour, we packed up camp and smacked our horses' hindquarters, sending them cantering into the forest. They'd find their way home. Láchlan took a rowboat across the shallows to get us. He'd traded his fisherman's attire for leather armour. A black-feathered cormorant circled overhead out of archery range.

"It followed us the whole way," Láchlan said, wiping sweat from his forehead. "Don't suppose you know who it is?"

"Nei," I said truthfully. "Quinil got me exiled."

He swished water around his mouth, rinsing out the salt. "Quinil. Weaselly fellow. Sorry, lass. My one blessing is I had no family in the old country to leave."

I'd expected to travel with just Láchlan and his crew, but that was when I thought we'd be hauling blackpowder through unpatrolled waters. Instead, we had to go past Rutnaast, heavily guarded by the navy. Láchlan's plan was to meet Iollan here, load everyone onto the *Róg Sál*, and combine our defenses.

Late that evening, wind whistled through the gorge, blowing sea spray into the harbour. A red-sailed schooner drifted in and dropped anchor. "Suriel," I murmured, and the gusts turned warm on my face.

The cormorant battled in the sky, wings twisting, blown one way then the other. It gave up and soared off. Likely to report that Suriel wasn't where expected, but by the time anyone arrived, we'd be gone. Iannah watched me like a falcon minding its chick. One wrong move would end us both.

I scanned the new ship's deck for Iollan. Makoril had described him. No longer gaunt or bearded from prison, he was now simply a pale, brown-haired itheran of average height. The only way to identify him would be his clothes, but no one onboard wore burlap robes or a druidic knot.

Láchlan's first mate rowed across to the *Róg Sál*. He explained that they'd gotten delayed dodging naval guards around the Algard Island fishery. Iollan, afraid of running out of time, had mounted a kinaru, left the ship, and flown ahead to prepare the rift site. His acolyte and a team of mercenaries were with him as protection.

My only reassurance was seeing the antayul. All fourteen climbed up from below deck, squinting in the light, hands tied behind their backs. Runed cuffs glinted on their wrists. They were thin, but not skin-over-bones like when I left them. Gallnach mercenaries prodded them with crossbows, shepherding them onto rowboats to come over to the *Róg Sál*.

The leaders permitted to look after them during the ceasefire were there, too. The Beru representative was their okoreni, the young man who'd been Fendul's second-in-command during the invasion. A necklace of shark teeth hung under the whale tattoo on his neck. The Nuthalha had appointed a matriarch and spirit-seer, a leathery woman with a black soapstone bar through her nose. Two respected leaders, and I couldn't speak openly to either.

As they boarded our ship, the matriarch suddenly looked at me. I recoiled. One eye was white with a cataract, and it felt like that eye had seen straight through my skin. Maybe Nuthalha beliefs about spirit possession came from people like me.

Ignore her, Suriel soothed, stroking a finger of air across my white roots. *She does not understand what we share now.*

Once we got away from land, a perfectly aligned gale puffed out the sails. The *Róg Sál* sped through the night. A sailor tossed out a weighted rope that unwound, rattling on its coil. He counted knots that vanished into our foaming wake. Four in a quarter-hour, a speed of sixteen knots, twice what this ship could usually do.

Wind curled around me. Suriel whispered into my ear. Despite having two Corvittai captains present, his new Cattil and Nonil, he'd chosen me as his mouthpiece.

"A dolphin and a finback whale are following us," I announced. Makoril must've buried his pride and brought the biggest, fastest scout he could find. Finbacks could grow almost the length of the *Róg Sál*. "They keep surfacing for air. Suriel tried driving them off, but they dove underwater."

Láchlan peered into the darkness beyond the stern's lantern. "Smart. A finback whale can keep this pace easy, and a dolphin can follow in its path. Same way geese fly. They could swim this whole inlet without tiring."

Iannah shrugged with resignation. "Let them come. Not much else we can do."

She followed me into the hold where the antayul were chained. Water dripped down and ran off tarps covering the blackpowder kegs. Carrying candles or lanterns around explosive material would be a death wish, so we had to get around by what little light came from above. The reek of seaweed and urine wafted up from the bilge.

Uqiat, the young Nuthalha woman I met on Innisbán, gave me a withering look to compete with Rhonos's. From her viewpoint, I'd sided with the Corvittai again, not helped by anything her matriarch said about looking inside me, I was sure. As I picked mould off their flatbread rations, she spoke.

"My family," she rasped, the words fuzzy with her accent. Not once had she shown any sign of knowing Aikoto, and the old Nuthalha man only knew a few words.

Uqiat pointed at the two eldest Nuthalha. "Mother-father. Mother-mother." At the middle-aged woman. "Mother." At the man with whip scars who'd fainted on the amp rune. "Mother-brother." At the teenage boy whose nose got broken by Cattil's mercenary. "Mother-brother child."

Likely only a fraction of her family. Nuthalha tended to have more children since bloodweed didn't grow that far north. Cattil's whip cracked in my mind, but the sailors guarding the ladder to the upper deck didn't silence Uqiat. It was my job to manage the antayul.

"What about the rest of your family?" I asked.

She spoke to the Okoreni-Beru, who answered in fluent Nuthalha. He must've been an emissary to their confederacy often enough to know the language. As he spoke, he touched her arm with the softness of a lover. That explained how Uqiat learned Aikoto. A lot had happened in two months.

The man turned to me. "Uqiat's father was like an okorebai, sworn to protect an extended family of seal hunters. When raiders attacked their camp, the Nuthalha warriors and exiled Iyo fought so others could escape. Everyone who stayed got killed or captured. Uqiat's father, aunt, and two of her cousins were killed for the blackpowder trap."

"And the woman who attacked Cattil with the amp rune?"

"Uqiat's older sister. She would've become leader after their father."

Uqiat jerked her wrist. Her chains snapped taut. She wanted me to know what I did to her family, to Ilani and Ganiam, people from my own confederacy. What I was still doing.

I set the flatbread on a crate and sat cross-legged. Shifting wind outside told me Suriel was listening. "Will you tell Uqiat something?"

The Okoreni-Beru nodded.

"My older sister will have a baby soon," I said, looking at Uqiat. "I've got a brother the same age as your cousin and an ex-lover in prison. It's hard not to think about them, but I had to leave to devote myself to Suriel. I'm sorry for what happened to your family, sorry you weren't given a choice. I'm here to protect you, though. This will be over soon."

He translated. Uqiat frowned. Someone who risked her life for her family would have trouble believing I had truly abandoned mine, which was my intent — at least it was in my head. It'd been easy to refer to Airedain as my past. Even my memories of him were fading.

Pitching waves made everyone too ill to sleep. Near dawn, raised voices lured Iannah and me to the deck. Rutnaast's lighthouse shone through the gloom. Last time I had seen it was at sunset after Esiad's death. Anchored ships rocked in the harbour next to the one capsized on a pier.

Láchlan's men scurried about, adjusting sails as the wind changed direction. We tacked away from land and skirted the town. The lighthouse beacon flashed, signalling us to stop. We slipped between two patrolling ships. Suriel drove them away while pushing us onward. Their masthead lights shrank until they were like stars on the horizon, then vanished.

No other ports stood between us and the inlet crux. But as we lurched through the water, I felt a thrumming by our prow. I leaned over the bulwark.

"Seasickness," I told a nearby sailor.

Searching the dark expanse of waves, I sensed a thread underwater across the inlet. Our hull plowed through it like a duck cleaving apart an algae-coated pond. Once we passed, the ends swirled back into a continuous thread. The thrumming faded.

A tripwire that did nothing. Mystified, I went through every form of magic I knew. Runes for Folk wouldn't affect us, and druids put wards near water, not in it. Eventually my fur trapping experience gave it away. I'd once rigged snares with bells so I could wait in my tent and hear when I caught game. This wire would trigger a signal in Ingdanrad to indicate someone was approaching their waters.

Our canoes hadn't set it off last year. It was deep enough to only catch ship hulls, and it must've been tweaked so whales didn't trip it. I'd abandoned my bells after birds kept landing on them. Some mages would've stayed to defend Ingdanrad while others went to Ile vi Pumèze, but I doubted they'd care about us hitting the wire. Navy patrols would do it all the time these days.

I wondered what they could figure out from the tripwire. Tiernan said much of magic was just advanced mathematics. Based on how much space got interrupted, someone could measure a ship's width and distinguish between a tiny cutter, medium schooner, or massive galleon. And if there were multiple wires between Rutnaast and Ingdanrad, they could gauge how fast a ship was sailing.

Which meant they'd notice a ship flying along at impossible speeds.

As the sky lightened behind the mountains, I felt the thrumming of another wire. I pictured some tired night-shift guard scrambling up as he realized Suriel must be helping the ship. The mages would realize the Corvittai were heading for the inlet crux and not Ile vi Pumèze. While we sailed east, those still at Ingdanrad would rush to sail west toward us. The race was on.

Deep in the eastern range, with the sun dragging itself above snowy peaks, a sailor in the crow's nest called out. Everyone crowded onto the forecastle. A wall of mist stretched across the inlet, high enough for birds to get lost in, fading into a green blur where it met the far shore leagues away. Iannah gave me a questioning look. I shrugged.

The wall stayed as we hurtled toward it. Suriel soared ahead, cleaving through the fog, only for it to swallow the gap. Vapour rose into the sky and shredded apart. The man next to me uttered a Gallnach oath to his dead.

Sailors went below deck and confirmed the antayul were still cuffed. I could've told them so. I, trained by generations of respected antayul and exposed to all sorts of endurance testing by Tiernan, struggled to hold a fraction of that much water during the heist. A team of people couldn't hold it against a tel-saidu.

I threw my mind ahead. A voice brushed back in a strange language. I bit down on my shock. Each syllable rippled, not the hollowness that was Suriel's voice.

Kae scholars in Ingdanrad had spoken of an anta-saidu that lived in Burren Inlet's south arm. It was ancient, well beyond the fifty thousand years most saidu lived. After waking from dormancy, it'd ignored everyone and everything — the saidu war, Suriel reigning over the inlet's north arm, humans trying to communicate. The spirit version of an old man cranky about being interrupted from a nap. It didn't even bother repairing the world.

The Kae must've finally got through to it. Guilted it, maybe, for leaving Suriel unchecked. Or pointed out that if the edge of its territory got torn open to form a rift, it'd spend the rest of its life annoyed by things drifting through from other worlds.

"It's an anta-saidu," I told Iannah and Láchlan. "Humans can't stop it. The best we can do is keep afloat."

Láchlan and his first mate conferred in rapid Gallnach. The other man shook his head, but Láchlan slapped the bulwark. "Carry on, lads," he shouted. "Never back down from a challenge, eh?"

They hustled to storm-rig the sails. The wall loomed like an iceberg. I braced myself, half-expecting our prow to crumple into splintered wood. Dampness folded around us. The sunlight dimmed.

Waves struck our starboard side, sending us careening toward shore as Suriel and the anta-saidu battled. We tacked back toward open water, only to whirl on our axis. Two sailors clung to the spinning ship's wheel to keep us on course.

Láchlan held a compass in one hand and the forestay rope in the other, swaying with perfect balance, shouting orders. Iannah snapped her fingers at her men, who fetched half the antayul. Together, we strained against oncoming waves to keep the *Róg Sál* from tipping. Iannah and her men bailed out the flooding deck. Shouts went up as we skirted a whirlpool. An enormous finback whale whisked past its edge.

The remaining antayul took over to let us rest. Fog pressed in. The crow's nest vanished, then the stern and sails. The bowsprit plunged into a void. I was soaked to the skin, shivering, my hands locked around a rope. Wind and water, water and wind, creaking timbers and straining ropes.

Whatever was happening to Suriel, it hurt. First, as if my own body were getting battered, then like death itself. His pain ripped through my skin and bones into the part of his spirit that lived in me. He was screaming — not with words, and yet I understood. *Kill me*, he cried. *End it now.*

But he'd tried this before. Saidu could only die by true defeat, and the old anta-saidu couldn't best a younger, stronger spirit. Suriel tore at the other saidu, his rage growing. His screams worked into me until they came from my own mouth. *Then surrender*, he demanded. *Give in. Give in!*

Abruptly the waves flattened. The gusts dropped from our sails. We drifted to a stop and floated in the doldrums. I wiped my face with my sleeve, shaking. All around, mist floated in sheets and tendrils and eddies, an aurora of grey and white.

"Suriel?" I breathed, my throat raw.

No answer. The name was wrong, I recalled, given to him by itherans. I sank into myself, seeking the deepest point his pain had touched, and found a different sound. I spoke again. Hollowness left my lips.

I am here, he replied.

In those few words were all the emotions I'd lost, half-formed and vulnerable as spring buds. Pride, shame, tenderness, concern. Not his or mine alone, but ours. Confusion. Discomfort at this sudden connection. And underneath, the anguish that drove him to choose death over continued suffering. The sense that we had changed too much to ever belong in this world again.

Someone grabbed my hand. I shrieked.

"Hush," Iannah hissed, her face appearing in the mist. "Let's go."

"What?"

"Suriel's weakened. The antayul are free. We can escape now in this fog and avoid Iollan. His whole plan falls apart without them—"

"No." I pulled my hand back. "We're staying with Suriel."

Láchlan sent some sailors to the oars and others to patch holes in the ship. We edged forward with rhythmic splashes. The time-keeper, smacking his pocket watch to make it work, guessed we'd spent six hours in the maelstrom. We had no idea how far we had to go. Iannah watched me, but I could no longer read her flat expression.

I sank my mind through the ship timbers into the ocean and sent out shockwaves like whalesong. A faint reply pulsed back. Makoril had kept up with the whale scout. Someone else was catching up, too. The tracking stone's pulse grew in my thigh. Fendul must've realized I was heading into the mountains and told everyone still in Toel Ginu, though I wasn't sure who he'd entrust to carry the stone's match, my only way of finding the Rin again.

When the fog thinned, the sun was on its descent through the sky. Kinaru wailed in the distance. One soared toward us and landed on deck. A black-armoured woman slid off its back, her severe bun and slight limp unmistakable. Arril had abandoned her veil, showing me her face for the first time. Handsome was the wrong word. She was a *force*. Brick-jawed, dark-eyed, tanned from years spent in sunshine and wind.

"What in holy hell happened?" Arril demanded. "Where's Suriel?"

"Around," Láchlan said. "Some water spirit finally got off its arse and challenged him. Minor delay. We've got all of Abhain ahead."

"Not anymore. Two galleys with Ingdanrad's flag are rowing toward the crux."

Láchlan swore. "Double speed, lads!" he shouted to his sailors. "Heave those oars!"

Arril clapped her hands. "Nonil, I want a full update. Kateiko Rin, someone will be here soon."

As promised, another kinaru deposited a woman in burlap robes, Iollan's acolyte from Innisbán. The woman's cold manner had been replaced with fevered energy. Chittering in Coast Trader sprinkled with Gallnach, she took me to inspect the antayul and get them drying blackpowder. The kegs weren't large — a sailor could carry one under each arm — but there were hundreds, and the storm's humidity had caked the powder like wet sand.

We were nearly done when Iannah came below deck, crouched next to the Okoreni-Beru, and whispered to him. He frowned as he answered.

Stop them.

I twisted, searching for Suriel. His voice was faint through the ship timbers.

They want to take you from me. They will enlist the spirit-seer. Suriel reached through our link, pulling me closer, into him. My white roots sent a tingle into my scalp and down across my body. *We are joined now. We will leave this world together.*

I crossed the hold and called up the ladder. Arril climbed down, looking annoyed by the interruption. Láchlan followed.

"Another Nonil wishes to betray us," I said.

Iannah's shoulders sank. She searched my face, then rose and unsheathed her sword. Láchlan swung toward me, seeming to expect something.

Arril drew hers, too. "Damn the ceasefire. Kill whoever we don't need."

Láchlan pushed in front of her. "I'll not be party to murdering our own forces. I left that behind with Fíannula."

"Need I remind you who commands here?" she snapped.

"It's my ship, my crew, and my ceasefire. Bind Nonil down in the bilge where she can't plot with anyone. None of this will matter soon."

We faced off across the blackpowder kegs. Outside, the oars stopped splashing. The anchor chain rattled as it sank into the ocean. We'd reached the crux.

Arril scoffed. "Bind her, then, and hurry. We have work to do."

35.

THE CRUX

Four inlet arms met in a valley so broad I had to squint to see the far side. The surrounding mountains were prickly with pines. Spring rivers were swollen by snowmelt that cascaded down cliffs in crystalline waterfalls. More kinaru than I'd ever seen flew overhead or bobbed in the water. Iollan was here somewhere. Ingdanrad's mages weren't. With luck, they wouldn't arrive by the time Abhain started at sunset, when our water-calling would supposedly grow stronger.

"Peimil is building fifteen rune sites, one per water mage," the acolyte told me as sailors stacked kegs on deck. "They'll magnify the force of the blackpowder. We also made gear to help you keep your sites dry from afar. Hold out your hand."

I lifted the one without my rope bracelet. I couldn't remember why I was wearing it, just that I didn't want her touching it.

She tied a cord with two etched iron beads around my wrist.

"One's an amp rune, one's a focal rune. The design you provided from Tiernan Heilind was extremely helpful."

With her fingertip, she copied the focal rune onto twenty kegs, leaving faint glowing lines. When she pressed her palm against the last rune, all twenty lit up along with the one on my wrist. It felt like concentrating without trying. I tasted sea spray on the timbers, trying to seep through the resin seals.

Sailors loaded the runed kegs into nets. Kinaru swooped down to the cramped deck one at a time, grabbed a net in their bill, and rose into the air. I felt a pull as the nets moved apart, like I was a twenty-armed octopus reaching into the sky. No wonder the Corvittai needed so many antayul. One person couldn't handle more than this.

The kinaru flew toward the southern point of land, the fire direction according to druidism. They landed in the forest halfway up a mountain. The pull was more draining with distance, yet still I sensed the kegs like they were next to me. I sank into meditation and sorted varying patches of moisture into a hazy picture. Around the kegs was a ring of dry stone monoliths, a colossal druidic knot amid the damp trees.

"Where will we be?" I asked, handing the cord back. The octopus feeling faded.

"Over there." The acolyte waved west, the earth direction. "We have a camp where Peimil will trigger the explosion. It is safely out of the impact radius. Acceptable?"

I nodded.

"Good, then get the others."

I called into the hold. The antayul shuffled up, nudged by guards with crossbows. Arril tapped her foot. As the acolyte started linking powder kegs to cords for the other sites, strung across the mountains like a garland, a kinaru screeched an alarm.

"So it begins," Láchlan muttered.

Dots appeared on the northeast horizon, growing into galleys with oars low in the water. Láchlan directed archers to the bow. Kinaru flocked close. Arril lifted her face to the clouds and whispered.

Like a hurtling falcon, wind sliced through the ocean and slammed into the galleys. They rocked, turning broadside as Suriel pushed them off course. Sails unfurled as the crews fought to turn the gusts in their favour, but the ships shrank, pushed back. In minutes, they were gone.

Then a man up in the crow's nest shouted, "They're raising an island!"

Arril grabbed a spyglass. I peered through one I'd taken from Iannah. A rocky crag thrust up from the ocean, sheets of water falling from the stone. As the galleys passed it, sailors high on the rigging flung out hooked ropes that snagged in low crevices, anchoring them. They looped straps over the ropes and rappelled down to land. Others dove over the bulwarks and swam.

On the island, they clustered together, wielding stone slabs against the wind. Iannah had taught me about military formations from around the world. The shield wall was an old Sverbian one. Suriel drove at them from every side and couldn't separate them. The anta-saidu had worn him out.

"Fight," I urged him. "We're stronger than them!"

But the island grew. An earthen bridge rose like rope lifted from the water. The mages edged forward, a massive stone caterpillar straining against the squall, feet shuffling below their shields. Their bridge hit the mainland. A tunnel opened ahead, straight into the mountainside. The mages tumbled inside and sealed it. Suriel tore up trees along the shore, enraged at their escape.

"Where are they going?" a sailor asked.

"The far rune sites," the acolyte said. "But they won't bother climbing all that way. My guess is they'll tap into the mountains' power directly."

Arril snapped her fingers. A kinaru landed and hunkered down for someone to get on. "Get the water mages to the camp."

A soldier pushed Uqiat forward. She dug in her heels, stretching her arm back toward her family. Arril yanked a crossbow from a mercenary and fired into a spar. Wood exploded out the other side. I reached for my weapons, readying for a fight — then birds hurtled through the sky.

They came from the west, Iyo from Toel Ginu. My tracking stone throbbed. More warriors flew from the northeast, probably Kae from Ingdanrad. Suriel swept across the inlet crux. Birds spun and whirled, buffeted about. Some fell and spiralled toward the ocean.

I couldn't locate the tracking stone's match. Suriel took up too much space in my head. I barely noticed motion in the water, churning as Aikoto took their human forms. Wet bodies crept up the *Róg Sál's* hull, climbing the anchor rope, portholes, whatever possible.

Before I could shout a warning, someone body-slammed me. My skull struck a mast and I dropped. Lights flashed across my vision. Figures swung over the bulwarks. Blades clashed.

Uqiat dragged me behind some blackpowder kegs. She straddled me, yanked up my sleeve, and bit my forearm. I shrieked. She spat and held up my arm, letting blood trickle down my skin. It was red. I'd expected it to be white.

"You," she said. "Not Suriel."

Makoril appeared, dripping. "Whatever you're doing—" He whirled and sank a dagger into a sailor's gut. They grappled, knocking over kegs.

Another man seized Uqiat. I grabbed her leg, pulling her back. He kicked me away and wrestled her onto a kinaru. They flew west.

Makoril slit his attacker's throat and let him fall. "Where's he taking Uqiat?" he panted.

"Peimil's camp," called the Okoreni-Beru, fighting two mercenaries at once.

"Then we're going after her." Makoril hauled me upright. "I kept my promise and followed you. It's your turn now."

As another kinaru dipped toward the ship, he grabbed its ankle. It squawked. I leapt and caught its other ankle. The bird sank under our combined weight, then beat its wings hard, rising above the masts. Massive webbed feet flapped in front of my face.

"Fly west!" Makoril told it.

The kinaru dithered. I repeated the command, and we soared away. Waves pulsed far underneath us. My arms throbbed and my billowing cloak weighed me down. *Don't let go, don't let go,* I chanted. Mountains loomed ahead, bands and flecks of rock showing through the snow mantle. But we were too low, heading for forest midway up a slope.

"Jump!" Makoril yelled. He thrust one foot toward a white smudge. "Aim for that snow!"

The moment we passed above it, I shut my eyes and opened my hands. My insides stayed put while my body fell. Air rushed past.

I landed with a *whump*. Snow folded over me, sending me into a coughing fit. I dug myself out, gasping. We'd hit a steep hill, maybe an old mudslide. The barren white incline rose into a vast mat of ladder pines.

Makoril surfaced nearby, brushing snow off his shaved hair. His elbow bent oddly. He popped it back into place and swore, strange with his soft voice, then crawled toward me. "Kateiko. Look at me. What happened?"

I didn't answer. Suriel had felt me bleed. Felt me leave. He was calling me back, flooding my mind, grasping my white roots.

"You talked to that kinaru in some weird language, then it tried to knock us off on the trees. Even it doesn't know whose side you're on. Ai—" Makoril grabbed my chin to keep my head from lolling. "Yan taku, Kateiko. Stay with me. What was Uqiat doing to you?"

"Fixing her," called Iannah.

A kinaru sailed overhead and alighted, its black feathers stark against the snow. Rhonos and Iannah slid off its back. Her wrists were red from being tied in the bilge. The bird shifted into Yironem, wearing the other tracking stone on a cord around his neck.

Iannah crouched next to us. "Suriel's taking her over. I asked the Nuthalha spirit-seer how to fight it but didn't get her answer."

"This, apparently." Makoril lifted my arm and showed them the bite marks.

"Blood," Yironem said. "We carry our ancestors in our blood-lines. Maybe Uqiat was trying to ward Kako." He drew his hunting knife and cut me.

The pain had a strange clarity. I dipped my fingers into my blood and painted streaks from my forehead to my chin, feeling it, tasting it. Remembering my bodies. This one, gifted by my parents when they were alive, and my wolf body, gifted by my aeldu. Suriel would have to kill me to claim those.

Which he wanted. I sat up, the haziness lifting from his words. *We will leave this world together.* He was afraid to die alone.

"Come back to us, Koehl," Iannah said. "Let's finish what we started. Once we save the Nuthalha, they can fix you properly."

"I . . ." My eyes focused on Yironem. My brother, no matter how much Suriel wanted to claim him as well. "You're too young to be here."

He gave a choked laugh. "I'm too young to fight. Fendul let me bring Rhonos. I wasn't supposed to go near the ship, but we couldn't leave Iannah there."

Back in the crux, the colossal finback whale rammed the *Róg Sál*, splintering the hull where it'd taken damage in the maelsrom. I wished I could see better, then realized Iannah's spyglass was in my cloak pocket, cracked but intact. I held it to my eye. Sailors flung harpoons into the whale. Its blowhole erupted, a mist of half-digested fish I was glad I couldn't smell. And in the sky — a pair of kinaru flying straight at us.

They landed on the incline above us. Láchlan and two Corvittai archers dismounted. Rhonos already had an arrow nocked.

"I won't fight unless I gotta," Láchlan said. "We can end this now, peacefully."

"How?" Iannah asked.

"Most of the antayul escaped. I need Kateiko, Yironem, and Makoril to take their places."

She snorted. "You talk about being different than the last Cattil, but look what you've come to. Forcing children, the broken, and the wounded to serve a murderous spirit."

"If this is a moral pissing contest, *I* kept Arril from killing you. *Your* side broke the ceasefire and butchered my men." Láchlan skidded down the slope, leaving a furrow in the snow, and stretched out a calloused hand to me. "C'mon, Kateiko. You wanna help Suriel, right, lass?"

I didn't know anymore. Suriel's call had become a demand. But through that storm, my aeldu called, too. They wouldn't hand over our people. Facing Láchlan now, a thought surfaced. *He* turned

Airedain into an arsonist. *He* got my lover arrested. My ancestors' rage at everything itherans had taken from us welled up inside me, forcing out Suriel.

"Go fuck yourself," I said, and punched Láchlan.

Arrows whirred. Láchlan struck me, tossed me over his shoulder, and whistled for a kinaru. Shrieking curses, I froze everything in reach, stabbing with ice spikes that shattered on his armour.

Iannah slammed her sword hilt into Láchlan's head. He dropped me. She dove at him. They slid down the hill on glassy ice and tumbled into the forest.

Rhonos lowered his longbow. He'd taken down the archers before they landed a hit on us. We half-ran, half-slid through the forest, pine needles scraping our skin, trees swinging past — until the ground fell away. I scrabbled on the edge of a ravine. Pebbles came loose under me.

Looking down, I saw Iannah and Láchlan tangled together in a snowdrift, dazed. Their groans echoed up the rock walls. Rhonos hesitated. He couldn't get a clear shot at Láchlan, and he wouldn't risk harming Iannah.

Yironem peered into the ravine. "I can't get them out. I won't fit down there as a kinaru."

"I climbed mountains in my ranger days," Rhonos said, uncoiling a rope. "There is no time to lose, though. You must go on without us."

Makoril eyed me. "Are you back to normal?"

"Nothing's normal," I said. "But Suriel's not controlling me anymore."

We found a clearing so Yironem had room to shift and I could look through the badly cracked spyglass over the trees. The finback whale was nowhere to be seen, but it'd taken down the *Róg Sál*. Bubbles rose around the sinking ship. Survivors clung to drifting flotsam. Kinaru hauled nets of blackpowder, salvaging what they could. The fight had moved to Iollan's camp.

I climbed onto Yironem with Makoril behind me. We took off and zigzagged, gaining altitude. The temperature dropped. I scanned the peak of the mountain we'd just left and pointed at dark smudges that looked like tents. We thumped down behind a rocky ridge a safe distance away. Up here still felt like winter. I fumbled my gloves on. Makoril drew his dagger and kept watch.

"Suriel won't harm you," I told Yironem. "Rescue whoever you can carry, then fly straight to Toel Ginu. Don't look back. You have to look after Nili and her baby and our tema. Promise you will."

He rubbed his head against my shoulder, then soared toward the *Róg Sál*'s wreckage. Makoril and I crept around the ridge and hid behind boulders. Uqiat, her teenage cousin, her mother, and the Okoreni-Beru were on their knees in the snow, wrists bound. Arril paced with her slight limp. Iollan's acolyte frantically marked runes onto powder kegs. Mercenaries flanked a brown-haired man in burlap robes, standing with his hands folded.

"Iollan," I breathed.

"Give me that spyglass." Makoril peered through it. "That's not Iollan in the druid robes."

"What?"

"I was in his test group on Innisbán, remember? I know his face. See that man in the tan woolwrap and leather armour? *That's* Iollan och Cormic. He must've swapped clothes as a decoy."

I squinted. They both looked in their late thirties, pale and beardless, though the armour seemed loose on the tan-clad one. He wove patterns in the air with tiny gestures of his fingers. On a log in front of him, faint runes shimmered into existence. Tiernan's research had included notes on remote triggers. Once the log caught fire, the blackpowder at the rune sites would, too.

"Do we go after Iollan or the antayul?" I asked.

Makoril frowned. "Wait and see what they do. We'll only get one chance at surprising them."

A kinaru landed in the camp. Wincing, a bloodied scout dismounted and headed for Arril. Attuning was my only way to hear them, and I hadn't tried since making my sacrifice to Suriel. I cut my palm. Holding the clarity of my blood, calling on my aeldu, I shifted into my wolf body. Sound roared into my head along with the sulphurous smell of blackpowder.

The scout reported that attuned viirelei had gotten past Suriel and tried to flood the rune sites. Magical traps killed a few, but the rest realized the traps were all on land and started working from the sky. Ingdanrad's mages were still concealed deep inside the mountains.

Arril glanced up. The sun was half-hidden behind the peaks, scorching the sky red. Abhain would start soon. "Prepare the water mages."

Mercenaries knotted beaded cords onto the Nuthalha's wrists, five each. Uneasiness latched onto me like leeches. Nothing could help someone focus on keeping a hundred powder kegs dry at five different sites. Across the inlet crux, fog appeared above the southern point of land. Our Aikoto warriors were dampening every stone circle. If they had amp runes, too, both sides would be at a stalemate, bringing themselves closer to death.

Arril approached the Nuthalha. "We have no time for belligerence. Obey, or you choose who dies." She mimed slitting her throat.

The Okoreni-Beru translated, his voice soaked with disgust. Uqiat's face twisted. Saving her mother, cousin, and the man she'd fallen in love with wasn't a hard choice. A mercenary unclasped her runed cuff. Her eyes flew wide. I could imagine the feeling, her mind shattered like glass, split a hundred ways. Sweat streaked down her forehead.

I shifted back to human. "We can't take down all these Corvittai in one strike," I told Makoril. "Only Iollan and his acolyte can finish those trigger runes, though. If we kill them, there's no explosion. And when the guards come for us, maybe the antayul can escape."

Our eyes met. We knew what *our* chances of getting out were.

"You know," he said, like the words were nettles, "I'm sorry about attacking your brother last year."

I smiled bitterly. "Sorry I couldn't save Ilani and Ganiam."

Makoril edged along the boulders, getting closer to the acolyte. I drew Nurivel and positioned myself with a clear shot at Iollan's neck, exposed above his armour. It felt strange to have hunted him for so long and now to see him for so little time before his death. Makoril signalled he was ready. I took a deep breath and aimed.

Someone shouted.

Iollan ducked. Nurivel sailed over his head. A rock shield ruptured up from the ground. Arril spun, drawing her sword.

Ice wrapped around the acolyte's chest, cracking her ribs. She dropped to her knees gasping. *Keep going*, I mouthed at Makoril, and scrambled along the boulders. Maybe I could bluff long enough to get near Iollan—

A bolt whizzed in front of me. Mercenaries streamed over the boulders. One hit me in the jaw, putting my tooth through my lip. Makoril made a fist. The acolyte screeched in the distance. A bolt hit his thigh, and he buckled.

Arril limped into sight. "Kateiko Rin. I should've known. Suriel won't let me kill you, but if you want your companion to live, I advise surrender."

My aeldu answered through the blood in my mouth. I raised my hands.

Mercenaries took Antalei and Kohekai. One snapped a runed cuff on my wrist and bound my hands. I gritted my teeth as his fingers brushed my bracelet. They did the same with Makoril and dragged us into the camp. The acolyte lay in a heap of burlap robes, her chest collapsed and her face blue. Iollan came closer, stepping over the woman's body. The red wool of his druidic knot pendant was studded with volcanic glass that glinted in the sunset.

Everyone described Iollan och Cormic as an average-looking itheran. Despite that, I'd pictured him as skeletal and twisted, so inhuman he murdered a teenage acolyte for his research. Neither were true. Something very much alive glittered in his brown eyes. I was being broken down into parts under his scrutiny.

"Impressive," he said. "That's the closest anyone's gotten to killing me."

I bared my bloody teeth. "Tiernan Heilind sends his regards."

He flinched. "Good thing you kept Makoril Iyo alive," he told Arril. "We may need a replacement."

That was all the attention paid to us. I chanced a look at the distant rune sites. As expected, three antayul with amp beads weren't strong enough to stop our warriors' attempted sabotage. Indigo clouds hung over the mountains like ripe huckleberries ready to burst. If I could stall the Corvittai—

Arril tore open Uqiat's shirt, exposing the wave tattoo below her collarbones. I felt faint. Iollan pressed a bone knife to Uqiat's chest.

"Apologies," he said. "I would've had a woman do this, but alas, my acolyte is unavailable."

She screamed as he sliced into her antayul tattoo. Guards held her still. Among the onlookers, I spotted a familiar grey coat.

"Quinil!" I shouted. "What happened to protecting our people?"

Falwen's mouth drew tight. "She is not Aikoto."

"Who fucking cares? She's not an itheran!"

A blue-clad mercenary hit me in the mouth. I swallowed blood and choked. Iollan cut a sunburst of lines into Uqiat, curved as if someone dripped dye into water and swirled it. He wiped his knife on his woolwrap and stepped back.

Uqiat crumpled. The clouds above the nearest rune sites shuddered. Black shot through the veins in her chest. Tiernan had lived through this, but he was a trained soldier, not a twenty-year-old girl who'd spent the winter starving in an underground cell. I pulled at my bonds in vain. Iollan moved onto Uqiat's cousin. The boy looked terrified.

"Falwen!" I shrieked. "*Falwen!*"

The blue-clad mercenary slammed his crossbow into my skull. When I came to, all three antayul had runes in their chests. Uqiat's mother convulsed, her eyes rolling back. Blood bubbled from her lip. The rain clouds pulsed in an erratic dance as the Nuthalha fought with our faraway Aikoto warriors.

I had to get free. I tried shifting my hands into paws but couldn't focus. The connection to my aeldu was warping, corrupted by whatever Suriel left in me. The more I bled, burning through my ancestors' power, the weaker I got. *Think*, I told myself. What did I have? No weapons, no water-calling. Just a fragment of Airedain's spirit and an Iyo who didn't much like me.

"Makoril," I hissed. "Sing something."

He stared like I'd been hit in the head too often. Which, well, I had.

"Trust me. You know that Iyo song about the ocean depths?"

He sang. Not as well as Airedain soothing me during Suriel's blizzard, but his Iyo accent was right. The blue-clad mercenary glanced at him strangely and went back to watching the Nuthalha. I sank into the feeling of Airedain's hair grazing my wrist, the memory of his touch in Toel Ginu's shrine, the sense of being loved and protected.

My hands shrank. Fur rippled across my skin. The runed cuff slid off into trampled snow, followed by the ropes around my wrists. I snapped back to fully human, shoved the bracelet into my purse, and froze Makoril's bonds. Wincing at the cold, he twisted his wrists. The brittle ropes snapped. It wouldn't work on his iron cuff, but I slipped him an ice spike, then froze the Okoreni-Beru's bonds, too. He caught his surprise before anyone noticed.

Now, I mouthed.

The Okoreni-Beru tackled Arril. Makoril stabbed the blue-clad guard. I yanked a stalagmite of ice up from the snow, straight between Iollan's legs into his gut. Whirling, I coiled a water whip around a man's leg and toppled him.

Iollan, impaled but alive, raised his hands like he was unsealing a tomb. The ground shook. A fissure opened under my feet. I dove and rolled. Gorges appeared on either side, hounding me through the camp. Only when Makoril yelled did I turn back.

He collapsed, holding his ribs. A mercenary raised his sword. Behind them, Falwen aimed a crossbow — and shot the mercenary.

I didn't know why, until I saw Uqiat cradling her mother and screaming. Iollan's rune had killed the older woman. Makoril and I were the only ones who could take her place.

The mountain stilled. Iollan went limp like a scarecrow, blood flowing down his legs. The Okoreni-Beru and three mercenaries lay in a patch of red snow. I spun, looking for Arril.

She held a knife to Uqiat's cousin's throat. "Finish the job," she called to Uqiat.

A bluff, I thought. Arril needed the boy, too. Makoril was hurt and Uqiat couldn't do it alone. Then I looked up. The sun vanished behind snowy peaks, leaving a bleeding glow. Abhain had begun.

All that grew stronger for me was the ache in my head. But for Uqiat — whether Iollan's faith had sunk into her subconscious or whether she was overcome by pain and rage and grief for her dead family and lover — I saw a surge within her eyes.

A furrow shot through the ocean. The rainclouds vanished. Red-brown patches bloomed in the forest around the rune sites. Only once had I seen slopes like that, in a summer of beetle plague that killed huge swaths of pine. Trees withered and bent under a gale from Suriel. Birds flocked away, surrendering.

Arril smiled like a satisfied cat. "There we go."

As fast as it came, her smugness faded. The ground trembled again. Dead trees crumbled in waves. Deep within the mountains, Ingdanrad's mages were shaking the rune sites, trying to topple the stone circles.

Arril hesitated. In that second, her grip loosened. The Nuthalha boy sprinted away and caught Uqiat as she fell.

I forced everything I had at Arril. Snow melted and swirled in an orb around her. She floated in a suspended pool. She gagged, thrusting her hands through water to tear at the edges, but I held fast. Bubbles swelled to the surface. *Drown*, I thought, *drown*. The world dissolved into screaming.

Then everything went quiet.

Arril's limbs drooped. The bubbles stopped. I released the orb. Her body hit the ground, rocking in water flowing down the mountainside. The Nuthalha boy, sobbing, held Uqiat. Her heart had given out. Nothing else moved in the camp.

I ran to Makoril. His shirt was blood-soaked. His chest stuttered, face pale, eyes drifting. I'd seen that look on Esiad moments before he bled to death. "Nei, nei, nei. Come on, Makoril. Look at me. *Mako!*"

An orange glow caught my eye. A flaming bolt.

Falwen fired. The trigger log burst into flames, bigger than a bonfire. My face blistered.

Across the crux, white-hot circles erupted like volcanoes. Fire roiled into the sky. A shockwave rolled out, exposing the ocean floor. It slammed against our shore and I toppled. The *booms* hit a second later.

And the ground gave way beneath us.

36.

WITH GRACE

Avalanche. That's all I had time to think.

A fracture shot across the peak. The slab of packed snow under us broke off and slid down the mountain. Makoril tumbled away. Screaming, I grabbed a boulder. My nails tore. Streaks of blood vanished into the chaos. The slab tipped, then there was nothing but surging whiteness.

Swim, my father's memory commanded.

I thrashed. Snow and ice flowed around me. My flailing kept me on the surface. But I was tired, aching, dazed from blood loss and skull trauma. Powder filled my lungs. I kept going, on and on, until my limbs gave out to exhaustion.

With a last swell of strength, I clamped my hands to my mouth. A torrent rolled over me. Everything went dark.

Weight. Stale air. And blackness like the inside of a barrel.

My chest had no room to expand. I loosed numb fingers from my face. When I was young, my father had drilled avalanche survival into me. Thanks to him, I'd captured a pocket of air that'd last ten, maybe twenty minutes. Enough time to dig out if I was near the surface. Not that I knew which way that was.

I pushed. Nothing happened. I reached out with my mind and found endless snow. A hundred tons pressed in from every direction, packed like brick. Hot panic swelled through me. My breaths came rapid and shallow. Colours flashed across my vision.

Calm down. Conserve air.

But why bother? No one was left to rescue me. Makoril was too weak to have stayed afloat, Uqiat's cousin was from the tundra and wouldn't know how to survive an avalanche, and Rhonos and Iannah would've gotten the brunt of it farther down the mountain. I was buried alive in my grave.

"Fuck that."

I jerked.

Airedain lay next to me, head propped on one hand like after we made love in the shrine. The rope bracelet with my hair circled his wrist. I reached out. Warm skin, the crunch of pine resin in his hair — but no pulse in his throat. I saw him, yet not my fingers. I shouldn't have been able to move my arm.

I closed my eyes. "You're not real. You're in prison."

"Yeah, waiting for you." He jabbed my chest. "C'mon. Since when do you give up, Rin-girl?"

"I can't get out!"

"You ain't even trying!"

I flinched. Anger was one thing — he couldn't do more harm than my impending suffocation — but I knew him. Anger was his veil.

Airedain cupped my face. "Kako. Know what scares me about dying in prison? If the Elkhounds don't return my body for an Iyo burial, my spirit won't pass to Aeldu-yan. I'll never see my family or friends there. I can't spend the rest of time with you. Know what happens if you die like this?"

"The snow will melt. My body will find the earth. It's enough."

"You're forgetting something." He fingered my cut hair. "You gave Suriel your spirit. If you die without getting it back, you're stuck forever between worlds. Like the void he wants to reach. Are you really gonna do that to yourself? To Fendul and your family? To me?"

"What else *can* I do?"

"Find the surface. If you're underwater on a cloudy night, no moonlight to guide you, how do you know which way's up?"

"Down is where you sink." That tugged at a memory of something else my father taught me. I spat. It hit my cheek. So I was on my back facing up, more or less. I thought my way through the snow, not turning back this time. There — a sudden thinning where I touched air. "It's too far."

Airedain scoffed. "You're the smartest antayul I know. Forget amp runes, forget Abhain. Think."

"Fine. If you sing for me."

He sang. From him, it was perfect. I forced myself to meditate. I didn't need out yet, I just needed air. I melted a finger-sized hole down from the surface, pushing water out the top so it wouldn't drown me. Airedain sang faster, urging me on. My focus flickered. My lungs seared. *Keep going*, he said through his song. *Almost there*.

I slammed my hand upward. The remaining snow shattered onto my face. I gasped cold air. Airedain grinned — and vanished.

"Nei!"

It was too late. I only got one or the other, him or life. I rested, restoring feeling to my limbs, then melted enough space to roll over. I set to work on a steep tunnel, softening the snow enough to dig. I'd lost my gloves, and I'd never gotten my weapons back from the Corvittai, so I unbuckled my knife sheaths and used them as shovels. Slowly, I wriggled upward like a weasel in a den.

While I rested again, I felt vibrations. Another avalanche, I thought with a flare of terror, but they stayed steady. Someone else — or some*thing* — was digging. I spread my mind out and found another tunnel far above, the size of a person, coming from the surface.

"Ai!" I shouted. "Down here!"

I couldn't tell if there was a reply. My ears were ringing louder than stavehall bells. I made a new breathing hole above me and shouted up it, then angled my digging toward the other tunnel. We worked together like that, getting closer. Finally I punched through the snowpack — and a hand grabbed mine.

We scrambled to clear the opening. It was too dark to see a face. They didn't speak, just crawled backward, allowing me to follow. I broke the surface into murky moonlight, sucked in air — and found myself facing Falwen.

"I heard you scream," he said. He held a shovel. A pickaxe and rope lay nearby. Behind him flew a kinaru.

"I don't need you. Go save someone else."

"There is no one else. Our people fled. This is a cursed place now."

Across the inlet crux, the southern tip of land was half its former height. The mountains had collapsed, spilling rubble into the ocean. The only sign of the rune sites was a few scorched craters. The mages in the mountain might've survived if they'd stayed low enough, but digging out would be an ordeal even for earth-callers.

Smoke hung in thick clouds, blocking the stars. Yet at the centre of the wastes, a sliver of green forest continued up into a sliver of clear sky. The sword of the tel-saidu glittered in the night, a cross constellation mirroring the inlet crux below. No matter how I turned my head, I couldn't make it disappear.

"That's a real rift?" I asked.

"So it seems. Suriel left without you. I do not know if he reached the void or went past into the shoirdryge."

"You set him loose in another world?!"

"Better than our world." He held out his hand. "Come. We can look for survivors if you wish."

I laughed. "I'll never go anywhere with you again. Neither will anyone else."

His brows drew together.

"You know what the Rin did during all this? The moment you left Caladheå, Fendul sent messengers to every jouyen and itheran town on this coast. Now everyone knows you're Quinil. They'll discover you triggered this explosion. You'll wander the land alone, more of an exile than you were with the Dona. No jouyen, no status, no protection. People will wash their mouths after saying your name. They'll burn your image in effigy for as long as that rift is open. Maybe thousands of years, maybe forever.

"And your nieces and nephews you adopted into the Yula-jouyen? They know everything you did while claiming to care about me like a daughter. They know you didn't keep Parr from me. They know you got me exiled at risk of tearing apart the Rin. The Yula elders will cut off your hands before letting you near those kids, and any Aikoto woman will cut off your nethers before letting you father your own. Your only legacy will be your crimes."

Falwen's mouth worked soundlessly. He had no defense against something that he truly, utterly deserved.

"If this is where we part," he managed to say, "you should know there is one other survivor. Down this slope and to the left. But they are beyond saving."

"Who?"

"You will see." He tossed his tools at my feet. "Goodbye, Sohikoehl. You will never believe me, but I am sorry."

Using the shovel and my cracked flint to make sparks, I ignited a branch for a torch, then hurried down the mountain, going sideways so I didn't tumble head over rump. The snow was so high that only scattered treetops showed through. In the sputtering light, they all looked like bodies against the bleak expanse. Giving up on sight, I shifted into my second body long enough to search for a human scent.

Rhonos. My wolf ears picked up his juddering heartbeat.

I found him on his side, buried from the waist down. It looked like he'd started digging himself out and given up. A bit of snow was stained dark around him, but not enough for it to be a fatal injury. I dropped to my knees at his side. He smiled weakly.

"Where are you hurt?" I asked.

"My back." His voice scraped. "I climbed a tree. It kept me above the snow until the trunk broke."

I looked behind him. In horror, I realized the problem. A branch had impaled his ribs next to his spine. It plugged the wound, so when it was removed, he'd bleed out — if he didn't die of internal bleeding first.

"What happened to Iannah?" I asked as I melted the snow around his legs.

He closed his eyes. "I rescued her and Láchlan from the ravine. We were debating what to do with him when the avalanche hit.

Iannah is an excellent soldier, but . . . I do not expect she lived. The Colonnium does not teach outdoor survival."

I swallowed a hill-sized lump. He was probably right. And I'd thrown away the kinaru makiri, her last chance of protection.

"Tell me, Kateiko. Did she love me?"

No secrets, no lies. "She cared about you, more than any man I've known her to. Beyond that, I'm not sure. She still loved Pia Rossius."

Surprise flickered across his face. So she'd never told him about Pia.

I finished freeing his legs and the branch, which had broken away from its tree, then unbuckled his quiver and eased him into an awkward lying position. He couldn't support his upper body, whether due to pain or blood loss, I wasn't sure. We'd lost our cloaks, so I piled snow under his head for a pillow.

"I may have frostbite," he said. "I cannot feel my legs."

It wasn't that cold this low on the mountain, but I built a fire and pulled off his boots and socks. His feet hadn't gone black or white. I rubbed them with snow to get the blood flowing. He didn't react. Most people screamed during this part.

"Try moving your toes," I said.

Moments passed. He shook his head.

"Legs, then."

He shook his head again. I sat back on my heels, stunned. Paralysis meant he was stuck on this mountain. I hardly had the strength to walk, let alone carry a man.

Rhonos caught my expression. "God have mercy on my soul."

"Gods give no mercy. The closest thing to a god I know just abandoned this world." I looked to the sky. A few kinaru lingered despite the smoke. Without Suriel, I couldn't find the old words of the wind to command them, but if Falwen meant his apology, maybe he'd command one for me. I started to rise.

Rhonos reached out. His fingers circled my arm but slipped loose. "Stay."

"I can bring help—"

"The nearest medic is hours away." He gave a rattling cough. His face contorted, and blood seeped from his back. "I will not last that long."

I set out the contents of my herb pouches. Most of it was damaged, the vials shattered, the bogmoss swollen with melted snow. All I had of use was hellseed powder to calm the nerves and half a vial of needlemint tincture for pain. It wasn't enough for this kind of wound.

"Anything else you want to know while I'm spilling secrets?" I said to distract Rhonos.

He deliberated so long I glanced up to check he was alive. Finally he said, "Did a Rin kill my father?"

"Yes." My voice was quiet over the snapping fire. "I did. With Fendul's help. If Parr lived, we'd never be safe."

Rhonos sighed. "I am grateful I saw him once more. To be sure he deserved his end." He coughed again, spitting up blood. His breath came in spasms. "God, but it hurts. I should be thankful . . . to only feel half my body."

"It's that bad?"

"Growing worse."

The crushed remains of my bloodweed gave me an idea. Airedain had warned me that mixing it with alcohol could make people seriously ill, far more than either would alone. I sprinkled hellseed into the needlemint and shook the vial.

"What is that?" he asked.

"Mercy. If you're ready for your end."

He nodded. I tipped the vial into his mouth, pausing while he coughed.

"A favour," he said. "May I be upright when . . ."

I understood. Better to keep a fragment of dignity. He groaned as I lifted him into a sitting position and rested his weight against me, avoiding the wood embedded in his back.

"I owed you more," he murmured. "Serving on the Council . . . helping your nation . . ."

"You've repaid it." I stroked his straight black hair. "I wish I could speak to you in Aikoto. I'd tell you so many things I can't find words for. How grateful I am. We've known each other, what, a year and a half? Yet look at all we've endured together. Betrayals, deaths, battles. Famine. You vowing to kill me."

Rhonos laughed softly. "Look in my quiver."

I upended it. Of course, all his arrows had fallen out in the avalanche — including the one he'd marked for my death.

He seemed to grow heavier. Closer to the earth. "If I spoke in Ferish . . . I would tell you a military quote. 'To die in a friend's arms is to not truly die.' And though I am afraid . . . I could not have chosen a braver friend. I would say . . . thank you. Even for this."

I kissed his hair. I'd bundle his fear inside me and hold it for him. "Go with grace," I whispered. "May we meet again on the other side."

Too exhausted to move, I slept with Rhonos draped over me. I woke shivering hours later. The fire had gone out, as had his body heat. The stench of death had settled in.

It was then that the crushing realization hit. There wasn't anyone I could return to in the whole world. After Airedain's arrest, my exile, and Iannah's likely death, Rhonos was my last friend and protector.

"Aeldu guide me," I said into the sky. "No one else can."

I knew the concept of Ferish burial rites, but not the words, and my chances of finding soil were roughly none. The Rin had rites for when burials weren't practical, though. Usually it was when attending the dead endangered the living, like in a war zone. I cut Rhonos's palms and placed them downward to bleed into the earth. Animals would climb over the avalanche wreckage and feed on his body. Life sprang from death in so many ways. Every autumn, some salmon spawned and died, while others became food for bears and eagles who dropped the remains in the rainforest. Those remains nourished the plants. Maybe trees would grow here again one day.

Right now, Rhonos looked small amidst all that snow. His longbow and dagger were lost. I arranged branches around him in the shape of a three-blossom flower, a holy marker to get the Ferish god's attention. I pulled his brass military tag from under his shirt so he could be identified.

My clothes were stained with his blood. I needed to burn them to send his spirit on, but I didn't want to freeze. It seemed hopeless until I went to gather kindling and grabbed something soft in the snow — his green cloak snagged on a branch. With Falwen's rope as a belt, the cloak worked as a makeshift dress.

Everyone who died here deserved a proper burial. Iannah, Makoril, the antayul, even Láchlan, Arril, and Iollan. But I was in no shape to search a mountain range. Someone else would have to. Everyone from Ingdanrad to Toel Ginu had probably felt the shock-wave. This time, I chose to look after myself. *I must leave the dead behind so I can live.* That's what attuning taught me years ago.

I took stock of my belongings. No food, no weapons, just a shovel and pickaxe. A few healing supplies, my flint, and a coil of snare wire. Not much, but I could survive on it. The fireweed and arrowhead leaves sewn into my purse were intact along with my bracelet. I touched them gratefully. Losing my father's knives and my flail, gifted from my parents, was hard enough.

I had one other comfort. The tracking stone in my thigh tugged faintly to the west. Yironem must've made it back to Toel Ginu. No matter where I went, I could find my way home.

Once a glimmer of dawn appeared, I climbed down the mountain. My stomach grumbled. I waded into the cold ocean and used water-calling to nudge a surfperch into my hands. While the fish roasted, I wandered along shore and found a sheet of splintery wood, probably flotsam from the sunken *Róg Sál*. It'd work as a raft. I used the pickaxe to break a sharp flake off a rock, then used the flake to shape driftwood into a paddle.

My last task was the hardest. Ever since leaving Airedain in prison, I'd kept his hair close, but I couldn't risk losing it where I was going. His spirit belonged in this world. I kissed my rope bracelet and set it in the fire. The scent of burning pine resin wafted up with the smoke.

Finally, I pushed my raft into the water and set a course for the green sliver across the inlet, steering around burnt trees that floated by. The sword of the tel-saidu was faint over the sunrise. Even with the tide, the ocean was calm as a mirror. Suriel had mentioned once that other tel-saidu would claim his territory and take over managing the wind, but if that was true, they'd have to come from very far away. I didn't know of any still alive on this whole coast.

The green sliver was a valley, I saw as I drew closer. The fabric of the world had disintegrated. Framed by looming slopes of tumbled rock was a smudge of somewhere else — hemlock trees draped over a burbling creek, rushes swaying along its banks, sunshine glittering on the dew. Birdsong drifted to me even as I breathed the scent of sulphur.

With it came a steady stream of voices. Shrouded words, laughter, screams, songs, weeping, like the speakers were underwater and I couldn't reach through the surface. But for the first time, I could. I could.

Maybe Suriel had found the void between worlds and the solace of nothingness. Maybe he passed beyond into the next world. All I knew was he alone could return my spirit. Whether he left it here or took it with him, finding it was my key to becoming whole again. To regaining my life in this world and ensuring my afterlife in it. To truly going home to my loved ones.

I skimmed my hand across the ocean, feeling the water of my homeland. There was a chance I'd never touch it again. "Today I fly," I said to the mountains.

And I sailed into the rift.

GLOSSARY

etymology: A: Aikoto, F: Ferish, S: Sverbian

Abhain: Gallnach sowing festival in spring
aeldu: spirits of the dead in Aikoto mythology
Aeldu-yan: land of the dead in Aikoto mythology
Antalei: [A. *anta* water, *leiro* 'to fall'] Kateiko's flail
antayul: [A. *anta* water, *-yul* caller] viirelei who have learned to
    control water
attuning: shapeshifting into an animal; a rite of passage for
    viirelei adolescents
Blackbird Battle: a devastating battle in which Nonil and the
    Corvittai mutinied and attacked the Rin-jouyen, hoping to
    destroy the Rúonbattai's last allies
bloodweed: semi-poisonous leaves used as birth control by viirelei

bogmoss: moss used for dressing wounds; antiseptic and highly absorbent

Bódhain: Gallnach harvest festival and day of the dead in autumn

Bøkkhem: [S. *Bøkkai*, *hem* flatlands] a barren land in Sverbian mythology

brännvin: [S. *bränn* burn, *vin* wine] several varieties of clear rye liquor, including vodka

Coast Trader: a pidgin trade language derived from Aikoto, Sverbian, Ferish, Gallnach, and others

Corvittai: [F. *corvide* blackbird, S. *vittai* ghost] Suriel's human soldiers

duck potato: underwater root of arrowhead plants; ground up for flour by viirelei

Elken Wars: a series of wars fought between Ferish colonists and a Sverbian-Aikoto alliance for control of the coast and its natural resources

Folk: dangerous spirits in Gallnach mythology, said to emerge from the otherworld on Bódhain

Hafelús: [S. *hafe* ocean, *lús* light] Tiernan's sword, named after the mythical lantern on the ferry to the land of the dead

hellseed: a poisonous plant, used in small doses to calm the nerves

irumoi: a wooden rod covered with glowing blue mushrooms, used as a light source

itheran: [S. *ithera* 'out there'] viirelei term for foreign colonists

jinrayul: [A. *jinra* fire, *-yul* caller] mages who have learned to control fire

jouyen: viirelei tribe(s) typically belonging to a confederacy

kinaru: giant waterfowl sacred to tel-saidu and the Rin-jouyen

Kohekai: [A. *kohesamu* blood, *kairo* 'to bring'] Kateiko's hunting knife

makiri: Aikoto charms carved in the shape of animals that protect
    a home from cruel spirits
needlemint: evergreen-scented leaves native to Sverba; used as
    numbing painkiller
Nurivel: [A. 'shimmer of light on water'] Kateiko's throwing
    dagger
okorebai: political, spiritual, and military leader of a jouyen
okoreni: successor to an okorebai, typically passed from parent to
    child
pann: a denomination of the sovereign currency; 100 pann to 1
    sovereign
plank house: a large building and social unit of the Aikoto,
    housing up to ten families
rioden: massive auburn conifer trees used for dugout canoes,
    buildings, bark weaving, etc.
Rúonbattai: [S. *rúon* rain, *battai* guard] radical Sverbian militant
    group who swore to drive off the Ferish, but were massacred
    by Suriel's mercenaries several years after the Third Elken War
saidu: spirits that control the weather and maintain balance in nature
    ANTA-SAIDU (WATER), EDIM-SAIDU (EARTH AND PLANTS),
    JINRA-SAIDU (FIRE), TEL-SAIDU (AIR)
sancte: Ferish holy building
shoirdryge: [S. *shoird* shard, *ryge* realm] parallel world that
    splintered off from other worlds
stjolvind: [S. *stjolv* shield, *-ind* male] Sverbian groom's guardian
Skaarnaht: [S. *skaar* red, *naht* night] Sverbian new year festival
sovereign: a form of currency introduced by the Sverbian
    monarchy
stavehall: Sverbian holy building
Thaerijmur: land of the dead in Sverbian mythology

tulanta: hallucinogenic painkiller made from tularem leaves; used
    by viirelei

viirelei: [A. *vii* they, *rel* of, *leiga* west] colonists' term for coastal
    indigenous people, including the Aikoto, Nuthalha, and
    Kowichelk confederaries

War of the Wind: war between Eremur's army and Suriel,
    fought for control of border lands

woolwrap: a long skirt worn by Gallnach men and women

Yanben: [A. *yan* world, *benro* meet] Aikoto winter solstice festival
    when the worlds of the living and dead unite

PHRASES, SLANG, PROFANITY

akesida: Aikoto term for 'young woman'

Antlers: slang for Colonnium guards

Elkhounds: slang for Caladheå city guards

kaid: any insult to the aeldu, used as strong profanity by the
    Aikoto

någva: [S. 'to fuck'] highly versatile Sverbian profanity; adjective
    form is *någvakt*

pigeon: slur for itherans

takuran: [A. *taku* shit] highly offensive slur alluding to Aikoto
    burial rites, referencing someone so foul they must be buried in
    shit because dirt rejects their blood

tema: Aikoto affectionate term for 'mother'

temal: Aikoto affectionate term for 'father'

yan taku: [A. *yan* world, *taku* shit] profanity with religious
    connotations

CULTURES

Aikoto: [A. *ainu* mountain, *ko* flow, *toel* coast] A confederacy of seven (formerly eight) jouyen occupying a large region of coastal rainforest.

Ferish: Colonists from Ferland who landed on the west coast of the Aikoto's continent. Later, a mass exodus from Ferland of famine victims caused a population boom in Aikoto lands.

INDUSTRIES: wheat farming, manufacturing, naval trading.

RELIGION: monotheist.

Gallnach: Settlers from Gallun, persecuted by Sverbians. They fled to Aikoto lands and built Ingdanrad as a refuge for mages.

INDUSTRIES: barley farming, sheep herding, mining.

RELIGION: pagan.

Kowichelk: A confederacy of jouyen in the rainforest south of the Aikoto. Largely wiped out from disease brought by foreign colonists.

INDUSTRIES: fishing, textiles, jade carving.

RELIGION: animist.

Nuthalha: A confederacy of jouyen in the tundra north of the Aikoto. Largely isolated.

INDUSTRIES: whaling, trapping, bone carving.

RELIGION: animist.

Sverbians: Settlers from Sverba who landed on the east coast of the Aikoto's continent, migrated west, and later allied with the Aikoto against the Ferish.

INDUSTRIES: rye farming, goat herding, logging.

RELIGION: polytheist.

AIKOTO JOUYEN: NORTH

Beru-jouyen: "People of the sea." Live in Meira Dael on the
coast of Nokun Bel.

CREST: grey whale.

INDUSTRIES: whaling, soapstone-carving.

Dona-jouyen: "Nomad people." Lived in Anwen Bel. Formed
when members of the Rin and Iyo split off. Wiped out in a
recent war with the Rin.

CREST: white seagull.

INDUSTRIES: none.

Haka-jouyen: "People of the frost." Live inland in Nokun Bel.

CREST: brown grizzly bear.

INDUSTRIES: fur trapping, tanning.

Rin-jouyen: "People of the lakeshore." Live in Aeti Ginu in
central Anwen Bel. Oldest jouyen in the Aikoto. Large in
territory and influence, but small in population these days.

CREST: white or black kinaru.

INDUSTRIES: woodcarving, embroidery, fur trapping.

Tamu-jouyen: "People of the peninsulas." Live in Tamun Dael
on the coast of Anwen Bel.

CREST: orange shark.

INDUSTRIES: fishing, boatcraft.

AIKOTO JOUYEN: SOUTH

Iyo-jouyen: "People of the surrounds." Live in Toel Ginu and
Caladheå on the coast of Iyun Bel. Largest and most powerful
jouyen in the Aikoto. Historic allies with the Rin.

CREST: blue dolphin.

INDUSTRIES: stone carving, textiles.

Kae-jouyen: "People of the inlet." Live on the coast of Ukan Bel alongside Burren Inlet. Allies with the Gallnach due to centuries of trade and intermarriage.

CREST: green heron.

INDUSTRIES: fishing.

Yula-jouyen: "People of the valley." Live inland in Ukan Bel in a network of river valleys.

CREST: copper fox.

INDUSTRIES: weaving.

A BRIEF HISTORY OF EREMUR
AND SURROUNDING LANDS

-70   The Iyo-jouyen constructs a shrine in Toel Ginu, one of the oldest surviving buildings in the Aikoto Confederacy.

-60   Sverbian sailors land on the east coast of the Aikoto's continent and begin migrating west.

1   The Sverbian monarchy introduces a new calendar, marking the birth of a empire.

24   Rånyl Sigrunnehl, queen of Sverba, invades Gallun and begins killing druids. Gallnach refugees flee to the Aikoto's continent and migrate west ahead of the expanding Sverbian front.

366   Gallnach druids build a refuge, Ingdanrad, in the mountains bordering Aikoto territory. They establish trade with the nearby Kae-jouyen.

428   Sverba founds the province of Nyhemur across the mountains from Aikoto lands. The two groups begin trading.

487   Ferish sailors land in Aikoto territory. They clash violently with Aikoto and Sverbians over trade routes and natural resources. Ingdanrad declares neutrality and offers refuge to all mages.

513   Barros Sanguero, lord of the New Ferland Trading Company, builds the Colonnium stronghold in Iyo territory. He quickly dominates regional trade.

533   FIRST ELKEN WAR

Sverbians and Aikoto ally to drive out the Ferish. Fighting spans the entire Aikoto coast. Some Rin and Iyo refuse to go to war, and instead split off to form the nomadic Dona-jouyen.

The Sverbian-Aikoto alliance kills Sanguero and repels the NFTC. Iyo, Rin, and Sverbian settlers build a fort around the captured Colonnium to ensure Ferish soldiers cannot retake it. They name the fort Caladheå.

535   Imarein Rin, traumatized from the war, abandons his jouyen. He climbs Se Ji Ainu and swears devotion to the air spirit Suriel.

545   Sverba founds the province of Eremur in Aikoto territory, declares Caladheå the capital, and establishes a local military. The Aikoto Confederacy refuses to recognize these actions. Imarein briefly returns to the Rin-jouyen.

547   Famine hits Ferland. Thousands of Ferish immigrants flee overseas to Eremur and nearby lands. Caladheå blooms into an international trading port.

557–8 SECOND ELKEN WAR

A Ferish naval captain attempts to retake the Colonnium and claim land for new immigrants. The Sverbian-Aikoto alliance nearly defeats him – until his soldiers raze Bronnoi Ridge, the Aikoto district in Caladheå. The Rin-jouyen abandons the city and returns north.

Sverba agrees to share control of Eremur with Ferland via an elected council. The Iyo surrender Bronnoi Ridge in exchange for land and housing in the Ashtown slums. Sverbian dissenters form the Rúonbattai, a radical militant group, and vow to drive out the Ferish.

An influenza epidemic ravages Eremur, killing thousands. Ferish rebels, angry about treaties from the previous war, take advantage of the weakened military and hold a coup. The Rúonbattai have a resurgence of support and retaliate against the Ferish rebels.

The wartorn Rin and other northern jouyen refuse to come south and fight, breaking the Aikoto alliance. The Iyo temporarily abandon Caladheå. After great losses, the Council regains control of the city.

606 Several Sverbian mages, accused of helping the Rúonbattai massacre Ferish immigrants, are murdered in Council custody. Ingdanrad cuts diplomatic ties to Eremur.

618 Suriel learns that the Rúonbattai leader, Liet, plans to wake other saidu as a weapon against the Ferish. He hires Ferish mercenaries, who successfully massacre the Rúonbattai.

619 The Dona-jouyen attack the Rin-jouyen to prevent them from carrying out Liet's plan. The Rin wipe out the Dona, then wake the saidu, causing the Storm Year.

623 A military expedition from Caladheå is massacred in Dúnravn Pass. A few survivors and the Iyo claim Suriel was responsible.

625   Suriel's mercenaries massacre a logging camp near
       Dúnravn Pass then destroy the mining town Rutnaast.

626   WAR OF THE WIND

Eremur declares war on Suriel, whose mercenaries become
known as Corvittai. Eremur's military fails to breach Dúnravn
Pass, but their navy successfully cuts off the Corvittai's supply
lines. The Corvittai begin pillaging and razing farms.

In summer, Suriel vanishes. The Corvittai mutiny and attack
the Rin-jouyen in what becomes known as the Blackbird Battle.
The Rin are victorious, but both sides suffer devastating losses,
including the deaths of their leaders.

ACKNOWLEDGEMENTS

My gratitude to the following:

Rob Masson, my life partner, for your patience during the long mind-melting process of writing a novel, your help with world-building logistics, and your love and support. You'll always carry part of my spirit.

Susan Renouf, my editor, for understanding the story's needs better than me. Jen Albert, my secondary editor, for insight and solidarity. All the other talented, hardworking people at ECW Press who have helped this series take shape.

Simon Carr, my cover illustrator, and Tiffany Munro, my cartographer, for your beautiful and attentive artwork. Sera-Lys McArthur of the Nakota, my audiobook narrator for *Flight*, for breathing so much life into my characters that I heard their voices while working on this book.

All my wonderful writer groups. Squid Squad: Roy Leon (THALL), Rochelle Jardine, Shannon O'Donovan, Lilah Souza, and Bo Jones for encouragement, memes, and writing help at all hours of the day. Cythera Crew: special thanks to Jessica Smith #453 for being my most loyal beta reader. CRLiterature: special thanks to Jay Knioum (the best skeleton friend I could ever want) for insightful advice, unwavering support, and shouting from the rooftops about my book.

Kathleen and Douglas, my parents; Florence and Nic, my siblings; and our extended family for all your help and love.

Dr. Rob Budde for continuing to teach me things from afar. Jackson 2bears of the Kanien'kehaka (Mohawk) and Luke Parnell of the Haida and Nisga'a for teaching me how to blend old and new culture. Nicolas Brasch for your support despite never having me as a student.

The Wurundjeri, in whose territory this novel was written; and the nations of the Northwest Coast and the Gulf of Alaska, in whose territory it's set.